PASSIONS OF THE HEART

Harry escorted her to her room and stood looking down at her. Alessa searched his face for a sign, for help with the words she could not bring herself to say, but she saw nothing but fatigue and a kind benevolence. She did not want kindness, nor pity. Pity could not warm the chill that threatened her heart.

Alessa turned away and opened the door to her room. The candle she had left burning on the bedside table flickered in the draft. She could dimly see her bed, a large shapeless mass. There she would find warmth of a sort and oblivion. But not the oblivion she wanted.

She was about to close the door when Harry called her name. Surprised, she looked up and met his gaze. His eyes reflected the candle flame, and in their naked depths she saw a need as great as her own.

"Alessa," he said again. He set the candle down on a table that stood just inside the door and took a step toward her. Alessa held her breath, terrified at the sudden knowledge of how much he could hurt her.

If he saw her hesitation, he gave no sign. With a cry like that of a drowning man gasping for air, he drew her into his arms . . .

A Sensible Match

Anthea Malcolm

ZEBRA BOOKS
KENSINGTON PUBLISHING CORP.

For the other Alessa and Fiona

O ceremony, show me but thy worth!
What is thy soul of adoration?
Art thou aught else but place, degree and
form,
Creating awe and fear in other men?
Wherein thou art less happy being fear'd
Than they in fearing.

Shakespeare,
Henry V

Prologue

Alessandra di Tassio stepped from the warmth of the sunlit garden into the cool quiet of the green parlor, contemplating the wisdom of the decision she was about to make. Marriage was a subject for dispassionate thought, not giddy transports and romantic yearnings. She had learned that lesson three years ago and she had no intention of repeating her mistake.

Alessa pulled the French windows shut behind her, conscious of a constriction in her chest at the memory of her youthful folly. It would pass, her friends had told her, and it had, after a fashion. At least, the sharp pain had dimmed to a dull ache. At the time she had sworn she would never marry anyone, but that had been foolishness, born of her bitterness and grief. She was now one-and-twenty and it was time she put all that behind her, time she had her own establishment, time she acquired a husband who would be a credit to the Tassio name.

Banishing the past to the recesses of memory where it belonged, Alessa glanced at the mantel clock. It lacked but five minutes to four, the appointed hour for Lord Milverton's call. She walked toward the chimney glass and paused for a moment to study her reflection. The coming interview might not be the stuff of romantic novels, but for the sake of self-respect, if nothing else, she wanted to look her best. Her walk in the

7

garden had lent color to her cheeks, but the late afternoon breeze had loosened a few strands of hair. Alessa pinned them into place and decided she would do. Her heavy dark hair was swept back and coiled into a loose knot; her face was framed by discreet pearl earrings and a stiff, high-standing lace collar. She looked like a woman who knew her own mind, not a frivolous young girl whose words were not to be taken seriously.

The clock struck four. Alessa turned from the glass and surveyed the room. Her mother had refurbished it when she purchased the house three years ago, and it had a look of newness about it, in keeping with a family that had been recently transplanted to England. Shimmering sea green silk covered the walls, setting off swags of fringed curtains in a rich, ornate pattern which recalled her mother's native Russia. There were fresh flowers on the sofa table and a faint smell of polish hung in the air. The servants had been especially diligent this morning, readying the room for the scene which was about to take place. There wasn't a soul in the house who didn't know the reason for Lord Milverton's call and wonder what her answer would be.

Alessa walked across an expanse of Aubusson carpet to the sofa, straightened the profusion of chintz cushions, and settled herself to wait. At three minutes past, Christopher, the first footman, stepped into the room and cleared his throat. "Lord Milverton, my lady."

Conscious that she was more nervous than she would have wished, Alessa got to her feet and extended her hand to Harry Dudley, Sixth Earl of Milverton.

Her first thought was that he was taller than she remembered. Perhaps it was merely the effect of seeing him here, in the green parlor, rather than on Rotten Row or in a crowded reception room. They said he had been a wild young man, the despair of his father, but that was before he had succeeded to the title. Now, in buff-colored breeches and a tan coat, his dark brown hair neatly combed, his cravat carefully tied, he appeared perfectly respectable, even a trifle sober.

Alessa indicated that Christopher should withdraw, motioned her guest to be seated, and returned to the sofa. Milverton settled himself in a straight-backed cane chair. If he was nervous he gave no sign of it, save perhaps in the gravity of his demeanor.

After they had exchanged words of greeting, Alessa folded her hands in her lap and waited for him to speak. Though they must have met a dozen times, she had the sense that she had never looked at him properly before. Her memory was of an attractive man with easy manners who sat a horse well and was a more than adequate waltzing partner. Now she noticed the strength in his lean face, the determination in the set of his mouth, the intelligence in his dark eyes. He was only six years her senior, but there was a maturity about him lacking in other men of seven-and-twenty.

When the silence between them had stretched just long enough to be uncomfortable, Milverton gave a sudden, unexpectedly boyish smile. "There's no avoiding the awkwardness, is there? I take it you know the reason for my visit."

"My mother spoke with me yesterday, after you called on her," Alessa said. Her mother's words, well modulated and tinged with impatience, echoed in her head. *Three years ago I left matters in your hands, Alessa. Perhaps I was mistaken. A mother has a responsibility to see her daughter suitably settled. Lord Milverton is an estimable young man, the family is unexceptionable, and the title is old.* Finally and inarguably, *It's time you were married.*

Milverton leaned back in his chair and crossed his legs. "And is my proposal unwelcome?" he asked in a conversational tone.

Alessa lifted her chin. "If it were unwelcome, my lord, I would not have agreed to see you."

Milverton smiled again. There was something about that smile which Alessa found disconcerting. It threatened to put her too much at her ease. She sat up straighter, determined to maintain her self-possession.

"I fear I have little experience of scenes such as this," Milverton said. "Marriage is a serious business, especially for a woman. Perhaps before you commit yourself further, you should tell me what you expect of it."

Alessa was taken aback. She had received a number of proposals in the last three years, and no gentleman had begun by asking for her opinion of marriage. Lord Milverton was proving a more interesting man than she had expected. Like his smile, it was disconcerting. Still, she had every intention of making her views on marriage clear and he had given her the opening she needed.

"I expect you have heard that I was betrothed once before." The words were harder to say than she had expected, but they had to be said. "My fiancé pretended to be in love with me and I was silly enough to believe him. It was an embarrassing experience. I trust you would never make the same mistake."

Alessa spoke more sharply than she had intended. Perhaps it had something to do with the disturbing effect of his smile. Milverton did not appear to take it amiss. Nor did he betray surprise at her words or offer romantic protestations, as many men would have done. "I hope we will always be honest with each other," he said mildly. "It would seem to me a minimum requirement for marriage."

"Certainly," Alessa agreed. She adjusted one of the embroidered cambric bands which confined her sleeves. "It goes without saying that I wouldn't expect you to dance attendance on me."

"Nor, I take it, would you expect to dance attendance on me in turn."

"I don't intend to sit quietly at home."

"I see." Milverton regarded her thoughtfully. "In other words, we would lead separate lives."

Alessa fixed him with a level gaze. "You needn't fear that I'll take lovers. I've had my fill of romance. What you do with your own time is your own affair."

Alessa was pleased to see that she had taken him by surprise. Hitherto he had appeared entirely too much in command of the scene. But though he was surprised, he was certainly not shocked. "Generous of you," he murmured, an appreciative glint in his eyes.

"I'm one-and-twenty," Alessa told him. "I know how the marriage game is played in our circles. I, in turn, would expect to choose my own friends and my own clothes and my own entertainment. And I would expect to retain complete control over my own money."

She flung this last out like a challenge and waited for him to object, or at least suggest that the matter be left to her mother and the solicitors. Instead he inclined his head. "I'd be grateful if you did. Looking after my own estates is complicated enough. I've no desire to add to the burden."

Startled by his ready agreement, Alessa looked into his eyes and felt a shock of surprise. Lord Milverton had the clothes and manners of a typical English gentleman, but they were no more than a carefully cultivated facade which he employed quite deliberately. The real Harry Milverton was someone very different, someone she could barely glimpse and could not begin to understand.

He had agreed to all her demands and yet Alessa felt a panicked impulse to refuse his proposal and ask him to leave the house. She could have dealt with the man she had thought he was. The reality was an unknown quantity. Unknown and intriguing. Alessa was not at all sure she wanted marriage to be intriguing.

"Now you can answer a question," she said, determined to turn the conversation away from herself. "Why did you offer for me?" Though they had been acquainted for some time, he could hardly be said to have been courting her.

"I thought the answer was obvious. I'm in need of a wife. And," he added, with a smile which robbed the words of offense, "you fit the qualifications better than any woman I know."

"Because my father was the Prince di Tassio and my mother's cousin is the Emperor of Russia?"

"It's more than that." Milverton leaned forward, suddenly direct. "Before my father's death I was employed as an attaché at the British embassy in St. Petersburg. I still undertake diplomatic missions and I'm frequently called from home at unexpected moments. I would scarcely be able to dance attendance on my wife even if she wished it. I thought you would understand that. And . . ." He hesitated. For the first time she sensed that he was unsure of himself. "Like you, I've had my fill of romance," he said abruptly. "I thought you would understand that as well."

A dozen questions which she could not possibly ask sprang to Alessa's lips. "It seems you thought a great deal," she said, a hint of tartness in her voice.

"I told you marriage was a serious business." He sat back and folded his arms. "The consensus in my family is that I wasn't cut out to be an earl. I've been doing my best to prove them wrong. I think you can help me."

"You seem to be doing very well on your own."

"Every earl needs a countess."

"And an heir," Alessa said coolly.

Milverton regarded her for a moment. "That too," he agreed.

Alessa forced herself not to look away, though her mouth had gone dry and her pulse had quickened. She knew perfectly well what intimacies marriage entailed and she would admit to being more than a little curious about them. But never, not even during her betrothal, had she come so close to discussing it with a man, and it was difficult to keep her imagination from running riot. She would never consent to marry a man she held in distaste. That would hardly be a problem with Lord Milverton. But to marry a man who had such a disturbing effect on her senses might prove equally unwise. It gave him entirely too much power over her.

"I would like children," she said, looking steadily at him. "It's one of the reasons I wish to marry. I'd do my best to give you a son, though I can make you no promises."

"I want an heir, of course. It is one of the reasons *I* wish to marry. But should an heir fail to materialize, I have a very adequate younger brother." Milverton's tone was grave, but there was a glint of amusement in his eyes.

Alessa found herself smiling in return, then felt suddenly awkward.

"Since we are speaking of children," Milverton continued, "we ought perhaps to discuss the matter of religion."

"I considered that at the time of my former betrothal,"

Alessa said, relieved at the change of subject. "My mother was raised in the Russian Orthodox Church. My father was a Roman Catholic and my stepfather is an Anglican. If we are to live in England, I have no objection to my children being raised in the English church."

Milverton inclined his head. "You are very generous."

"We Tassios may be proud," Alessa told him, "but we aren't strangers to compromise."

"We Dudleys, I fear, have a tendency to be pigheaded." Milverton gave a rueful smile. "You must know that if you marry me you'll be taking on my family as well. My two youngest sisters are still underage. If I marry, my mother will no doubt offer to remove to the dower house, but —"

"But it would hardly be fair to ask your sisters to do so as well, and as your mother would not wish to be separated from them, they will all make their home with us."

"It would appear to be the most logical arrangement." He grinned suddenly. "I imagine you'll be more than a match for my mother."

Alessa, who had met Lady Milverton, was not sure she concurred. The countess had cut an important figure in society for some thirty years, and it was unlikely she would be pleased to relinquish any of her authority to a younger woman. Still, Alessa had never been one to shrink from a challenge and her battles with her own mother had left her a toughened veteran. "I have no objection to sharing the household with your family," she told him, knowing she could say nothing else and wondering if she was making a great mistake. "We are hardly young lovers eager for privacy. Indeed, I hope my own family will be frequent visitors. My brother Simon and I have always been close. It would be hard to be separated from him."

"I believe I caught a glimpse of him on my way in here. A serious-faced boy looking out the library door."

"I imagine *he* was trying to catch a glimpse of *you*. Simon is only fifteen but he takes his responsibilities as head of the Tassio family very seriously."

"Is he likely to forbid the match?" Milverton asked, a glint in his eyes again.

"Not if I tell him I'm satisfied."

The laughter left his eyes and he regarded her in silence for a long moment. "And are you?" he asked softly.

It was the point of the whole interview, the question she had thought to answer with dispassionate logic and which now seemed muddled by a host of conflicting impulses. But as she looked into Milverton's eyes, Alessa realized she had already made up her mind. Perhaps she had known it the moment he walked into the room, with an instinct which should have no place in the convenient alliance she was about to enter.

"If you wish me to be your wife, my lord, I will endeavor to be a creditable Countess of Milverton"

For a moment she thought she saw relief in his eyes, quickly masked. He got to his feet. Alessa did likewise. For a moment they regarded each other. Alessa sensed that he was as uncertain as she about who should make the first move or even what was the correct move to make.

Milverton stepped forward with sudden decision. Alessa felt her face grow warm and realized, with surprise and alarm, that she very much wanted him to kiss her. But instead of taking her in his arms, he held out his hand. An appropriate gesture, after all, to seal a marriage of convenience. Alessa placed her hand in his and felt his fingers close around hers in a friendly clasp which sent a tremor through her that had nothing to do with friendship.

Willing herself to be sensible, she looked into his eyes. They were dark and serious and strangely vulnerable. "Are you frightened?" he asked softly.

Alessa considered a number of clever lies and discarded them in favor of the unvarnished truth. "Yes," she admitted. "I'm frightened."

Milverton smiled, a sweet, engaging, utterly disarming smile. "So am I."

Chapter One

Tsarkoe Selo, near St. Petersburg
Summer 1818

Elisabeth Alexeyevna, wife of the Emperor of Russia, studied the two young men seated across from her on stiff-backed chairs covered in blue and white flowered silk.

Simon di Tassio returned her regard with shrewd brown eyes set between straight level brows. There was pride in his face and a touch of hauteur which reminded Elisabeth of his mother.

But though Simon had a gravity and assurance which far exceeded his seventeen years, the present circumstances were enough to strain even his self-command. His friend, Peter Carne, looked equally apprehensive. Beside the dark-haired Simon, Peter, a handsome, sturdy boy with light brown hair which fell over his forehead, appeared very English. Elisabeth was reminded that both boys were a long way from home. They were also, she thought, with a pang of regret, of an age to be her sons.

"I want to help," she said, "truly I do. But first I must understand. What possessed Alessa to travel all the way to St. Petersburg in her condition?"

Simon hesitated, glanced at Peter, then turned back to Elisabeth. "She came to look for her husband," he said in perfectly accented French, the language of the Russian court.

"She . . ." Elisabeth put a hand to her head and smoothed

her hair, as if by doing so she could make sense of this bewildering statement. "I know that Lord Milverton was once employed at the British embassy here. I remember him. But he returned to England some years ago, long before he married Alessa. I did not know that he had come back to Russia."

"He's not here on a diplomatic mission, Cousin Elisabeth. That is, I don't think he is." Simon drew a breath. "Perhaps I should start at the beginning?"

"I think that would be best."

Simon hesitated and stared at his hands. Beside him, Peter was very quiet. In the tumultuous two days since they had appeared at the country palace at Tsarkoe Selo, both boys had avoided giving an account of the reasons for their abrupt and unannounced arrival. As for Alessa, she had been in no state to discuss anything. But she was now out of danger, and though Elisabeth sympathized with the boys, she was determined to have some answers. "You were traveling on the Continent, I believe," she prompted gently. "You and Alessa and your friend Mr. Carne."

"That's right." Simon seemed relieved to be given a place to start. "I hadn't been back to Sardinia or Savoy since we came to England, you see. *Maman* thought it was time I visited the Tassio estates, but she's expecting again and she didn't want to leave Michael—my stepfather. So Alessa was to travel with me instead and Peter's parents said he could come along. It was a sort of Grand Tour."

"I see." Elisabeth adjusted the folds of her lilac silk gown. "And your mother and Lord Milverton were willing to allow Alessa to travel despite—"

"They didn't know," Simon said quickly. "About her condition, I mean. Anyway Harry—Lord Milverton—wasn't in England when we left. He'd been sent to Denmark on a mission two months before. Alessa was wild to make the trip so she didn't write to him and she didn't tell *Maman*. She didn't even tell Peter and me at first. Well, she didn't tell us at all actually. But after a while it became pretty obvious. That is . . ." Simon's pale skin flushed with color. "Peter and I may not know a lot about that sort of thing, but we know what a

16

woman looks like when she's going to have a baby."

"Quite so." Elisabeth gave him an encouraging smile. "But by then I suppose you had been traveling for some time."

Simon nodded. "We went to Paris first, and then to Savoy and Sardinia to see the Tassio estates. We were in Sardinia before Peter and I were really sure—about the baby, I mean. We got Alessa to admit it, but she told us not to worry as the baby wouldn't be born for several months yet. She didn't want to go home and be fussed over." Simon shifted uncomfortably in his chair. "Alessa doesn't always have a very easy time at home. Harry travels a lot and she doesn't get on well with his mother."

Elisabeth nodded, her eyes flickering to the portraits of her husband's ancestors which hung against walls covered in the same blue and white silk as the chairs. She could sympathize with the loneliness of a young wife. She herself had been only thirteen when she had been sent from her native Germany to become the bride of the future Emperor of Russia.

"I thought about writing to *Maman* about the baby," Simon continued, "but she was about to be confined herself and Alessa told me not to upset her. As for Harry, Alessa said it was up to her to decide when to tell him. I couldn't argue with that."

"Lord Milverton was still in Denmark?" Elisabeth asked.

"No, he was back in England by then. At least, he was supposed to be." Simon stared at the floor, tracing the inlaid pattern of the wood with the toe of his boot. "After we left Sardinia, we went to Italy and then on to Vienna. That's where Alessa got the letter."

"Letter?" Elisabeth prompted when Simon paused.

"Yes, it was from Georgiana, Harry's sister. She's only thirteen and she's terrible at keeping secrets. She said Harry had come back from Denmark, like everyone expected, but less than a month later he started making plans to leave England again. He was very mysterious about it and he wouldn't tell the family where he was going. He said the matter was personal. Then one night Georgiana overheard him talking to his secretary about St. Petersburg." Simon paused again. For a moment he looked like the seventeen-year-old boy he in fact was. "Georgiana was probably eavesdropping. She always does. Anyway, she decided Alessa had a right to know."

"And Alessa decided to follow her husband."

Simon nodded. "We hadn't intended to come to Russia, but Alessa said traveling to St. Petersburg wouldn't be any more strenuous than visiting Prague and Dresden, like we'd planned." Simon's brows drew together. "I should have stopped her."

Elisabeth recalled the high-spirited child Alessa had been when she last saw her. "I doubt you would have been able to do so."

"That's true enough," Simon admitted, though he continued to frown.

"He tried to talk her out of it, Your Majesty," Peter said, coming to his friend's defense. His accent was not as good as Simon's, but he too spoke fluent French. "But Alessa can be very stubborn. Besides, at the time it didn't seem so bad. It was spring, so the roads were in good condition. The baby wasn't due for more than two months."

"But then we were delayed," Simon said grimly, "and Alessa got sick, and by the time we arrived here . . ." He looked at Elisabeth, his anxiety breaking through. "She *is* going to be all right, isn't she, Cousin Elisabeth?"

"The doctors assure me that she will be," Elisabeth told him, her own fears of the past two days fresh in her mind. "And the baby as well. He was a month early, but he is not as small as such children frequently are."

"When can we see them?"

Elisabeth smiled. "As soon as she is awake. I have instructed my maid-of-honor to inform us."

Simon sat back in his chair, his relief evident. "I should write to *Maman*. And Peter's parents should know where he is. Do you know how long it will be before it's safe for her to travel?"

"The doctors say perhaps a month, if Alessa continues well and the baby thrives. We are very happy to have you as our guests, but you are quite right, you must inform your families

18

of what has happened." Elisabeth looked at Simon, thinking again of his mother, the Princess Sofia, her husband's favorite cousin. Sofia, who had married the Prince di Tassio and gone to live in Savoy and then after his death had gone to England and married an Englishman, was known in the family for her temper. Breaking the news to her would not be easy. "If you wish," Elisabeth suggested, "I would be happy to write for you."

Simon shook his head. "Thank you, Cousin Elisabeth, but it's our responsibility."

Elisabeth smiled. It was what she would have expected him to say. She clasped her hands and looked down at the gold of her wedding band, puzzling over the story she had just heard. "Simon—Alessa had no idea why her husband wished to travel to St. Petersburg in such secrecy?"

"No." Simon's eyes were troubled. "Harry's a very decent fellow. He wouldn't be so secretive without a good reason." Simon hesitated and frowned again. "I hate to be a bother, Cousin Elisabeth, but do you think you could possibly help us find him?"

"I have every intention of doing so," Elisabeth assured him. "And you may be sure the Emperor will feel the same when he learns the story. I will write to Lord Cathcart, your ambassador here, to see what he knows of the matter. I'm sure there's a simple explanation."

"Yes. Very likely," Simon agreed, though Elisabeth knew he no more believed it than she did. She was searching for some way to offer reassurance when one of her maids-of-honor knocked at the door to say that Lady Milverton was awake and was asking for her brother.

Alessa pushed herself up in the vast four-poster bed and looked at the ornate Italian cradle of carved and gilded wood. If she craned her neck, she could see the top of his head with its downy cap of black hair. The nurses had told her she should count herself fortunate if he slept, but she felt bereft when he was out of her sight for more than five minutes. He had been born less than twenty-four hours ago and already he was the center of her world.

Satisfied that her son was sleeping peacefully, Alessa leaned back against the damask-covered headboard. She had known she wanted children, but she hadn't dreamed of the fierce joy and pride and tenderness she would feel when her baby was first placed in her arms. With an involuntary smile, she thought of the softness of his skin and the feel of his mouth at her breast and the wonder that she had produced such a tiny, perfectly formed creature. Though in fairness, she must acknowledge that Harry had done his part.

Harry. If Georgiana was to be believed, he was here, in St. Petersburg, for reasons he had not seen fit to share with his family. Would he have told her if she had been in England? Probably not. She and Harry might have been married close to two years, but they were scarcely confidantes. They had, after all, agreed to lead separate lives. Harry had certainly stuck to his side of the bargain. She had control of her fortune and, apart from the times when their duties as Earl and Countess of Milverton brought them together, the freedom to order her life as she chose. Harry was polite and considerate and could be a most engaging companion. But in many ways Alessa felt she knew him little better than she had on that afternoon in the green parlor when she agreed to be his wife.

Surely that would change when he learned she had given him a son and heir. Now that they shared something as miraculous as a child, there would not, could not, be such distance between them. With a stab of longing, Alessa recalled the night when their son must have been conceived. Harry had not visited her for over a fortnight and she had long since given up waiting for him each night. She had been woken from a light sleep by the pressure of his lips against her own, and in that languorous state she had felt no awkwardness or constraint, only joy and a pleasure which even now she blushed to recall. It seemed fitting that such a night had produced their son.

But the next day, Harry had been as politely distant as ever. Indeed, he had not visited her bed again before he left on his mission to Denmark. By the time she was certain of her pregnancy, he was not there to share the news with her. Alessa had been relieved to escape to the Continent with only Peter and Simon for company.

Would Harry feel that in following him to St. Petersburg she had broken her side of their agreement not to interfere in each other's lives? Whatever had caused him to travel to Russia in such secrecy must be very serious. Surely as his wife she had a right, even a duty, to know about it. Alessa was still puzzling over the reasons for her husband's mysterious journey when the gilded pedimented door opened and the Empress Elisabeth ushered Simon and Peter into the room.

Alessa looked at the boys' familiar faces with affection and relief. Until now, she hadn't realized how far from home she felt. She stretched out her hands. "Simon. And Peter. I'm so glad to see you."

The boys responded with awkward greetings. Elisabeth murmured that she would leave them to talk alone and discreetly withdrew. As the door clicked shut behind her, Simon looked up from contemplation of the carpet. He studied his sister in silence for a long moment. "I say," he exclaimed, a note of surprise in his voice, "you look just like you always do."

"I'll take that as a compliment." Alessa pushed back the embroidered silk coverlet and swung her legs to the floor. "It's all right," she said, noting the looks of alarm which crossed both boys' faces. "All I've done is have a baby. Women do it all the time and most can't afford to take to their beds afterwards."

Actually, despite her euphoria, the ordeal had affected her more than she would admit. Her head swam when she stood up. There was a sharp soreness between her legs. Her muscles ached in unexpected places and her body felt as if it was not quite held together properly.

Moving gingerly, Alessa picked up the soft green wool dressing gown which was laid out at the foot of the bed and shrugged it onto her shoulders, then walked toward the cradle. The baby stirred slightly at her approach, but did not open his eyes. Alessa looked down at him fondly for a moment, then looked back at the boys. "Well?" she said. "Don't

21

you want to meet Rutledge?" The baby did not yet have a name, but as the Earl of Milverton's heir he would be the Viscount Rutledge and that was how Alessa thought of him.

Simon moved forward cautiously, Peter following a step or so behind. They stood beside the cradle and looked down solemnly at the small figure peeking out from a profusion of linen and lace.

"He looks very well," Peter said politely.

"He's very small," Simon observed.

"He's quite splendid," Alessa retorted, "but I think only mothers notice that at this age." And fathers too, she added, but only to herself. She looked from one boy to the other. "I owe you both an apology. These last days haven't been easy and I have no one to blame but myself."

Simon gave a sudden grin. "It wasn't your fault the coach broke down in Kalisz, or that we took so long crossing the Baltic, or that you were so sick on the last part of our journey. And Peter and I were silly enough to go with you, so I suppose it's our fault as well."

Alessa pulled a face at him, greatly relieved to find that the events of the past forty-eight hours had not changed things so very much. She tucked the covers more closely about Rutledge, then moved to a nearby chair upholstered in the pale rose brocade which also covered the walls. She found that it was a relief to sit down.

Simon and Peter seated themselves on a settee opposite her. Peter was visibly more relaxed, but Simon had turned serious again. "I told Cousin Elisabeth," he said, fixing his sister with a level gaze. "About Harry and why we came here. She insisted, and quite honestly we did owe her an explanation."

Alessa started to protest, then settled back in her chair and nodded. Simon, as was the case provokingly often, was right.

"She was very decent," Simon continued. "She's going to write to Lord Cathcart to see if he's heard anything about Harry."

The thought that she might soon have word of her husband banished any qualms Alessa felt at sharing with others the news of the journey which Harry had been at such pains to keep secret. Surely Cathcart, on whose staff Harry had once been employed, would know if Harry was in St. Petersburg. He would send word to Harry and in a few days, perhaps only a few hours, Harry would come to Tsarkoe Selo and she could present their son to him.

"What are you grinning about?" Simon demanded.

"Nothing," Alessa said happily, in charity with all the world. "I may have been a great fool, Simon, but I think perhaps everything is going to turn out splendidly after all."

"So far so good," Simon agreed. "But there is one other thing. I promised Cousin Elisabeth that I'd write and tell *Maman* the whole. She'll be furious, but she won't be able to do anything. With luck she'll have calmed down by the time we get back."

"I'll write to my father," Peter said. "I daresay he'll be able to make her see sense. Or if not, Fiona will."

Alessa smiled. If anyone could cope with *Maman's* bursts of temper, it was Fiona, who had once been Simon and Alessa's governess and was now Peter's stepmother. But at the thought of what Fiona would say about her own behavior, Alessa's smile faded. She valued her former governess's opinion considerably more than her mother's. "Fiona is going to think I've acted like a fool when she hears what happened."

"No she won't," Simon said. "She'll just think you've acted like yourself."

Simon was grinning impudently. Beside him, Peter was trying very hard to keep a straight face. Alessa reached behind her for a tapestry-covered cushion and threw it at her brother. She might now be a mother, but she hadn't stopped being Simon's sister.

Harry Dudley, Sixth Earl of Milverton, paced restlessly down the length of the study in the suite of rooms his friend Edward Clifford kept on Moika Street. After the turmoil he had felt when Ned's letter reached him in England, the hurried preparations, and the nerve-wrackingly slow voyage through the North Sea and the Baltic, this further delay was

23

damnable. Harry banged his fist against the windowsill and stared down at the placid waters of the River Moika below.

Bathed in the soft pastel light of early evening which was uniquely its own, St. Petersburg glowed with radiance. In the careless, heedless days of his youth, Harry had been at home in these streets, as he had been at home in other, less decorous parts of town. But there was nothing careless or heedless about the way he felt now. St. Petersburg might be one of the most beautiful cities in Europe, but it could be a Lancashire mining town for all its beauty mattered.

The sight before him was suddenly blotted out by an image of fine sable hair and smoky almond-shaped eyes, of an enticing mouth and an imperious chin and a soft, supple body. Harry had not seen his wife in over six months, and the mere thought of her was enough to make him ache with desire and longing.

Hell and the devil. He hadn't realized he would miss her so much. How, when he still knew her so little, could she have come to mean so much to him? His feelings were unnerving. He did not want to make himself vulnerable, and he had no right to make emotional demands on her. She had made that clear when she accepted his proposal.

He had returned from Denmark as eager for news from her as a callow stripling with his first mistress. There had been only one letter from her awaiting him, a cheerful, impersonal catalog of gossip about the foreign courts she and the boys had visited and accounts of the sights they had seen. The letter had left him with the impression that she was having a glorious time and did not miss her husband in the least. Harry wondered if she had written again since he had left England. She and Simon and Peter would be in the German states by now, on the last leg of their Continental tour. They would probably return to England about the time he did.

And then he would have to tell her of his journey to Russia, and the reasons for it, and the result.

Harry tugged at his cravat, seeking relief from the summer heat and the weight of his own feelings. Would Alessa understand? Or would his news shatter the fragile bond of friendship they had built up over the last two years? And if so, what would be left to them?

The opening of the door put a stop to his reflections. He spun round, every nerve keyed for the news he both longed for and dreaded. Edward was standing on the threshold, and the look on his face told Harry that his friend had something to report.

"You've had word?" Harry demanded, striding forward. "Out with it, man, what is it?"

"You'd better sit down, Harry." Edward stepped out of the shadows of the doorway. The blue eyes that were generally filled with laughter held nothing but concern.

Harry held his worry at bay. "I won't collapse at your feet," he said evenly. "What's happened?"

Edward tossed his gloves onto a side table, swept his hat from his fair hair, and wiped a hand across his forehead. "I have news, but it's not the kind you're thinking of," he said, crossing to a cabinet of Karelian birch which held a set of decanters. "I was at a meeting at the French embassy all day," he continued, filling two glasses with the whisky which he imported from home, claiming he'd never been able to acquire a taste for vodka. "When I returned to report to Cathcart, he told me he'd had a message from Tsarkoe Selo last night. From the Empress. He wanted to know if I knew anything of your whereabouts."

Edward crossed back to Harry's side and pressed one of the glasses into his hand. "Here, I have a feeling you're going to want a drink. I know I need one." He swallowed half the contents of his own glass and met his friend's gaze. "Harry . . ." Edward looked at him as if knowing there was no way to break the news easily. "Your wife's here," he blurted out. "At Tsarkoe Selo."

Harry groaned. He should have realized there was a chance his wife and her brother would decide to pay an impromptu visit to their royal cousins. It must be Alessa's doing. Simon never acted so impulsively. "Does she know I'm here?" he asked, rapidly turning over various ways to handle this new complication.

"Oh, yes. Apparently that's why she decided to come to Russia. Someone wrote to tell her you were on your way to St. Petersburg."

Harry swore, quickly and fluently. Then he ran a hand through his hair and tried to order his thoughts. Time enough later to puzzle over who might have betrayed his plans, though he could make a fairly shrewd guess. Damn Georgiana and her eavesdropping. But at the moment it didn't matter. He had to cope with the result.

"Harry," Edward said in a soft voice which held an undercurrent of warning.

"Yes?" Harry looked back at his friend, wondering what further complications there could possibly be.

Edward, a six-year veteran of the diplomatic service, seemed at a loss for words. He swallowed the rest of the whisky, hesitated, and finally spoke. "Did you know Alessa was with child?"

Harry stared at him. "Don't be ridiculous," he said sharply. "She'd have told me if there was any chance . . ." But he bit the words back even as he spoke them. Alessa had never been in the habit of confiding in him, and in those last weeks before he left for Denmark she had seemed more reserved than ever.

A sudden image flooded his memory, an image of that night when he had gone late to her chamber and she had responded so ardently to his lovemaking. In spite or perhaps because of his own desires, he had always been careful not to impose on her too often, but that night he had gone to her room on impulse, without first asking her permission. The result had surprised them both. It was the last time he had bedded her before he left England. The last time in all these months. He had been too frightened of his feelings to approach her again. "God," he muttered. "Oh, dear God in heaven."

He dropped into a wing chair, scarcely aware that he had moved. To have the child he had longed for materialize now, when he had decided it was a blessing that he and Alessa did not yet have any children of their own. The situation might be funny, if he could see beyond the pain of it.

His fingers clenched and he realized he was still holding the untouched glass. He swallowed the whisky in one draught, with no thought for its subtle flavor, and carefully set the glass down on the table beside him, because his impulse was to hurl it into the fireplace. "When's the baby due?" he demanded, looking up at Edward again. "Should she be traveling in this condition?"

Edward drew a breath. "Alessa is well. The Empress wanted you to be assured of that. Two days ago your wife was delivered of a son."

The words shattered the remnants of Harry's self-command. He pushed himself out of his chair and stared unseeing at the oak-paneled wall. A son. He had a son. Alessa was here, in the palace at Tsarkoe Selo, and she had just given birth to their son. It was sharp, bitter irony. It was everything he had once longed for.

It was a disaster.

Chapter Two

Alessa studied her reflection with dissatisfaction. Her face was pale, her eyes were shadowed, and her hair, badly in want of washing after days of travel, was dull and uncurled. She pushed it back from her shoulders and found herself staring at her breasts. They had swollen during her pregnancy, but her milk had come in last night and now they seemed enormous, straining against the thin lawn of her nightdress. This was the first time she had taken a proper look at herself. She felt a stab of mingled pride and self-consciousness. "I didn't realize having a baby affected one so much. I was never flat-chested, but—"

Elisabeth laughed. "Your husband will find it most becoming, I assure you."

Her husband. Harry. He could arrive at any moment. Cousin Elisabeth had sent word to Lord Cathcart as soon as she learned of the story, Lord Cathcart had managed to locate Harry the following day, and Harry had sent a message to Tsarkoe Selo late that night, saying that he would visit his wife the next morning. As she prepared for the meeting, Alessa's joy of the previous day had given way to nervousness.

"It's the only part of me he might possibly find becoming," Alessa said with an attempt at raillery. She picked up a silver-backed brush from the dressing table and dragged it through her hair. "I look positively haggish."

Elisabeth took the brush from Alessa and smoothed back the long waves of dark hair. "You're the mother of his child. He'll think you look radiant. And you do. There. You see?"

Her hair now hung in a smooth waterfall down her back. Though it would still be better for washing, it was a vast improvement. Alessa turned to thank Elisabeth, but she had set down the hair brush and was walking to the settee where she had placed something when she came into the room. Alessa, preoccupied with the problem of her hair, had paid little attention.

"I thought you might prefer this to the green wool," Elisabeth said. "It's woefully impractical, but then this is hardly a time for practicality."

She held up a dressing gown of pale pink silk, the sleeves lavish with lace, the skirt graceful and trailing. With a cry of delight, Alessa hurried across the room to give her cousin a hug. "You've been so good to me, Cousin Elisabeth. *Maman* couldn't have been kinder. In fact, I daresay she would have been far less sympathetic."

"Don't crush the silk," Elisabeth admonished, laughing and holding out the garment for Alessa to slip on.

The fabric was luxuriously soft and gossamer light. And, Alessa noted when she looked in the cheval glass, it made the most of her new shape, emphasizing the curve of her breasts. "Thank you," she said, turning back to Elisabeth. She hesitated a moment, adjusting the full sleeves. "This meeting is very important," she ventured suddenly. "That is, it would be important in any case, but Harry and I—It wasn't a love match. I thought that was what I wanted, but now . . ."

"You wish there was more between you?" Elisabeth's eyes were kind.

Alessa bit her lip. "Yes."

"Are you in love with him?"

It was a question Alessa had scarcely dared allow herself to consider, except perhaps after that last night they had spent together and later, when she learned she was expect-

29

ing the baby. "I don't know," she said truthfully. "But I do know I wish I knew him better."

Elisabeth sighed and sank down gracefully on the settee. Small and delicate, with thick, unbound ash blond hair, she appeared far younger than her thirty-nine years. But suddenly her face was tinged with weariness and her lovely eyes were troubled. "People of our sort don't marry for love, Alessa. Sometimes it comes after marriage, if one is lucky. You are fortunate. You have given your husband a son. That is important to a man."

The sadness in her voice was unmistakable. Alessa looked searchingly at her and for the first time saw not her cousin, who belonged to her mother's generation, but a fellow woman. Elisabeth had had only two children, both girls, who had died in early childhood. It was no secret that the Emperor kept a mistress, but Alessa had never considered what this might mean to his wife. That was how such things were arranged among European royalty, even among minor branches of the family such as Alessa's mother belonged to. *Maman* had married for love the second time, but that was an aberration in the general scheme of things.

Cousin Sacha had come to see Rutledge last night. He had sat on the edge of Alessa's bed and teased her, as he had teased her when she was a girl. Alessa had always looked on him as an honorary uncle. Now, for the first time, she felt a flash of anger at this handsome, careless, good-humored man who was her mother's favorite cousin and the Emperor of all Russia. Cousin Elisabeth deserved more. Although, Alessa thought, recalling the stories about the Empress and the handsome Polish Prince Adam Czartoryski, Elisabeth had not been unconsoled. Still, it seemed a sad and lonely sort of life.

Alessa was searching for something to say when one of the maids-of-honor entered the room to tell her that Lord Milverton had arrived and was on his way upstairs.

The news of Harry's arrival drove all other thoughts from Alessa's mind. Elisabeth, her melancholy gone, embraced

30

Alessa and then whisked herself and her maid-of-honor out of the room. They would not intrude on the reunion between husband and wife. Alessa smoothed the skirt of the new dressing gown, ran a hand through her hair, and crossed the room to look down at Rutledge. He had fallen asleep after his morning feeding, but as Alessa bent over the cradle, he opened his eyes and gave a loud, demanding cry.

"Darling, what's the matter?" Alessa gathered him into her arms to offer comfort and discovered the cause of his distress. His napkin was damp. Dismayed, she glanced at the door. Hitherto, she had rung for one of the nurses to attend to changing him, but she could not do so now, with Harry about to arrive. Nor could she leave the child in his present discomfort. There was only one solution. She would have to change him herself. She had watched the nurse do it, and she would be a poor mother if she could not manage such a simple task herself.

Murmuring softly to the squalling baby, Alessa shifted him against her shoulder and crossed to the chest of drawers where his things were kept. It was awkward to move while he squirmed against her, but she managed to extract clean towels, a fresh napkin, and a laundry bag. She carried the things to a table, spread a towel over the bedding in the cradle, and settled Rutledge on it, very pleased with how well she was managing. But when she set him down, he only cried more loudly, and when she tried to untie the tapes on his napkin, he would not lie still. Helpless infants, it seemed, had surprisingly strong muscles.

Soothing words had no effect whatsoever. Feeling hopelessly incompetent, Alessa tugged at the tapes. At last, she managed to ease the soiled napkin out from under him. She straightened up with a sigh of relief and reached for the laundry bag. But instead of picking it up, she froze, the napkin held in one hand. Just inside the doorway, regarding her with a quizzical expression, stood her baby's father.

With Rutledge's cries filling the air and all her attention

on her task, she must not have heard him come in. How long had he been standing there?

Alessa drew a breath. Her lovely dressing gown was crumpled, her angelic baby was bawling, and she was holding a dirty napkin, but she was a Tassio and Tassios were equal to anything. "You must forgive me, Harry," she said. "I'm afraid I've never done this before."

"Neither have I, if it comes to that." Harry crossed the room with long easy strides, picked up the laundry bag, and calmly held it out to her. "He has strong lungs, doesn't he? Would it help if I held him?"

"No, it's easier when he's lying down." Alessa dropped the dirty napkin into the bag and reached for a towel. "It's just that he won't hold still."

But Rutledge's cries, Alessa realized, were not as loud as before. They said children couldn't recognize people at this age, but he seemed to know there was someone new in the room. Harry held out a tanned, long-fingered hand. Rutledge grasped hold of Harry's forefinger. The cries stopped, and when Alessa wiped him clean with the towel, he held remarkably still. She slid the fresh napkin beneath him and contrived to do up the tapes. It was not as neat a job as the nurse would have done, but it would do. She had managed it. She and Harry together.

Flushed with triumph, Alessa lifted the now complacent baby into her arms. This was the moment she had been waiting for. "Harry, may I present the Viscount Rutledge."

It seemed to Alessa that a shadow crossed Harry's face, but it was quickly gone and she told herself she must have imagined it. He looked down at Rutledge and in his eyes she saw the same wonder she had felt when she first held the child. "Would you like to hold him?" she asked, feeling a surge of pure happiness.

Harry gave the crooked grin he used to mask moments of feeling. "You aren't afraid I'll break him?"

Alessa smiled in return. "Babies are sturdier than they look. My nurse told me that when Simon was born. Just be sure you support his head. So. You see? It's really remarkably easy."

Alessa stepped back and watched with satisfaction as her husband cradled their child. Harry held the baby carefully, but he did not appear overly awkward. He was going to make a splendid father, just as she had expected. "He has your mouth, I think," Harry said, studying the baby's features. "And the Dudley chin, I fear. He's going to grow up as stubborn as the rest of us."

He looked up and met her eyes. It was the first time they had looked at each other properly, without the baby's needs to divert them. Harry seemed leaner than before, his skin was tanned and roughened by the wind, his hair longer and lightened by the sun. His eyes looked darker and more serious somehow. Alessa had the sudden conviction that it was a long time since he had laughed.

"It's a great relief to see you looking so well," Harry said. "Both of you." He hesitated. "I'm so very sorry I wasn't here."

"You didn't know. And you're here now." Alessa felt surprisingly awkward. She wished he would kiss her, but he couldn't, of course, while he was holding the baby. "It was an easy birth, considering he came so early."

"They said you'd been ill."

"That was mostly because of the journey. Harry . . . you're not angry I came to Russia?"

"You had every right to come to Russia. Your family is here."

Alessa looked steadily at him. "That's not why I came."

Harry returned her regard and it seemed to Alessa that the light went out of his eyes. "No," he agreed. "I know it isn't. Alessa . . ."

His words were drowned out by a determined cry from Rutledge. "He's hungry," Alessa said and found she was relieved at the interruption. The look in Harry's eyes before he spoke had disturbed her more than she cared to admit.

When Harry put Rutledge into her arms, she caught a

whiff of shaving soap. The familiar, spicy smell was reassuring. Whatever had happened, whatever he had to tell her, some things were still the same.

The scent also brought back aching memories, which were perhaps not best dwelled upon in Harry's presence. Alessa sought refuge on the settee and loosened the pink silk dressing gown so she could ease it off one shoulder. Then, studiously avoiding Harry's gaze, she unbuttoned the lawn nightdress and settled Rutledge at her breast. Distracted by the sharp feel of Rutledge pulling at her nipple yet gratified to know she was suckling him, she told herself her fears were no more than foolish imaginings.

Harry sat on a chair opposite his wife and watched her nurse their son. He had forgot how beautiful she was. Or perhaps the baby's birth had given her a new beauty, a sort of inner radiance which had nothing to do with lustrous hair or fine features or a tempting body. Not that her body was easy to ignore, especially now, with the baby drawing on her swollen breast. How could a sight that was so maternal also be so potently erotic?

Aware of his quickened pulse, Harry drew an uneven breath. He tried to concentrate on the baby. His son. No longer an abstract idea, but a living breathing creature. Christ, but he seemed fragile. Yet before long he would be an independent person with his own thoughts and wishes. Wishes, Harry vowed, which would be respected better than his own had been.

But even these thoughts were treacherous, for looking at the baby Harry found it impossible not to remember the night the child had been conceived. That small person was part of his flesh and of Alessa's, the creation, if not of their love, at least of their passion. For a moment, the memory of Alessa clinging to him in the throes of release was so vivid it almost seemed anything was possible between them.

Then, with all the chill of a dash into the snow after a Russian steambath, Harry reminded himself of why he had

34

come to St. Petersburg and what he had to say to Alessa. This moment, which seemed so full of promise, was merely a prelude to a scene which might devastate all they had between them.

Determined to savor these few moments of tranquillity, Harry asked his wife about Simon and Peter, relieved to find that at least his voice was steady. Alessa answered him with tolerable composure. By tacit agreement, nothing was said about his reasons for coming to Russia or hers for following him.

At last the baby released her second breast and fell back against her arm. Murmuring endearments, Alessa settled him in the cradle and spent a long time tucking the blankets around him. Harry stood beside his chair, his gaze never leaving her. He longed to touch her but knew he did not dare. He would need every ounce of control he possessed to get through the next half-hour.

Alessa straightened up and looked at Harry. She wondered if he would take her in his arms, now that the baby was asleep, but he made no move toward her. Save for when she had given him Rutledge to hold and when he had given Rutledge back to her, they had not touched at all.

"I owe you an explanation," he said.

"You owe me nothing," said Alessa, moving back to the settee and speaking with deliberate calm. "We agreed to lead separate lives."

Harry gave a faint, strained smile. "Did that agreement include unexplained visits to foreign countries?"

"At the time it never occurred to me that that would be an issue," Alessa said, seating herself and adjusting the folds of her dressing gown.

"Nor to me either, God knows." Harry dropped down into his chair. "You know I was stationed here for several years before my father's death."

Alessa drew in her breath. Something in Harry's matter-of-fact words filled her with a painful certainty. She should have guessed and it shouldn't matter, but she hadn't let herself think about it and it did. "There was a woman, wasn't there?" she said.

"There were several," Harry said ruefully. "I was rather indiscriminate in those days." His face grew serious. "They all knew the rules of the game. Except for Nadia."

Icy cold clamped about Alessa's chest where before she had felt warmth and joy. "Nadia?" she asked, her voice brittle.

Harry's eyes darkened as though with remembered pain. "This isn't a pretty story and it doesn't show me to advantage," he said, "but remember it was before our marriage. Before I had even met you."

He spoke gently, but it was a rebuke. She had no right to be jealous, but she was, bitterly. Not so much because Harry had once shared his bed with this woman Nadia, but because he still felt tenderly toward her. That much was clear from his tone. "I understand," Alessa said with what dignity she could muster.

"Nadia's father was a shopkeeper," Harry continued, speaking rapidly. "Respectable, though not particularly prosperous. She had a sort of understanding with her cousin Grigor Lychenko, though they weren't formally betrothed." Harry grimaced and Alessa knew that his feelings toward Lychenko were far from charitable. "Nadia's family doted on Grigor—he's a captain in the Guard and the son of a minor nobleman. They didn't worry much about where Nadia went when she was with him. One night he took her to a tavern—a damned fool thing to have done, for it was no place for a girl of eighteen. I happened to be there that night. Grigor drank too much and got into a fight, and before long, half the people in the tavern were brawling. Nadia was terrified. I took her home."

"To her home?" Alessa asked, though she knew what the answer would be.

"No." Harry met her gaze. "To mine. I was drunk myself," he added after a moment. "Nadia was furious with Grigor. It never should have happened. But it did. At the

36

time it didn't occur to me that there might be consequences."

Alessa bit back a cry. It was obvious where all this was leading, but somehow she had refused to see it. She should not be surprised—her own father had sired a bastard daughter—yet she found the thought that Rutledge might not be Harry's firstborn inexpressibly painful. "You're telling me you have a by-blow in St. Petersburg?" she demanded. "Is that why you came?" Dear God, had he come all this way because Nadia sent him word about their child? Did she still mean that much to him?

"No." Harry ran his fingers through his hair, his face drawn with the effort to contain his feelings. "I don't have a by-blow. But three months after the night at the tavern, Nadia turned up outside my lodgings. She was with child. Grigor would have nothing to do with her, her family was in a rage, and she had no one else to turn to."

"She lost the baby?" Alessa asked, ashamed that she should feel such relief at someone else's suffering.

"Six months later I received word that she died giving birth to a stillborn child. By then I was back in England."

"But you had provided for her before you left." Not all men would have done so, but Alessa knew Harry would never neglect his responsibilities.

"You might say so," Harry said. He hesitated. "I married her."

Alessa stared at him. "That's not funny," she said sharply.

"It wasn't meant to be."

Alessa's heart thudded to a standstill. "But—you don't mean—you don't mean you actually *married* her?" A shopkeeper's daughter, a girl he had known for scarce more than a drunken hour.

"I thought it was time I began to take some responsibility for my actions," Harry said evenly.

"Yes, but to marry the girl . . ."

Harry's brows drew together. "Is it so hard to believe that

37

I have some vestiges of honor? Or that she was worthy of them?"

"No, of course not," Alessa said with impatience. "I know you would never cast off a woman who was"—she hesitated; it was painful even to say it—"who was carrying your child. But there are ways of handling these things. No one expects a gentleman to—"

"She was a virgin until I took her to my bed." Harry's eyes were colder than Alessa had ever seen them. "The man she expected to marry had cast her off. No other man would have her. To her family she was at best an embarrassment."

"But—"

"She was eighteen, Alessa. The same age you were when you were first betrothed."

Alessa flinched inwardly. She found any mention of her first betrothal almost too painful to bear. To have Harry refer to it in such a context was like a blow to her gut. How could he be so unfeeling?

"You didn't tell me," she said, beginning to understand the full implications of his story. Anger welled up in her, pushing the pain aside. "How could you? How could you ask me to be your wife and not tell me you had been married before?"

"I scarcely told anyone except Nadia's family. I knew my own family would be in an uproar if they heard of it. Time enough when the baby was born and I took it and Nadia back to England." Harry tented his fingers and stared down at them. "Two months before the baby was due, I received word that my father was failing fast and I must return home immediately. Nadia was in no condition to travel, so I left her with her family, intending to return for her after the baby was born."

He sprang to his feet and took a turn about the room, then stood with his arms resting on the back of his chair. "I arrived home to find my family in confusion. It was no time to make revelations about my marriage. A month later

Nadia's sister wrote to tell me that Nadia and the baby were dead. There was no point in burdening my family with the story. My father died shortly after and I found myself Earl of Milverton."

Harry stared at the floor, as if haunted by the demons of the past. Ashamed of her anger, Alessa got to her feet and crossed to his side. "I'm so sorry," she said, laying a hand on his arm. "But it is in the past. You must learn to forget about it."

"Forget?" Harry gave a bitter laugh which made Alessa draw back.

"Harry?" she said uncertainly. "Why did you come to St. Petersburg? To see Nadia's family?"

"You could say that. Oh, Christ." Harry gave another laugh, which changed to a groan. He dragged his hands over his face. "Shortly after I returned from Denmark, I received a letter from Ned. He was one of the few people who knew about my first marriage."

Alessa nodded. She'd met Edward Clifford when he'd last been in England.

"Grigor Lychenko had got in touch with him. Grigor said he had information he thought I might be interested in. He asked Edward how to reach me."

Alessa swallowed and clenched her fingers on the soft silk of the dressing gown. "What sort of information?"

Harry lifted a hand, then let it fall, as if to acknowledge that he couldn't soften what he was about to say. "It seems the baby wasn't stillborn after all."

The breath caught in Alessa's throat. "I see," she said. Then, "No, I don't. Why did they tell you it had died?"

"Nadia's sister Irina knew I'd take the child to England. She wanted to raise it herself."

"And now?" Alessa could feel the tension between them. Harry seemed to be drawing farther and farther away from her and there was no way to bring him back.

"Irina was carried off by a chill last winter. She was a widow and both her parents had died since I left Russia.

Grigor became the child's guardian and decided I should know of its existence." Harry drew a breath. "The child's four years old now. I came to Russia to fetch it."

"It?" Alessa asked, looking into his eyes and seeing her son's future, her own efforts, her value to Harry as the mother of his heir—the only thing he had really needed her for—all crumble to dust.

"He," Harry said. "It's a son."

Chapter Three

Harry watched his wife's lovely face, the face he saw in his dreams, the face he longed to cover with kisses, contort with bitterness and rage.

"How could you?" Alessa's rich, throaty voice trembled with fury. "You never breathed a word of this. For two whole years. Not when you asked me to be your wife, not when we were married, not when—"

She broke off, her breath catching, but the unspoken words hung between them. *Not when you came to my bed.* In her eyes Harry saw the memory of that last night when she had surrendered to him so completely. By keeping such a secret from her, he had betrayed all they had shared in that hour of passion.

"I thought it didn't have anything to do with us," Harry said and knew it was no kind of answer.

"Didn't have anything to do with us?" Alessa gave a sharp brittle laugh which was on the edge of hysteria. "Oh, no, of course it didn't. Why should it concern me that I wasn't your first wife? Why should I have any right to know that our son wouldn't be your heir?"

Harry drew in his breath. "If I'd had any notion that the child was alive, I'd have told you before I asked you to be my wife. You must believe that."

"Oh, I believe it." She laughed again, but the sound was

as harsh as the grating of a knife. "If you'd known you already had an heir, you'd have had no reason to marry me at all."

"Stop it, Alessa," Harry said, moving toward her. "You know that's not true."

"Don't, Harry. Don't touch me." Alessa sprang back, putting the chair between them.

The simple, economical movement was like a slap in the face. Harry held himself rigid. She was breathing quickly, her color high, her eyes lit with anger. He wanted to shake her and make her listen to what he had to say. He wanted, even more urgently, to take her in his arms. He could do neither.

Alessa folded her arms in front of her, as if to protect herself. "How can you be sure he's your son?" she demanded. "Is he the image of one of the Dudley ancestors?"

Harry tried to smile. "I'll tell you when I've seen him."

Alessa's eyes widened. For a moment, incredulity overcame anger. "You haven't seen him yet?"

"No," Harry admitted, goaded by this reminder of all the other frustrations he had faced since his arrival in St. Petersburg. "It took nearly a fortnight for Ned and me to locate Grigor."

"He was hiding? I thought he wanted you to come for the child."

"He was at a summer house on the Volga with a married lady whose husband is a Cossack and a fellow officer."

"I see. For a tradesman's nephew, he has expensive tastes." Alessa moved to a chair some distance away and sat down, her back very straight. "I still don't understand why you didn't visit your"—there was a slight catch in her breath—"your son once Captain Lychenko reappeared."

Harry controlled the urge to bellow. It was Grigor, not Alessa, whose neck he wanted to wring. "Because Grigor's been away on maneuvers. And because he won't tell me where the child is."

Alessa's finely arched brows drew together. "Why not?"

Harry knew there was no easy way to put it. "He first wants to be assured that I will adequately compensate him for the care of the child."

Alessa stared at him. "You're a fool, Harry," she said. "This is straight out of Mrs. Radcliffe. The secret heir who's been hidden away for four years. Your precious Nadia's cousin is out to line his own purse. And perhaps to get revenge. After all, you debauched the girl he wanted to marry. He's probably trying to foist his own bastard off on you. Or someone else's."

The fact that she had touched on the dark fear which had haunted Harry ever since he learned of the child and especially since his meeting with Grigor did nothing to improve his humor. "I doubt Grigor would have the initiative for such a scheme," he said. "But it's true there's no way to be sure."

"No. There's no way to be sure." Alessa pushed herself out of the chair and walked to the fireplace, tossing back her long dark hair. The hair he had once seen spread in all its shining glory against a linen pillowcase. For a moment, the memory of how it had felt to bury his face in that silky softness overcame all else.

"And when you see him, Harry?" Alessa asked, her back to him. "Is there a mysterious Dudley birthmark which will let you know for sure?"

Harry tried to order his thoughts and senses. "Dudleys have always been marked more by personality than appearance," he said.

"Then you'll never know for sure." Alessa's voice was well modulated, but he could hear the tension rippling through it, like the stirring of wind which warns of a storm. "This child who may be the son of God knows who will come back to England and be raised as your heir,

43

and our son . . ." Alessa turned to face him and he saw the storm break in her eyes. "My God, Harry, how could you do this to us?"

There was anger in her voice, but also a stab of anguish, a plea for understanding. Harry strode forward without thinking and gathered her to him. She stood rigid, but she did not try to pull out of his arms. Encouraged, he began to stroke her hair. Alessa drew a shuddering breath which drained some of the tension from her body. Harry felt the wetness of tears against his shoulder.

"You have every right to be angry," he said, his lips against her hair. "But you must see that if there's any chance the boy is my son, I have to accept him. I owe that to the child. And I owe it to Nadia."

Alessa had begun to relax against him, but at his words she suddenly stiffened. "And what do you owe to me?" she said, looking up at him.

His fingers trembled with the urge to pull her to him again. A host of images chased each other through his mind. Alessa admitting she was frightened the day she agreed to be his wife. Alessa aloof and breathtaking in white silk and pearls on their wedding day. Alessa, her breath warm on his skin, her body moving urgently beneath his own the night their son had been conceived.

"I owe you a husband who is a man of honor," he said.

"And is it honorable to disinherit your son?" Alessa demanded.

For a moment Harry again felt the baby's featherlight weight in his arms and saw the delicately veined head and impossibly tiny hands. "One day our son will understand," he said, fervently hoping this would prove true. "As I pray you will."

"No." Alessa wrenched herself out of his arms and drew back. Her eyes were dark, not with tears but with fury, as if she had armored herself against vulnerability. "I agreed to be the Countess of Milverton, Harry. I'll honor my side of the bargain. But don't expect me to understand why you insist on this folly. It would be too much if our son was betrayed by both his parents."

"Alessa . . ." Harry stretched out a hand to her, but as he did so, she drew back still farther. Her face, which could be so full of life, was cold and set, like smooth, implacable marble.

Harry let his hand fall to his side. It was impossible to reason with Alessa when she was in a temper, and his own temper was frayed to the breaking point. If he remained in the room much longer, he would only worsen the rift between them. "As you wish," he said, his voice hard. "I will, of course, remain in Russia until you are able to travel home. But we can speak of that later. I won't trouble you further with my presence."

He turned, wanting only to be gone from the room. But then, yielding to a compulsion, he crossed to the cradle and looked down at the baby for a moment. So small. So fragile. So alive. Why hadn't anyone warned him how he would feel when he first looked at his child?

"He needs a name," Alessa said. "I can't go on calling him Rutledge. I thought you might want to name him after your father, but that, of course, was when I thought he was your heir. Does the other child have a name?"

"Nikolai." Harry felt his throat close. "He's called Niki."

"Then I won't call my son Nicholas." Alessa's voice was expressionless. "Other than that, do you care what name I choose?"

Harry felt a moment of blinding rage. Care? Of course he cared. But perhaps he owed it to Alessa to let her make the decision. "I'll call in a few days," he said. "We can discuss the name then."

Unable to face her any longer, he turned and strode to the door. His chest was tight with something more than anger and guilt. Alessa's voice echoed in his head. *I agreed to be the Countess of Milverton.* Not *I agreed to be your wife.*

She had made it clear that her primary concern was for her own position and the child's. It should come as no surprise. He'd known from the first that she hadn't married him, she'd married the Earl of Milverton. He had no right to want more.

But he did.

"You can understand why she's upset, Harry." Edward Clifford transferred a second helping of broiled herring onto his plate, an unaccustomed frown on his face. "Alessa's the sort who's been raised to think of position as everything. I mean, if you hadn't been the Earl of Milverton . . ." Edward broke off, coughed, and became very busy cutting up the herring.

"If I hadn't been the Earl of Milverton, she wouldn't have married me." Harry set down his coffee cup and leaned back in his chair. "It's all right, Ned. It's no secret."

Edward looked up and met his friend's gaze, his eyes filled with earnest sympathy. "Her family wouldn't have let her look twice at any man who wasn't at least an earl. That doesn't mean there wasn't a reason she chose you."

"Of course there was. I offered for her and I wasn't wholly repulsive." Harry turned away from the table and glanced out the window. The morning sun streamed into the study, warming the woodwork and casting an unremittingly cheerful light on the breakfast dishes. Though it was not yet nine, already the heat was oppressive. He and Ned were breakfasting in their shirtsleeves. But the oppression Harry felt had little to do with the weather. It was two days since his visit to Alessa, but time had done nothing to ease the turmoil he felt. He had woken yesterday morning with a strong urge to borrow one of Ned's horses and gallop back to Tsarkoe Selo. Only the knowledge that he had to give her time to overcome her pain and anger had prevented him from doing so.

Aware that he had been appallingly bad company since

46

his arrival in St. Petersburg, Harry looked back at his friend with a sudden grin. "Sorry, Ned. At this rate I'll put you off marriage entirely. Julia will never forgive me."

Edward's concerned expression gave way to an abashed smile. He had known all the Dudley children since childhood, but on his last trip to England he had begun to stare at Harry's sister Julia in a moonstruck sort of way which had made Harry feel a pang of regret for what he and Alessa would never know.

"That's one advantage of being a younger son," Edward said. "At least I don't have to worry that Julia wants me for my title. Of course," he added, in a tone of forced lightness, "I do have to worry if she wants me at all."

Harry regarded his friend with a mixture of amusement and envy. "You wouldn't say so if you'd seen Julia's face whenever your name's been mentioned for the past year or so. And at least you know you have her guardian's consent. Provided you behave yourself, of course."

"Devil a bit," Edward said in a far more cheerful voice. "There's always Gretna Green."

"I detect a distinct lack of respect in your tone, Clifford," Harry said, reaching for the coffeepot.

"Do you?" Edward asked, finishing up the last of the herring. "That's what comes of talking with people who knew you in your misspent youth."

Harry set down the coffeepot rather too quickly, so that some of the dark liquid sloshed onto the white linen table cloth. "Quite," he said in an expressionless voice.

"Oh, Lord," Edward said with a groan, "I'm sorry, Harry. I didn't mean it that way. I can't seem to say anything right this morning."

"It's not you, it's the situation." Harry mopped up the stain with his napkin. "Sorry about the damage."

"Oh, that's all right." Edward waved aside the apology. For a moment, the only sound was the muffled noise of traffic from the street below. "You said you wanted a marriage of convenience," Edward said, staring fixedly into his egg cup.

Harry laid the napkin aside and looked at Edward. A good friend could be counted on to remind one of one's own folly. "So now that I've got it, I should have the grace to stop complaining?"

"Not necessarily. I just wondered when you changed your mind."

"I'm not sure I have. Alessa and I have hurt each other enough as it is. God knows what sort of damage we'd do if we actually started caring for one another."

"Meaning you don't care for her?" Edward asked, regarding him steadily.

There were drawbacks, Harry decided, in having a friend who was trained to read the smallest nuance in a comment made across a diplomatic negotiating table. "Damn it, no, meaning nothing of the sort."

"So I suspected." Edward gave a faint smile. "It's understandable. She's very beautiful."

"It's not that." Harry dropped his head into his hands and massaged his temples which were beginning to throb. "Or not just that. She's . . ."

He hesitated, searching for adequate words to describe Alessa, and was interrupted by footsteps and the sound of the door being pushed open. Edward's valet Wilton stepped into the room, an apologetic look on his face. "Excuse me, my lord, Mr. Clifford. There are two young gentlemen outside. One of them says he is Lord Milverton's brother-in-law."

Harry looked up, not sure whether to laugh or to curse. He should have suspected Simon would come seeking an explanation. "Show them in, Wilton. And bring us two more place settings."

Edward regarded his friend with sympathy. "Is young Simon likely to challenge you to a duel?" he asked when the valet had left the room.

48

"I shouldn't think so. But only because he doesn't approve of them. Simon's very modern in his thinking. Whatever you do, don't treat him like a child. It can be fatal."

Though he spoke lightly, Harry knew that the coming interview might be crucial to any hope he had of salvaging his marriage. He got to his feet and walked forward when Wilton ushered Simon and Peter into the room. Harry had not seen the boys for over six months, and it seemed to him that they had both aged in the interval. But perhaps it was merely that he had never seen them in such a grave humor. Simon had wrapped himself in the princely demeanor he only adopted on occasions of great formality or great crisis. Peter looked at once determined and uncomfortable.

After a stilted exchange of greetings, Edward asked if the boys would like breakfast. A look of relief crossed Peter's face — he and Simon must have left Tsarkoe Selo before seven o'clock and Harry doubted if they had eaten — but it was quickly masked.

"Coffee would be welcome," Simon said with dignity.

When they were all seated at the table and supplied with fresh coffee, Harry voiced the question he had been longing to ask since Simon stepped into the room. "How is she?"

"She's been crying." Simon delivered the words with the precision of an expert sword thrust.

"The doctor says she's doing well, sir," Peter added quickly. "He came to see her yesterday. He says the baby's well too."

"When are you going to see them again?" Simon asked.

"I don't know. At the moment I think your sister would prefer that I left her alone." Harry sipped his coffee. It was hot and burned his mouth. "How much do you know?" he asked.

Simon folded his arms. For all their squabbling, Harry

knew he was fiercely loyal to his sister. It had taken Simon weeks to decide Harry was a man to be trusted, not someone who would hurt Alessa as her first betrothed had done. Eventually he and Harry had become friends. With a pang, Harry realized that he risked losing that friendship as well as his marriage.

"Alessa says you were married before," Simon said, his eyes hard and uncompromising.

"That's true."

"And that you have a son from your first marriage."

"That's true as well."

"And that you didn't tell her until two days ago."

"True again." Harry gave a faint smile. "Am I totally damned?"

Simon met Harry's gaze. "I can't say until I know the whole story, can I? That's why Peter and I came here."

Harry laid his hands palm down on the table top and stared at them for a moment. Then, as calmly and matter-of-factly as he could, he told Simon and Peter what he had told Alessa two days before.

The boys listened in silence. Peter looked fixedly at his coffee cup. Simon kept his eyes on Harry. Harry was reminded of a tutor he'd had at Oxford who would listen to his students in just such judicious silence and then proceed to tear their argument to ribbons.

When Harry finished, Simon was silent. "Alessa has a corker of a temper, just like *Maman*," he said at last. "Very often I don't agree with her. But this time I can understand. It's not just herself she's upset about, it's the baby."

Harry had an acute memory of how he had felt when Alessa placed the child in his arms. "I know," he said, surprised to find his voice so even.

Simon's brows drew together. "She thinks you should have told her the truth before you were married, but I can see why you didn't. You thought it was all in the past." He looked at Harry, some of the tension gone from

50

his face. "It's a beastly mess, but I expect in your place I'd have done the same."

Harry felt a wave of intense relief. It was a small victory, but it gave him strength to face the rest of the battle. "I'm glad to hear it," he said. "Now," he added, looking from Simon to Peter, "would you like some breakfast?"

The last of the tension was shattered. Simon and Peter fell upon the food with unabashed enthusiasm. "It's been months since we had a proper English breakfast," Peter said, helping himself to bacon and boiled eggs.

"Ned likes everything to be as English as possible," Harry said, handing Simon the orange marmalade. "That's why he's been a diplomat since he left university."

"Only doing my best to keep up the standards of my country," Edward retorted.

Peter grinned, but Simon had turned serious again. "I'll try to help smooth things over," he said, spreading marmalade on a piece of toast. "But I don't know what good it will do. Alessa doesn't always listen to me."

"I'm sure she'll come round with time," Peter said. "She usually does."

"Yes," Simon agreed. "Of course."

Both boys looked at Harry with determined optimism. Harry realized they were trying to bolster his confidence. He was touched, but far from reassured. As he debated an appropriate answer, Wilton entered the room once again, bearing a sealed paper. "This just came for you, Lord Milverton. The boy who delivered it said it was urgent."

"Quite a busy morning," Edward said. Then he looked at Harry and his expression changed. "Is it . . ."

Harry gave a brief nod, then slit open the paper and stared at the familiar black scrawl. There was a quiet click as Wilton discreetly withdrew.

"Is it bad news?" Simon asked. "It's not about Alessa, is it?"

51

"Not directly, no. And I wouldn't say it's bad news." Harry folded the paper and looked at Edward and the boys. There was no point in keeping this a secret. They were all in his confidence now. "It's from Grigor Lychenko," he said, folding the paper. "He's completed his maneuvers. I'm to meet him tomorrow at an inn in Krasnoe Selo, and he'll bring the child."

As their coachman pulled away from the curb and made his way down Moika Street, Simon slumped back against the silk-covered squabs. "*Maman* is going to be furious."

"She'll be furious about us coming to Russia anyway," Peter pointed out. He had grown accustomed to the Princess Sofia's rages in the five years he and Simon had been friends. "This may not make it any worse."

Simon shook his head. "This is different."

"Because she'll think Harry betrayed Alessa?"

"Because she'll think her grandchild has been disinherited."

Peter frowned. "But the other boy was born first. Alessa's baby wasn't the heir to begin with. So he can't be disinherited."

"I didn't say he was. I said that's how *Maman* would see it." Simon shifted his position on the carriage seat. "It was *Maman* who convinced Alessa to marry Harry. She wanted Alessa to be a countess. And she wanted her to be the mother of an earl. I doubt *Maman* would have encouraged the marriage if she'd known Harry already had a son."

"Surely your mother of all people understands that marriage has to do with more than inheritance," Peter objected. He'd heard the story often enough. How in her youth Princess Sofia had fallen in love with a young English diplomat, only to have her parents interfere and see that she married someone of her own rank. How years later, after her husband's death, she had met the diplomat again and married him. Peter did not consider himself overly romantic, but he thought it was a touching story.

"Oh, *Maman* loves Michael," Simon said. "But that's not the way she was raised to think of marriage. It's not the way things are done in her family. Our family."

Peter shook his head in puzzlement. As the son of a viscount, he knew he had been born to privilege, but he would never fully understand the rarified world to which Simon and Alessa belonged. He said as much.

Simon grinned. "I'm not sure I understand it either."

The carriage lurched as their coachman made a sudden turn. Peter grasped hold of the leather strap and glanced out the window. Despite the circumstances of their visit, St. Petersburg fascinated him. They were moving across a small stone bridge with a wrought iron railing. The expanse of water below must be the River Moika. A stately barge was headed toward the bridge, with liveried men at the oars and two elegantly dressed ladies seated beneath a pink velvet canopy. But the dignified picture was marred by a young boy in a bright red cap sitting on the pavement at the edge of the river with a fishing pole in his hands.

"We're on the Nevsky Prospekt now," Simon said as they clattered onto a sweeping cobbled avenue, broader than any street in London.

Peter pressed his face to the cool glass and looked about in fascination. Accustomed to London, where medieval courts jostled modern squares and crescents, he found it odd to be in a city where no building was more than a hundred years old. "What's that?" he asked, gesturing toward a massive baroque building with a sloping red tile roof.

Simon frowned. "The Stroganov Palace, I think. It's a long time since I've been here." He gave a sudden sigh, a rare acknowledgment of the strain of the past few weeks.

"Things seemed a lot simpler in England, didn't they?"

"Things were a lot simpler," Peter said. But then he thought back to his visits to the Milverton estate, to rare moments when he had seen Harry and Alessa laughing together and more frequent glimpses of them apart, in separate spheres of the vast, coldly formal house. "I don't know a lot about marriage," Peter ventured, "but I'm not sure things were ever right between Harry and Alessa. Even in England."

Simon met his friend's gaze and nodded slowly. "I know," he said. "That's what's worrying me."

It was early afternoon by the time they reached Tsarkoe Selo. Simon at once made inquiries about his sister's whereabouts and learned she had taken the baby out into the park surrounding the palace. He was determined to go in search of her, and after having spent four of the previous six hours in the carriage, Peter was relieved at the excuse for a walk.

They found Alessa seated on a stone bench in the shade of a cluster of oak trees beside one of the smaller ponds. A pair of swans glided gracefully across the water, but Alessa's eyes were on the baby, who was in a carriage beside her. She was wearing a loose white dress and an embroidered shawl in the same soft green as the leaves of the tree above. Her hair tumbled unpinned down her back. Peter thought she looked very pretty. And very unhappy.

At the crunch of leaves along the dirt path, Alessa looked up quickly. She seemed disappointed when she saw who was approaching. Peter wondered if she had been hoping Harry had come to see her.

"Hullo," Simon said, ducking beneath a low branch and coming to stand beside his sister.

"Hullo," Alessa returned, her back straight, her gaze aloof and composed. "Did you have a pleasant trip?"

There was a challenge in her gaze. For once, she'd

managed to take Simon by surprise. Which, Peter knew, was not easy to do.

"You know where we've been?" Simon asked.

Alessa reached over and smoothed the baby's covers. "Cousin Elisabeth said you'd asked to borrow a carriage so you could go into St. Petersburg," she said in a tone of disinterest. "I assume you went to visit Harry."

That, Peter thought, accounted for the aloofness. Alessa took their going to see Harry as a betrayal.

Simon put his hands behind his back and stared fixedly at his sister. "Don't you want to know how your husband is?"

Alessa continued to smooth the already pristine blankets. "I assume you'd tell me if he'd fallen ill or met with an accident." She looked round suddenly, concern in her eyes.

"He's fine." Peter made haste to reassure Alessa as he had reassured Harry earlier. Sometimes he thought Simon was too hard on his sister.

"I see." Alessa became remote again. She'd been like that ever since Harry visited her two days ago, though Peter could read the telltale signs and knew she had been crying in private.

There was an awkward silence. A slight breeze stirred the leaves and ruffled the surface of the pond. One of the swans climbed onto dry land and shook the water from its wings.

Peter stepped forward and looked down at the baby. He had a younger brother and two younger sisters and he liked children, even very small ones. "Does he like the park?" Peter asked Alessa.

"He seems to. That is, he's been sound asleep since we came outside, so at least he doesn't have a strong objection to it."

Simon remained where he had been standing, a little apart from the others, a look of calculation on his face. "Harry got a message while we were there," he said.

"Did he?" Alessa was looking at the baby again.

"From his first wife's cousin. He's going to bring the little boy to see Harry tomorrow."

Alessa stiffened. Then she swung round to look at her brother. "Where?"

"An inn in Krasnoe Selo." Simon looked immensely pleased with himself.

Peter watched the cold mask Alessa had worn for the past two days dissolve before his eyes. She did not look happy, but she certainly looked alive. Her eyes burned with a sort of suppressed excitement and her cheeks were flushed with color. "Krasnoe Selo," she said. "That's about ten miles from here, isn't it?"

"I think so." Simon's tone was wary, as if he were beginning to realize that in shaking Alessa out of her melancholy he might have got more than he bargained for.

"Good." A smile crossed Alessa's face, not of joy but of triumph. "It should take us less than two hours."

"Us?" Simon asked.

"I assume you'll want to come with me. And we'll have to take the baby; I can't leave him for long." Alessa got to her feet and shook out the folds of her gown. "Don't look at me like that, Simon. Surely I have every right to meet my stepson."

Chapter Four

At first Harry thought he must have imagined seeing her. He was standing in the entrance hall of the inn, staring out the narrow windows for some sign of Grigor and thinking that he seemed to have spent the greatest part of the past month waiting. At midday the inn yard was crowded by officers of the Guard, and a number of them were accompanied by well-dressed ladies. Harry, on the lookout for Grigor, paid the women little heed. Until suddenly he found himself staring at his wife.

Or so he thought. His brief glimpse of her was quickly obliterated by a trio of soldiers, rather the worse for drink, who galloped into the yard and made a great commotion shouting for the ostlers. Harry told himself that his mind must be playing tricks on him. It had a way of doing that where Alessa was concerned.

But then the soldiers dismounted and the horses were led away and he saw her again. She was standing not twenty feet from the inn, a net bonnet framing her face, an elaborate pelisse of a shiny pale gray material falling in crisp folds about her. Even surrounded by the dust and chaos of the stables, she looked glorious. And she was the last person in the world Harry wanted to see.

Cursing under his breath, Harry pushed his way through the main door of the inn. Alessa was making her way across the yard now, her head turned to speak to Simon and Peter, who were walking beside her. Simon carried an oblong bas-

57

ket under his arm. Phillips, Alessa's maid, walked a little behind them, a blanket-wrapped bundle carefully cradled in her arms. The baby. Of course. The basket was for the baby to sleep in. Dear God in heaven, could it possibly get any worse?

Harry stopped, waiting for them to reach him. Simon saw him first and gave a helpless shrug. Alessa followed the direction of her brother's gaze. She looked directly at Harry, and for a moment he thought he saw uncertainty in her eyes. Then she gave a cool, controlled smile. She took another half-dozen steps and stopped in front of him, so near he could touch her, so aloof he would not have dared to.

"Hullo, Harry." At their last meeting she had been stripped of her self-control. Now her manner was as stiff and formal as the brim of her bonnet and the elegant folds of her pelisse. "You really should have told me you were to meet the boy today," she said. "Surely I have as much right to be present as you do. After all, I will be his stepmother."

There was no way Harry could argue with her without denying Nikolai the position in the family which he had been at such pains to uphold. "You must forgive me," he said. "I wasn't sure you'd be well enough to travel."

Alessa lifted her chin. "Men frequently make the mistake of thinking women are more fragile than we are. Captain Lychenko and the child aren't here yet?"

"No. Lychenko is always notoriously late. You'd best come inside. I'll see if I can procure a private room."

With a smile which made Harry think he vastly preferred her anger, Alessa moved past him into the inn.

"I'm sorry," Simon murmured to Harry as they followed. "I told her you'd be here. I didn't dream she'd take it into her head to come after you." He looked at Harry with a faint frown. "Though I suppose she does have a point: The boy will be a Dudley, and Alessa's a Dudley now."

"So she is," said Harry. It was just that he found it difficult enough to face the upcoming meeting without also having to worry about Alessa's response. A cowardly way of thinking perhaps, but true nonetheless.

The inn was crowded, but Harry found that, as in England, traveling with Alessa was a distinct advantage. One look at her assured ostlers and innkeepers alike that here was a lady of distinction. Within a very short time they were shown to a private room at the back of the inn, and a maidservant brought in a samovar and a plate of cakes.

Alessa saw the baby settled in his basket, then seated herself in a high-backed chair, stripped off her pale gray gloves, and began to serve the tea. The room had become her domain. Harry felt like a guest who is not quite sure of his welcome.

"You plan to take the child with you today?" Alessa asked, handing Harry a tall steaming glass.

"Yes." Of this at least Harry had no doubt. He sipped the tea, grateful for its bracing flavor. He'd never learned to drink it with sugar as most Russians did.

"Edward's lodgings are hardly the place for a child," Alessa observed.

This, Harry knew, was all too true, but he was determined to begin doing his duty by Nikolai as soon as possible. "We'll manage," he said.

"Edward may feel differently." Alessa's eyes were on the tap of the samovar as she filled a second glass. "I have spoken with Cousin Elisabeth. She agrees it would be best if you and the child remove to Tsarkoe Selo."

Harry drew a breath. He had been married to Alessa for nearly two years and she could still take him completely by surprise.

"It's very kind of the Empress to offer," Harry said. "But—"

"You're my husband. It would look odd if we lived fifteen miles apart." Alessa stirred a spoonful of sugar into the glass, then handed it to Simon. Simon carried it over to Phillips, who was sitting near the baby.

Alessa continued to pour the tea as if the matter was settled. Harry felt a moment of intense rebellion, the way he had as a boy when his father issued dictatorial commands about what was expected of the future Earl of Milverton. But Alessa had a number of points on her side. Edward had readily agreed to have Nikolai at his lodgings, but there was no denying it would be awkward. And neither he nor Alessa was anonymous. If he remained in St. Petersburg while she stayed at Tsarkoe Selo, it would cause talk, at court and at the embassy. He had caused Alessa enough pain already without subjecting her to that as well.

"If it's no inconvenience, I'd be most grateful," Harry said, swallowing his pride as he'd never learned to do with his father.

"I told you. It's all arranged." Alessa handed glasses of tea to Simon and Peter. "Cousin Elisabeth has already ordered a suite of rooms prepared for you." She looked up at Harry as she said this last. The message was plain. He was to move into the palace, but they would occupy separate chambers. As with so much of their marriage, it was appearances that counted.

Harry, who had stood throughout the exchange, retreated to a chair. Alessa sipped her own tea. Simon handed round the plate of cakes.

"We had a cracking drive here," Peter said into the silence. "The countryside is beautiful."

"Yes," said Simon, "it was more familiar than I thought it would be. *Maman* brought us here once to see the soldiers drilling. Remember, Alessa?"

Alessa took one of the cakes and handed the plate to Peter. "Distinctly. I was bored to tears."

Peter and Simon exchanged glances and lapsed into silence. Harry sent them a look of sympathy.

"The baby did splendidly in the carriage," Alessa said. "I was afraid the motion would make him sick, but he scarcely cried at all."

"I'm glad," Harry said.

Alessa set her glass down with a click and looked him full

in the face. There was a flash of anger in her eyes, the first sign of real emotion she'd shown. "You haven't looked at him," she said in a low voice. "Not once."

Harry swallowed. Even before Alessa arrived, he had been terrified that he would not feel the same instinctive love for Nikolai that he had felt when he first saw the baby. So much tipped the scales in the baby's favor. The fact that it was a child Harry had wanted, not a child conceived in a moment of drunken passion. The fact that Harry knew beyond a doubt that the baby was his. The fact that Alessa was its mother. If he looked at the baby now, when Grigor and Niki might arrive at any moment, the comparison would be unendurable. Even seated several feet away, he was aware of the baby's milky smell. That in itself threatened his determination to do what was right.

"I don't want to wake him," Harry said.

"Yes," Alessa said, her eyes cold once again. "Of course. Would anyone like another cake?"

The creak of the door saved all of them from answering. The moment Harry had been dreading and anticipating for weeks had arrived, and all he could feel was that it could not possibly be as bad as sitting here making painstaking conversation with his wife. He got to his feet and turned to the door, braced for his first sight of Nikolai, though he knew it was likely that Grigor would first come in alone.

As he had expected, only Grigor stood in the doorway, a look of surprise on his face as he took in the company before him. He would have expected Harry to come alone. Harry felt a moment of satisfaction. After waiting for Grigor for nearly four weeks, it was gratifying to have a momentary advantage.

"Late as usual," Harry said, stepping forward. He fixed the other man with a level gaze. "Where's the boy?"

"In the kitchen. I thought we should talk first." Grigor made an effort to recover his customary self-assurance. "I didn't know you meant to bring a party with you."

"It was a somewhat impromptu decision." Harry turned back to Alessa with a smile. Two could play at the business of keeping up appearances. "Captain Grigor Lychenko, my dear." He looked at Grigor. "My wife, Lady Milverton. Her brother Simon and his friend Peter Carne." Harry saw no need to inform Grigor of Alessa's and Simon's titles and relationship to the imperial family.

A look of amazement crossed Grigor's face, quickly replaced by a practiced smile. "Clifford did not tell me you had taken another wife. My felicitations, Lady Milverton. I see that Harry is a lucky man."

Alessa inclined her head and studied the man who had wreaked such havoc on their lives. Captain Lychenko was not quite as tall as Harry, but he carried himself with an air of easy arrogance. His hair, dark and thick and curly, fell rakishly over his forehead, he sported neatly clipped side whiskers and a dashing mustache, and his eyes, a dark, startling blue, surveyed her with appreciation. At eighteen he might have made her pulse beat a little faster. At twenty-three Alessa thought he looked shallow and weak beside her husband. The sort of man who wouldn't hesitate to palm a bastard child off on his cousin's husband if the rewards seemed great enough.

"I want to see the boy," Harry said. "We can talk on the way to the kitchen."

"There's no need to be in such a hurry, Harry," Lychenko protested. "I'll send for him when we've talked."

"No. Take me to him now."

Lychenko hesitated, then shrugged his shoulders. "Very well."

Alessa got to her feet. "I'm coming with you."

She met Harry's gaze, daring him to deny her. Harry looked at her for a moment, then nodded. "As you wish."

He did not offer her his arm. Not sure whether she was glad or sorry, Alessa looked back at her brother. "Come for me if the baby wakes."

She turned to the door to find Lychenko watching her

with fresh surprise. His eyes went to the basket in sudden comprehension. "I see you are to be doubly congratulated. A child."

"Yes. A little brother for Nikolai. I do hope they get on well." Alessa gave Lychenko her most brilliant smile and walked into the corridor.

The men followed her, but once there Lychenko caught Harry by the arm and detained him. "I've brought the boy here as we agreed. You haven't forgot your side of the bargain?"

Harry looked at Lychenko. For the first time, Alessa became aware of the palpable tension between the two men. They looked more like opponents in battle than relatives settling the fate of a child. "You'll get your money," Harry said.

Lychenko shook his head. "Compensation, Harry. I did assume the burden of the boy's care for four months. Your anger is misdirected. It was Irina, not I, who kept the child from you."

"Irina at least stood by Nadia when she was in trouble. Which is more than can be said for some of her relatives."

Lychenko's eyes hardened. "My dear Harry, if it wasn't for you, Nadia would never have been in trouble in the first place."

Even in the dimly lit corridor, Alessa saw the pain in Harry's eyes. She felt a moment of compassion, followed by a stab of bitterness because she doubted Harry would ever feel so deeply where she was concerned.

"What's done is done," Harry said evenly. "Let's get on with it."

Lychenko gave the smile of a swordsman who has unsettled his opponent. "Of course. That's what we're here for, isn't it?"

With an ease which indicated he was well acquainted with the inn, Lychenko led the way through a maze of corridors. Alessa and Harry followed, walking side by side but not touching or looking at each other. Alessa found her mouth had gone dry. Her stomach felt hollow and a tight knot had formed in her chest. She stole a glance at Harry. His face was set with grim determination, and she could see the strain about his mouth and eyes. She felt a sudden impulse to reach out and take his hand, both to give comfort and to receive it. Surely this was something they should face together. But she doubted if Harry would welcome such a gesture. Not after she had made it very clear that in this matter she was not his ally but his opponent.

At last Lychenko opened a door onto the heat of a cooking fire and the pungent smell of roast meat and rye beer. A plump, fair-haired maidservant stepped out of the room balancing a tray loaded with tankards and covered dishes. At the sight of Lychenko she stopped and gave him a familiar, knowing smile. Lychenko grinned back and patted her on the bottom, then led the way into a large room crowded with kitchen staff preparing food and servants bearing dishes to and from the common room and private parlors. No one seemed to take Captain Lychenko's presence amiss. It seemed he had many friends among the inn staff, at least among the young women. Alessa was aware of some curious looks sent her way, but she ignored them.

Lychenko walked toward a trestle table in an alcove at one end of the room, away from the bustle. Another maidservant, also fair-haired but slighter than the other girl, was standing beside it, bending over to speak to someone who was hidden behind her full skirts. At Lychenko's approach, she looked up with an expression of relief. "Thank goodness, I was wondering what had become of you. Though I must say, he's been quiet as a mouse."

"Thank you, Galina, I knew I could count on you." Lychenko switched from French to the Russian the girl spoke. "Come on, Niki," he said, looking beyond her. "Don't be shy."

Alessa felt a chill of expectation. As Galina stepped back, Harry drew in his breath. All they could see of the boy was a wheat-colored mass of thick hair shading a face that barely cleared the table top and two hands holding a mug of milk.

"There you are, my sweet," Galina said, bending over the child. "See who's come for you."

The boy continued to stare solemnly at the milk. Beside her, Alessa could feel Harry's absolute stillness. Lychenko took an impatient step forward, but Galina checked him with a frown. "It's your father, Niki, come all the way from England to see you." Galina lifted the boy in her arms and set him on his feet, facing Harry and Alessa.

He was so small. It was Alessa's first thought as she looked at the child who had supplanted her son. Somehow, despite the fact that she had two younger brothers, she hadn't considered how small the boy would be. Niki stood in front of them, staring down at his shoes. His hair fell over his face, so it was difficult to make out his features. Alessa turned to look at Harry and saw that the grimness and strain on his face had been replaced by a look of stunned, intense longing.

Harry stepped forward with a hesitancy in sharp contrast to his usual decisive stride and crouched down in front of the boy. The child flinched at the sudden movement and Harry went still. "Hullo, Niki," he said in Russian. He spoke cheerfully, but Alessa could hear the tremor in his voice. "I'm very pleased to meet you at last."

Niki made no response and did not even raise his eyes. The laughter of the inn staff and the banging of plates and sloshing of ale suddenly seemed deafening.

"For heaven's sake, he's terrified," Alessa said. "Let's at least get him back to the parlor where there's some quiet. He seems to feel comfortable with you," she added, turning to Galina. "Can you come with us?"

"Of course." Galina moved forward and bent over Niki. "Come on, love, let's go with the nice people."

Niki still did not speak, but he took Galina's hand without protest. Harry got to his feet, his eyes on the child. They made their way back through the corridors to the parlor in silence. Lychenko led the way with Galina and Niki following. Harry walked a little behind. He did not once look at Alessa, and she made no attempt to speak to him.

When they reached the parlor, Lychenko held open the door and Alessa went in first. Simon and Peter looked up expectantly at her entrance. Alessa motioned for Galina to bring Niki in. "This is Niki, and he doesn't feel like talking just yet," Alessa told her brother and Peter.

Niki did not look up, but he did sit on Galina's lap and accept one of the cakes. Alessa returned to her chair and poured fresh tea because it seemed appropriate and it served to fill up the silence. Harry continued to look fixedly at Niki, but made no further attempt to approach the child. Lychenko sipped his tea and watched the scene with a detachment which convinced Alessa that, whoever's child Niki was, Captain Lychenko's interest in the boy was strictly mercenary.

Her impression was confirmed when Lychenko set down his glass and made to rise after the shortest of intervals. "Now that I have seen Niki restored to the bosom of his family, I fear I must be on my way," he said, smiling at Alessa.

Alessa was not sorry to see him go, but it seemed callous to abandon Niki among strangers so quickly. "You didn't bring his nurse with you?" she asked, for the first time realizing how difficult it would be to take the child into a wholly alien environment.

"Unfortunately no, Lady Milverton. But I know you and Harry will provide him with excellent care. Harry, we have some business to settle before I leave."

Harry got to his feet as well, but this time the reference to money didn't seem to rouse his anger. Once he had seen Niki, all else seemed to fade to insignificance.

As the two men left the room, Alessa looked at the boy. He seemed oblivious to the departure of his former guardian, but she could imagine how great his terror would be when they took him from the strange inn to the equally

66

strange but far larger, far more confusing palace. She raised her eyes from Niki to Galina and again spoke on impulse. "We're going to take Niki to Tsarkoe Selo. Could you come with us?"

Galina's eyes widened in surprise, perhaps at the mention of the palace, perhaps at the offer itself. "I'm not a trained nursemaid."

"He trusts you," Alessa said. "That's more important." She hesitated a moment, then added, "Whatever they pay you here, I promise we will double it."

The surprise deepened. "It's not that, my lady. But I never considered . . ." Galina looked down at the small boy in her lap, then looked back at Alessà. She could not be much more than twenty, but her face showed both strength and intelligence. "I never cared for waiting on tables."

"It's settled then." Alessa smiled, pleased to have won her point.

"Yes." Galina laughed in faint disbelief. "I suppose it is." Her clear blue eyes registered sudden decision. "I'll have to have a word with the innkeeper." She bent her head and murmured something to Niki, then put him onto the settee beside her and left the room, promising to return shortly.

Simon looked at his sister. "*Maman* couldn't have done it better," he murmured. "You got that girl to change her whole life in five minutes just to suit your purposes. I don't suppose it occurred to you that she might have friends or family or God knows what other reasons to stay in Krasnoe Selo."

"Obviously she doesn't or she wouldn't have agreed." Alessa was in no mood to cope with her brother's blandishments. She looked at Niki, who seemed to have shrunk back into the settee, and tried to think of what she could say to him. She offered him another cake, but he shook his head. Simon studied the boy in puzzlement.

There was a sudden jangle as Peter, who had sat silent while they spoke in Russian, reached into his pocket and fished out a handful of coins. Smiling at Niki, Peter set the

67

coins on the table and began to pile them up into towers of various sizes. Niki raised his head, his eyes fixed on the glittering towers. Slowly, he inched forward on the settee. Peter held some of the coins out to him. After a moment's hesitation, Niki took the coins and began carefully building his own towers.

Alessa sat very still, afraid of disturbing him. As he leaned forward, intent on the coins, she had her first good look at his face. He had a broad forehead and a rounded chin and wide-set, enormous dark blue eyes set beneath level brows. Her first thought was that she wished he could smile. Her second was that he didn't look remotely like Harry or any of the Dudleys.

At the sound of the door opening, Alessa looked round and saw Harry standing on the threshold, watching Niki carefully lay another coin atop his tower. "Peter's found a game Niki likes," she said.

"So I see." Harry stepped into the room and smiled at Peter. "Thank you." There was a note of heartfelt gratitude in the two words. "It seems you've succeeded where the rest of us have failed."

Peter seemed embarrassed by the praise. "It's a game my brother and sisters always liked. I think he's just a bit shy, sir."

"Yes." Harry looked back at Niki with concern. "Where's Galina?" he asked Alessa.

"Speaking with the innkeeper. She's agreed to come with us and help look after Niki for a time. That way Niki will have someone familiar near him."

Harry stared at his wife in surprise. "He's only known her a few hours."

"Yes, but he trusts her and he doesn't seem to trust us yet."

Harry glanced at Niki, then turned back to Alessa. "Thank you," he said softly.

Alessa looked into his eyes and for a moment saw a chance to bridge the hostility between them. Whatever their

68

differences, they both had Niki's welfare at heart. It gave them common ground. But before she could speak, the quiet in the room was shattered by a loud cry from the baby.

Alessa was on her feet at once. "He'll be hungry," she said, crossing to the basket. As she bent down and lifted the baby into her arms, she felt a stab of guilt. For a few moments, Niki's plight had been more present in her mind than the needs of her child. She might feel compassion for Niki but she could never let herself forget her loyalty to her own son.

"I didn't realize he'd be so — so . . ." Alessa stopped pacing the parquet floor and looked at Elisabeth, searching for the right word.

"Young?" Elisabeth asked with a faint smile. "Vulnerable? Sweet?"

"All of those things," Alessa admitted, leaning against one of the twisted faience columns which supported the ceiling of the exquisite bedchamber that had been designed for Catherine II and now belonged to Elisabeth. A small statue of Cupid stood on a green marble pedestal in a niche across the room. Alessa looked at the curly-haired figure, no more than a boy despite his wings and quiver of arrows, and saw again Niki's solemn face staring at her across the expanse of the carriage on the journey from Krasnoe Selo to Tsarkoe Selo. She had yet to hear him speak a word to anyone but Galina and even to her he talked only in monosyllables.

"The truth is I hadn't thought about *him* at all, only about what he meant to me and the baby," Alessa said, dropping down onto a chair covered in a pale green satin which echoed the color of the walls. "And then all of a sudden there he was, standing in front of me. He's obviously had a beastly time of it, and if Harry and I don't look after him, he hasn't got anyone but Captain Lychenko, and Captain Lychenko is despicable . . ."

69

Alessa put her hands to her temples, which were beginning to throb. "But that's just it. Captain Lychenko is despicable, and I don't trust him the least bit."

"You think he is lying about the boy being Harry's son?" Elisabeth looked at Alessa across the small gilded table which stood between them, her gaze calm and steady.

Alessa dragged her hands away from her face. "He doesn't look remotely like Harry. I know that doesn't prove anything, but Captain Lychenko is obviously only interested in whatever money he can get. And it's clear that the two men have no use for each other. I suspect Captain Lychenko would like nothing better than to do Harry a mischief. It would be revenge for . . ." She broke off, because she had not told Elisabeth all the details of Harry's seduction of Nadia.

"What does Harry think?" Elisabeth asked.

"If Harry had any doubts, they ended the moment he set eyes on Niki." Alessa felt a flash of jealousy as she recalled the longing in Harry's eyes when he had first looked at the boy.

"But that isn't enough for you?"

"Would it be enough for you?" Alessa demanded.

Elisabeth folded the embroidery she had been working on when Alessa came to see her. "My husband's mistress bore his child fourteen years ago. She chose to tell me about it at a ball, in between dances. I had a child myself not long after. My child did not survive. Hers did." Elisabeth's hands stilled on the embroidery. "I think I know how you feel, Alessa. What do you mean to do about it?"

Alessa fingered the soft pleated cambric of her gown. "I mean to find out the truth."

"Without telling Harry?"

"There'll be time enough to tell him if I discover anything." Alessa stared at one of the panels of medallions which adorned the walls, classical figures in white set against circular backgrounds of bright blue. They reminded her of her mother's Wedgewood dishes. Alessa had written to her mother about the baby, but not about Niki. That was too painful. But when they reached England, *Maman* would have to know. The whole family would. Alessa was determined to learn the truth about Niki before then.

Clasping her hands firmly in her lap, Alessa looked at Elisabeth. "Can you employ someone to learn whatever possible about Captain Lychenko?"

Elisabeth regarded her gravely. "Marriage is a fragile thing, Alessa. It can't be broken, but it can be damaged beyond repair."

Alessa gave a bitter laugh. "You think I don't know that? Ours may already be irreparable. But there's no hope for us with this hanging between us. And I'd be a poor mother if I didn't defend my child's rights." She leaned forward across the table. "I have to know."

Elisabeth carefully adjusted a lace frill on the cuff of her gown. Then she looked up and met Alessa's gaze. "Very well," she said in a tone which suddenly reminded Alessa that Elisabeth was the Empress of Russia. "It will be done."

Chapter Five

Harry knelt on the sun-warmed ground at the edge of the lake and pushed the small boat out onto the water. As the boat was propelled by the current, he sat back on his heels and glanced carefully to one side.

Niki was watching in frowning concentration. "Boat." The voice was small and soft and heavily accented, but the English word was unmistakable.

Harry looked from Niki to Galina, who was sitting on a bench beside the lake, a basket of sewing in her lap. "Master Peter taught him," she said.

Of course. In the ten days since they had brought Niki to Tsarkoe Selo, it was only Peter and Simon to whom Niki had been at all responsive. Harry knew the boys had been trying to teach Niki English, but he hadn't realized how many words Niki had managed to pick up.

"Boat," Niki said again.

"Boat," Harry agreed, pleased to be able to communicate even in so small a way. At least Niki was talking to him.

"Boat," Niki said more insistently, the word almost a wail.

Harry was overcome by a sense of hopeless inadequacy. It was becoming a familiar sensation.

His face screwed up with concentration, Niki stretched a hand toward the lake. With sudden understanding, Harry leaned out over the water, caught hold of the boat, and placed it before Niki.

Niki's frown was replaced by an intent look. Slowly, he ran a finger along the boat's miniature deck.

Harry shook the water from his sleeve and watched with a wry smile. He had managed to give Niki what he wanted, but now Niki had no further interest in him. Leaning back on his hands, Harry looked at the solemn face beneath the thick tangle of hair and wondered what had happened to make Niki so withdrawn and mistrustful. Was it just the trauma of losing the woman he thought of as his mother and being given into the care of strangers? God knew that would be enough to make most children fearful of the world around them. Yet Harry could not rid himself of the sense that something else was bothering the child.

Harry shut his eyes for a moment, feeling the warmth of the afternoon sun and the coolness of the moist air from the lake. He seemed capable of coping with no one's needs, least of all those of his wife and children. Since the day they had gone to fetch Niki, Alessa had not sought him out once. In public she was careful to give no sign of the discord between them. When he went to her apartments to visit the baby, she treated him with cold formality. Harry almost thought he would welcome another quarrel. The only member of his immediate family who hadn't wholly rejected him was the baby. It might have been encouraging save that the nurses said infants of this age couldn't yet discriminate between people.

Harry opened his eyes and looked out over the water. A gardener's boy was pushing a barrow across the expanse of lawn which stretched down from the palace. A well-dressed man and woman were strolling in the direction of the Grotto, an elegant, blue and white domed building on the edge of the lake where the Emperor often went in the morning to feed the birds. Harry had encountered the Emperor there two days ago while taking Niki on an early walk. Alexander, not a man to stand on ceremony, had greeted them politely, but there had been a definite reserve in his manner. Harry knew the Emperor had not forgiven him for what he had done to Alessa.

But Alexander was not above questioning Harry about the political situation in England. With the international conference at Aix-la-Chapelle to discuss the withdrawal of foreign troops from France only two months away, the Emperor and his advisors were quite prepared to take advantage of having an English diplomat in their midst.

There would be more questions at the reception the Emperor and Empress were giving that night. Harry grimaced. Alessa would be there at his side, playing the part of Lady Milverton to perfection. It could never be said that she had not fulfilled her duty as his countess. For some reason the thought made him violently angry.

Niki was now running his fingers over the boat's masts. Harry leaned forward cautiously. "Mast," he said, touching one of the masts. Niki raised his head and Harry found himself looking directly into the boy's blue eyes. For a moment, he thought Niki meant to mimic the word. He waited, aware that his heart had stopped beating.

Niki looked at Harry a second or so longer. Then he lowered his head and continued his perusal of the boat. Harry let out an audible sigh.

"I suppose I just don't have the knack for it," he said, turning to Galina.

Galina broke off a thread. "I shouldn't take it so hard, Lord Milverton. He talks to Master Peter and the prince a bit, but he's just as quiet with the countess as he is with you."

Harry grimaced, then frowned. "The countess?"

"Lady Milverton." Galina held the needle up against the light so she could thread it.

Harry drew a breath. He had visited Niki every day and not once had he encountered Alessa. He had visited Alessa every day and not once had she spoken of seeing Niki. After the sympathy she had shown the boy at Krasnoe Selo, Harry had been surprised and a little hurt, but he had told himself he had no right to expect Alessa to lavish attention on the child he had foisted on her. "When did Lady Milverton visit Niki?" Harry asked, as casually as he could manage.

There was a glimmering of understanding in Galina's eyes, quickly masked. "Afternoons, mostly. While the baby's napping."

"So she's been to see him several times?"

Galina knotted the thread and began mending a rent in one of Niki's socks. "Every day. Just like you."

Harry released his breath. The wind came up, stirring the trees and sending a scattering of leaves over the lake.

"Lady Mil-ver-ton," Niki said softly, giving the lie to Galina's assertion that he was as distant with Alessa as he was with Harry.

Harry turned back to his son, feeling a constriction in his chest. He wondered if Niki would ever say "Papa." And then he wondered if he would ever understand Alessa.

Peter had been to balls his stepmother gave, but he had never seen anything approaching the luxury and formality of a court reception at Tsarkoe Selo. Candles blazed everywhere, their flames reflected in the highly polished, intricate parquet floor over which the dancers were moving through the lively figures of the mazurka. The scent of the candles vied with the scent worn by the ladies, just as the ladies' jewels competed with the shimmering crystals of the chandeliers and the profusion of gilt paint on the walls and ceiling. Peter's stepmother's country house was accounted one of the great showplaces in England, yet the restrained grandeur of Sundon was nothing compared to the ornate and playful opulence of Tsarkoe Selo.

"It's overwhelming," Peter murmured to Simon, who was standing beside him.

Simon, looking very much a prince in an impeccably fitting dark blue coat, cream-colored knee breeches, and white silk stockings, pulled an expressive face. "It's stuffy," he said under his breath. "Look at the way the men and women hover on different sides of the room. That doesn't make for a lively evening."

Peter appreciated his friend's point. It was difficult enough to know how to speak to a girl in the ordinary course of things. It was quite impossible in such a setting. Some of the girls dancing the mazurka were probably no older than he was himself, but they seemed infinitely more experienced.

Alessa had been that age when he first met her, Peter realized. At the time he had thought her thoroughly grown up, but looking back he could see how much she'd changed since then. She was more thoughtful and less impulsive. And she didn't laugh nearly as much.

Peter sought out Simon's sister among the dancers. He hadn't seen her since the mazurka started, but now he spotted her in a set on the opposite side of the room. To his surprise and relief, the man holding her gloved hand was Harry. "They're dancing together," Peter whispered to Simon.

Simon followed the direction of Peter's gaze. "Of course," he said. "They were bound to at least once tonight. Alessa would see to it. We've been brought up to believe in appearances."

Peter looked back at Alessa and her husband. She was turning, her gown billowing about her in a swirl of gauze and wine-colored satin. The rubies at her throat and ears and the silver embroidery on her gown caught the candlelight. Both she and Harry moved gracefully, varying their steps and even improvising new ones, which seemed to be the point of the mazurka. But as Peter watched, he saw that the smile on Alessa's face was fixed and set and that there was a certain rigidity in the way she clasped Harry's hand.

Harry's smile was as practiced as Alessa's, yet it seemed to Peter that there was something different about it. He watched them for a moment longer, frowning. Then he re-alized what it was. "Harry looks as if he doesn't quite take it all seriously," Peter said. "Like an actor playing a part."

Simon, who had also been frowning, turned to Peter. "You're right. That's it exactly." He paused, a thoughtful look on his face. "Sometimes I don't think Harry likes being an earl."

Peter looked at Harry, dressed in knee breeches and a pristine black coat. And then he thought of Harry in buck-skins and an open-necked shirt, galloping over the fields of his estate in England. "You can't blame him," Peter said. "Aren't there times when you don't like being a prince?"

Simon grinned. "Lots," he said with feeling. Then he frowned again. "Alessa likes being a countess. Or she thinks she does. I wish she were more like Harry. Then perhaps they'd get on better."

"At least they're together," Peter said, "even if it's only for appearances. Maybe they'll talk."

"I doubt it," Simon said with certainty.

"Why not?" Peter asked.

A footman passed by carrying a silver tray filled with glasses of champagne. Simon took two glasses and gave one to Peter. "Because," he said, taking a sip of champagne, "no one can be more stubborn than my sister when she puts her mind to it."

The mazurka came to an end soon after. Peter lost sight of Harry and Alessa as the company rearranged themselves and took their places for a waltz. Then a few minutes later Harry was beside them, smiling in a far more genuine way than he had during the dance. "Well?" he asked. "What do you make of it?"

"I like the mazurka," Peter said. "It looks like fun."

Harry looked at Peter, thinking how painful it had been to dance the mazurka with Alessa. "It can be," he said. And then, realizing he might have betrayed too much, he added more lightly, "If you'd like to try it, I'm sure we can find a young woman to teach you the steps."

A look of alarm crossed Peter's face. "No. Thank you," he added quickly. "But I'd rather just watch."

Harry laughed, remembering how it felt to be seventeen, though at that age he'd been rather more precocious than Peter or Simon. "What about you, Simon?" Harry asked, turning to his brother-in-law. "As I remember, you danced quite well last Christmas."

"That was fun," Simon said.

"And this isn't?"

Simon looked squarely at Harry. "Do you think it is?"

Harry grinned. "Is it that obvious?" he asked. "I thought I was putting on a good show."

Simon grinned back. "The best," he said. "I've done it often enough myself to know the signs."

Harry turned to look at the dancers, wondering if the boys had watched him dancing with Alessa and if so what they had made of it. The sweet, seductive strains of a waltz rose above the murmur of conversation around them. He would have liked to waltz with Alessa, to hold her, however lightly, and whirl her around the floor. But Alessa had made it very clear after the mazurka that she felt one dance was enough to demonstrate to the company that there was no estrangement between them.

Alessa was now dancing with Prince Nikita Volkonsky, one of the Emperor's aides-de-camp. Harry grimaced, for Volkonsky was known for his attentions to women, but Alessa looked elegant and remote as she moved about the floor in Volkonsky's arms. No doubt every bit as remote and elegant as she had looked when dancing with her husband.

Watching Alessa, Harry was struck by how well she fit into this world. She was not an outsider as he had always been as a member of the diplomatic corps. Nor was she merely another court lady. She was a royal cousin, one of the elite, and it was a role she slipped into with perfect assurance. Like him, she had been trained from the cradle to assume the position that was hers by birth.

And unlike him, she had not rebelled.

"Your wife is charming, Lord Milverton. Very like her mother. They say half the men in St. Petersburg were mad about the Princess Sofia."

Harry turned round. The Foreign Minister, Count Nesselrode, had appeared at his side.

Nesselrode smiled. "Though I must admit I'm surprised you aren't dancing with her yourself," he said. "It's a brave husband who trusts his wife to Volkonsky."

"My wife can be trusted," Harry said in an even voice.

"My dear fellow, of course. I meant no disrespect. If she's anything like her mother, she's well able to look after herself." Nesselrode pushed his spectacles up onto his nose. He was a kind man, known to be devoted to his bluestocking wife. Harry knew he had not meant to imply anything about Alessa. But where his wife was concerned, Harry had a way of jumping at shadows.

"In truth, I'm glad to find you not dancing," Nesselrode continued. "I was hoping for a few words with you."

"Of course." Then Harry said to Simon and Peter, who were standing by silently, "Sorry, chaps, duty calls."

Nesselrode was not the first person that evening to approach Harry about news from England in general and England's negotiating posture at the coming conference in particular. Harry had spoken with Lord Castlereagh, the English Foreign Secretary, more recently than had Lord Cathcart, and was not bound, as the embassy staff were, to stick to formal government pronouncements. As Harry had expected, a number of people had tried to extract information from him in the course of the reception. Some asked bold-faced questions which bordered on impudence. Others circled round the subject in the hope that Harry would let something slip. Still others made assertions which were really questions in disguise.

Nesselrode was more straightforward. "Now," he said with a friendly smile when he and Harry had reached a painted alcove at one end of the room, "tell me more about Lord

Castlereagh's views on Spain's late South American colonies."

Harry answered as directly as he could without betraying Castlereagh's confidence. If it was not everything Nesselrode wanted to know, it was probably a more honest assessment than he had hoped for.

"You're an intelligent man, Milverton," the Foreign Minister said as they returned to the main room. "I hope Castlereagh has the sense to include you in his delegation to the conference."

Harry nearly groaned aloud at the thought of yet another foreign trip. "I think family business will keep me in England," he said. "My wife has just had a child."

Nesselrode looked surprised. "Your sentiments are admirable, Lord Milverton. But I'm sure Lady Milverton would understand if your country required your presence in Aix-la-Chapelle. She must appreciate the duties of a man in your position."

Harry made an evasive answer and excused himself. He had no doubt that Alessa would understand his absence—he feared she would welcome it—but he was damned if he'd let the gulf between them widen any further. Even before he'd known about Niki and the baby, Harry had decided he was away from home too much. When he had accepted the mission to Copenhagen last spring, he had told Castlereagh he would not be able to attend the conference in the autumn. Castlereagh had not been pleased. Though he and Harry often disagreed about matters of policy, he valued Harry's opinion as an expert on Russian affairs. Harry suspected that once he returned to England, the Foreign Secretary would try to persuade him to change his mind about the conference.

Not thinking much about where he was going, Harry made his way through the close-pressed crowd and found himself back where he had left Peter and Simon. The boys were still there. And they were talking to his wife.

Alessa was laughing at something Simon had said, her

face softened, the formal veneer momentarily broken. Then she looked up and saw Harry. Her face closed. She even seemed to stand a little straighter, as if holding herself aloof from him.

"Hullo, Harry," she said. "Are you enjoying yourself?"

"About as much as you are, I should think," Harry replied. "Did Volkonsky try to seduce you?"

He saw a flash of anger in Alessa's eyes. That sort of question, even in jest, was a violation of the rules of their marriage. But tonight Harry didn't feel like playing by the rules.

"I expect he would have," Alessa said, "but I think he draws the line at women who've given birth within the past month."

It was a crushingly effective rebuke. Harry inclined his head in acknowledgment of the point she had scored, then turned to the boys and found they were already beginning to move off into the crowd.

"We'll be back in a few minutes," Simon said. "We're going to get Alessa some lemonade."

Alessa frowned at her brother. "I didn't ask for lemonade."

"No, but you look as though you need it," Simon said cheerfully.

He and Peter were gone before Harry or Alessa could protest further. Harry looked at his wife and saw the color rise in her cheeks as she realized why the boys had left. "Evidently Simon thinks we need some time alone together," he said.

"Simon thinks entirely too much," Alessa returned. The pulse at the base of her throat had quickened, drawing his eye to the décolletage of her gown. The tops of her breasts were visible beneath a film of ivory-colored lace, stirring errant thoughts which threatened to wreak havoc with his composure.

Harry drew a steadying breath. "If we can play the

81

happy couple while we're on the dance floor, there's no reason we can't do it when we're not."

"None at all," Alessa agreed coolly.

Harry studied his wife with concern, noting the pallor of her face. Her health seemed to have mended remarkably well since the baby's birth, but he knew what a strain the endless round of dancing and talking and standing could be. The heat in the room was enough to overpower the strongest constitution, let alone a woman who had just gone through the ordeal of childbirth. "Are you feeling all right?" he asked. "Would you like to sit down?"

"Thank you, I prefer to stand." Alessa shifted her position slightly, so she was even farther away from him.

Harry looked searchingly at her. He knew that if she was feeling ill, he was the last person she'd admit it to.

"I'm all right, Harry," Alessa said sharply. "I rested all afternoon."

There was an uncomfortable moment of silence. Harry recalled similar silences when he visited Niki. And then he remembered what Galina had told him. "You didn't mention that you'd been to see Niki," he said.

Alessa's painted silk fan trembled slightly, as if she had tightened her grip on it. "You didn't ask."

"True," Harry agreed. Then, in a softer voice, he added, "Thank you. I had no right to ask you to pay such attention to him."

"Whatever's between us, I couldn't very well take it out on a child." Alessa hesitated a moment. "Harry . . ." She laid a hand on his arm, then drew it back quickly, as if disconcerted by such intimacy.

"What is it?" Harry asked, looking down at her.

"It's Niki," Alessa said in a quick, urgent tone. "Something's bothering him. Not just all the confusion and the new people. Something specific. I've tried to get him to talk about it, but he won't tell me anything. Or else he doesn't know how to."

For the moment her eyes held nothing but concern.

82

Harry was shaken by the strength of her feeling for the child he had forced her to accept. He lifted his hand, wanting to brush his fingers against her cheek, to make some gesture of comfort and understanding. Then, knowing she might shrink away, he let it fall. "I think you're right," he said. "We'll have to wait until he's more comfortable with us. At least he'll talk to you. He'll scarcely say a word to me."

"There must be something we can do," Alessa insisted. "Could Captain Lychenko—"

"Alessa! My dear, you look ravishing. I'd never know you'd just risen from childbed." A stout, dark-haired woman wearing a diamond tiara and a heavily embroidered blue satin gown swept down upon them.

"Cousin Olga." Alessa's social mask was once again in place. She leaned forward and kissed the woman's cheek, then turned to Harry. "My husband, Lord Milverton. Harry, *Maman*'s cousin, the Princess Matisova."

"Lord Milverton and I met when he was stationed here." The princess nodded familiarly at Harry, who had only the vaguest recollection of meeting her. Half the nobility in Russia seemed to be related to Alessa's mother. "You had some other name then," the princess continued. "Rutledge, that's it. Impossible to pronounce, these English names. I never dreamed you'd be one of the family."

"Nor did I," Harry murmured.

"But I must congratulate you both," the princess went on, scarcely pausing to allow him to respond. "So fortunate there weren't complications with the baby coming early. I must say, Alessa dear, I don't know what your mother was about letting you travel in such a condition."

Alessa lifted her chin. *"Maman* no longer makes such decisions for me."

The princess blinked in surprise. "Well, it's all turned out for the best," she said, a faint note of disapproval in her voice. "I daresay the baby will have a settling influence on you—they usually do." She glanced from Alessa to Harry,

83

her eyes sharp, as if she was only now coming to the real point of the conversation. "I understand there is another child as well?"

Harry drew in his breath to respond, but Alessa spoke first. "Yes," she said pleasantly. "My husband's son from his first marriage."

"I see." The princess's tone implied that she did not see at all but was determined to do so before the end of the discussion. She fixed Harry with a hard stare. "I did not know you had been married before, Lord Milverton."

Diplomacy taught one how to answer difficult questions. "I don't believe I was at the time of our earlier meeting, Princess," Harry said.

"The marriage was quiet owing to the wishes of the bride's family," Alessa added smoothly. Harry felt her draw imperceptibly closer to him, as if in solidarity against the princess's prying.

"And the child was raised in Russia?" the princess persisted, implying that she didn't believe the half of it.

"By his aunt," Harry said.

"Harry came to St. Petersburg to fetch him. He will now make his home with us," Alessa said, as if she couldn't be happier with how things had turned out. She stepped even closer to Harry and linked her arm through his. Harry knew she was trying to keep up appearances in front of the princess, but regardless of the reason, for the moment she was his ally, not his enemy. He felt his spirits soar.

The princess adjusted the heavily fringed shawl draped over her shoulders. "This is all very surprising. Dear Sofia said nothing of it when she wrote to me of your marriage."

"Oh, *Maman* doesn't know about it yet," Alessa said, smiling with easy assurance. "But I'm sure when she does, she'll be as delighted as the rest of the family. And she's sure to love Niki. He's a darling."

"Niki?" the princess asked.

"Nikolai." The faintest edge crept into Alessa's voice, though Harry thought only he could hear it. "Harry's son.

84

The Viscount Rutledge."

"The viscount?" The princess frowned, trying, Harry suspected, to sort out the English system of titles. "I see," she said, as if she had only just realized how very bad it was. "Of course, he will be the eldest son and Lord Milverton's heir. These things can lead to the most shocking rivalry between brothers, can't they? But I'm sure you'll be able to smooth all that over. Does your own son have a name yet, Alessa dear?"

For the first time since the princess's arrival, Alessa hesitated. "No," she began, "we haven't—"

"We haven't come to a definite decision," Harry said, drawing Alessa closer to him. "But we're thinking of calling the boy Alexander."

"Alexander? But how charming," the princess exclaimed, as if for the first time they had done something she approved of. "In honor of the Emperor, of course."

"No," Harry said, smiling at her. "In honor of my wife."

Alessa looked up at him, her eyes wide with surprise. Harry squeezed her arm.

"Well, Alessa is named for the Emperor," the princess said after a moment, "so I suppose it's all the same." She opened her mouth, as if about to say more, then closed it abruptly, her eye caught by something across the room. "Oh, dear, there goes Colonel Rostov. You must forgive me, I've been looking for him all evening. He's the perfect match for my Sonia. Alessa dear, remember me when you write to your mother. Do take good care of her, Lord Milverton, you know how fragile women can be at a time like this."

"Horrid woman," Alessa said under her breath as the princess moved off. "She's always been a fearful gossip."

"Laugh at her," Harry advised. "It's the only way to handle such people."

"Yes, I suppose so." Alessa still had her arm through his and she seemed in no hurry to relinquish it. "Harry . . . when did you decide you wanted to call him Alexander?"

"I've been thinking about it for some time," Harry said

truthfully, wondering if it had been a mistake to mention the name. "But we can call him something else if you'd prefer."

Alessa looked up at her husband, trying to sort out her feelings. It was as if in offering to name the child after her, Harry had somehow acknowledged her place in the family. "No," she said. "I like Alexander, though we'll have to think of something to call him for short."

"Sacha?" Harry suggested.

"Not for an English child. *Maman* named me Alessandra because that was the Italian form and we lived in Savoy." Alessa thought of her recent trip to Savoy with Simon and Peter, which in turn made her think of Peter's parents. She wanted Peter's stepmother, Fiona, to be the baby's godmother, although such a thing would never have occurred to her ten years ago, when an unknown woman named Fiona Alastair arrived in Sardinia to be governess to her and Simon.

"I know," Alessa exclaimed, seized by a sudden inspiration. "Alastair is a Scottish form of Alexander. If we call him Alastair, he'll be named after Fiona as well."

She looked at Harry, wondering if he would think it odd to name the child after her former governess, but Harry nodded. "That's a splendid idea. We can ask Gideon and Fiona to stand as godparents."

"It's settled then," Alessa said, pleased they were in agreement. Harry had always liked Fiona, and her husband, Gideon, had become Harry's mentor in political matters.

Harry smiled, his expression open and unforced, as it rarely was these days. Alessa was aware of the warmth of his body and the stirring of his breath on her skin. She felt a sudden longing to pull his head down to her own and kiss him.

"Thank you," she said, searching for words that might begin to close the distance between them. "I—"

"Harry, I've been looking all over for you. Oh, Alessa, I say, you do look smashing."

It was Edward Clifford. Alessa turned from Harry, not sure whether she was glad or sorry for the interruption, and gave Edward her hand. "Hullo, Edward."

Edward lifted her fingers to his lips. "I hope the baby's well. And—"

"Niki," Alessa concluded for him, recognizing his embarrassment. She had not seen Edward since her arrival in St. Petersburg and she realized he was afraid she would bear him a grudge for the role he had played in recovering Niki. "He's thriving. So's the baby."

Edward's face relaxed into a smile. "I'm glad to hear it. And I'm glad to see a couple of friendly faces. I've just spent half an hour listening to an argument between the French chargé and one of the Emperor's aides-de-camp and trying to remain impartial. By God, you're well out of the diplomatic corps, Harry. Bow a fraction of an inch too low or speak two minutes longer to one dignitary than another and it's a matter of gossip in every embassy in town."

Harry grinned. "Don't tell me you still haven't mastered the perfect bow." He turned to Alessa. "When Ned and I first came to St. Petersburg, we used to practice in front of a mirror before these functions to be sure we got it right."

"Which didn't stop you from nearly falling flat on your face in front of General Kutuzov," Edward retorted.

"Ah, well," Harry said with mock gravity, "these minor annoyances are the price of handling such weighty affairs, my friend. Think of the excitement of the diplomatic life, the intrigue—"

"Excitement nothing," Edward retorted. "Do you know what 'weighty affairs' occupied me yesterday? We—not just a few of us, but the whole diplomatic corps—went to a convent school and watched the students being examined in geography, music, dancing, and God knows what else. The dam—dashed thing lasted six hours. Not that the girls weren't charming and the school isn't a worthy enterprise, but—"

Edward broke off and gave a helpless laugh. Harry

laughed as well. Alessa joined them, feeling suddenly care-
free. She had not forgot about Niki and the baby and all
that lay between her and Harry, but for the moment she
could laugh at the world, the way Edward laughed at the
diplomatic service. She glanced at Harry. His face was
etched with lines of humor, making him appear younger.
This was the way he must have looked before he became
Lord Milverton. It almost seemed that if she reached out
she could find a part of him she had thought lost long before their marriage.

"Harry . . ." Alessa began, not sure what she wanted to
say, save that somehow she must find a way to hang on to
the moment.

But as she spoke, she saw the laughter fade from Harry's
eyes. He was looking beyond her, to the room's main doorway. Alessa followed the direction of his gaze and felt her
own laughter still within her. The crowd had parted, and
she had a clear view of the woman who was entering the
ballroom. A tall, slender woman, with dark gold hair and a
magnificent figure. A woman of whom Alessa was instantly
and passionately jealous.

"Good God," Harry breathed with wonder and something
that sounded horribly like delight. "It's Marina."

Chapter Six

"Marina?" Alessa asked Harry, her voice brittle.

Harry turned back to her, as if he had forgot she was standing beside him. "The Countess Chernikova." He looked at Edward. "I didn't know she was in St. Petersburg."

"Nor did I." Edward appeared uneasy. "The last I heard she was with her husband's family in Moscow."

"Poor Marina, she deserves more freedom," Harry said, a reminiscent smile playing about his lips.

The smile and the tenderness in his eyes made Alessa's stomach clench painfully. It reminded her all too well of the way Adrian, the man she had loved and almost married, had looked when he spoke of his mistress. A married woman. An older woman. Like Marina Chernikova.

"Come and meet her," Harry said, taking Alessa's hand and drawing her forward. "You're sure to get on famously."

He was smiling, as if nothing could be more agreeable. He wouldn't even acknowledge that Alessa had the right to be jealous. It made it all the worse. "No, Harry," Alessa said, pulling her hand from his clasp. "You go ahead. I'm sure you and the countess have many things to discuss."

"One of them being my marriage." Harry was still smiling. "I want Marina to meet you."

Alessa felt a surge of anger sweep through her. She could think of only one reason why Harry would want to introduce his wife to a woman who was at the least an old friend and very likely his former mistress. She was not going to let Harry use her to make his Marina jealous. Some things were beyond even the bounds of a convenient marriage. "Don't be silly," she said, not trying to disguise the edge to her voice. "I know how tiresome a third party can be at a reunion. Edward will keep me company, won't you, Edward?"

Edward nodded, looking acutely uncomfortable. He understood the awkwardness of the situation even if Harry did not.

"Very well." Harry looked hurt, for all the world as if it was she who had rebuffed him. "I'll find Marina and bring her over."

Determined to maintain her *savoir faire*, Alessa smiled at Edward. "The countess looks charming. Is she a friend of yours as well?"

"More of Harry's." Edward swallowed. "Alessa . . ."

Alessa waved her fan, stirring the warm air. "Yes, Edward?"

"I know how it looks," Edward said, his expression earnest, "but I knew Harry better than anyone when he was in St. Petersburg, and I never thought he and the countess were more than friends. Even if they were, it ended when he left Russia."

Alessa closed her fan abruptly. "Presumably it had to. I never heard of a liaison being conducted across hundreds of miles."

"Oh, Lord, I didn't mean it that way." Edward straightened his already immaculate cravat, a flush creeping up his neck. "It's just that you may hear talk and I wanted you to know that whatever was between them ended a long time ago."

Alessa hesitated, curiosity warring with her determination to remain aloof. Curiosity won. "Then there *was* something between them?" Despite all her efforts, there was a note of strain in her voice.

"Harry never told me there was," Edward said, not meeting her gaze directly.

"But he never told you there wasn't?" Alessa fixed her husband's friend with a hard stare.

"He . . ." Edward cleared his throat, looking like a man who is sinking deeper and deeper into a quagmire and doesn't know how to extricate himself. "Actually, I don't think he talked to me about the countess at all."

"But other people did?"

Edward shifted his weight from one foot to the other. "You know the sort of things that are said whenever a man and a woman are much together. That's why I wanted to warn you. People may remember the stories about Harry and the countess from five years ago. And now that she's a widow . . ."

"A widow?" Alessa asked, more quickly than she intended.

"Yes, a recent one." The flush suffused Edward's face. "It's one of the reasons I don't think there was anything very serious between her and Harry," he said in a lowered voice. "The count wasn't . . ."

"Complacent?" Alessa asked, gripping her fan tightly.

Edward nodded. "To put it bluntly."

Alessa swallowed, aware of the bitter taste of fear in her mouth. If Harry had not been the countess's lover, perhaps the count's death had removed the one impediment to their liaison. Harry clearly did not expect Alessa to stand in his way.

"Oh, there you are," Simon said, wending his way between a young couple and a pair of gossiping matrons. "Sorry we took so long. I brought both champagne and lemonade. I wasn't sure which you'd want."

"Champagne," Alessa said without hesitation, taking the chilled glass from her brother.

"I was afraid of that," Simon said. "I'll have to drink the lemonade myself. Hullo, Ned."

Edward greeted Simon and Peter as if greatly relieved to

have his talk with Alessa interrupted. Simon answered Edward's questions about the ball, but Alessa knew her brother sensed something was wrong. "Where's Harry?" he asked her.

"Talking to an old friend." Alessa took a long drink of champagne. The light, bubbly taste was in marked contrast to the leaden feeling in her stomach.

Simon regarded her, his brows drawn together, but before he could speak, Peter gave an exclamation of amazement. "I say, she's exquisite."

Alessa turned round. There must be over two hundred women at the reception but, of course, Peter was looking toward the doorway where Harry stood beside the woman with the golden hair while a thin girl in white hovered behind them. Overwhelmed by the hurts of the past few minutes, Alessa spoke without thought or restraint. "I suppose so. Though she must be nearly as old as *Maman*."

Peter looked at her in surprise. Simon grinned. "Don't be a dunderhead," he said. "Peter doesn't mean her. He means the young one."

Startled, Alessa looked back at the delicate, fair-haired girl standing beside the countess.

"Radka," Edward said. "The countess's daughter. She must be about fifteen by now."

"I see. She's lovely." Alessa's spirits sank even lower. Much as she had disliked the thought of Peter admiring the countess, somehow it was even worse that the object of his attention was a girl eight years her own junior.

"Does Harry know them well?" Peter asked, an eager note in his voice.

Alessa scarcely heard Edward's reply. A new dance was forming and in the swirl of movement she lost sight of Harry. The musicians began to play another waltz. Her throat closed at the sound. That waltz had been very popular in England. She and Harry had danced to it at the first ball she had given as Countess of Milverton.

"Don't do anything foolish, Peter," Simon said, "but

Harry seems to be bringing them over to meet us."

The view had cleared again, and Harry was escorting the countess and her daughter around the edge of the dance floor in their direction. With sudden decision, Alessa turned to Edward. "Shall we meet them?" she asked, taking his arm and starting forward before he could reply. If confrontation was inevitable, she would meet the enemy head on.

Edward looked at her in concern, but he could scarcely deny her. Alessa lifted her head high, armoring herself against the coming scene. She heard Peter and Simon following, but she kept her gaze fixed ahead. Meeting one's husband's mistress was one of the accomplishments of a married woman, much like planning an evening's entertainment or arranging the seating at a large dinner. For all she knew, more than one of the women she received in London had shared Harry's bed. The fact that she had heard so little gossip about her husband since their marriage was probably sheer chance.

They had to stop once to exchange greetings with an elderly man with a great many medals pinned to his coat who claimed to have been a friend of Alessa and Simon's grandfather. Then they moved on, and suddenly Harry was only a few feet away. Alessa's hands felt clammy and she knew it was due to more than the damp heat that was so pervasive around St. Petersburg in the summer. She met Harry's gaze. He smiled, as if her coming to meet them was an overture of peace, not an act of confrontation.

"The Countess Chernikova and her daughter, the Countess Radka," he said, at least granting Alessa the higher precedence in the introductions.

"Lady Milverton, I'm so glad to meet you," the countess said when Harry had introduced Alessa and the boys. "Harry wrote that you were beautiful, but I think he grossly understated the matter."

"You're too kind, Countess." Alessa shot an accusing look at Harry. He had written to the woman? It seemed there was no end to the things she didn't know about him. "You have the advantage of me," Alessa told the countess. "Harry has never mentioned you to me at all."

The countess laughed, a lilting, musical sound. "I'm not surprised. I imagine he has far more important things to talk to you about." Close up she was every bit as beautiful as she had been at a distance. Fine lines about her eyes betrayed her age, but the eyes themselves were a clear blue. Her smile was generous, and her gown, of pale blue crêpe, was discreetly elegant yet revealed that the years had not impaired her figure.

"I'm delighted to meet you gentlemen, too," the countess said, turning her dazzling smile on Simon and Peter. "I wonder . . ." She hesitated, glancing down at her daughter, who had been looking fixedly at the tips of her satin slippers ever since the introductions. "Radka scarcely knows any young men her own age," the countess said. "Perhaps one of you would care to dance?"

Radka looked up quickly. "Oh, *Maman,*" she said, flushing beet red.

"Peter's been longing to dance, haven't you, Peter?" Simon said, looking at his friend who seemed to have momentarily lost the power of speech.

"What? No. That is, yes, of course. I mean, I'd be honored, Countess." Peter offered his arm to Radka, though he seemed afraid to meet her eyes.

Radka hesitated, glanced at her mother, then shyly placed her hand on Peter's arm. She was, Alessa admitted, an extraordinarily pretty child, shorter and slighter than her mother, with a thin face dominated by enormous blue eyes and framed by pale blond ringlets threaded through with a pink ribbon. But she hardly seemed old enough to be dancing. Alessa had been seventeen before her mother allowed her to dance and eighteen before she was permitted to waltz. She had, of course, believed herself old enough to dance far earlier, but that was beside the point.

"I'm so glad," the countess said, as Peter and Radka

joined the dancers. "I hope your friend will forgive my forwardness," she added, turning to Simon. "I fear Radka is very shy."

"So's Peter," Simon said. "At least with a girl that pretty."

"An hour ago he was vehemently insisting he didn't want to dance at all," Harry said. "It seems Radka can work wonders."

Alessa stood by silently throughout this exchange, feeling rather forgotten. Just when she had decided she could safely fault the countess with rudeness for ignoring her, the countess said with a smile, "I understand I am to congratulate you on being a mother yourself, Lady Milverton."

Even the woman's manners were impeccable. "Yes," Alessa said. "And I am a stepmother as well. Has Harry told you about our little Niki?"

Something flashed in Harry's eyes that might have been anger or might have been a warning. "No," he said in a pleasant voice. "There hasn't been time."

The countess, Alessa was pleased to see, was looking puzzled. "Oh, dear, don't you know?" Alessa exclaimed, sending Harry a look of open challenge. "Forgive me, I was sure that being such an old friend of Harry's, he would have told you of his first marriage."

There was a moment of silence. To Alessa's satisfaction, a look of genuine astonishment crossed the countess's face. Edward coughed. Simon turned to his sister with a hard stare.

Harry met Alessa's gaze, as if he had suddenly realized she was in a less than agreeable humor. "How odd," he said in a pleasant voice. "I thought I had made it clear that no one but the bride's family knew of the marriage."

"Did you?" Alessa gave her husband a sweet smile laced with venom. "I'm afraid I don't remember, Harry."

Harry turned to the countess. "It's a long story."

"Please." The countess laid a hand on his arm, a simple gesture which Alessa found inexpressibly painful. "There is no need to tell me—"

95

"It's no secret," Harry began, but as he spoke, the musicians stopped playing and silence suddenly rippled through the crowd around them. Alessa turned and saw the Emperor on the threshold of an adjoining room where guests were also gathered, the candlelight playing off his gold hair and the braid on his uniform jacket.

Alexander signaled the musicians to resume playing, but the crowd remained subdued as he began to make his way about the room. Harry made no further attempt to speak, and they all stood by in virtual silence until the Emperor stopped before them.

Waving aside their bows and curtsies, Alexander turned to Alessa with a warm smile. "The evening hasn't been too much for you?" he asked.

"Not at all," Alessa assured him. It was a half-truth. The evening had indeed been too much for her, but it had nothing to do with her health.

"Good, good," Alexander said. "See that you take care of her, Milverton," he added, in a tone that implied his words were not entirely in jest.

"I am endeavoring to do so, Your Majesty," Harry returned. If there was irony in his voice, Alessa thought only she could hear it.

Alexander nodded to Edward and Simon, then smiled at the countess. It was as warm a smile as the one he had given Alessa, but it was not the smile of an honorary uncle to his favorite cousin's daughter, but of a man to a beautiful woman. Alessa felt a flash of anger that was only partly on Elisabeth's account.

"It's good to see you back in St. Petersburg, Countess," Alexander said. "I hope we will see more of you at court in the future."

"Thank you, Your Majesty," the countess murmured. "But my daughter and I plan to live a retired life."

"Can't hide yourself forever," Alexander said. "Or that charming daughter of yours. You'll be looking for a husband for her soon."

96

It seemed to Alessa that a look of alarm crossed the countess's face. "Radka is only fifteen," she said.

"Fifteen already. Good Lord, she's practically a young lady," Alexander exclaimed with a laugh.

The countess gave a strained smile but made no reply. Alexander stayed to talk a few minutes longer, then moved off, returning them to the uncomfortable moment before he had entered the room. Alessa smoothed a crease from one of her gloves. She looked at Harry but he was looking at the countess who still seemed troubled. "You're Radka's mother," he said softly. "No one could deny you a say in her future."

The countess looked up and smiled at him in gratitude. Harry smiled back. Alessa found the unspoken communication between them more distressing than anything that had gone before. Swallowing past the lump in throat, she turned to Edward and Simon. "Well?" she said, with a brightness that rang false to her own ears. "Isn't one of you going to ask me to dance? I'm sure Harry and the countess have a great deal to say to each other."

Alessa adjusted her straw hat against the morning sun spilling across the exquisite gallery designed by Charles Cameron. "Tell me about the Countess Chernikova."

Elisabeth stopped walking and turned to look at her. "What do you want to know?"

"I met her at the reception last night. Harry introduced us." Alessa swallowed. "It seems he and the countess are old friends."

"I see," Elisabeth said, resuming their promenade.

"You didn't know?" Alessa asked, looking at her cousin.

"Should I have?"

Alessa stared at the ranks of gray pedestals and gleaming bronze busts which lined the colonnade. "I understand there was talk about them when Harry was stationed here."

Elisabeth smiled. "My dear Alessa, I can hardly keep

track of all the gossip in St. Petersburg. You know as well as I do that at least half of it is utter nonsense."

"They're on very intimate terms," Alessa said, her voice sharp. "*That* isn't nonsense."

"I daresay the countess can use all the friends she can get," Elisabeth said quietly. "Her life hasn't been easy."

"Then you do know something about her." Alessa gripped Elisabeth's arm. "Tell me."

Elisabeth sighed and moved to a stone bench which stood between two of the Ionic columns that supported the roof of the colonnade. "I don't know the countess well," she said, as Alessa dropped down beside her. "She seems to be a nice woman, but she's never spent a great deal of time at court. I believe her marriage to Count Chernikov was arranged by her parents. The count was a wealthy man but at least twenty years her senior and rather forbidding. Not at all the sort of husband to make a young girl happy."

"The marriage was said to be unhappy?" Alessa asked.

"There were rumors." Elisabeth gave a faint smile. "Rumors I *did* hear. The few times I saw them together they did not appear a happy couple—not that a great many couples do. It was widely known that the count had married chiefly to have an heir, but they only had one child, a daughter. I imagine he wasn't pleased that his wife couldn't give him a son." Elisabeth hesitated a moment, toying with one of the satin ribbons which adorned her sleeves. "I remember the first time the countess came to court as a bride. Sacha was quite taken with her. For a time there was some gossip that she would supplant his present mistress, but nothing came of it. Among other things, the count was said to have a jealous temper, and Sacha couldn't afford a falling out with him. Besides, as far as I know, the countess never gave Sacha any encouragement."

Alessa recalled the meeting between Alexander and the countess the previous evening. "Did the countess ever give anyone else any encouragement?" she asked, her voice tight.

Elisabeth looked at her directly. "Not as far as I know."

It was not nearly enough reassurance. Alessa gripped her hands together in her lap. "When did the count die?"

"Last year. The title went to his younger brother. The countess and her daughter made their home with him and his wife in Moscow until recently."

When, coincidentally, Harry had also come to St. Petersburg. Had he written to the countess after his arrival? Was that the real reason she had returned to the capital? "Does she plan to stay long?" Alessa asked.

"I don't know. I only had the chance to say a few words to her last night." Elisabeth was silent for a moment. Then she leaned forward and touched Alessa's arm gently. "You may not believe this, Alessa, but a man may be a woman's friend without being her lover."

"I know." Alessa got to her feet and looked over the wrought metal railing at the edge of the colonnade. The summer air felt damp and heavy against her skin. The smooth, glassy surface of the lake spread before her. Two young women wearing the sashes of maids-of-honor were walking across the lawn. Birds called to each other in the nearby trees, sounding incongruously joyful.

"I don't know if you want to hear about it," Elisabeth said quietly, "but I have received a report on Captain Grigor Lychenko."

In her concern over the countess, Alessa had almost forgot her worries about Niki. She turned round quickly, relieved at the distraction yet disturbed by the reminder of this other cause of discord between her and Harry. "And?" she asked, leaning back against the railing and looking at Elisabeth.

Elisabeth's eyes were troubled. "Nothing conclusive, I'm afraid. Captain Lychenko's father was an impoverished minor noble with an estate near Moscow. His mother was the daughter of a reasonably prosperous Moscow merchant."

"His mother's sister was Nadia's mother?" Alessa asked

forcing her voice to stay even as she spoke of Harry's first wife.

Elisabeth nodded. "Nadia's mother married a shopkeeper in St. Petersburg. Her family thought she had married beneath her and the two sisters weren't close, but when Captain Lychenko joined the Guard and came to St. Petersburg, he looked up his aunt and her family."

"And met Nadia." Alessa kept her voice flat. "Harry said they were betrothed."

"After a fashion. It was never official. As cousins, they would have required a dispensation to marry, though it shouldn't have been difficult to come by. Her family seems to have felt they were betrothed, but Captain Lychenko's friends doubt he ever would have gone through with the marriage. He needs a bride with money." A welcome breeze came up, stirring the air and scattering a few leaves onto the stone floor of the colonnade. Elisabeth pushed some loosened strands of hair off her face. "From what I've heard of Captain Lychenko, he doesn't sound like a man who would hesitate to seduce a young girl if he thought he could get away with it."

"From what I've seen of him, I heartily agree," Alessa said, recalling her meeting with Captain Lychenko. "Did you learn anything more recent about him?"

"Very little. My sources obtained most of this information from his fellow officers. None of them knew anything about the child, merely that Lychenko's cousin Irina — Nadia's sister — had died recently and Lychenko had been seeing to the estate." Elisabeth hesitated. "Apparently, there is a general impression that Captain Lychenko lives wildly and well beyond his income."

"Harry says he has a mistress whose husband is a Cossack," Alessa said.

Elisabeth smiled. "I didn't hear that, but I'm not at all surprised. He also gambles freely and is heavily in debt."

Alessa's fingers clenched on the sun-warmed metal of the railing. "So he might be willing to take drastic measures to

100

recoup his fortunes. Such as producing a child and claiming it was Nadia's."

Elisabeth regarded her steadily. "He might. But none of this proves anything."

Alessa moved away from the railing. "No. It merely makes me even more convinced that I have cause not to trust him."

But Elisabeth was right, Alessa acknowledged as she returned to the bench. She was no closer to learning the truth, and she did not know where else to seek for it. And she was still determined to find out. It was more than just learning whether or not Niki was really Harry's son. Alessa suspected that Captain Lychenko held the key to whatever was troubling Niki.

Having persuaded Elisabeth to make the inquiries, Alessa had been more than content to leave the matter up to her cousin's agents. That was how her mother would have handled it. It was not the sort of thing in which a lady was expected to involve herself firsthand. Yet, Alessa realized, that was exactly what she would have to do if she wished to learn more.

As she listened with half an ear while Elisabeth talked of more cheerful subjects, it occurred to Alessa that there was one other person in the palace who might know something about Grigor Lychenko. It had never occurred to her to question a servant, but Galina was the obvious person to talk to. After she had returned to her apartments and fed the baby and tucked him back in his cradle, Alessa went in search of Niki's nurse.

The rooms that had been made into Niki's nursery were far less formal than most of those in the palace, with bright print curtains and cheerful, white-painted woodwork. There were a great many toys—Elisabeth had produced some from a mysterious store and Harry had added more on a foray into St. Petersburg—and the rooms held an unmistakable smell of child which stirred a discomfiting longing.

Niki was sprawled in a patch of sun on the flowered carpet, building towers out of a colorful set of blocks. Galina knelt beside him, admiring his handiwork, but at Alessa's entrance both looked up in surprise.

A smile broke across Niki's usually solemn face. "Lady Milverton."

Feeling a treacherous rush of joy and pride at the sound of Niki saying her name, Alessa walked over to him and ruffled his hair. "Hullo, lambkin," she said in Russian.

The endearment came easily to her lips. She had come to talk to Galina, but she found herself sitting beside Niki and helping him build towers. Time passed more quickly than she realized. All of a sudden, a footman came in to lay luncheon in the adjoining room.

"Will you join us?" Galina asked as Niki clambered onto one of the chairs at the table.

Alessa hesitated, then nodded. Perhaps because of the distraction of the food or perhaps because of the shared adventure of building towers, Niki was more talkative than usual over the meal. He made a game of pointing at things and getting Alessa to say their names in English and French. He had already learned some of the words from Peter and Simon. He was a quick study. Alessa thought of the illustrations she had drawn for the history books her friend Fiona had written for children. In a few more years, Niki would be old enough for such books. Even now, as his English improved, she would be able to read to him. And she could give him drawing lessons. . . .

It was only when Niki returned to his blocks in the other room, leaving Alessa and Galina sitting at the table drinking more tea, that Alessa remembered the reason for her visit. She was reluctant to break the comfortable feeling in the room, but her determination to learn the truth was as strong as ever. "Galina," she said, "how well do you know Captain Lychenko?"

A look of surprise and confusion crossed Galina's face. "I'm sorry," Alessa said quickly, realizing how her words must have sounded. "I didn't mean it that way. It's just that I know so little about him, and I thought perhaps you could tell me more. Had you met him before the day he brought Niki to the inn?"

Galina nodded, her composure recovered. "A great many officers of the Guard came to the inn when they were drilling in Krasnoe Selo. Everyone who worked at the inn knew Captain Lychenko. He was a favorite with many of the girls. But," said Galina, regarding Alessa steadily, "I never shared his bed."

Alessa smiled. "I didn't think you had. You have better taste than that."

Slowly, an answering smile spread across Galina's face. "I am more cautious at least," she said. "To tell the truth, I was surprised Captain Lychenko asked me to look after Niki, for he doesn't know me well."

"I'm not surprised," Alessa said. "He must have realized you could be trusted with a child. Had you heard anything about Niki before that day?"

"Nothing. Everyone was astonished to see Captain Lychenko arrive at the inn with a child. Niki was obviously terrified. Whatever I thought of Captain Lychenko, I wanted to help the little boy."

"Yes." Alessa looked through the open door at Niki, once again absorbed in the blocks. "I feel much the same myself."

Galina smoothed the white kerchief which covered her hair. "Lady Milverton?" she asked, an uncertain note in her voice. "You fear something is wrong?"

"I don't know," Alessa said. "I'm afraid Captain Lychenko hasn't told us the whole truth about Niki. Something's troubling Niki. I'd like to know what it is."

"So would I," said Galina, glancing at the child.

Alessa smiled at the other woman. It occurred to her that for the past quarter-hour she had conversed with Galina not as a servant but as a friend. Alessa had grown up surrounded by servants, but this was the first time she had had such a frank conversation with one. And yet, even in retrospect, it did not seem at all odd to have spoken thus with the serving maid she had hired to be Niki's nurse.

Alessa glanced at the clock over the mantel. "I must go," she said, getting to her feet. "The baby may wake up." She went into the other room to say goodbye to Niki. "I'll come and see you again tomorrow," she promised, kneeling beside him. "We can build more towers."

Niki nodded, solemn once again. Alessa realized he did not want her to leave. She was touched, yet she had to go. She couldn't leave the baby for long. Unless . . . Alessa hesitated, weighing a decision it would not have occurred to her to even consider a few hours before. With sudden resolution, she held her hand out to Niki. "Would you like to come with me and see the baby?"

At her words he sprang to his feet and seized her hand in a tight grip. "It's all right," Alessa told Galina. "Enjoy some time to yourself."

As she led Niki through the labyrinth of corridors, Alessa realized it was the first time she had had him with her without Galina being there as well. He walked beside her in silence, though she noticed him glancing about with curiosity as they moved into a region of the palace where he had never been.

Alessa rather liked the feel of his hand in hers, but she was already beginning to question the wisdom of her hasty decision. At Krasnoe Selo, and in the carriage on the way to the palace, he had seemed too frightened to show any interest in the baby, and Alessa had made no effort to introduce the two children to each other. Taking Niki to see the baby now was one more step which bound him irrevocably into their family.

But it was too late to go back now. "We have to be quiet," Alessa told Niki at the door of her bedchamber. "The baby may be asleep."

Niki nodded, his face serious, but his eyes wide with curiosity. Alessa eased the door open. The muslin subcurtains were drawn, filling the rose silk room with a soft, muted light. The baby was making noises, not cries of discomfort—Alessa was getting very good at interpreting the different sounds he made—but an announcement that he was awake. He was squirming on the table near his cradle, while one of the nurses bent over him.

"I've just changed him, my lady," the nurse said, looking up and curtsying at Alessa's entrance.

"Thank you, I'll take him now." Alessa crossed to the table and lifted her son into her arms. He smelled of clean linen and dusting powder. One of his hands closed around the jade beads she was wearing. Alessa kissed him on the forehead.

There was a quiet click of the door as the nurse withdrew. Niki was still standing uncertainly where Alessa had left him. "It's all right," Alessa said, realizing she had abandoned him when she went to pick up the baby. She wasn't used to looking after two children at once. She carried the baby over to the settee and motioned Niki to join her.

Niki crossed the room hesitantly. Alessa said nothing, merely held the baby and watched as the boy who might or might not be Harry's son by a woman she had never met stared down at the child she and Harry had produced.

Niki's eyes were round and enormous. Cautiously, he lifted his small hand and touched the baby's even smaller one. The baby stirred. Niki's eyes widened still further. He looked up at Alessa. "What's its name?" he asked.

"Alastair." Alessa called her son by the name for the first time, pushing aside memories of how happy she had been last night when she and Harry chose the name and how much Harry had hurt her afterward.

" 'Stair." Niki stroked the baby's hair gently, almost reverently. Then he climbed onto the settee beside Alessa. "Is he your baby?" he asked.

"Yes." Alessa looked down at the little boy beside her. Niki was still watching Alastair. He seemed entranced by the baby and Alessa felt a great welling of warmth for him. "My baby and Lord Mil—your father's," she said.

Niki looked up at her in puzzlement.

"You're the baby's brother," Alessa explained.

To her astonishment, at the word "brother" Niki's lips trembled and tears welled up in his eyes.

"Niki." If she hadn't been holding the baby, Alessa would have gathered him in her arms. "What is it?"

The trembling increased. Niki made a strangled sound that sounded like "Rara."

"It's all right, darling," Alessa said soothingly. "Only tell me what is the matter."

Niki's face crumpled, but this time the word came out more clearly. "Zara."

"Zara?" Alessa asked. "Who is Zara?"

As if he had suddenly found his voice, Niki let out a wail. "I want Zara back."

Alastair, who had been drowsing in Alessa's arms, woke up and howled. Alessa looked from one crying child to the other, then quickly got to her feet, carried Alastair into the adjoining room, and gave him into the nurse's care. She returned to the settee and gathered the sobbing Niki into her arms, heedless of the way his tears drenched her embroidered muslin dress. Finally, when the tears had ceased, she wiped his eyes and nose with her handkerchief and settled him on her lap. "I want to help you, Niki," she said, bending over him. "But first you must tell me more. Who is Zara? Your nurse?"

Niki shook his head. His face was still red from the crying and his eyes were glassy with tears.

"Who then?" Alessa persisted.

Niki rubbed his hand across his eyes. "My sister," he said in a soft voice.

Alessa stared at him in astonishment. "Sister?" she repeated, not sure she had heard correctly.

Niki nodded. "Sister," he repeated, his voice clearer and stronger.

Alessa tried to order her thoughts. Dear God, was this proof that Niki was not Harry's son? Or was it possible that

Nadia had had twins? Then Alessa remembered that Niki had been raised by his aunt from babyhood. He might well regard his aunt's children as siblings. "Is Zara your Aunt Irina's little girl?" she asked.

"Irina," Niki said with recognition. "My mama."

Alessa drew a breath. Having lost his adoptive parents, Niki had then received the further blow of being separated from the girl he thought of as his sister. Who had fathered Niki now seemed less important than the fact that she finally saw a way she could help him. "Where is Zara now?" she asked.

Niki's brows drew together. "He took me away. Cousin Grigor."

"Yes, darling, I know," Alessa said, mentally cursing Grigor Lychenko in English, Russian, French, and Italian. "Where did he take you away from?"

"Our cousins' house."

"You were staying with cousins?" Alessa asked.

Niki nodded vigorously. "They make bread."

A bakeshop. After Irina died, Niki and Zara must have been sent to stay with cousins who owned a bakeshop. "Do you know their name?" she asked.

"Petrov," Niki told her.

Alessa smoothed Niki's hair, wondering how much else he could reasonably be expected to remember. "And do you know where the Petrovs live?"

"St. Petersburg."

Alessa forced down her frustration. "Do you know the name of the street? Did you ever hear any of your cousins say it?"

Niki's face screwed up in concentration "Mik-lov-skaya," he said at last, sounding the word out carefully.

Mikhailovskaya. Alessa let out a whoop and kissed him. Niki looked at her with concern. "You'll find Zara?"

"I'll try to find her," Alessa said, forcing herself to be sober. But the thought that she might at least be able to solve Niki's problems made her spirits lighten tremendously.

Half an hour later, when she had returned Niki to Galina and fed Alastair, Alessa made her way to her husband's apartments. However bitter she felt about the countess, this was something she and Harry should share. He would want to come with her to look for Zara. Alessa felt a satisfying sense of triumph at the thought of telling Harry that it was she who had solved the mystery of what was troubling Niki.

But the door of Harry's room was opened not by Harry but by Lytton, his valet. Alessa smiled at him, buoyed by a sense of purpose. Lytton was far less stuffy than most valets. The son of one of the tenants on the Milverton estate, he had grown up with Harry and then served as a footman before Harry, with typical disregard for convention, had employed him as a valet.

"Is Lord Milverton here?" Alessa asked.

"I'm afraid not, my lady. His lordship went out this morning. He took the prince and Master Peter with him."

"I see." Harry had every right to go out, of course, though he might have sent her a note telling her of his plans. And Simon might have told her, the wretch. Alessa wondered how soon Harry would return and if she should wait for him or go in search of Zara and the bakeshop cousins on her own. "Do you know where his lordship has gone?" she asked.

Lytton hesitated. "I believe," he said, "that his lordship meant to pay a visit to the Countess Chernikova."

Chapter Seven

Peter was disappointed by his first sight of the Countess Chernikova's dacha. They were traveling along a winding road with a forest of fir trees on one side and a scattering of leafy oak on the other when they suddenly came round a bend and caught sight of the house set on a slight rise in the flat countryside. It was a rectangular building of pale stone with orderly sash windows and shallow steps leading up to a stately Ionic portico. An upper story rose like a small, flattened tower from the center of the roof but did not destroy the classical symmetry of the whole.

"It looks just like a villa at Richmond," Peter said.

Simon grinned. "It is just like a villa at Richmond. I warned you a dacha isn't any more than a country house."

"I know, but . . ." Peter broke off, abashed both at having offered criticism and at having sounded naive.

Harry sent him a sympathetic look. "I felt the same way when I first came here. It seems as if everything should be as exotic as it sounds."

Their coachman drew the calèche up in front of the house, and a footman admitted them to a spacious marble-tiled entrance hall, brightened by several vases of flowers. Like the facade of the dacha, it looked little different from a country house in England, but the sweet, clear melody of a waltz came from behind one of the doors opening off the hall. Peter recognized the sound of a clavichord. His pulse quickened. Radka had mentioned last night that she played the clavichord.

The footman led them to the door from which the music came and flung it open. Beyond was a sunny room with soft lavender-gray walls, but Peter took little notice of it. His eyes went directly to the clavichord, where Radka was sitting, her hair bright in the sunlight as she picked out the melody of the waltz.

"Harry. Prince. Mr. Carne." The Countess Chernikova rose and came toward them, nodding to the footman to withdraw. "I'm so glad you could come."

Peter forced himself to turn his attention to their hostess, who had given Harry both her hands and was smiling up at him with easy familiarity. They were expected, Peter realized. Harry must have arranged the visit with the countess last night. Peter wondered if Alessa knew and how she would feel about it.

Radka rose from the clavichord and came to stand beside her mother. She was wearing a simple white muslin dress and her hair was uncurled and caught back from her face with a ribbon, but she looked every bit as pretty as she had last night. Some things *were* different in Russia, Peter decided. He'd never seen an English girl half as enchanting as Radka Chernikova.

"We'll have luncheon in about an hour," the countess was saying. "I thought perhaps you young people would care to explore the gardens first."

Obviously the countess wanted to talk to Harry alone and Peter wasn't at all sure that this was a good thing. He glanced at Simon. Though Simon was smiling, Peter knew his friend found it troubling as well. On the other hand, Peter could hardly find fault with the prospect of a stroll in the gardens with Radka.

Radka led them down a gentle slope of lawn toward an ornamental stream. Though she seemed more at ease than she had last night, she was still quiet. Peter felt painfully awkward. He was comfortable talking to women, but girls his own age were another matter. Simon, he noted with a twinge of jealousy, appeared distressingly relaxed.

"This is a beautiful house," Simon said, breaking the silence among the three of them.

"Thank you." Radka gave a quick, shy smile which Peter wished had been directed at him. "It belonged to my father. It's my uncle's now, but he's letting *Maman* and me live here. I'm grateful to him but somehow it doesn't—it doesn't seem quite the same as when it was our own."

"My father died when I was ten," Simon said, looking at her with sympathy. "And Peter lost his mother when he was eleven. It's beastly."

Seeing the troubled look in Radka's blue eyes, Peter cursed himself for staring at her like an idiot instead of offering sympathy as Simon had done. But before he could say anything, Radka spoke. "I didn't know my father very well. I'm sorry he's dead, of course," she added quickly. "But he was away a great deal and he—well, he wasn't much interested in me. He wanted a son."

"That's despicable." Peter spoke up at last, filled with an intense dislike of the late Count Chernikov.

Radka shrugged her thin shoulders. "He wanted an heir," she said matter-of-factly. "Most men do."

Peter started to say that he didn't and then decided that perhaps it was premature. They had reached the edge of the stream, an expanse of bright, rippling blue. Though the air was still and damp, it carried the clean, welcome scent of the nearby fir trees. "This is my favorite view," Radka said, leading them onto a curving stone bridge which spanned the stream. She stopped in the middle of the bridge to look out over the water, her expression grave, almost sad.

"You've been away for a long time, haven't you?" Peter asked.

Radka nodded. "We were staying with my uncle's family in Moscow." She looked back at the water, her delicate brows drawing together. "It's awkward, living in someone else's house. And my uncle . . ."

"Isn't much better than your father?" Simon asked.

111

Radka looked at him in surprise. Then she gave a whole-hearted smile. "I can't admit it to very many people."

"I have an uncle," Simon said. "He had to go abroad and we aren't allowed to speak of him at all. It's a great relief."

"Come to think of it, my uncle tried to embezzle my father's money," Peter said, his eyes on Radka.

"My uncle never tried to do anything like that. But he's my guardian." Turning away abruptly, Radka led them across the bridge, onto a path that wound between trees and beds of summer flowers, and finally to a grouping of wrought-iron benches, overshadowed by a spreading oak tree and a pair of classical statues.

Radka sat down on one of the benches. Simon moved to another, letting Peter sit beside Radka. Peter sent his friend a look of gratitude.

Radka began pleating the fabric of her skirt between her fingers, an intent look on her face, as if she were trying to come to a decision. "There's no one I can talk to about it," she said suddenly, looking from Peter to Simon. "That's what makes it so horrid."

"You can talk to us," Simon said, leaning back against the bench with an ease Peter envied. "We're trustworthy, and anyway we're going back to England soon so we can't make trouble for you."

Radka smiled again, but the look on her face made Peter want to go out and slay dragons. "I think it's because of my uncle that *Maman* decided to come back to St. Petersburg," she said. "I think she's afraid he's going to arrange a marriage for me and she won't be able to stop him."

"But surely she has some say in the matter. She's your mother," Peter protested, shocked at the thought of Radka being old enough to marry. Disconcertingly, it made his mind stray to the other things she might be old enough to do.

"It doesn't always work that way," Simon said. "Even in England." He looked at Radka with the appraising air he adopted when there was a problem to sort out. "Has your uncle said anything to you about marriage?"

"Not directly. But he and my aunt made a point of inviting unmarried young men to the house. Well, they weren't all so young actually. Some of them were older than my uncle. And one night I heard him arguing with *Maman*." Radka reached up to tuck a stray curl behind her ear. "My uncle is an ambitious man. I think he would like an alliance with a powerful family. I'm not sure how big my dowry is, but it's large enough that people won't leave me alone."

"That's what it was like for my sister," Simon said. "She almost married a man who wanted her money more than he wanted her. Our mother approved of him too," he added grimly.

"There must be something we can do," Peter said, brushing angrily at the ever-present mosquitos. "I mean," he amended when Radka looked at him in surprise, "we can't just leave you at your uncle's mercy."

Radka smiled, this time directly at him. Peter's heart caught in his throat. "That's very kind of you, Mr. Carne," she said, "but it's my problem. I didn't mean to burden you with it."

"No, he's right," Simon said, leaning forward. "We wouldn't be very good friends if we didn't try to help. You must think of us as friends or you wouldn't have told us all that."

"Exactly," Peter said. "And you'd better call me Peter and him Simon. He doesn't like to be reminded he's a prince unless it's useful."

Radka looked from him to Simon, first in uncertainty, then in gratitude. Watching her, Peter made a surprising discovery. She wasn't a creature of spun glass, but a girl, a very pretty, very human girl. He found the thought vastly reassuring.

"Right," said Simon, as if he were calling a meeting to order. "Now we just have to think what's to be done."

* * *

113

"I'm worried about Radka." Releasing her grip on a fold of the white damask curtain, Marina turned from the window where she had been watching her daughter and the boys walk toward the stream. "Sergei controls her money now and her fate along with it."

"He let you bring her to St. Petersburg," Harry said, leaning against the clavichord.

"He did." Marina sank into an upholstered chair. "But I expect he'll follow soon himself. He wants to increase his influence at court." She passed a hand over her face. "I was married at seventeen. I don't want the same thing to happen to Radka."

"Radka's fifteen," Harry reminded her, dropping down in a nearby chair. "If you aren't careful, you'll make me feel ancient."

His words did not divert her as he had hoped. "Old enough for Sergei to be considering possible husbands," Marina said, leaning back in her chair. The light from the windows revealed the shadows of strain on her face. "There's nothing quite like having a child. I didn't know how all-consuming it would be."

"Nor did I," Harry said softly.

Marina looked up quickly. "I'm sorry. I've been shockingly selfish and talked of nothing but myself. Do you like being a father?"

"Very much." Harry hesitated, fumbling for the right words. "I didn't expect—"

"You don't," Marina said with a quick smile. "Not until you actually hold them in your arms. At least that's how it was for me when Radka was born."

Harry thought of the first time Alessa had given him the baby to hold and of the moment he had seen Niki in the kitchen of the inn in Krasnoe Selo. "It was for me too," he said. And then, without planning to, he added, "With both of them."

Marina's blue eyes were understanding. "It can't have been easy, acquiring two children at once."

114

She had given him an opening to talk, but she was not going to push him. Last night had been no place to explain the tangled history of his first marriage, but Harry was determined to tell Marina the story. She was his friend and she deserved to know. More than that, he discovered that he wanted to talk about it.

Hands clasped before him, voice level, Harry told Marina about his first meeting with Nadia and all that had followed, including his estrangement from Alessa and his inability to reach Niki.

Marina listened in silence, her face grave but free from censure, as he had known it would be. He had always admired Marina's calm, soothing acceptance as much as her beauty. "It must have been a great shock for your wife," she said when he had done. "Especially since she had just had a child herself. But I'm sure with time you'll be able to —"

"No." Harry pushed himself to his feet, surprised at the bitterness in his voice. "We might work it out if we had a real marriage. But we don't. We have an arrangement of mutual convenience."

"That, I suppose, is why your wife looked ready to kill me when you introduced us last night," Marina said quietly.

Harry swung round to look at her. "You think Alessa was jealous of you?"

"I'm sure she was," Marina said with a smile.

Harry raked a hand through his hair, recalling Alessa's coldness when he'd tried to take her to meet Marina. Only a few moments before he'd thought they were getting on better. At the time, he had thought her change of mood had been because of Niki, yet nothing had been said about Niki in that moment. He felt a surge of triumph at the thought that he could arouse Alessa's jealousy. At least it was some sort of emotion. And yet, he reminded himself, it was an emotion which could spring as much from pride as from love. "If she's jealous, it's of her position as my wife," he said.

Marina shook her head, her wrought gold earrings stirring against her clear skin. "You're a fool, Harry."

"Perhaps. But I'm not such a fool as to believe my wife feels something for me that I know she doesn't." Harry moved across the room, longing for more exercise than this elegant chamber allowed.

"Are you in love with her?" Marina asked.

Harry froze, staring at a small, exquisitely painted icon which stood on the mantel. The brilliant colors blurred before his eyes. The denial which should have been automatic caught in his throat. To speak the words seemed like sacrilege. "I scarcely know her," he said in a low voice.

"Romeo scarcely knew Juliet," Marina said.

Harry drew a steadying breath. His mouth was dry and his brain felt as befuddled as if he'd downed a tumbler of vodka. "I needed a wife," he said, forcing himself to turn and meet Marina's questioning gaze. "More than that, I needed an heir. If I'd known about Niki . . ." He broke off, realizing that if he had known he already had a son, he might have never asked Alessa to be his wife, realizing what an unspeakable loss that would have been.

"The marriage was arranged," Marina said.

"You could say that. Though Alessa and I did most of the arranging." Harry clasped his hands behind him, seeing again Alessa on the day she had agreed to be his wife. Even then, she had stirred him far more than he had been willing to admit. "In all the years of my growing up I don't remember one moment of intimacy between my parents," he told Marina. "I thought of marriage as a contract. After Nadia, I didn't want anyone else who might be hurt. God, that's rich, isn't it," he said striding back to his chair, "after what I've done to Alessa."

"You didn't mean to hurt her," Marina said.

"No," Harry agreed, his voice kept carefully free of emotion. "I didn't mean to hurt Nadia either." Suddenly finding the heat in the room stifling, he reached up and loosened his cravat. "When I proposed to Alessa, my father had been dead less than two years. I never wanted to be Earl of Milverton — you know that," he added, recalling the evenings Marina had listened to his drunken tirades against life in general and his father in particular. "But since I was, I was determined to make something of it, whatever the rest of the family thought of me. Alessa had been trained for that sort of life. She seemed a sensible choice." Harry bit back a cry of anguish and frustration. If there was one thing he didn't feel now when it came to his wife, it was sensible.

"There's nothing wrong with falling in love, Harry," Marina said. "Even with your own wife."

Harry stared down at his hands, remembering the moment he had slipped his ring on Alessa's finger at their wedding. The thought of admitting he loved her filled him with a terrible, frightening exhilaration. Was it true? Did he want it to be? He pressed his hands to his temples, trying to massage away the confusion.

When he looked up, he found Marina watching him, a smile playing about her lips. "Perhaps I should have taken you as a lover when I had the chance," she said. "I have the feeling you'll be no use to any other women now."

Harry returned the smile, feeling a wave of affection for the woman who sat across from him. Her eyes were lustrous, her hair more brilliant than the gold of her earrings. When he had first met her at a ball at the Winter Palace nearly six years ago, he had thought that she was the most beautiful woman he had ever seen. Later he learned that she was one of the kindest. That he had not become her lover was not due to any lack of desire on his part.

She was every bit as beautiful now as she had been then. Yet it was as if his awareness of her had been muted. Since Alessa, he had looked at women in a different way. It was not that he couldn't recognize that other woman were beautiful or clever or desirable. It was simply that none of them was Alessa.

Harry got to his feet and crossed to Marina's side.

"You're a good friend, Marina," he said, lifting her hand to his lips. "But you didn't ask me here to talk about my own problems. You're worried about Radka and the future. Is there something you want me to do?"

Marina's eyes, which had seemed so worldly-wise when they talked about his problems, were suddenly troubled. He heard her draw in her breath and felt her fingers close around his own. "Yes," she said. "That's why I asked you here. I need your help, Harry. Quite desperately. I hope your wife will understand."

Mikhailovskaya Street was a small, quiet thoroughfare off the more fashionable Nevsky Prospekt. Alessa signaled the coachman to stop at the first bakeshop they reached and sent the footman she had brought from the palace to inquire whether the proprietors were named Petrov and if they were related to Irina Varsenina.

They were not. Sighing, Alessa wondered if she would be able to keep her promise to Niki. She looked down at Alastair, whom she was cradling in her arms. He had borne the two-hour journey better than she had expected. She had even managed to feed him in the swaying carriage. Now his eyes were fixed on the light coming in through the window. On the opposite side of the carriage, Phillips sat quietly, hands folded in her lap. Around them were all the paraphernalia required to take a baby on even so short a journey as this—a sleeping basket, fresh napkins, extra blankets.

At the second bakeshop they reached, they repeated the same procedure. But this time when the footman emerged from the shop, his expression told Alessa he had been successful. Feeling a stab of triumph and wondering what she had got herself into, Alessa lowered the carriage window.

"The proprietor, Petrov, is the cousin of Madame Varsenina's late husband," the footman told her.

"Thank you, Misha." Drawing a breath, Alessa closed the

window and gave Alastair to Phillips. "I shouldn't be long," she said.

Phillips took the baby and smiled happily down at him. In the last weeks she had smiled more than in the four years she had worked for Alessa. Phillips, who had always seemed very conscious of her position as a lady's maid, was entranced by Alastair.

When the footman had handed her down from the carriage, Alessa told him to wait with the coachman and then surveyed the neat building in front of her. It looked prosperous but far from grand. Ruffled curtains on the upper windows showed that the top story housed the family. Nadia, who might have been Countess of Milverton, had probably come from a home such as this.

Banishing thoughts of Harry's first wife, Alessa made her way into the shop. The warm, yeasty smell of freshly baked bread and the rich aroma of chocolate greeted her. Glass fronted cases displayed trays of elaborate pastries and more prosaic bread and rolls. A thin, bespectacled man was waiting on two middle-aged women, respectably but not fashionably dressed. As Alessa moved forward, a dark-haired woman wearing an apron over a print dress hurried from behind the counter and came toward her, no doubt alerted by the footman.

"Madame Petrova?" Alessa asked in Russian.

The woman nodded, regarded Alessa uncertainly, then dropped a quick curtsy. "You were a friend of Irina's?" she asked, as if doubting that her cousin-in-law and Alessa could have been acquainted.

"No," Alessa told her, "I never met Madame Varsenina. I am Nikolai's stepmother, Lady Milverton."

Surprise and realization showed in Madame Petrova's eyes. "Please," she said, "you must come upstairs." Without further speech, she led the way behind the counter, stopped to say a few words to her husband, then took Alessa into the back of the shop and up a narrow staircase to the family quarters. She showed Alessa to a small sitting room, shabbier than the shop but clean and tidy, and insisted on fetching tea and a plate of cakes. Only when she had served Alessa a cake and glass of tea, did she ask, the concern in her eyes evident, "Niki is staying with you?"

Alessa nodded. "For almost two weeks now. But he seems unhappy. I think he misses his cousin Zara."

Madame Petrova's brows drew together. She had a kind-looking face and was probably only ten years older than Alessa herself. "I knew no good would come of separating those two. There was a fearful scene when Captain Lychenko took Niki away." She sighed, her eyes troubled. "Before Captain Lychenko came, it never occurred to me that they weren't brother and sister."

Alessa set down her untouched tea glass abruptly. "But surely Irina told you . . ."

Madame Petrova shook her head. "My husband and I are from Kiev," she explained. "We came to St. Petersburg less than a year ago. My husband and his cousin, Irina's husband, had only written to each other occasionally, but after we came here we visited Irina. She was a widow by then with two young children who called her mama. We assumed they were both her own, and she never told us otherwise. We only saw them a half-dozen times before Irina became ill."

"And you became their guardians after her death?" Alessa asked.

"There was no one else, so we took them into our home. Then one day Captain Lychenko arrived and told us about Niki. I was never more shocked."

"But you believed him?" Alessa persisted, gripping her hands together.

Madame Petrova looked at Alessa in surprise. "Why should he have lied? It's to his credit that he interfered at all. I would have thought a young man like him would be likely to just have left the children with us."

"Of course." Alessa gave her a reassuring smile, her brain in a whirl. Were Niki and Zara brother and sister in fact?

Had she been right to think Lychenko had invented the story of Nadia's baby for money and vengeance?

"In some ways it was a relief to learn Niki had other people to look after him," Madame Petrova continued, smoothing her skirt, "for we have four little ones of our own and it's no denying it's a lot of mouths to feed. But I didn't like seeing him and Zara separated. I still don't."

"That's why I came." Alessa leaned forward. "I'd like to take Zara to Tsarkoe Selo to visit Niki, at least for a week or so."

At the mention of Tsarkoe Selo, Madame Petrova gave a slight start. But she nodded her head slowly. "The children are out for a walk now with our maid, but they should be back soon. If Zara wishes to go, and I think she will, I have no objection."

"I'm so glad." Alessa picked up her tea again and this time sipped it.

She sat drinking tea and eating the cake, which was delicious, and making conversation with Madame Petrova, which was easier than she would have expected, until a clatter of feet in the corridor outside announced the return of the children. Madame Petrova excused herself. From behind the closed door, Alessa heard the sound of high-pitched voices and Madame Petrova's calmer accents. A few minutes later, she returned to the sitting room, shepherding a small girl.

The child looked so like Niki that the breath stopped in Alessa's throat. The rounded face was the same and the blue eyes and the thick fair hair, save that Zara's hung down her back in a neat braid. She looked to be an inch or so taller than Niki. Could she be old enough to be his sister? Or could she be his twin? One thing was certain. Whoever Niki's parents were, he and Zara were related by blood.

"Hullo, Zara." Alessa smiled and held out her hand. "Niki told me to give you his love."

At the mention of Niki's name, Zara's face broke into a

121

smile. "This is Lady Milverton," Madame Petrova said, leading Zara forward. "She's Niki's stepmother."

Zara studied Alessa gravely. She did not seem as frightened as Niki had been that day at the inn, but then her life had not been upset as much as Niki's. "Our mother is dead," she told Alessa.

"I know," Alessa said, her throat tightening at the thought of what both the children had been through. "But Niki's father—Niki's other father," she added, realizing Zara would think of Irina's husband as his father, "is my husband. That makes me Niki's stepmother."

It sounded hopelessly tangled to Alessa's ears, but Zara nodded. "Did you bring Niki with you?" she asked, looking around the room eagerly.

"No, I'm afraid not," Alessa said, wishing she had when she saw the disappointment in the little girl's eyes. She paused, afraid Zara would be frightened of leaving the Petrovs' house. "But I want to take you with me to visit him. Would you like that?"

Zara did not even hesitate. She smiled again, this time with wholehearted delight, took Alessa's hand, and looked up at her with an expression of complete and utter trust.

As the calèche made its way back to Tsarkoe Selo, Harry sat in silence. He was worried about Marina and troubled by the potential consequences of the promise he had given her. But more than anything, he was disturbed by the memory of their talk about Alessa. Marina had forced him to confront feelings he had tried to keep on a tight rein. If he ever loosed his hold, he feared those feelings would overpower him.

As if sensing his mood, Simon and Peter were quiet as well. Simon looked serious, but there was a half-smile on Peter's face. Harry recalled the way Peter had stared at Radka across the luncheon table. He had seemed less moonstruck than he had last night, but more tender some

122

how, as if his admiration for her was changing into sincere affection. Not that it could amount to anything, of course. They were children.

Harry caught himself up short and shook his head. At seventeen, he had certainly not thought of himself as a child. And Peter and Simon had proved their maturity more than once. In the past weeks, their behavior had been considerably more adult than his and Alessa's.

The gilded wrought iron of the main gates of Tsarkoe Selo was suddenly before them. As they drove beneath the eagles and crown which topped the gates in a delicate yet unmistakable reminder of imperial power, Harry stared at the thousand-foot facade of the palace. The bright blue and stark white of the walls were softened by the northern sunlight. Corinthian columns, classical statuary, wrought-iron balconies, square-paned French windows, and bronze-washed caryatids vied for attention and yet blended into a harmonious whole. It was a creation of shimmering beauty and wild ostentation, of stately pomp and theatrical glitter, a fitting symbol of the world Harry had spent years trying to understand. The world into which his wife had been born.

When they dismounted and went inside, a footman informed Harry that Lady Milverton was by the lake and had asked that he join her as soon as he returned. At the thought that Alessa wanted to see him, Harry felt a burst of sheer happiness. Accompanied by Peter and Simon, he quickly made his way up to the first floor, through the hanging garden which linked the palace and the Cameron Gallery, and along the gallery's colonnade. At the top of the great curving double staircase, he paused and looked down at the lake below, scanning the grounds for some sign of his wife.

And then he saw her. She was sitting on a blanket a little way up the slope from the water. Her bonnet was pushed back and the sunlight lent a sheen to her hair. A baby carriage was drawn up nearby. Galina and Niki were sitting on

123

the blanket beside Alessa. And so was another child, a little girl about Niki's size with a long braid hanging down her back.

"Whose little girl is that?" Peter asked.

"I don't know." Filled with a sense that his life was about to become even more complicated, Harry hurried down one side of the double staircase and then down the second tier of steps which spilled onto the grass. He heard Peter and Simon's footsteps echoing on the stone behind him, but his eyes were on Alessa.

As he strode across the grass toward her, Alessa looked up and met his gaze. And in that moment Harry knew that whatever her reason for wanting to see him, it was not because she regretted the coldness between them last night.

Alessa smiled, a steely, determined smile. "Hullo, Harry. I hope you had a pleasant visit with the Countess Chernikova. As you can see, I had a busy day as well." She looked at Niki and the little girl, who had both turned toward Harry when Alessa spoke. Niki, Harry was relieved to see, was smiling. Harry glanced at the girl, who was regarding him with curiosity. His blood stilled. She was the image of Niki.

Alessa put her arm around the girl, and the girl, unlike Niki, who did not like to be touched, cuddled against her. "This," Alessa said, "is Zara."

Chapter Eight

"We have to take her with us, Harry."

Leaning against the balustrade of the Palladian bridge which spanned the far end of the lake, Harry turned to look at his wife. She was staring not over the water but at the patch of lawn to one side where Peter stood, his tall, gangly frame bent low as he showed Niki how to throw a ball. Radka Chernikova was watching with admiration in her eyes, the pink ribbons on her bonnet fluttering in the breeze. Zara, who was perched on Simon's shoulders, clapped enthusiastically as Niki threw the bright yellow ball to Galina. Niki looked around at the circle of faces, flushed with triumph.

"He's a completely different child since she's been here," Alessa said.

Harry could not argue with that. In the two weeks since Alessa had brought Zara to the palace, the change in Niki had been miraculous. He laughed and shouted and, though still on the quiet side, behaved very much as a normal four-year-old. Only when their departure for England was mentioned did Niki again become the solemn, withdrawn little boy they had found in Krasnoe Selo.

A merchant ship was scheduled to leave for England at the end of the week, and the doctors said both Alessa and the baby were well enough to travel. They would have to be on their way before the Baltic froze over. Edward, who was going home on leave, was to travel with them, as was Galina, who had agreed to continue as Niki's nurse. Only Zara's future remained undecided.

Looking at his son's laughing face, Harry was overwhelmed by a host of conflicting emotions. Tenderness; regret for the years of Niki's life he had missed and all that Niki had been through; gratitude that Alessa had found Zara; and more than a touch of jealousy, because Niki still seemed closer to Alessa than to him.

"It isn't entirely our decision," Harry said. "Zara's guardians may not want to let her go."

"I doubt it. They want to do what's right, but they have four children of their own and looking after a fifth is a strain. I think Madame Petrova would like Niki and Zara to be together." Alessa perched on the balustrade, leaning against one of the arches which supported the bridge's roof.

Harry rested his shoulders against the opposite side of the arch and turned to study her. The gray Siberian marble of the bridge emphasized her pale skin and the rose-colored stuff of her dress. Something about her relaxed pose made her seem more approachable than she had been of late. The arch enclosed them, and though they did not touch, it struck Harry that it was the most intimate moment they had shared in weeks. He was aware of her scent, tuberose and jasmine, as elusive and exotic as Alessa herself.

"You wouldn't mind?" he asked. "Taking a second child into our home?"

Alessa stiffened. "I'm not a monster, Harry. Protecting my son's birthright has nothing to do with denying a home to a motherless child." Her eyes were bright and her quickened breathing emphasized the curve of her breasts, swollen with milk. She looked magnificent, like an angry Madonna.

"I know it," Harry said, clenching his hands to prevent himself from touching her. "And I never called you a monster. A man would have to be blind to do so."

Alessa's breath caught. He was aware of her sudden stillness. For a moment, their eyes held, the air heavy and charged between them. Then she looked beyond him. "I'm surprised you could persuade the Countess Chernikova to

126

visit Tsarkoe Selo. I understood she wished to avoid court."

Harry turned and followed the direction of Alessa's gaze to a tree-shaded bench a little way removed from the young people where Marina sat talking with the Empress. "Marina wants Radka to meet people her own age," he said. "You could hardly call this a court function."

"She and Cousin Elisabeth appear to be getting on famously." Still looking at Marina and the Empress, Alessa added in the same tone, "Cousin Elisabeth is a tolerant woman. She told me Cousin Sacha was quite taken with the countess, though he never became her lover."

"That's true." Remembering Marina's words about Alessa's jealousy, Harry looked fixedly at his wife. "Nor did anyone else."

Alessa met his gaze, her mouth curved in a smile, her eyes hard. "The credit, I'm sure, is all hers."

Harry felt his face grow warm, a sensation he had not experienced in years. There was no way he could deny what Alessa implied. Whatever he felt for Marina now, there was a time when he would gladly have been her lover if she had encouraged him. "The countess has always been known as a virtuous woman," he said. The words sounded stiff and pompous to his own ears, but he could think of nothing else to say that would not make matters worse and drag Marina into a matter which should be between him and Alessa.

Willing the color to fade from his face, Harry stared down at the water lapping against the red granite base of the bridge. The rumbling of the waterfalls where a small stream ran into the lake sounded preternaturally loud in the sudden silence.

Alessa stood and moved out of the archway, breaking the intimacy between them. "I should get back to Alastair," she said, glancing at the baby, who was being pushed in his carriage by one of the nurses. "It's settled then? We'll take Zara with us?"

There had really been no question about that from the first. Perhaps, Harry thought, he had not agreed at once simply because he wanted to keep Alessa talking to him. "I'll call on the Petrovs tomorrow," he promised.

Alessa gave him a cool smile. "Then there's nothing more to talk about, is there?" she said in a well-modulated voice. "Thank you for your time, Harry. I won't keep you from the countess any longer."

Without thinking, Harry swung away from the arch and seized his wife by the arm. "Hasn't it occurred to you that I might prefer your company?"

His face was inches from her own. She stared up at him in confusion, the composed facade momentarily shattered. It was a small victory. Then she spoke, the tension in her voice razor sharp. "Unfair tactics, Harry. We agreed never to use such words between us."

If they had been alone, he would have crushed her to him and covered her mouth with his own, showing her how much his feelings differed from the cold agreement which had formed the basis of their marriage. He might have done so anyway, but before he could respond, there was a burst of applause and a shout from the lawn below.

"Come and see Niki," Simon shouted, speaking in Russian as they did with the children. "He's becoming an expert."

Alessa pulled away from Harry as if his touch burned her and hurried down the steps to the lawn. By the time Harry followed, she was hugging Niki. Harry stood a little way off, waiting until Alessa released his son. He was still careful not to push Niki too far.

As he watched, Harry felt a tug at his hand. He looked down to find Zara smiling at him. "I like this game," she said. "I'm going to be as good as Niki."

Harry found that the warmth of the small hand eased the chill around his heart. Preoccupied with Niki, he had perhaps not shown Zara as much attention as he should. She seemed to be a happy child, less troubled than Niki and far more outgoing. She had been affectionate with Alessa from the start, but this was the first time she had approached Harry on her own.

"I'm sure you will," he said. "We have a very nice meadow for games at my house in England."

At the mention of England, the smile left Zara's face. A few

128

feet away, Niki stiffened in Alessa's arms. Alessa released him and met Harry's gaze. The message in her eyes was clear. Harry had intended to wait until they returned to the nursery before he spoke to the children, but to put it off would be cruel.

Crouching down to the children's level, Harry looked at Niki, then turned back to Zara. "You know we'll be leaving for England soon and Niki will be coming with us?"

Zara nodded, eyes wide and intent.

Harry swallowed. So far all he had managed to do was state the obvious. He was aware of the boys and Radka and Galina watching from a little way off. "Lady Milverton and I were wondering if you'd like to come with us as well. I'll speak to your cousins about it, but only if it's what you'd like."

The instant the words were out of his mouth, Zara's blue eyes lit with happiness. She took a step forward and flung her arms around Harry's neck. A moment later, Harry felt a small body hurtle against him as Niki ran over and hugged him as well. Harry fell backward onto the grass, wrapped in a confused embrace of children and not minding in the least. He was dimly aware of Simon's voice saying something to Alessa in approving accents. By the time he sat up, Alessa, Galina, Simon, Peter, and Radka had all gathered round.

Simon gave Harry his hand and helped him to his feet. Niki looked beyond the group at Elisabeth and Marina, who were walking down the slope of lawn toward them. "Papa says Zara can come to England."

Elisabeth smiled. "I'm pleased to hear it, though we'll be sorry to lose all of you."

Harry nodded in response to the Empress's words. Then he swung round and looked at his son, realizing what Niki had called him. Niki and Zara were now running about in circles, chanting "England" with cheerful glee. But before Harry could fully savor the moment, Radka spoke. "Look," she said, gesturing toward the palace.

A footman was hurrying across the grounds toward them. Elisabeth smoothed her skirt and ran a hand over her hair, quickly assuming a more stately demeanor, as if in expectation of a summons. But when the footman reached them, he turned to Harry. "Forgive me, Lord Milverton, but there's a gentleman asking for you. A Captain Lychenko. I wouldn't have come after you, but he says it's urgent."

Harry saw Alessa's face go pale. For some reason, she cast a quick, anxious glance at Elisabeth. Harry suppressed a groan. He did not want to see Grigor, not now of all times, but he knew he should discover what the man wanted. "Thank you," Harry said to the footman. "I'd best speak with him."

He smiled at Niki and Zara, who had stopped running and were looking on with wary curiosity. The mention of Grigor's name would have troubled them. "It's all right," he said. "Cousin Grigor wants to see me, not you. He isn't your guardian anymore."

Niki and Zara both nodded. Bolstered by the trust in their eyes, Harry excused himself to the others. Alessa avoided his gaze. As he followed the footman back across the grounds to the palace, Harry recalled his wife's words to him on the bridge. *Unfair tactics, Harry. We agreed never to use such words between us.* The words had angered him, yet Alessa had spoken no more than the truth. She had warned him never to speak of love. Having already burdened her with Niki, he had no right to impose additional demands on her. And even if he managed to put his confused feelings into words, Alessa had made it clear she would not believe him.

Grigor had been shown into a sitting room which was relatively simple by palace standards but luxuriant by any other. He was sitting in a chased steel armchair of Russian design, hands clenched, one booted foot tapping impatiently on the inlaid floor. At Harry's entrance he sprang to his feet and strode across the room. "God curse you," he said, seizing Harry by the lapels of his coat and pushing him against the wall. "What the hell do you think you're doing?"

Harry, who had been expecting another demand for money, was pleased at the prospect of a confrontation. "Leaving my wife and children in order to answer a summons from a man I have little cause to respect," he said, grasping Grigor's wrists and disengaging him with rather more force than was necessary.

"Respect." Grigor fairly spat the word. "That's rich. I'm not the one who asks a man's friends questions about him behind his back."

Harry looked at Nadia's cousin in puzzlement. He was not surprised that Grigor wanted to knock him senseless, but he did not understand the immediate cause of the other man's anger. "What the devil are you talking about?"

"What does it sound like I'm talking about?" Grigor waved his hand impatiently. "Your inquiries, Harry. Your clever little agents asking half the regiment about what I do and where I sup and whom I take to bed. By God, I could strangle you."

"The sentiment is mutual," Harry assured him, moving toward the fireplace, less to avoid Grigor than to ensure that he would not be tempted to further violence himself. "But I haven't employed any agents, clever or not, to ask any questions about you. My interest in you ended the day you gave Niki into my care."

"You miserable liar, do you expect me to believe that?" Grigor demanded, his body tense, as though coiled for another attack. "Who else would have done it?"

Harry raised his brows. "A jealous husband?"

"They were imperial agents," Grigor said, the words as distinct as rifle shots. "There's no doubt of it. Hiding behind your wife's skirts, Harry?"

Words of denial froze on Harry's lips. The blood rushed from his head, replaced by a cold, sickening chill. He saw again the nervous look Alessa had given Elisabeth when she learned Grigor was at the palace. And he knew, with angry certainty, who had set the inquiries in motion. All the time Alessa had been winning Niki's trust and love she had been trying to prove he was a bastard. Behind her husband's back.

"I already know more than enough about you, Grigor," Harry said, controlling his voice. He would not give Grigor the satisfaction of knowing he had been shaken. "And if I wanted to destroy you, I wouldn't hide behind anyone.

"Fine words." Grigor gripped the back of the chair as if he wished it were Harry's neck. "I want the questions to stop."

"They will."

"Then you admit responsibility."

"I admit nothing."

"If you didn't start the inquiries, you can't stop them. Unless . . ." A slow smile spread across Grigor's face. His posture relaxed slightly, as if he knew he had regained the upper hand. "Unless your lovely wife has acted without your knowledge. Oh, Harry, you never did have much luck with women, did you? You know, you really should have told me Lady Milverton was connected to the imperial family."

"So Niki would have been worth a few pounds more?" Harry tugged at the bell rope with a viciousness he would have liked to use on Grigor. "A footman will see you out. You'll forgive me if I don't stay. I imagine you welcome my presence even less than I welcome yours."

Dreading the confrontation he faced with Alessa, yet knowing he could not rest until they had had the matter out, Harry started for the door. When he reached it, he stopped and looked back at Grigor. "By the way, we have Zara with us. We're taking her to England."

A look of genuine surprise crossed Grigor's face. "Irina's daughter? Why in God's name? She's no kin to you."

"No. But she is to my son. And there's more than kinship involved." Harry took a firm grip on the door handle. "Good day, Grigor. I pray neither of us will have cause to inflict our presence on the other again."

Before Grigor could respond, Harry strode through the door and went in search of his wife.

"You mustn't worry, Alessa. There are many reasons why Captain Lychenko might have come to the palace." Elisabeth's voice was soothing, but there was concern in her eyes, and Alessa knew her cousin was not as confident as she sounded.

"Of course." Alessa forced her voice to sound soothing as well. She looked down at Alastair, who was cradled in her arms, industriously draining the milk from her left breast.

She was aware of his mouth tugging at her skin, but it was no longer as uncomfortable as it had been when she first began to nurse him. They both seemed to be getting better at it. His body felt heavier against her arm too and his muscles firmer. He had grown, greatly to her relief. Though he still seemed impossibly tiny, the doctors assured her that premature babies were often much smaller. He slept and ate more regularly than he had at first and she thought perhaps he could recognize her voice. After nearly a month in the world, Alastair was beginning to settle into life. Alessa only wished she could do the same.

On the lawn, another game of catch was in progress. This time Radka had persuaded her mother to join in. The countess appeared to be having as much fun as the young people. Alessa looked at her, a creature of white and gold with her gauzy gown and loosely dressed hair, and felt a pang of jealousy that was sharper than the sensation of the child at her breast.

"The countess likes you," Elisabeth said quietly. "She told me how much she admires your ease with the children."

Alessa suppressed a derisive snort. "She'd hardly criticize me to you, would she?"

"Perhaps not," Elisabeth agreed. "But after being at court for over twenty years, I think I've learned to recognize sincerity when I hear it."

Alessa transferred Alastair to her right breast, avoiding a reply. She had to admit that the countess was a pleasant woman. But Alessa most emphatically did not want to like her.

The sound of footsteps behind them saved her from further discussion of the countess. Alessa looked over her shoulder to see her husband approaching. He was walking more quickly than usual, but it was the carefully controlled tension in his face which made Alessa's heart plummet somewhere beneath her ribcage. Now she knew beyond a doubt why Lychenko had come to Tsarkoe Selo. Despite the comforting solidity of the baby in her arms, she felt frighteningly alone.

Harry stopped to speak with Alessa and Elisabeth, his expression veiled, his voice courteous. Alessa was not deceived. As the game came to an end and they all partook of light refreshments at the table set up nearby, Harry remained polite and self-contained. He laughed with the children and chatted with the countess and teased Radka and rarely even glanced at Alessa. Only when they had returned to the palace and said their farewells to the countess and Radka did he turn to Alessa and look her full in the face.

"I need to talk to you." His voice was even, but his eyes were hard.

"Of course," Alessa said, her head held high. Elisabeth gave her arm a sympathetic squeeze. Even Peter and Simon seemed to realize something was amiss, though they could not know what.

There were still details to be taken care of—the children sent off to the nursery with Galina, Alastair settled in his cradle in Alessa's room with one of the nurses. Finally, Alessa led Harry into the boudoir which adjoined her bedchamber.

Harry closed the door behind them with a quiet click, but did not at once speak. The silence grated on Alessa's already worn nerves. She turned to find him watching her, arms folded in front of him.

"I can understand your wanting to ask questions," he said in an even voice. "What I can't understand is your doing it behind my back."

At the clipped, detached words, a surge of anger cut through the guilt Alessa had felt since Grigor's arrival. "If I'd asked you, you'd have forbidden me to do anything."

"And that would have prevented you?" Harry countered.

"You wouldn't have tried to stop me?" Alessa demanded, feeling her face grow warm from the heat of the argument.

"When have I stopped you from doing anything?"

That brought Alessa up short. Unlike most husbands, Harry had never tried to exert such authority over her. Chastened, she sank down onto a small gilt chair. "I had to know," she said, echoing the words she had used with Elisabeth. "And I knew you would dislike it. I'd have told you if I learned anything."

134

"And did you?" Harry asked. His voice was still even, but it had a dangerous edge.

Alessa straightened her back and lifted her chin. She didn't like to be challenged. "Captain Lychenko is an adulterer and a gambler and heavily in debt."

"I could have told you all that had you asked me. Did you learn anything to suggest Niki isn't my son?"

Alessa looked straight into her husband's dark, cold eyes. "No. But I didn't learn anything to suggest he is either."

Harry's hands clenched on the sleeves of his coat. "And if you had?" he demanded, his voice suddenly savage. "What were you planning to do then? Tell Niki we'd made a mistake and ship him back to the Petrovs?"

"If you think I'd abandon Niki, then you don't know me," Alessa said, her skin tingling as if she had been slapped.

"You're right," Harry said. "I don't."

Alessa put her hand to her cheek. The sting of those words was even more bitter than his previous attack. "Tassios don't shirk their responsibilities to those dependent on them," she said, drawing on her dignity for protection.

Harry took a step forward, then checked himself. "It will never stop, will it?" he said, his voice low and so bitter that Alessa felt it stab through her.

She had an impulse to reach out to him, but it was swept aside by the need to lash out and protect herself from further hurt. "I didn't start this, Harry. And I don't think anything short of the truth will end it."

"If you'd come to me first . . ." He broke off and stared at her. Perhaps it was a trick of the late afternoon light, but the lines beside his mouth stood out in stark relief, making him appear older and more hardened. "I thought if nothing else, we at least had honesty between us," he said.

Alessa stood, holding her body rigid to armor herself against the pain that threatened on all sides. "So did I. Until you told me about Nadia."

For a moment, the hurt she was trying to save herself from was reflected in Harry's eyes. Then it was gone, replaced by defenses every bit as strong as her own, and she knew she could not reach him. "True enough." His mouth twisted with bitter mockery. "It seems we're even. You've done your work well, Alessa." Without another word, he turned and strode from the room.

Alessa watched the door close behind him. Then she sank down on the chair again and clasped her arms over her stomach, aware of a hollow ache which seemed worse than the pangs of childbirth. Elisabeth was right. Marriage was fragile. And the fragile bond between them had just been smashed to bits.

Grigor rode back to St. Petersburg in a vile mood. The questions would stop. Harry, damn his soul to hell, was a man of his word. It remained to be seen whether the talk which had been stirred up would reach Vera's husband. Grigor had no desire to find himself forced to duel with a man who had killed his last three opponents. All of whom were said to have been his wife's lovers.

The question of money remained as well. He had known better than to try to get more out of Nadia's husband. Having given up the boy, Grigor had no further hold over Harry. But there was another avenue he could try. Besides, he needed someone on whom to vent his anger.

When he reached the city, Grigor made his way to a familiar house and climbed the steps to a familiar set of rooms. Pushing his way past the valet, he strode into the bedchamber where the man who, Grigor thought bitterly, had got him into this mess, stood before the looking glass, tying his cravat.

At Grigor's entrance, the man swung round, the cravat now crumpled in his hands. "What the devil are you doing here?" he demanded. "I thought we agreed not to meet again unless there was an emergency."

"This is one." Grigor glanced about the room, flung himself into the most comfortable chair, and crossed his legs. "His bitch of a wife's been asking questions about me."

"Alessa?" The other man's brows drew together in a quick frown.

"Lady Alessandra di Tassio, now Countess of Milverton, favored cousin of our august Emperor. Why the hell didn't you warn me I was tangling with the imperial family?"

"It didn't seem relevant." The other man tossed the crumpled neckcloth aside and selected a new one, turning it over thoughtfully in his hands.

"Relevant? Oh no, not at all. It's just that now I've got imperial agents poking into my affairs."

"Have they learned anything?"

"Not about the boy," Grigor admitted.

"Well then." The other man turned back to the looking glass and began to arrange the cravat with deft fingers. "It's not my problem, is it?"

"The devil it isn't," Grigor said indignantly. "You got me into this."

"As I remember, it was you who came to me first." The other man picked up the white waistcoat laid out on his dressing table bench and shrugged it onto his shoulders.

"But the plan was your idea," Grigor said, leaning forward. "And the risk is mine." He settled back in his chair, eyeing the other man fixedly. "Unless, of course, I decide to confide in someone."

The other man finished buttoning up his waistcoat and gave a sigh of resignation. "What do you want, Grigor?"

Grigor smiled, feeling his spirits improve for the first time since he had learned of the inquiries. "Compensation. What else?"

The other man grimaced, but tugged open his dressing table drawer and pulled out a handful of bills. "Here," he said, giving them to Grigor. "This ought to make Alessa's inquiries a little less offensive."

Grigor counted the bills carefully. "Always nice to know you can count on a friend," he said cheerfully, stowing the money in his pocket.

The other man reached for his coat. "Did I mention that I have a dinner engagement?"

"No, but I won't trouble you further." Feeling in charity with the world once again, Grigor got to his feet. "Harry likes the boy, you know," he said as he reached the door. "I didn't expect him to."

"Nor did I. But it doesn't change anything. And it won't stop Harry from rotting in his own particular hell."

The venom in the man's voice as he spoke these last words was unmistakable, quite unlike his usual pleasant tones. Grigor looked at him in puzzlement, wondering, not for the first time, why he had embarked on this course of action. "Why do you hate him so much?" Grigor asked abruptly. "I thought you were friends."

"So we were. Once," said Edward Clifford.

Chapter Nine

The English air was cool and damp and heavy with soot. Aware of an equally heavy feeling in her heart, Alessa tucked the blankets closer around Alastair, who was being remarkably quiet as their ship moved into position at London's busy docks. Beside her at the rail, Alessa could hear Harry explaining the sights to Niki and Zara, with Peter and Simon putting in a word now and then. Edward was standing by quietly, thinking, no doubt, about his reunion with Harry's sister Julia. The sailors called cheerfully to each other as they maneuvered the ship, pleased to be home.

Alessa sighed. That was the rub. She wasn't pleased to be home. Home meant facing her mother and Harry's mother and trying to pick up the shattered pieces of her life. Painful as it had been to be in the confined space of the ship with this coolness between her and Harry, it seemed preferable to attempting to be the Countess of Milverton again.

Elisabeth had insisted that Alessa write to tell her mother of their departure and the name of their ship. *Maman* might even be here to meet them, though she would not normally be in London at this time of year. Reminding herself that she was not a coward, Alessa scanned the jostling crowd on the quayside. *Maman* always stood out in a crowd, and any woman of fashion would stand out in the throng of sailors and dock workers who milled about before them.

As Alessa watched, the crowd shifted and she caught a glimpse of a plaited straw bonnet and pale gray ribbons. Drawing a breath, Alessa snuggled Alastair for comfort. If things had been different, she could have looked forward to the moment when she could first show him to her mother. As it was—

"Alessa." Simon reached in front of Harry to tug at her sleeve. "Look!"

Alessa looked back at the quayside. The woman had moved farther forward and was now fully visible. The hair showing beneath her bonnet was fair, but several shades paler than *Maman's*. And her face was not *Maman's*, though it was nearly as familiar. Farther down the rail, Peter gave an excited cry. Feeling as if she had received an unexpected reprieve, Alessa smiled at the woman who was her former governess, Peter's stepmother, and one of the few people in England in whom Alessa felt able to confide.

"I'm glad they were able to come," Harry said, waving to Fiona, her husband Gideon Carne, and their children, who were now gathered at the front of the crowd.

Alessa looked up quickly, not sure he was speaking to her. They had exchanged as few words as possible during the voyage. "It will make it easier for you, won't it?" Harry said quietly.

"Yes," Alessa said, disconcerted that he could understand her so well when there was such distance between them. "Yes, it will."

Harry nodded and for a moment Alessa thought he might say more. Then he bent down to speak to Niki and Zara and their brief conversation was at an end.

It seemed to take an unconscionably long time before they were able to disembark. On the quayside, Peter's brother Teddy, a sturdy boy of twelve, and his sister Beth, a tall nine-year-old with long blond hair and a serious face, jumped up and down and called out greetings. Their sister Fenella, a fair-haired child who would be four in January, perched on her father's shoulders, clapping and waving. Alessa was sure Fiona must have noticed Niki and Zara standing at the rail, taking in the scene far more quietly than the young Carnes, but Fiona did not look at all surprised. Perhaps she assumed Niki and Zara were the children of other passengers.

When they were finally able to disembark, Harry hung back

with Edward and Galina and the children, allowing Alessa and the boys to greet the Carnes first. There was a medley of cries and a flurry of running feet as Teddy and Beth flung themselves on their brother. While Gideon bent down to let Fenella join her siblings, Fiona surveyed Alessa and Simon with one of the warm, generous smiles which had been such a comfort in Alessa's childhood.

"Motherhood agrees with you," Fiona said, stepping forward to look down at the baby. "He looks very handsome."

"He looks like a baby," Simon said, "but he's quite endearing actually, considering how little he can do."

"He can do all sorts of things," Alessa retorted, as Alastair seized hold of the gloved finger Fiona held out to him. Fiona smiled at the baby. At four-and-thirty she was every bit as beautiful as she had been ten years ago when she arrived in Sardinia to be Simon and Alessa's governess. Aware of her own quick temper, Alessa had always envied her governess's cool elegance and unshakable composure.

"I'm so glad you're here," Alessa said, wishing she could ask about her mother but unable to see how she could gracefully do so.

Fiona looked up at her, her eyes filled with understanding. "Your mother's still in the country. But I promised faithfully to write to her as soon as you arrived."

"Oh, well," Simon said. "Can't put off the inevitable. And I must admit there were times I actually missed her."

Alessa drew a breath. Simon, she knew, was right. One could not put off the inevitable. She was searching for words to try to explain the situation to Fiona, when a high, clear voice rose above the babble around them. "What's your name?"

As the words were spoken, Alessa turned to see that Fenella had wandered away from the rest of the family and was looking with curiosity at Niki and Zara. Plainly overawed by the confusion, Niki was clinging to Galina's skirt and Zara had her arm hooked around Harry's leg. Teddy and Beth and Gideon were looking toward Niki and Zara as well. Peter cast an uncertain glance at Alessa.

"This is Niki and this is Zara," Harry told Fenella. "But I'm afraid they don't speak English yet." Actually, both Niki and Zara now spoke enough English to understand the question, but Alessa knew they would be too shy to answer it.

Harry straightened up and met Alessa's gaze. In all but name, this was her family. It was her place to speak. "Come and meet the other new additions to the family," Alessa told Fiona. "Harry's son Niki, and Niki's cousin Zara."

Not a flicker of surprise crossed Fiona's face. "What charming children," she said. "Fenella will be delighted to have someone her own age to play with."

Out of the corner of her eye, Alessa saw Simon grinning. Fiona had always been equal to anything. But as she drew Fiona forward, Alessa knew that of all the introductions she would have to make in England, this was by far the easiest.

"It's going to be beastly. *Maman* won't understand and Harry's mother will think Harry and I have taken leave of our senses." Alessa pushed her hair from her eyes and sank back against the cushions on the sofa in Fiona's sitting room. They were spending the night at the Carnes' London house, a welcome respite before they traveled to Moresby, Harry's country seat, tomorrow. With dinner over and the children tucked in bed, Alessa had at last been able to tell Fiona the full story of the past weeks.

"It would seem to me that you've both behaved with remarkable good sense." Fiona took a sip of tea and set her cup down. "It can't have been easy, Alessa. I'm proud of you."

Alessa looked up quickly, finding the praise more warming than the tea or the cheerful fire burning in the grate. "I don't feel as if I've been acting very sensibly. I went into the most awful rage when Harry told me about Niki. But these past weeks on the boat there were moments when I almost felt as if Niki and Zara were my own children. And then I'd look at Alastair . . ." Alessa's throat closed with the now-familiar anguish of divided loyalties. "Does it ever bother you that Peter is Gideon's firstborn?" she asked Fiona. "That if you had a son, he could never be Viscount Carne?"

"No," Fiona said, her eyes honest. "But my case is different than yours. I knew Peter and Teddy and Beth long before I married their father."

Alessa linked her hands together and stared at her gold wedding band, warm and solid in the lamplight, so different from the state of her marriage. "If *Maman* had known Harry already had a son, she might not have been so eager for me to marry him."

"Are you sorry you did?"

Fiona's question took Alessa by surprise. She raised her eyes to find her former governess regarding her with the challenging look she had often worn in schoolroom days when she had posed a difficult question and was waiting for her charges to think the answer through.

"No," Alessa said with a vehemence she had not intended. "I'm not sorry, but I . . ." She put her hands up to her face, trembling with the long suppressed grief she could no longer contain. "Oh, God, I'm not sorry I married him, but we don't have any marriage left. I've been the most awful fool, Fiona. I've lost Harry and ruined everything and there's nothing I can do to put it right."

Hot tears spilled between Alessa's fingers. For weeks she hadn't let herself cry and now she seemed unable to stop. She heard a swish of silk skirts and then she felt a soothing hand on her back as Fiona sat beside her. " 'Nothing' is a big word, Alessa. Perhaps you'd better tell me about it."

Alessa rubbed her hands across her eyes, heedless of the red marks she would leave. When she had explained about Niki, she had kept herself under careful control, remembering that she was a married woman and the Countess of Milverton and that she had her dignity to preserve. Now, in an untidy, over-wrought muddle she spilled out the story of how she had set the inquiries about Captain Lychenko in motion and how Harry had learned of them and what had followed.

"All those days on the boat he scarcely spoke to me unless he had to. We were never alone together. He was perfectly polite, but his eyes — dear God, I wouldn't have believed they could look so cold. If only I hadn't lost my temper. I'm just like *Maman*."

"I wouldn't go quite that far," Fiona said dryly.

Alessa tried to laugh but the sound was closer to a sob. "Well, maybe not quite. *Maman* never had you for a governess. But say what you will, Fiona, this whole mess is my own stupid fault. I was so busy trying to defend Alastair's birthright, I forgot about us being a family. I should at least have talked to Harry instead of going behind his back."

"It's no good blaming yourself." Fiona smoothed the hair back from Alessa's forehead, a familiar gesture which brought fresh tears to Alessa's eyes. "People in love often do foolish things."

Alessa straightened up abruptly. "I never said I was in love with Harry."

Fiona smiled. "People in love also frequently don't admit it, even to themselves."

"It wouldn't do me much good if I was," Alessa said, the bitter taste of her own folly sharp in her mouth. "I don't think Harry will ever forgive me."

"I doubt that," Fiona said, her voice gentle.

"You don't know," Alessa said, taking a bleak satisfaction from her certainty of the hopeless state of her marriage.

"On the contrary," Fiona said. "I know that forgiveness is remarkably easy if you love someone enough."

Something in her friend's tone jolted Alessa out of her preoccupation with her own affairs. She studied Fiona with curiosity. Though Fiona had never told her the complete story, Alessa knew there had been something between Fiona and Gideon long ago, when Gideon's first wife was still alive. Alessa could remember the palpable hurt and bitterness between her governess and Gideon Carne five years ago. And she knew how happy they were now. But she also knew that they loved each other.

"It's not the same," Alessa said, feeling the weight of her despair pressing down on her. "Even if I admit I love Harry, I know he doesn't love me. He has a mistress. Or an old love at any rate. She's beautiful and sophisticated and ten years older than I am and probably much better than I am at—at all the things that really matter to men. Don't look at me like

144

that, Fiona. I know men prefer older women. Adrian did."

"Adrian having a mistress had nothing to do with you, love," Fiona told her. "It simply doesn't occur to some men that they owe fidelity to their wives. But Harry isn't like that."

"But it was part of our agreement," Alessa said. "I told him I wouldn't mind if he had mistresses. I was sure he would, and I suppose I thought it would be easier to bear if I knew I'd given him my permission."

"Adrian's legacy," Fiona said with a grimace. She put her arm around Alessa. "Marriage can be so very different. I wish . . ."

"No, don't blame Adrian for this," Alessa said. "He taught me a valuable lesson."

Alessa stared about the room with its yellow silk hangings and elegant beechwood furniture, thinking how odd it was that she might have been mistress here. When she first visited this house, it had been the London residence of Adrian Melchett, Eighth Marquis of Parminter. Alessa had come to meet Adrian's family, accompanied by Fiona, who had been acting in the role of chaperone. Neither of them had known that Fiona was really Adrian's half-sister, the product of a youthful indiscretion committed by his mother. But a few weeks later, the proof that Fiona's parents had been secretly married had made Adrian's parents' marriage bigamous and cost him the marquisate.

"The first time we came here," Alessa said, turning to Fiona, "I never would have dreamed . . ."

"Nor would I," Fiona said, smiling. "It was more than a year before I felt comfortable living in this house."

"Yet it seems as if you were born to it," Alessa said, feeling a flash of envy. Fiona, who had been raised as the bastard daughter of a country gentleman, not only managed a vast inheritance and raised four children, but found time to write books and run the school she had started on her Cornish estates. All with the same quiet competence she had shown as a governess. While Alessa, who had been trained from the cradle for such a life, felt as if she had failed utterly.

The yellow hangings on the walls reminded Alessa of the yellow curtains in Fiona's sitting room when she had been their governess, of evenings spent drinking tea and talking, when life had seemed simpler. Then, Alessa had longed to be out in the hectic glamour of society. Now, she wanted nothing more than to burrow into the chintz cushions on the sofa and hide from the world.

But she wasn't a girl of eighteen any longer. She was a woman with responsibilities, and however much of a mull she had made of things, she had to try to get on with her life.

"It's all right," she said, reaching for her tea and taking a fortifying sip of the fragrant brew, so different from what they had drunk in Russia. "I only behave like a watering pot with people who know me very well indeed."

Gideon Carne leaned back in a comfortable leather-covered chair in his study and studied his son and Simon di Tassio. They looked older. Knowing all they had been through in the past months, Gideon felt a surge of pride, accompanied by a sense that they were growing up far too quickly. And then again, Gideon thought, recalling the way Harry and Alessa had studiously ignored each other at dinner, behaving with maturity sometimes grew more difficult as one grew older.

"All things considered, it was fairly grim on the voyage here," Peter said, stretching his long legs out in front of him. "We're not sure what went wrong between them, but it must have been horrid."

"Alessa did something," Simon said with conviction. "She's been looking guilty as the devil."

Gideon eased his left leg, the one that had been shattered by a bullet in the Peninsular War, over the right one. The boys were looking at him expectantly, as if there was something he could do to help. But though Gideon was fond of both Harry and Alessa, he knew it was damnably dangerous to involve oneself in the affairs of others, particularly affairs of the heart. He wished Harry felt able to confide in him, but Harry had retired early, partly, no doubt, so as not to intrude on the family reunion, partly, Gideon suspected, because whatever his problems with Alessa, he wanted to keep them to himself.

"It's a difficult situation for both of them," Gideon said.

"But it was getting better," Peter insisted, leaning forward. "Alessa was furious when she first found out about Niki. He was displacing her baby and she didn't believe he was really Harry's son . . ."

Peter brought himself up short and looked at his father. Feeling a pang, Gideon smiled and to his relief saw the uncertainty fade from his son's eyes. "But when Niki came to the palace, Alessa got to like him," Peter continued. "And then she found Zara, and she liked Zara too. But then she and Harry—"

"No," Simon said, "the trouble started before that. It was at the reception, when she saw the Countess Chernikova."

It seemed to Gideon that his son stiffened at the mention of the countess's name. "An old friend of Harry's," Peter explained.

"A not so old, very beautiful friend," Simon corrected. "We can't quite decide if she ever was his mistress or not, but we don't think she is now."

"We're certain she isn't," Peter said firmly.

"What makes you so sure?" Gideon asked, though he was fairly sure Peter was right.

"The way Harry looks at Alessa," Peter said simply.

"Ah." Gideon smiled. "Yes, I've noticed that myself, and I'm inclined to agree with you."

"But Alessa hasn't noticed." Peter scowled at a gilt-framed landscape which hung on the mahogany-paneled wall opposite. "I suppose women have to have these things spelled out for them."

Gideon grinned, recalling some of his more obtuse moments with Fiona. "Men too, frequently."

"There *is* something between Harry and the countess, though," Simon said thoughtfully. "Peter and I haven't quite been able to work it out. And then, of course, there's Radka."

Peter tugged down one of the cuffs of his shirt with great care. Even in the subdued lamplight, Gideon could have sworn his son's skin had reddened. "Radka?" Gideon asked, carefully keeping his face a polite, neutral mask.

"The countess's daughter." Peter looked up and met his

father's gaze. "She's—she's very pretty. But she's only fifteen. Too young for—for much of anything. But then I suppose we are too."

"Not too young," Simon said firmly. "Just too damnably well behaved. You and my stepfather did your work well, Gideon."

Gideon grinned at the prince. "I'll take that as a compliment," he said, remembering several conversations he had had with the boys about the impulses and responsibilities of adulthood. It was both reassuring and rather daunting to know that your son showed far better sense in such matters than you had yourself. He looked at Peter, wondering what pangs lay in store for him, hoping his son would be able to navigate love's waters with considerably more dexterity than he had himself.

"Radka's uncle's trying to force her to make a marriage of convenience," Peter said, scowling with an intensity which as much as anything convinced Gideon of the strength of his feelings for the girl. "But the last time we saw her, Radka told us her mother had a plan to make them safe, only it's a secret and even Radka doesn't know what it's about." Peter's scowl deepened.

"There wasn't anything else we could do, Peter," Simon said with the practicality of one not blinded by love. "The countess wouldn't lie to Radka. Besides, whatever her plan is, I expect it has something to do with Harry. And Harry's sure to be better at sorting out the countess's affairs than he is at sorting out his own." Simon linked his hands together and stared frowning at the Tassio ring he wore on his left hand. "Alessa may be jealous of the countess, but there's more to this latest trouble, I'd swear it. And the longer she and Harry go on being stubborn, the harder it's going to be for them to mend matters."

Gideon looked at his son's friend with sympathy. He had known Simon di Tassio since the prince was a boy of twelve. Even then, Simon had been inclined to take his responsibilities too seriously. "You can't always solve other people's problems, however much you want to," Gideon said. "Sometimes they have to work things out for themselves."

They sat in silence for a few moments until the door opened and Fiona slipped into the room, bringing a welcome air of brightness and good sense. "Not interrupting, am I?" she asked, looking from Gideon to the boys.

Simon shook his head. "We were just talking about Harry and Alessa. As you must have noticed, they're hopelessly muddled."

"I don't know about hopelessly, but certainly muddled," Fiona said, perching on the arm of Gideon's chair. Her voice was cheerful, but Simon's troubled look was reflected in her clear gray eyes. "But much as you may hate to admit it, Simon, Alessa has a great deal of sense."

Simon looked Fiona squarely in the eye. "You mean you're confident she and Harry will sort things out?"

Fiona returned his gaze. She made it a point, Gideon knew, never to lie to any of the children. "I very much hope they will," she said.

Simon nodded, as if it was the answer he had expected. Perhaps sensing little more was to be gained from discussing Harry and Alessa's problems, the boys went on to recount more cheerful incidents from their journey, seeming almost relieved to seek refuge in the mundane. When they finally rose to go up to bed, Peter hugged his father and kissed Fiona's cheek. "It's good to be home," he said simply, and Gideon knew that however much he missed Radka Chernikova, Peter meant it.

"It's good to have him home," Fiona said when the boys had left the room.

"I know," Gideon said, banking up the fire. "I missed him damnably." He set down the poker and turned to smile at his wife. "It's quite an honor, though, that Peter's pleased to be home. He met a girl named Radka in Russia, and he's quite taken with her."

Fiona seemed less surprised than he had been by the news of Peter's romance. "How old is she?"

"All of fifteen. But I don't think we need worry just yet. Peter assured me that she's too young for much of anything."

Fiona gave him a smile tinged with mischief. "You raised him well."

"We raised him well," Gideon corrected, watching the way the lamplight flickered against his wife's smooth skin. Some-

149

times it was hard to remember that there was a time when he hadn't been married to her.

Fiona moved to one of the lamps and turned it down. The smile had faded from her face and the troubled look was back in her eyes. "You're really worried about Alessa, aren't you?" Gideon said, taking her by the shoulders.

Fiona looked up into his eyes and nodded. "Yes. Though in some ways I'm less worried than I was when she and Harry became betrothed. Then I was afraid she was turning her back on life. Or at any event on love, and at the very least that makes life rather bleak."

"I won't argue with you there." Gideon slid his hand behind Fiona's neck and stroked his thumb against her cheek. "And now?"

"Now she's head over ears in love, whether or not she'll admit it. Far more genuinely in love than she ever was with Adrian. But that in itself can make problems more difficult to resolve." Fiona leaned forward and rested her head against Gideon's shoulder. "If only for one moment Alessa could forget that she's a Tassio and Harry could forget that he's a Dudley."

"My love, that's like asking them to forget who they are," Gideon said softly.

"I know." Fiona lifted her head and gave a rueful smile. "Oh, Gideon, how did we ever manage to be so happy?"

"It's a mystery," Gideon said, drawing her closer and feeling the familiar response run through her body.

Fiona twined her arms around his neck, the rueful smile replaced by a more playful expression. "None of this is going to be resolved tonight. Don't you think it's time you took me to bed?"

Gideon looked down at her, thinking, not for the first time, that he didn't deserve such happiness. "I can't imagine a better idea."

The silk-lined traveling carriage, one of several kept in readiness at Milverton House in London, was jostled slightly as the coachman negotiated the turn off the main road. As the wheels crunched against the smooth gravel of the long winding drive to Moresby, Alessa glanced at Alastair, asleep in his basket on the seat beside her. They were nearly there. Her fingers dug into the palms of her gloved hands. They had said goodbye to the Carnes at the last post stop, though at least she had the comfort of knowing her friends would be at Sundon, Fiona's country house, less than an hour away. Harry and Edward had elected to ride, leaving Alessa to travel in the carriage with Simon, Galina, and the children. A second carriage followed with Phillips, Lytton, Wilton, Alastair's nurse, and the luggage.

Alessa smiled at Niki and Zara, sitting on the seat opposite her on either side of Galina. They were dressed in some of the new clothes Alessa had had made for them before they left St. Petersburg, Niki in a dark blue coat more grown up than boys of his age usually wore, Zara in a merino dress and straw bonnet. They had managed to stay remarkably neat in the course of the journey, and with their blond hair, freshly combed at the last stop, they looked quite angelic. Whether or not Harry's mother would think of them that way was another matter.

"We're nearly at Moresby," Alessa said cheerfully in Russian. "Papa's house." Zara had taken to calling Harry "Papa" as Niki did, and Harry seemed pleased by it.

Niki nodded. Zara twisted a fold of her new pink shawl between her fingers and regarded Alessa across the expanse of the carriage. "Are you our Mama now?" she asked abruptly, as if it was a question she had been trying to puzzle out.

Alessa looked at the little girl in surprise. The children had continued to call her Lady Milverton, but Alessa felt vaguely uncomfortable with the title. Without quite admitting it, she had been increasingly jealous whenever she heard them call Harry "Papa." Alessa cast a quick glance at Alastair, then, recalling her discussion with Fiona, looked back at Zara and took a determined plunge into her new life. "Yes," she said, "if you want me to be."

"Mama," Zara said, trying out the word in its English form.

"Mama," Niki echoed, also in English. He grinned, something he was doing more and more of late. " 'Mama' is easy in English."

Out of the corner of her eye, Alessa caught Simon looking at her with approval. Galina smiled. Alessa smiled back, feeling a warmth which was more than the sense of having done the right thing. She had not made a concession to the children. They had extended a great privilege to her.

Alessa was still smiling when the carriage began to slow. The children looked at her expectantly. "Home?" Niki asked.

Alessa was taken aback, but it was a perfectly logical question. Niki had been told for weeks that Moresby was home. She turned to the window and caught a glimpse of tawny walls and mullioned windows. The warmth fled.

Alessa turned back to the children and summoned as cheerful a look as she could muster. "Home," she said.

Chapter Ten

The carriage rolled smoothly through the outer gateway and came to a halt in the forecourt. Smiling at the children, Alessa automatically adjusted the ribbons on her bonnet and smoothed the skirt of her pelisse. Through the window, she caught a glimpse of a footman in the green-and-buff Dudley livery and then another and then the dark skirts of one of the maids. Her heart sank. They must have had a stableboy watching at the lodge gates. The whole household would be drawn up to witness the return of Lord and Lady Milverton. That was going to make this even worse. Unless, perhaps, an audience would lend dignity to the scene.

Booted feet clicked against the flagstone paving as the coachman came round to let down the steps. The door was opened, filling the carriage with a burst of fresh air. Alastair made a faint protesting sound as Alessa lifted him from his basket, but then he settled against her arm. Grateful for small mercies, Alessa extended her hand so the coachman could assist her from the carriage.

But it was not the coachman who stood at the base of the carriage steps and took her outstretched hand. It was her husband. Startled, Alessa looked into Harry's eyes. He smiled, a slight smile but it lit his eyes and warmed his face. Strained as their relationship was, hard as he must find the return home himself, he was offering her his support. Her spirits bolstered enormously by the smile and the pressure of his fingers against her own, Alessa smiled back and carefully made her way down the steps.

As she had expected, the entire household, from Kittredge, the butler, to the youngest of the scullery maids, was drawn up in front of the house, filling the long distance between the two projecting wings which flanked the courtyard. On the stone steps which led to the front entrance, backed by high brick walls and blocks of mullioned windows, overshadowed by the gabled roof and the carved heraldic wolves which stood between the upper-story windows, the Dudley family was gathered.

Lady Milverton stood in the center, her back very straight, her dark hair impeccably dressed. Julia was beside her mother, wearing a thin pale blue gown too cool for the autumn afternoon, her cheeks flushed with color. Her eyes were already on Edward, who stood a little way off, holding the reins of his horse. Georgiana, grinning at Harry but looking uncomfortable in a ruffled muslin dress, stood on her mother's other side with her governess, Miss Beaton. John, Harry's cousin and secretary, sent Harry an apologetic look, as if to say this formal homecoming had not been his idea.

Kittredge took a step forward. "My lord. My lady. If I may be permitted to say so, we are all very pleased to see you home. And to welcome the new Viscount Rutledge to Moresby."

Harry's fingers tightened on Alessa's hand. Oddly enough, though Kittredge's words would once have reminded her of all her son had lost, Alessa found that she was the one who gave Harry's hand a sympathetic squeeze.

"Thank you, Kittredge." Harry released Alessa's hand and turned to the open door of the carriage.

As the servants moved to either side and Lady Milverton descended the steps to greet her son and daughter-in-law, Harry lifted Niki and Zara out of the carriage and gave his hand to Galina. Lady Milverton stopped, her eyes widening.

Putting an arm around each of the children, Harry turned

154

to his mother with a smile not of warmth but of assurance. "This is my son Niki," he said, "and this is his cousin Zara. They're going to live with us."

There was a stifled exclamation from the steps. Julia or Georgiana, Alessa could not be sure, for her eyes were on Lady Milverton. Whatever else she thought of her mother-in-law, Alessa had to admire Lady Milverton's composure in that moment. "I see." The two words were uttered with precise controlled calm. "We'd best go in then."

With these words, Lady Milverton turned and made her way back toward the house. Simon, who had followed Galina from the carriage, pressed Alessa's arm in sympathy. Harry sent Alessa another brief smile and they moved after his mother, Harry keeping his arms around the children. Simon, Galina, and Edward brought up the rear of the small procession.

At the base of the stairs, Lady Milverton turned to Mrs. Fitzherbert, the housekeeper, but Alessa spoke first. After all, *she* was mistress of Moresby. Moreover, she was the children's mother and she did not intend to allow her place to be usurped. "Could you see that the nursery is prepared for the children, Mrs. Fitz? I think Niki and Zara would be more comfortable if they could share a room, but we'll need another room for their nurse, Galina. And I'd like some light refreshments sent up to them as soon as possible."

"Of course, my lady." Mrs. Fitzherbert inclined her head, her expression carefully neutral, taking sides neither with the new countess nor with the dowager.

When they reached the top of the steps, Georgiana moved toward Harry and looked as if she might speak, then apparently thought better of it. Harry winked at her, but said nothing. The family moved into the house and stood in silence in the cool, stone-floored great hall while the servants filed past and discreetly vanished into the recesses of the house, save for two footmen who remained outside to see to the luggage. Alessa felt the weight of tradition settle about her as she stared at the wainscotted walls and breathed in the

155

cool air. Though it was not as extravagant as Tsarkoe Selo, Moresby's Jacobean grandeur had a power all its own.

"I'm sure you will wish to go upstairs and refresh yourselves," Lady Milverton said when the last of the servants had disappeared. "Dinner is at seven. Harry, I'd like to see you in my sitting room in an hour."

Harry met his mother's gaze. "No," he said in pleasant tones. "I think we'd best gather in the library. All of us. The whole family deserves to hear the story."

"Are you sure it's wise . . ." Lady Milverton began, a frown creasing her smooth forehead.

"Better than gossip, don't you think?" Harry asked, still looking steadily at her.

Lady Milverton returned her son's regard for a long moment. "As you wish."

"Harry," Julia burst out with sudden impatience, "you can't really mean—"

"Julia," Lady Milverton said. "Later."

Julia subsided but cast a pleading glance at Edward. Edward laid a hand on her arm.

Georgiana moved forward and knelt in front the children. "Hullo, I'm Georgy. I suppose I'm your aunt."

Niki and Zara looked up at her with uncomprehending eyes. "They're a little shy still, brat," Harry told his sister, "and they don't speak much English."

"We'd better get them upstairs," Alessa said. "Galina . . ."

Galina, who had been standing in the shadows, moved toward Alessa as if grateful to be able to escape the charged atmosphere of the hall. Harry spoke softly to the children, then shepherded them toward the archway that led to the staircase. When he reached the archway, he stopped to look back at his family. "The library. One hour."

He sounded as if he had no qualms about the coming scene. But as she followed him, Alessa was not deceived.

The library was a long, dark paneled room with orderly

156

tiers of books rising to a gallery and continuing still higher to the plaster ceiling. Heavy burgundy drapes lined windows which let in the muted evening light. Chairs and sofas were disposed about the room in arrangements which invited a quiet interlude with a book or at the very least subdued conversation. A well-worn Axminster carpet, worked in soft tones of burgundy and sage green and thick enough to deaden any footfalls, covered the floor. It was the sort of room in which it seemed quite impossible to shout or rail or create a scene. As she sat listening to her husband recount the story of his first marriage and the birth of his son, Alessa wondered if this was the reason Harry had chosen the room for this particular scene.

The family listened in silence. Lady Milverton sat in a high-backed chair, her hands tightly clasped, her gaze unwavering. Julia sat on a sofa beside Edward, clearly appalled by her brother's tale. Edward avoided her gaze. Georgiana regarded her brother with fascination, as if she hadn't dreamed he could be involved in anything half so interesting. John stared at his hands, a look of growing concern on his face. Simon, seated beside his sister, observed the whole with quiet assurance. Alessa was immensely grateful for his presence.

"So there you have it," Harry said. "I don't pretend to be proud of my actions, but what's done is done. My wife has shown great forbearance throughout the whole affair. I can only hope that the rest of you will welcome Niki as warmly as she has."

His words were greeted by a heavy, suffocating silence, very different from the usual soothing quiet found in the room. At last Georgiana leaned forward in her chair, tossing back her straight brown hair. "I think you've behaved splendidly." Her dark eyes were alight, making her round face appear almost pretty. "All except for the very first part, and you were drunk, so I suppose that's not your fault."

"Georgiana," Lady Milverton said, the tension in her voice razor sharp, "go up to Miss Beaton until dinner. Julia . . ."

157

Julia settled back in the corner of the sofa, her chestnut ringlets stirring about her face as she shook her head with defiance. "I'm not going anywhere, Mama."

Lady Milverton looked sharply at her elder daughter, then appeared to change her mind. "Very well, perhaps it's for the best. Georgiana, I believe I asked you to go upstairs."

Georgiana got to her feet with obvious reluctance. She looked at Harry and smiled, almost, Alessa thought, as if she were trying to bolster his spirits for what lay ahead, then retreated to the heavy, pedimented door.

"How could you, Harry," Julia exclaimed as the door shut behind her younger sister. "It's going to be the talk of London for months."

Harry made no reply. He was looking at his mother. Lady Milverton's hands were now resting on the arms of her chair and her knuckles had turned white. "My God," she said in a low voice, so heavy with bitterness that Alessa felt it as a physical force, "I was always afraid you'd be the ruin of the Dudleys, but I never dreamed of this."

"Nevertheless," Harry said, continuing to hold her eyes with his own. "I have accepted Niki as my son, and I expect the rest of you to do likewise."

"A tradesman's daughter," Julia burst out with horror.

Alessa looked at her sister-in-law with revulsion and then felt a stab of guilt, remembering that her own reaction had been very similar.

"If she had lived, she would have been Countess of Milverton," Julia continued, as if only now realizing how very bad it might have been. "How long have you known about this?" she demanded, turning to Edward.

"I was at the wedding, Harry's first wedding," Edward admitted. "But Harry asked me not to say anything."

"And you put him before the rest of us?" Her blue eyes darkened with anger, her mouth set with determination, Julia looked strikingly like her mother.

"He's my friend," Edward said helplessly.

"The marriage took place in a foreign country." Lady

158

Milverton ignored her daughter and continued to look at her son. "The child was claimed by another mother and another father. I see no need for you to acknowledge him as your son."

"None except honor," Harry said.

"Honor?" Lady Milverton gave a harsh laugh. "Don't mock me, Harry. When has the word ever meant anything to you?"

"Ever since I was old enough to understand what it really meant." Harry spoke quietly, but Alessa saw his mouth tighten and knew how much his mother's words had hurt him. She felt a surge of anger at Lady Milverton.

"You have a son," Lady Milverton continued. "How you ever had the sense to marry Alessa is beyond me, but you did and she's given you an heir you can be proud of. If you imagine I'm going to sit by while you allow the son of a Russian cit, conceived in a moment of drunken debauchery, to become the next Earl of Milverton —"

"Stop it." Alessa's voice filled the high-ceilinged room with an authority she'd never before been able to command when speaking to her mother-in-law. "I won't have any of you criticizing Niki. He's a little boy, a sweet, loving little boy who needs to be taken care of."

Julia stared at Alessa in amazement. "But his mother —"

"I'm his mother now," Alessa said, feeling the familiar pain at this reminder that she had not come first with Harry. "And Zara's. They're no different from Fenella Carne or my own little brother or any other children their age."

"You surprise me, Alessa." Lady Milverton's tone made these words the worst sort of disapproval. "The children themselves are immaterial. The Milverton succession is not." She looked back at Harry. "I know you once made it a point to drag the Dudley name through the mud, but you can't mean to let it go this far."

"No?" Harry said, a reckless edge to his voice. "Try me."

Lady Milverton clasped her hands tightly in her lap. "These things can be handled. We can discuss it with our solicitor, but I very much doubt the boy has any legal claim on us. Even if he does, he'd be too young to understand. If you raise him and the girl, they'll have done very well out of the arrangement. No one will comment at your seeing to the upbringing of a by-blow, though I think they should be removed from the house as soon as—"

"That's enough." Harry pushed himself to his feet in one swift, economical movement, his tall frame commanding the room. Though he did not shout, Alessa could feel his unleashed anger. "I know you've never liked me, madam," he said, looking at his mother with hard eyes. "I long since gave up trying to understand why. But for better or worse I am the head of the Dudley family. I wanted all of you to know about Niki, but the decision is mine and my wife's. I suggest you stop ranting and learn to accept your grandson."

For a long moment, Lady Milverton stared at her son, her face white with anger and, Alessa thought, with surprise. For all the tension between them, Alessa had never heard Harry speak to his mother in that tone before.

Without a word, Lady Milverton stood and swept from the room.

Silence followed the closing of the door. Julia drew in her breath sharply. Edward turned to her. "Ju—" he began, reaching for her hand.

"Don't." Snatching her hand away, Julia sprang to her feet and hurried after her mother.

Without a word Harry sank back into his chair and dropped his head into his hands. Alessa reached over and laid a tentative hand on his arm. To her relief, he did not flinch away, though she was not sure he was aware of her touch.

The silence was broken by quiet footfalls as John crossed to the table, where a set of decanters was laid out, and poured a generous amount of whisky into a glass. "Families are bloody hell," he said, pressing the glass into Harry's hand.

"From which one can never be redeemed." Harry took a

160

long drink, then looked up and gave John a quick smile. "You'd think I'd have grown used to it by now, wouldn't you?"

"No," said John, "thank God you haven't. You wouldn't be quite human if you had."

Harry took another sip of the whisky. Then, as if suddenly aware of Alessa's hand resting on his arm, he turned to look at her. Alessa smiled, uncertain if he was glad or sorry to have her beside him. Harry returned the smile and held out the whisky glass.

It was a sort of peace offering, an acknowledgment that what he had gone through she had endured as well. Alessa accepted the glass and took a small sip. The liquid burned her throat but gave her much-needed warmth after the coldness which had settled over the room.

Harry ran a hand through his hair. "It's done," he said. "All things considered, I suppose it could have been worse." He leaned toward Edward, who was now sitting alone on the sofa. "I'm sorry about Julia, Ned, but she'll come round. It's me she's angry at."

Edward nodded, his eyes on the carpet. "I don't know what got into her."

"Family pride," said Harry. "And Mother's upbringing." He got to his feet, his control seemingly restored. "I'm sorry all of you had to witness that. These next few days aren't going to be pleasant, but we'll get through them somehow."

There was little more to be said. A bell sounded, announcing that it was time to dress for dinner. Alessa found it almost a relief to be reminded of something so commonplace.

"There's one thing to be said for this," Simon murmured to her as they all moved out of the room and toward the stairs. "Telling *Maman* can't possibly be this bad."

Alessa nodded, knowing Simon was trying to be of help. But she suspected that for once her annoyingly acute younger brother might be mistaken.

161

With one last look at the two small forms curled beneath the quilts, Alessa tiptoed silently to the open door of Galina's room.

"They fell asleep almost at once," Galina said in a low voice, leaving the door ajar so they could hear the children.

"I was afraid they'd be anxious at being in a new place," Alessa said.

Galina regarded her with the forthright candor Alessa had come to expect of her, her eyes showing the same worry Alessa felt. "They were, but the journey wore them out. When they're less tired, I'm afraid they may be more frightened."

Worried their voices might wake the children, Alessa moved farther into the room, absently smoothing the silk skirt of her dinner dress. Her temples were throbbing with the beginning of a headache, which was not surprising considering the oppressive atmosphere this evening. She had escaped the after-dinner gathering in the drawing room to feed Alastair and then had looked in on Niki and Zara. Fortunately the children had been well away from the scene in the library and its aftermath, but Alessa knew they had sensed the surprise and hostility which had greeted their arrival at Moresby.

"You must come for me if they have nightmares or can't sleep," Alessa said, recalling frightened moments from her own childhood and the reassuring feel of her mother's hand on her forehead. "No matter what the time. You know where my bedchamber is? Two doors past the main staircase."

Galina gave a quick nod. Despite being in a strange house in a strange country, surrounded by people who spoke a language she barely knew, her composure remained unruffled. Not for the first time it occurred to Alessa that Niki and Zara's nurse was a remarkable young woman.

"Thank you for coming with us," Alessa said impulsively, laying her hand on Galina's arm. "I don't know what we'd have done without you."

Galina smiled. "A month ago I was waiting tables in Krasnoe Selo, Lady Milverton. I believe in taking what life has to offer."

Looking at Galina, Alessa saw the drudgery of a life spent waiting on drunken soldiers. It was disconcerting, the sense that she could put herself in the place of someone whose life should be wholly alien to her. And yet Alessa found herself wanting to sit down and talk to Galina about the life she had left behind and the potential chaos she had entered at Moresby.

But Alessa knew she had already been absent from the drawing room — *her* drawing room, she reminded herself — long enough, so instead she pressed Galina's hand and made her way to the main corridor and the staircase.

Light from the candle sconces cast bars of warmth on the golden oak of the open-well stairs and flickered against the grisaille paintings on the walls. Steeling herself for a return to the drawing room, Alessa descended the staircase slowly, running her hand along the smooth wood of the banister, pausing to stroke one of the carved wolves which stood on each of the newel posts.

As she reached the hall, John came toward her, a candle in his hand. "Alessa, we thought you'd decided to stay upstairs. Everyone decided to make it an early night. A good thing, too, if you ask me. Too many people not on speaking terms with too many other people doesn't make for anything approaching rational conversation."

Feeling the strain in her forehead ease at this temporary reprieve, Alessa smiled gratefully at Harry's cousin. Though he had the hazel eyes and red-tinged hair of the Dudley men — Harry was a rare exception — John was refreshingly free of the pride and discord that marked the Dudley family. He and Georgiana and Harry's brother Matt were the only Dudleys who had welcomed Alessa wholeheartedly into the family.

"They've all gone up?" Alessa asked.

"All except Harry. He went to his study to look over some

163

papers." John hesitated, a speculative look in his eyes. "I know Harry looked more or less his usual self at dinner, but a set-to with his mother always affects him more than he'll let on. Perhaps—Well, you're his wife. You'll know better than I."

Looking into John's sympathetic eyes, Alessa very nearly blurted out that she didn't know at all. But she was not quite ready to admit her marriage was a shambles. Recalling her talk with Fiona and the resolution she had found at the end of it, she smiled at Harry's cousin. "Thank you. Perhaps I will have a word with him."

By the time she reached Harry's study, Alessa was already doubting the wisdom of her decision. She had only visited the study on a half-dozen or so occasions, and she was cautious about invading his private domain. She hesitated a moment, then knocked on the door. Hearing a muffled "come in" from behind the sturdy oak panels, she pushed the door open.

The study was a low-ceilinged room with white-painted walls and plain dark floorboards, a surprising contrast to the splendor found in most of the house. Harry was sprawled in the chair behind his desk, his coat tossed over the chair back. The desk before him was strewn with papers but he was staring at the wavering flame of a candle which stood beside his ink blotter. Watching his drawn face and shadowed eyes, Alessa had the sense that she had intruded on him in a way that had to do with far more than entering the precincts of his study. Afraid to disturb him, unsure what to say, she stood still and waited. At last Harry looked up, his eyes widening in surprise.

"I'm sorry," Alessa said, sure now that she had made a dreadful mistake, "I didn't mean to disturb you. I'll let you get back to your work."

"No." Harry pushed back his chair and got to his feet. "Please," he added, with surprising determination. "I'm sorry, my mind was a league away. Sit down." He gestured toward a tapestry-covered chair which stood

164

near the desk. "Is anything the matter?"

Alessa shook her head. "When I came back downstairs, everyone else had gone up. John said you were in here. I thought . . ." Still unsure if she had made the right decision, she moved to the chair and sat down, then met Harry's questioning gaze. "I thought you might like to talk."

"Talk?" Harry looked at her in surprise and gave an unexpected, bitter laugh. "God help me, if only talk would mend matters."

"At least it can make burdens easier to bear," Alessa said, feeling emboldened because, whatever else he felt, Harry did not seem to take her presence amiss.

"Can it?" Harry asked harshly. "Forgive me," he said quickly, as if reading the distress in her eyes, "I didn't mean it that way. But it never occurred to me . . ."

He broke off but the unspoken words were as clear as the best family crystal. *It never occurred to me to talk about it to you.* Alessa clasped her hands together, trying to still the pain at this reminder of the state of their marriage. Comfort hadn't been a part of their bargain, but now it seemed to her that it should have been.

Harry pushed aside some papers and perched on the edge of his desk. He stared at the carpet for a moment, then spoke abruptly, as if he had come to some decision. "I thought I was prepared for today. But I wasn't prepared for how much it would affect me."

Alessa looked at him with a mixture of sympathy and curiosity. She had always known there was tension between Harry and his mother but she had never understood it, and she had never seen it so harshly displayed as it had been this afternoon. *I know you've never liked me, madam.* Alessa's insides twisted at the memory of the words. Whatever her difficulties with her own mother, she had never doubted *Maman*'s affection.

"Seeing Niki for the first time must have been a great shock for the whole family," she said, searching for some words that would ease his pain. "I'm sure with time . . ."

"Time heals all wounds?" Harry asked with a wry smile. "Perhaps. But it doesn't do away with the injury that caused them."

Not for the first time, Alessa wondered at how Harry had come to be such an outsider in his own family. But she did not yet feel she had the right to tread on such personal territory, so she said, "I looked in on Niki and Zara. They seem to have settled into the nursery very well. Galina says they fell asleep right away."

"Thank God for that at least." Harry regarded her for a moment, his eyes softening. "I haven't thanked you for standing up for the children this afternoon. That can't have been easy for you to do."

"On the contrary, I couldn't stop myself," Alessa said. "I was furious." She turned away, for the warmth in his eyes stirred a discomfiting yearning within her. "Not that anything I said made much difference."

"It made a difference to me," Harry said quietly. "And it will make a difference to Niki and Zara when they're old enough to understand all this."

"I pray to God they never do understand," Alessa said, recalling the cold look in Lady Milverton's eyes.

"So do I, but I doubt our prayers will be answered."

"Then we'll just have to do our best to protect them from the worst of it." Alessa looked up to find Harry watching her, an odd look in his eyes. "What's the matter?" she asked.

"You continue to surprise me. This isn't your fight."

At the suggestion that the children's welfare was more his concern than hers, Alessa felt a flash of anger. And yet, she realized, she had given him scant reason to consider her his ally. "I'd never let anyone hurt Niki or Zara," she said. "However badly you think of me, you must at least believe that."

"Badly?" Harry echoed. "Whatever gave you the idea I thought badly of you?"

"Be honest with me, Harry," Alessa said, her throat tight with the pain of the last weeks. "I deceived you, or at the very least I went behind your back. Don't patronize me by pretending it didn't happen."

"Oh, Christ." Harry gave a laugh, half rueful, half despairing. "My dear—would you believe I wasn't even thinking of that? It seems"—he ran a hand through his hair—"at the moment I must confess it seems trivial."

A short time ago Alessa would have sworn she couldn't believe that their last quarrel didn't weigh upon Harry as heavily as it weighed upon her. Yet now she saw how blindly she had been wrapped up in her own concerns. Suddenly aware of the chill of the evening, she rubbed her bare arms. How naive she had been to think that Harry thought about her as much as she thought about him.

"I wasn't thinking," she said. "Of course you have other things on your mind."

"I always find it difficult when I come back to Moresby, though it usually isn't this bad." Harry gave one of the quick, easy smiles Alessa found at once so comforting and so disconcerting. "John says there's a fair in the village the day after tomorrow. I thought we could take the children. They're sure to enjoy it, and I think we could both use a few hours of freedom."

"That's by far the nicest suggestion I've heard all day." Alessa found she did not feel nearly as cold as she had a few moments before. But the thought of the next few days brought the memory of another unwelcome prospect. "*Maman* should be here a day or so after that," she added.

"No rest, is there?" Harry said, his eyes warm with sympathy. "Would it help if I talked to her first?"

Startled and touched by his offer, Alessa shook her head. "No, she's my mother. I know how to handle her. At least, I know as well as anyone. It's just that she has a way of making me feel about twelve years old." Alessa adjusted one of the white satin roses on the bosom of her gown and added something she rarely admitted to anyone. "I've never quite felt her equal in anything."

"That's nonsense. She's not half as beautiful."

Glancing up, Alessa felt her face grow warm from the look in Harry's eyes. Though she knew he was trying to make her feel better, she was surprised, for he rarely paid her such compliments. "It will be all right," she said, trying to hide her embarrassment. "I'll just have to remember that no matter how badly *Maman* loses her temper, it's only because she wants me to be happy."

"Which your husband certainly hasn't made you."

The savage note in Harry's voice brought Alessa to her feet. Without quite knowing she had moved, she was at his side, her hand on his arm. "That's not true, Harry."

"No?" he asked in the same tone.

"If I've been unhappy, the fault is mine, not yours," Alessa said, pushing any thoughts of Marina Chernikova firmly to the back of her mind.

Harry's fingers closed over hers with sudden, crushing force. "I never wanted to hurt you."

The words were a plea. Feeling a great wave of protectiveness, Alessa stepped even closer to him. "I know that."

"If you knew," Harry said in a low voice. "If you knew how much I want . . ."

He raised his head and held her gaze with his own. Alessa felt his quickened pulse and the heat of his breath. With a shock of surprise, she realized he was now in the grip of a very different sort of demon. Her own pulse was racing, sending the blood to her face and making her fingers go nerveless and her thoughts tumble into confusion.

"Alessa."

Her name on his lips was a whisper of sound, another plea, every bit as desperate as the first. Beside them on the desk the candle flame wavered. Alessa's body tensed with a host of conflicting impulses. She wanted to move toward him and feel his arms close around her and his lips free her from the fears of the moment. Yet she feared the treacherous seduction of oblivion.

The image she had been trying to hold at bay rose before her eyes, the image of Harry handing the Countess Chernikova into her carriage that afternoon at Tsarkoe Selo. Subduing a cry of anguish, Alessa pulled her hand from Harry's grasp. They were both in need of comfort, but great as her longing was, pride was stronger. She could not give herself to him on those terms.

"I've kept you long enough. Alastair might wake. I should go up." Willing herself not to give in to the need in Harry's eyes, Alessa fled from the room.

Chapter Eleven

Feeling the warmth of the autumn sun on his face, Harry leaned forward and watched Will Talbot, the village cobbler, bowl against the visiting team from Little Whitcombe. Here, amid the cheerful, noisy, jostling crowd watching the cricket match, which was one of the high points of the fair, Harry found the joy of homecoming. He had known most of those gathered on Moresby common all his life. In some ways, he felt he knew them better than his own family.

Harry glanced at Alessa, who was sitting on the bench near him, with Niki and Zara between them. They had been to village cricket matches before but never quite like this. Today they had arrived unexpectedly and there had been no time to ready special seats for the lord of the manor and his family. Harry vastly preferred it this way, but he wasn't sure that Alessa shared his feeling. She had never seemed to show much interest in cricket in the past. Yet now she was leaning forward, her chin cupped in her hand, intent on the match. As Harry watched, she turned to him, her eyes bright with excitement. "I never knew cricket could be such fun."

"You never paid enough attention to it to find out," Simon said from the row behind. "Oh, I say," he added, his attention drawn back to the field. "Whitcombe's having terrible innings. Good show, Talbot."

Niki tugged at Harry's sleeve. "Could I learn to play this game?" he asked in Russian.

"Of course," Harry promised him, responding in the same language.

Zara clapped her hands as the audience burst into applause at a particularly clever bit of fielding by one of the Moresby men. "I want to play, too."

"I should think so," Alessa said, putting an arm around the little girl. "Papa can teach you and Niki together. And while you're showing the children how to play cricket," she added to Harry in English, "you might as well teach me the rules as well."

"I'll help too," Georgiana offered from beside Simon.

"Don't be stupid, Georgy, you don't know how to play cricket." Julia, who had been sulking all morning, was roused to speech by her sister's remark.

"Yes, I do, I've played with the Fletcher boys heaps of times. And if you tell Mama," Georgiana added quickly, "I'll put spiders in your bed."

As his sisters' squabbling subsided, Harry looked at Alessa. She was watching the match again, her bonnet slipping back from her forehead, a strand of dark hair tumbling over her cheek. A wave of longing tightened Harry's body and played havoc with his senses. In spite or perhaps because of the fact that his wife did not look particularly like a countess at the moment, he thought she had never looked more beautiful. Her pelisse and the ribbons on her bonnet, the color of ripe peaches, warmed her skin. Or perhaps it was her smile which did that. She seemed to be smiling more today than she had in weeks.

Harry looked away, trying to force his attention back to the match. The memory of that moment in his study when Alessa had fled from his unabashed plea stayed with him, an ever-present torment. In all the folly of his youth, he could not remember a moment when he had wanted a woman as badly as he had wanted her then.

His thoughts were interrupted by groans and shouts of laughter from the crowd as a ball sailed over the players' heads and into the hedge which bordered the common. "Just like old times, isn't it?" John said as there was a scramble on the field to locate a new ball.

"Not quite," Harry reminded him, grateful for the distraction. "We used to be out on the field instead of sitting tamely on benches."

John grinned. "Don't I remember. Matches at Eton never held a candle to cricket at Moresby. Playing was the highlight of visits here. Until—"

"Until Father put a stop to our playing," Harry finished for him, his eyes on the field, his father's words still vivid in his memory. *You're the next Earl of Milverton, Harry. It's beneath your dignity to be playing with village boys at your age. You're different from them. Don't ever forget it.* Harry's fingers clenched. It was impossible to forget it. His father had seen to that.

"As I recall, you didn't exactly heed his decree," John said, shading his eyes with his hand to scan the field as play was resumed. "I seem to remember a nasty whipping when we ducked out of lessons to take part in a match."

"Always leading you astray, wasn't I?" Harry pushed the unwelcome memories aside and grinned at his cousin.

"Thank God for it," John said with feeling. "It's the only way I escaped being an insufferable prig or an autocratic tyrant like most of the Dudley men." He glanced down at Niki. "Don't let your sons be stifled, Harry."

Harry looked from Niki to Alastair, who was asleep in his basket between Alessa and the nurse. "In that at least I won't fail them," he said, making the promise to himself as much as to John.

"Seems you've got a sensible nurse to start with," John said, his gaze straying down the bench. "She doesn't know much English, does she?"

"Louise?" Harry looked at the young woman they had brought from Russia to be Alastair's nurse. "Actually she does. She's French, but she worked for an English family in St. Petersburg."

"No, I mean the other one. Galina, isn't it? None of my nurses were ever half so pretty. Where did you find her?"

172

Harry glanced at Galina, who was sitting quietly beside Georgiana, who knew no Russian. "She was working in an inn," Harry murmured.

"How like you, Harry." John's eyes glinted with humor. "Don't worry, I won't tell anyone," he added, getting to his feet. "But I find I'm eternally grateful to you for teaching me Russian. I think I'll go and try to explain the game to her."

Watching his cousin make his way toward Galina, Harry wasn't sure whether to be amused or concerned. Flirtations with the servants were not generally in John's line.

Galina looked up in surprise when John approached her, but after a few moments she smiled, and as the match drew to a close, she appeared to have relaxed in his company. Harry pushed aside his concerns. He was already beginning to behave like a father. If he was any judge of character, John was too honorable to go beyond flirtation and Galina too sensible to let herself get into trouble.

The Moresby men won the match, causing the spectators to burst into furious, jubilant applause and spill onto the field.

"I should go and congratulate them," Harry said to Alessa. He hesitated, looking down at Niki, who was flushed with the excitement all around him. News of Lord Milverton's new heir would already have spread, for most of the Moresby servants had relatives in Moresby village. Deciding it was best to confront matters head on, Harry lifted Niki and swung him up onto his shoulders. Niki gave a cry of delight. Understanding in her eyes, Alessa looked at Harry and took Zara's hand.

A regrettable silence fell over the crowd as they made their way onto the field, still damp from the previous night's rain. Harry nodded and smiled at those he knew and ignored the curious looks. Beside him, Alessa held her head high and calmly lifted her skirt to avoid the mud.

When they reached Will Talbot, Harry stopped and held out his hand. "A splendid effort, Will. Congratulations."

Will accepted Harry's hand and met his gaze evenly. They

had once been team mates on this same field. "Thank you, my lord. It's good to see you back. My lady." He nodded to Alessa and refrained from staring at the children. Will had always been a tactful man.

"You've won two more converts to the game," Harry said, lifting Niki down from his shoulders. "Niki, my son from my first marriage, and his cousin Zara, my ward. I think they'd like to have a look at a ball and bat."

Will's face broke into a grin as he looked down at the children, who were regarding him with admiration and curiosity. "Well now, I think that can be arranged. Nat," he called to another of the men, "we have a couple of new recruits."

Half an hour later, Niki and Zara had both held a cricket bat and thrown a cricket ball and had a number of eager cricket players try to put the rules of the game into the few English words the children could understand. The children seemed to revel in all the attention. Alessa, who had been standing quietly by, turned to Harry with a smile. "Well done."

"It could have been worse," Harry agreed, subduing an impulse to take her hand. As he had learned, to his cost, touching her was fraught with peril.

By the time they returned to the others, they found their party had been joined by the Carnes and Edward Clifford, who had driven over from their respective homes. Harry and Alessa set off with the Carnes to show the younger children the sights of the fair. John, still talking to Galina, trailed along with them, but Peter and Simon decided to go exploring on their own and bore up very well when Georgiana asked to go with them. It was only as they began to move into the crowd that Harry realized his elder sister had disappeared.

"Where's Julia?" he asked, looking around for her, more in curiosity than in anxiety.

"Edward persuaded her to walk with him," Alessa said, settling Alastair in her arms. "I wouldn't have thought he could do it."

"Nor would I," Harry said. "But then Edward's always been a superlative diplomat."

Edward looked down at Julia as they made their way down the crowded aisles. With her clear skin and thick hair and appealingly rounded body, she was undeniably a lovely creature. Edward's affection for her was genuine, and he was more than eager to bed her. But London and St. Petersburg and even Bedfordshire were full of pretty, well-bred girls. If Julia were someone else's sister, Edward knew he would probably not be pursuing her so avidly.

But Julia was Harry's sister and a Dudley, and Edward was determined to have her. He had done his duty two days ago, standing by Harry, proving his loyalty to his friend. He had known when he did so that he risked Julia's wrath. Now was the time to mend matters.

"You don't have to like me to talk to me, you know," he said, steering her around an apple seller wheeling a large cart.

"I don't know why I came," Julia said. She had taken Edward's arm but was walking a good six inches away from him. "It's either hideously dusty or abominably muddy, most of the goods are impossibly vulgar, there are entirely too many children and animals running about, and the people push and jostle so."

"Then there's only one reason you could possibly have come." Edward gave a practiced smile which had worked particularly well on a princess in St. Petersburg. "Confess it, Ju."

"What?" Julia demanded, wrinkling her nose as they brushed close to a trio of day laborers.

"You wanted to see me."

Julia's fingers tensed on his arm. "Don't be ridiculous," she said, avoiding his gaze.

"Have it your own way," Edward said, well pleased with the progress he was making. "I know I came because I wanted to see you."

"But . . ." Julia looked up at him, confusion in her eyes,

175

then broke off as a yapping brown-and-white dog darted in front of them dragging a large bone.

"You're right," Edward said, taking advantage of the moment to pull her closer to him, "this is no place for a lady. I suggest we seek some privacy."

Before Julia could protest, he had steered her through a knot of people at the end of the aisle and behind the shelter of an ancient oak tree, heavy with acorns, which stood at the edge of the common.

"Harry is my friend," Edward said, turning Julia to face him and taking her by the shoulders. "God knows he's made his mistakes, but I couldn't turn on him in front of the family. You must understand that."

"You could have written to me when you found out about the boy. After all we were—"

"Practically engaged," Edward finished for her.

Julia pulled away from his grasp and turned away. "I don't know why I spent so long waiting for you. You're only a second son."

Edward's hands balled into fists. "Are you still waiting?" he asked, forcing himself to relax his fingers.

"I hope you don't think I'm still unmarried at twenty because I haven't received any other offers." She turned back to him, impatience and frustration on her face. "Why didn't you write to me about the children?"

"Because Harry asked me not to." And more importantly, because he would not for the world have spoiled the drama of Harry's homecoming.

"Then Harry means more to you than I do?" Julia demanded.

The filtered sunlight dappled her face, making Edward very much wish they could end this business so he could kiss her. "No one means as much to me as you do, Julia," he said, pulling her to him and lowering his mouth to hers.

Julia put up a token resistance, but before long she subsided in his embrace with quite as much ardor as she had shown the last time he was in England. A short engagement would definitely be in order, Edward decided, pleasantly drunk on passion and the knowledge that he had at least one Dudley completely in his power.

When he finally raised his head, Julia smiled up at him, her eyes bright and expectant. Edward remembered that there were still some formalities to be completed. "Marry me, Julia," he said, taking her face between his hands.

"Of course. I always meant to, you know. I was just so angry . . ." Her eyes darkened, as if she had been assailed by a sudden doubt. "Edward, promise me you'll never treat your duty to your family as lightly as Harry treats his."

Unexpected, unwelcome anger shot through him. "Never," he promised, tilting her face up for another kiss.

And that word at least he spoke with wholehearted fervor.

"I don't see why the cricket ball has to be called 'her'." Georgiana scowled at the footprint-scarred ground as she and Simon and Peter turned down an aisle fragrant with the smell of meat pies and the rich, pungent aroma of apple cider.

Peter looked at her in surprise. "I thought you wanted girls to be included."

"Oh, I'm all for girls being allowed to *play* cricket. But I do think it's a bit unfair that the only female allowed in most matches is something men go about bashing with a stick."

Simon laughed. "You may have a point there."

"Boys can do everything," Georgiana continued, turning up the dirt with the toe of her half-boot. "If I were a boy, I could go to the Continent like you or look for tombs and things in Egypt like Matt or be in Parliament like Harry. But since I'm a girl, all I can do is be like Julia."

This last was spoken with such disgust that Peter nearly laughed and with such genuine frustration that he carefully schooled his features. "You have a point there, too," he agreed.

"On the other hand," Simon said, casting a sidelong glance at Georgiana, "there are a number of things girls can do.

177

Simply writing a letter, for instance, can have all sorts of consequences."

Georgiana looked up quickly. "I was only trying to help. And if I hadn't written to Alessa and she hadn't followed Harry to Russia, she'd be as surprised as the rest of us about the children. She might even have sided with Mama and Julia instead of with Harry."

"Mmm. Yes, I think she might. Not," Simon added, looking speculatively at Harry's sister, "that you should know who sided with whom, considering the only time it was openly discussed you were sent out of the room."

"Don't sound so superior, Simon," Georgiana said, pushing some flyaway strands of hair beneath her bonnet. "If you'd been sent out of the room, you'd have been listening at the keyhole with me."

"We'll never know, will we?" Simon said in his stuffiest tone, then spoiled the effect by winking.

Georgiana pulled a face at him, but her eyes strayed across the road to a stall offering meat pies.

"Hungry?" Peter asked, recalling similar expressions on his brother's and sisters' faces.

"I'm always hungry," Georgiana said with feeling. "Julia says it's disgusting that I can eat so much and not swell up like a balloon, and Miss Beaton says I must still be growing and at this rate I'll be as tall as Harry. She sounds as if she thinks I could stop if I wanted to."

"Now that you mention it, you can work up quite an appetite watching cricket," Simon said. "Come on, child, we'll buy you lunch."

"I didn't mean it that way." Georgiana drew herself up. "I can pay for my own food."

"I'm sure you can," Simon said, fishing in his pocket. "But—"

"If you're going to say I'm a girl, I'll box your ears," Georgiana warned.

"I was going to say I'm older. More to the point, I'm sure my allowance is bigger." Simon pulled out his purse. "Meat pies or hot potatoes?"

They bought pies and large glasses of cider and, discovering that it was too much to manage while they walked, sought refuge on a fallen log at the end of the aisle. "I think Alessa's being splendid about the children," Georgiana said, pulling off her gloves. "It can't have been easy, especially since she has her own baby."

"It wasn't," Simon said. "You missed all the fun part."

Georgiana grimaced. "I was afraid of that. And now Mama's being beastly," she added, scowling at the meat pie the way Peter had seen her scowl when she talked about her mother. "That's not going to help things any."

"I'm not so sure about that," Simon said thoughtfully. "It may be good for Harry and Alessa to have a common enemy."

"You mean they'll be too busy fighting with Mama to fight with each other?"

"Something like that," Simon said.

Peter took a bite of the pie, which compensated for toughened meat with liberal amounts of spices and pepper. "They seem to be getting on much better today," he said, recalling his brief glimpse of Harry and Alessa on his arrival at the fair.

"Better," Simon agreed. "But you couldn't say they've mended matters."

His throat burning from the sharp taste of the pie, Peter took a drink of the cool cider. With the press of people, the lack of shade, and the heat from the cooking fires, the day was becoming uncomfortably warm. "There's something to be said for shady terraces," he said, reaching up and loosening his cravat.

"That's one advantage girls have over boys," Georgiana told him, brushing pie crumbs from her muslin skirt. "We don't have to wear so many clothes." She dampened her finger and began to rub at a grease stain on her bodice. "Maybe it's silly to expect Harry and Alessa to be any different."

"Different than what?" Peter asked.

"Well, Mama and Papa never got on very well. Most of the time they avoided each other—it's easy to do in a house as big as Moresby—but I know they fought. Once Mama even smashed one of the Chinese vases in her dressing room."

Uncomfortably recalling the days when his own mother had been alive, Peter was silent.

"Don't tell me you were listening at the door then too," Simon said lightly.

"Not quite." Georgiana gave up on the grease stain and picked up her glass. "I overheard two of the maids talking about it. It's funny, it doesn't seem at all like Mama. At least, not like the way she usually behaves." Georgiana stared at the sediment in the bottom of her glass. "I'm not sure she and Papa even *liked* each other very much."

The wistful undertone in her voice touched Peter's heart. "Things are changing. Marriages aren't arranged so much anymore," he said, though his hands clenched as he thought of Radka.

"I'm not so sure about that." Georgiana's eyes held a realism beyond her years. "I once heard Cecilia say that she wouldn't have looked twice at Tom if he hadn't been a viscount."

Peter could think of no response to this. He had only met Harry's eldest sister once, but she had certainly not appeared to be a woman deeply in love with her husband.

"At least Julia seems fond of Edward. I suppose that's one thing in her favor," Georgiana said, as if unwilling to grant her sister any finer qualities. "But Harry and Alessa—I wish . . ."

"What?" Peter asked.

"That they could be more like your parents," Georgiana said. "It would be nice to have a real family at Moresby."

Looking into her wide brown eyes, Peter was reminded of how young she was. He took her hand and gave it a sympathetic squeeze.

Simon got to his feet with sudden decision and looked down at them. "We won't do much good sitting here. Let's find them and see if we can help things along."

Georgiana's wistfulness vanished at the prospect of action. "How?"

Simon grinned. "To start with, we could take the children off their hands for a bit."

Harry looked from his brother-in-law to Peter. "You're sure you don't mind?"

"Not at all," Simon assured him. "We want to see *St. George and the Dragon*."

"They'll be all right, Harry," Alessa said, ruffling Zara's hair. "Simon can translate for them."

Harry cast one more glance at the children, who were looking with excitement at the makeshift stage where the play was to be performed. They were comfortable in Simon and Peter's care, and despite the language barrier they had become quite friendly with the young Carnes in the course of the day.

Teddy and Beth had already started toward the stage. Fenella was dragging Peter after them. "Don't worry, we'll take good care of them," Georgiana promised her brother, reaching for Niki's hand. "We'll come find you near the dancing pavilion when it's over. I think I'm going to like being an aunt."

As Georgiana led Niki and Zara to join the others, Fiona put a hand on Harry's arm. "It's all right. They're not as fragile as you think."

Harry smiled at her. "I'm still not used to being a father."

"You're looking older already," John told him. "As long as we're meeting at the dancing pavilion," he added, brushing a speck of dust from his coat with an elaborate show of unconcern, "I think I'll go there now." He turned to Galina and spoke in careful Russian. "I don't suppose I could persuade you to dance with me?"

Galina looked at him in surprise. "But the children . . ."

"The children will be fine," Harry said. "Lady Carne has

181

already convinced us of that. Enjoy yourself while you have the chance."

Galina hesitated a moment, then put her hand on John's arm. "Thank you, Mr. Dudley."

Harry intended to ask Alessa to dance, but she was already speaking to Fiona. "I need to check on Alastair. Do you want to come with me?"

The plea in her voice was unmistakable. Alessa didn't want to be with her husband. Fiona, who must have heard the plea as well, agreed at once.

"Come on," Gideon said, regarding Harry with sympathy, "I'll buy you some ale."

"I saw your uncle at a dinner in town while you were in Russia," Gideon said when they had carried the ale to the relative seclusion of a gap between two stalls.

Harry raised his brows. Though his Uncle George, John's father, held a seat in the House of Commons, he was a staunch Tory and did not move in the same circles as the reform-minded Gideon. "Must have been an interesting party. Where were you dining?"

"At Lord Parminter's. Fiona's cousin makes it a point to have a foot in every camp."

Harry settled his shoulders against the rough boards of the wall behind him. "Did Uncle George accuse you of corrupting my political soul?"

Gideon gave a grin which made him look far younger than his forty-two years. "In the most polite language. I told him I was flattered, but I must disclaim all credit. If you were going to the devil, you were doing it all on your own."

Harry laughed, but the sound rang harsh to his own ears. He was aware of the shouts of the children and the barking of dogs and the cries of hawkers. But beneath it he could hear his uncle's voice, so like his father's. *Damn it, boy, I don't know where we went wrong. You never were cut out to be Earl of Milverton.*

"It's the Habeas Corpus Act. Uncle George has never forgiven me for speaking against its suspension." Harry took a sip of ale to wash the bitter taste from his mouth. "At least now Uncle George has stopped fearing imminent revolution. Construction of Regent Street has resumed and all's right with the world."

"While a few streets away, men who fought at Waterloo and Trafalgar do battle with cold and starvation." Gideon pushed his unruly dark hair from his face, his quiet voice taking on the note of anger which lent such power to his parliamentary speeches.

Harry thought of the widowed sister of one of his tenants who had frozen to death in London the previous winter. Bitterly guilty when he learned of her plight, Harry had made an impassioned speech in the Lords which had prompted another fight with his uncle. "When I didn't take my responsibilities seriously, Uncle George thought I was a disgrace," Harry told Gideon. "Now that I do, he'd prefer I went back to being dissolute."

"Would you?" Gideon asked in a mild voice.

Harry met his friend's gaze and thought of his younger days, which seemed now to have been filled with anger rather than a search for pleasure. It was something to have a sense of purpose. "No," he said. "No, by God, I wouldn't." After a moment, he added, "My father never let me forget I was the next Earl of Milverton. I hated him for it."

Though he and Gideon had been friends for years, Harry had never made such a confidence before. To his relief, Gideon showed no surprise. "My father never thought about me much one way or the other," Gideon said. "I'm not sure which of us had the worst time, but I wouldn't call either situation ideal parenting." He wiped a streak of moisture from the side of his glass. "I've tried to do better by my own children. You seem to have made a good start with yours."

Feeling he had strayed too far into uncharted waters, Harry swallowed more of the strong, bracing ale. "Did my uncle say anything else?"

Gideon accepted the shift in the conversation without a blink. "Along the general lines of your political beliefs? He mentioned that it might be a good thing if you stuck to diplomacy in the future."

"All the more reason for me to do the opposite. There's too much to be done at home for me to spend my time abroad," Harry said, thinking both of politics and of his family.

"You're not going to Aix-la-Chapelle?" Gideon asked.

"No, I don't want to leave Alessa and the children," Harry said automatically and then realized that he had led the conversation back to the personal waters he had sought to avoid. He looked up to find Gideon watching him.

"I understand if you don't want to talk about it," Gideon said.

"There doesn't seem to be much to say, does there?" Harry swirled the ale in the bottom of his glass. "Alessa's been splendid since we've come home. Making the best of a bad bargain."

"Don't be so hard on yourself," Gideon advised. "Take from me, it doesn't get you anywhere."

"Giving in to self-pity, am I?" Harry asked. "Sorry. It's just—it's just that I don't seem to be able to reach her."

Gideon swallowed the last of his ale. "If I were you, I'd ask her to dance as soon as she comes back. Start with small things," he added in a more serious tone. "The rest will come."

Harry was not entirely confident of this last, but at least it seemed an effective strategy. If he wanted more warmth from Alessa, he could begin by courting her. "Come on," he said, feeling a renewed burst of confidence.

"Where?" Gideon asked.

Harry grinned. "I'm going to buy my wife a present."

Alessa bent and kissed her son on the forehead. "We'll be at the dancing pavilion, Louise," she said, turning to the nurse. "I'll check back in an hour or so."

"We'll do very well, my lady," Louise assured her. A neat precise young woman who had worked for several diplomatic families, she seemed well able to adapt herself to circum-

184

stances.

"She doesn't try to lord it over the nursery, thank goodness," Alessa told Fiona as they made their way back to the fair from the shady bench where Louise and Alastair were settled. "Some of my nurses acted as if *Maman* was intruding whenever she came to see us."

"I don't imagine they got away with it for long," Fiona said.

"No," Alessa agreed, *"Maman* never lets anyone tell her how to do anything." She hesitated, wanting to talk to Fiona but unsure where to begin.

"Has it been very bad?" Fiona asked, speaking in Italian, as they often did when holding a private conversation.

"Beastly. With Lady Milverton, that is. I don't think I'll ever forgive her for some of the things she said about the children. But Harry and I . . ." Alessa broke off, staring at a group of children engaged in a noisy game of quoits on the edge of the fair grounds.

"You seem to have made considerable progress," Fiona said.

Alessa was aware of a hollow feeling in the pit of her stomach. "I thought he couldn't forgive me for what I did in Russia, yet it seems he has. Only . . ."

"You haven't been to bed with him," Fiona said softly.

Though she felt her cheeks go hot with color, Alessa found she was relieved Fiona had said it. She was not sure she would have been able to do so herself. "Two days ago, he wanted to. And I suppose I did, too. But I couldn't—" She stared down at her wash-leather gloves. "Doesn't it ever seem to you that if you give in like that there won't be any part of you left?"

"Oh, yes." Fiona's eyes were soft with understanding. "I spent years armoring myself against those very feelings because I was afraid they would be my undoing. And," she added with a smile, "because there is regrettably little room for passion in the life of a governess. Yet I finally discovered that if you deny passion, you deny a part of yourself as well."

"But if I surrender myself to him like that, it's not an equal

185

bargain," Alessa said, smoothing a wrinkle from one of her gloves. "Harry would only be giving in to need, and that's not the same as love . . ."

Alessa drew in her breath sharply, aware of the pounding of her pulse. Despite the shouts from the game of quoits, the world seemed very still. Fiona's mouth curved in a smile, but she said nothing. Alessa lifted her chin and threw pretense to the winds. "There. I've finally admitted it."

"Do you feel the worse for it?" Fiona asked.

"Better, actually." Alessa found that it was a relief to no longer have to deny her feelings. Yet it also made her painfully vulnerable. She twisted her hands together, suddenly awkward. "I suppose we should get back," she said. "They'll be wondering what's become of us."

Determined not to reflect too much on what she had admitted, Alessa hastened to change the subject as they moved back into the fair grounds. The colorful crowd made her wish she had brought her sketchbook, and the thought of her sketchbook reminded her that she had something far more prosaic to say to Fiona. "I did some sketches in Russia. I was thinking perhaps we could do a book based on Russian history."

Fiona entered into the idea with enthusiasm. Delighted at the prospect of something that would be wholly hers, Alessa found that she had recovered something approaching composure by the time they joined Harry and Gideon near the dancing pavilion. Then Harry looked at her with a bone-melting smile and her composure fell to bits around her.

"The villagers will never forgive us if we don't dance at least once," he said, catching hold of her hand. Gideon took Fiona's arm and the four of them moved toward the pavilion, a grand name for a large canvas tent made festive with garlands of dried flowers. Inside, the air was heavy with the smell of scent and spilled ale and close-pressed bodies. Blinking at the contrast with the brightness outside, Alessa tried to sort out the swirl of movement and color before her. A trio of fiddlers was playing a lively country dance. There was a clear line between the local gentry at the top of the room and the country folk at the bottom, but when new sets began to form, Harry drew Alessa toward a group of the Moresby tenants.

Though there was a time when Alessa would have been shocked at such behavior, she was coming to understand her husband. These were his people.

Before any of the other dancers could express surprise at being joined by the earl and countess, the fiddlers struck up a new dance. Alessa gave herself up to the pleasure of dancing with Harry. Though she knew he had suggested the dance to keep up appearances in front of the tenants, when she looked at his smiling face she could not believe all was lost between them. Unlike the reception at Tsarkoe Selo, here Harry was plainly enjoying himself. And, Alessa found, despite the heat and the noise and the smells, so was she. There was something infectious about the enthusiasm in the room.

But when the dance came to an end and the fiddlers announced a short interval, silence settled around them. Alessa smiled at the thin, fair-haired woman standing opposite her, uncertain what to say. The woman inclined her head, plainly uncomfortable in the Milvertons' presence now that they did not have the business of the dance to distract them. Desperately wishing she could think of the right thing to say, Alessa tried to remember the woman's name. Felton, she thought. Or was it Flemming?

Harry smiled and held out his hand to the bearded man standing beside the woman. "If you still box as well as you dance, Bob, I wouldn't care to be matched against you."

The bearded man's posture instantly relaxed. "You're not so bad yourself, my lord. Glad to see London ways haven't ruined you."

Fletcher, that was it, Alessa thought. Bob and Mary Fletcher. And she had a clear image of the last time she had seen Mary Fletcher. "You've had another little one since Lord Milverton and I were last at Moresby, haven't you?"

Alessa asked.

"Yes, my lady." Mary seemed surprised that Alessa remembered. "A little girl. Our third."

"You must be very happy," Alessa said, feeling a great sense of satisfaction as some of the unease faded from Mary's face. "Lord Milverton and I have three children now as well."

"We've heard, my lady." Mary colored. "That is . . ."

"The talk's all over the village," Alessa finished for her. "It's all right, it saves us from explanations. I'll bring the children with me next time I come to visit."

"John says you've made some interesting improvements on the farm," Harry was saying to Bob. "I'll ride over later this week and have a look if I may."

As Bob launched into an enthusiastic account of the changes he had made on his farm, Alessa watched her husband, envying his ease in this setting. Many men of his station had played with the tenant children as boys. What was remarkable about Harry was that at nine-and-twenty he still knew how to talk to them.

"However do you manage it," she said, when Bob and Mary had moved off. "You always know just what to say."

Harry grinned. "When you've learned to talk to diplomats, you can talk to just about anyone." He took her arm and led her to the edge of the floor.

Disappointed, Alessa asked, "Don't you want to dance again?"

"Later perhaps. First I want to give you this." Reaching inside his coat, he pulled out a knot of pale peach ribbon, of the sort she had seen for sale in one of the booths, a simple rosette and flowing streamers with a pin to attach it to a dress or bonnet.

Alessa looked at her husband in surprise. In the two years of their marriage, this was the first time he had given her a spontaneous present.

"I know it's not much," Harry said, "but I thought it would match your bonnet."

"It's lovely. I—thank you." Alessa wanted to fling her arms around his neck, but she didn't dare. To hide her confused feelings, she took the ribbon and carefully pinned it to the bosom of her dress.

She looked up to find Harry watching her with a warmth in his eyes that made her heart turn over, but before she could speak, Georgiana pushed her way through the crowd toward them with two pieces of information. The play was over, and Julia was going to marry Edward.

Alessa rested her head against the squabs of the carriage and stroked the silky ribbon with one finger. The day had turned out far better than she had had any right to expect. Niki and Zara had enjoyed themselves, played with the young Carnes, and been accepted by the villagers. She had seen a comfortable side of Harry she had rarely glimpsed in more formal settings. He had danced with her and bought her a present. And then there was her own admission to Fiona, a terrible, wonderful secret she refused to let herself dwell on until she could be sure of privacy.

By the time they turned down the drive to Moresby, Alessa was filled with the best of intentions. She would go upstairs and sit with Niki and Zara while they had supper. She would try to make the evening festive for Julia and Edward, who had been asked to dine with them in honor of the engagement. She would be gracious to Lady Milverton and ask that Georgiana be allowed to sit up for dinner.

Lost in this happy reverie, Alessa did not pay attention to her surroundings until they reached the forecourt. "Carriage," Zara said, looking out the window and pronouncing the English word with great pride.

Alessa was surprised, for Harry and John were on horseback and they were ahead of the carriage bearing the rest of their party. But when she turned to the window she saw that Zara was right. The late afternoon sun shone against the gleaming dark green paint of not one but two carriages.

189

Alessa's heart lurched into her throat. She would have known those carriages anywhere. Ignoring the crowd of people milling about the forecourt, she raised her eyes to the steps and saw a familiar golden-haired figure standing beside Lady Milverton.

Alessa drew a breath, willing her breathing to slow. The day's brief respite was over. It was time to prepare for a new battle.

Her mother had arrived at Moresby.

Chapter Twelve

Her heart beating with anticipation and fear, Alessa stepped down from the carriage and moved toward the woman standing before the open door. The Princess Sofia gathered up her skirt and with a glad cry ran down the steps and enfolded her daughter in what Alessa had to admit was a comforting embrace. In the past weeks there had been so many times when she had longed for her mother, in the anxious last days of her pregnancy, in the wrenching hours of Alastair's birth, and in the lonely agonized days following when she had learned just how wide the gulf was that separated her from Harry. Now what should be a moment of joy was poisoned by the knowledge of what would follow when she told her mother that she had returned from Russia with not one child but three.

But there was no time to think of that now. Sofia released her daughter to embrace her son, who had just descended from the second Moresby carriage, and Alessa bent to embrace the small golden-haired boy who had wrapped his arms about her knees. Not so small, Alessa realized as she crouched down to speak to him face to face. Robby, her half-brother, the first child of Sofia's marriage to Michael Langley, had grown unexpectedly tall in the months of Alessa's absence. He would now be five, older by a few months than Niki and Zara. Throwing his arms around Alessa's neck, he planted a wet kiss on her cheek and told her he had a new baby sister and a new frog which his mother had refused to let him bring to Moresby. Then he left her abruptly to run to Simon, who threw him up in the air, leaving him breathless and squealing with delight.

Alessa was vaguely aware that Lady Milverton was standing nearby, receiving Julia's ecstatic account of her betrothal. Then her attention was claimed once more by her mother, who had caught sight of Louise cradling Alastair in her arms. "My dear child," Sofia said, pulling aside the folds of satin and lace that nearly covered the baby's head, "he's beautiful. Almost as beautiful as my Michelle. You'll see her later. It was time for her feeding and the nurse took her inside. How fortunate you had a boy." Sofia smiled at Alessa with obvious pride. "An heir. The Milverton heir."

Alessa felt a painful knot in the pit of her stomach. "We call him Alastair," she said.

Sofia lifted her beautifully arched brows. "After Fiona?"

Alessa could read her mother's face. Fiona had married well and she had become a very wealthy woman, but she had been Alessa and Simon's governess. "Not entirely," Alessa said, suppressing a smile. "Alastair is the Scottish form of Alexander."

Sofia's face relaxed. "Ah. A nice conceit. I long to hold my grandchild. You will permit?"

Alessa nodded and Louise gave the small bundle into the princess's arms. An unaccustomedly soft look came over Sofia's face. How tender she is, Alessa thought, and then she had a pang of jealousy because her mother seemed as much at ease with the child as she did herself.

"How peacefully he sleeps," Sofia said, "and what a wonder with all the noise and confusion."

"He has a hearty set of lungs," Alessa informed her, "but he's full and dry now. I fed him in the carriage."

Sofia looked up. "You feed him yourself? Well, perhaps that is good with one's firstborn. I nursed you in the throes of first motherhood, but with the others I employed a wet nurse. Else one has not a moment to call one's own." She

4 FREE BOOKS

TO GET YOUR 4 FREE BOOKS WORTH $18.00 —MAIL IN THE FREE BOOK CERTIFICATE T O D A Y

Fill in the Free Book Certificate below, and we'll send your FREE BOOKS to you as soon as we receive it.

If the certificate is missing below, write to: Zebra Home Subscription Service, Inc., P.O. Box 5214, 120 Brighton Road, Clifton, New Jersey 07015-5214.

FREE BOOK CERTIFICATE

4 FREE BOOKS

ZEBRA HOME SUBSCRIPTION SERVICE, INC.

YES! Please start my subscription to Zebra Historical Romances and send me my first 4 books absolutely FREE. I understand that each month I may preview four new Zebra Historical Romances free for 10 days. If I'm not satisfied with them, I may return the four books within 10 days and owe nothing. Otherwise, I will pay the low preferred subscriber's price of just $3.75 each; a total of $15.00, *a savings off the publisher's price of $3.00.* I may return any shipment and I may cancel this subscription at any time. There is no obligation to buy any shipment and there are no shipping, handling or other hidden charges. Regardless of what I decide, the four free books are mine to keep.

NAME

ADDRESS   APT

CITY   STATE   ZIP

TELEPHONE
(   )

SIGNATURE   (if under 18, parent or guardian must sign)

Terms, offer and prices subject to change without notice. Subscription subject to acceptance by Zebra Books. Zebra Books reserves the right to reject any order or cancel any subscription.

ZB0593

handed Alastair back to Louise and caught sight of Galina, who was urging the children to come down from the carriage. "The girl is Russian," she said. It was at once an observation and a question.

The moment could not be postponed. "Galina Yuskaya," Alessa said, drawing herself more erect. "I brought her with us to look after the children."

Sofia's face went blank, a sign of uncertainty and alarm. Alessa looked round for Harry, but he was several yards away, in earnest conversation with her stepfather, Michael Langley. And it was her problem, not his.

Alessa turned to the carriage and put on a welcoming smile for the children, who descended with obvious reluctance, their gaze going from the disapproving face of Lady Milverton, who had appeared at Sofia's side, to the golden-haired stranger whose face showed no welcome at all. "Niki and Zara, *Maman*. They're to live with us."

Her mother frowned. The children shrank closer together, as though taking comfort in each other's touch. Robby came to stand by his mother and watched the two newcomers with obvious interest. He might have moved toward them had not his mother put a restraining hand on his shoulder. "I would have thought you had quite enough to occupy you," she said to her daughter, "without picking up strays."

Alessa felt a hot flush rise in her face. "They're not strays," she said with what control she could muster. "The boy is Nikolai Dudley, Harry's son."

"His firstborn son." Lady Milverton's voice held a note of vindictive pleasure.

"The girl is his cousin," Alessa continued as though her mother-in-law had not spoken, "Zara Varsenina. You will oblige me, *Maman*, by welcoming them to England."

Sofia's gaze did not leave her daughter's face. "You will oblige me, Alessa, by answering some questions. Come inside where we may be private. Robby, go to Nurse." Sofia pushed her son away from the contamination of the hapless Russian children and, without regard for anyone standing in her way, made for the stairs and disappeared inside the house.

Alessa was furious. The children had been upset by Lady Milverton's obvious disapproval of their presence, and her mother's cold disregard had only added to their fright and bewilderment. "It's all right," she said in Russian, kneeling down before them. "That was my mother, the Princess Sofia. She's Russian too, and I'm afraid she has a fearful temper, but it never lasts long. It's just that she doesn't like surprises. I must go and explain to her how we came to bring you to England. The little boy is her son, Robby. He's my brother, and I think he would like to get to know you, but he doesn't speak Russian, so it may take some time."

The children stared at her with wide, uncomprehending eyes. "It will be all right," Alessa said again, feeling angry and helpless. She rose and shook out her wrinkled skirt. "Take them to the nursery, Galina. I'll be up later."

As she made her way to the house, Alessa was conscious of Lady Milverton's tight-lipped face and Julia's spiteful gaze. Edward had retreated to a safe distance. John shrugged and gave her a look that expressed his sympathy and his awareness that he could do nothing to help her. Louise, at least, had had the sense to take Alastair into the house.

Simon caught up with Alessa at the foot of the stairs. "Can I help?"

Alessa gave him a rueful smile. "It's between me and *Maman*. But you might come in later and see which of us is the more bloodied. At the moment I could kill her."

Simon grinned. "I'll talk to Michael. He has a calming influence."

Feeling somewhat more prepared by this exchange, Alessa mounted the stairs and entered the house, where she was informed by a footman that the Princess Sofia was waiting for her upstairs in the blue saloon.

It was Sofia's favorite room at Moresby, perhaps because its small scale and delicate furnishings were congenial to her size, perhaps because its hangings set off her coloring to advantage. In her early forties, the princess was still a remark-ably beautiful woman and vain enough to take delight in that fact. Alessa would have preferred to meet her mother in one of the more massive rooms of the house, where she was not quite so conscious of her mother's power to dominate any chamber in which she appeared.

Sofia was seated on a small settee, hands clasped in her lap, one foot beating a rapid tattoo on the thick-piled carpet. "Sit down," she said.

Alessa's chin went up. "I prefer to stand."

"Stubborn child. As you wish."

Alessa sat down quickly in a gilt-backed chair, feeling very much as if she were still in the schoolroom.

Sofia's foot ceased its rapid movement. "Is he legitimate?"

"He is." Alessa felt once more the pain of betrayal. "Harry was married while he was stationed in Russia. No," she added, forestalling her mother's question, "he didn't tell me. His wife died in childbirth after he returned to England. He was told the child died as well."

"And then?"

Alessa drew a deep breath. "And then he received a letter from Edward Clifford. Edward wrote that he had been vis-ited by a cousin of Harry's wife. The child, it seems, had lived. He had been cared for by his wife's sister, who had a daughter of her own."

"She raised him as her own son?" Sofia's voice was sharp.

"I don't know," Alessa admitted. "He speaks of her as his mother. She's the only one he's known."

Sofia frowned. "So this boy, whom the sister has raised without a murmur as her own son, the boy who has been a brother to her own daughter, has become suddenly incon-venient?"

Her mother was making it worse than it was. "No, *Ma-man*," Alessa said, stifling an angry retort. "The sister died. Her husband died two years before, and the children were left alone. Captain Lychenko was the sister's nearest relative. He could hardly keep the children himself. He's unmarried, and a soldier, and rather wild and disreputable. But he had some sense of obligation, and he came to Edward, thinking Edward could put him in touch with Harry."

Sofia's brows drew together, and her eyes, those beautifully shaped, long-lashed blue-green eyes Alessa had always envied showed sparks of light. *"Juste ciel.* How could you, Alessa? How could you possibly believe this improbable story? Who's to say whose son the boy is? No one but a man you admit is nothing but a disreputable soldier, a man who would find the children an inconvenient burden. How could you possibly believe him?"

"Maman, he's Harry's son. Harry saw the resemblance at once."

"Harry is a sentimental fool. And I fear you are little better. This Lychenko foists not one but two children on you."

"No, it was my choice." Alessa made no attempt to hide her anger. "Do you understand, *Maman?* I was the one who found Zara. I was the one who brought her to Tsarkoe Selo. I was the one who convinced Harry to bring her to England."

"I assume you had your reasons," Sofia said dryly.

"Of course I had reasons. The children were raised as brother and sister. They have no one but each other. Niki was miserable when Harry brought him to the palace. He would scarcely say a word. But with Zara nearby, he's a perfectly normal little boy. I couldn't separate them. Besides, they were living with a cousin of Zara's father, a baker in St. Petersburg who could barely feed his own children."

"A baker. *Mon Dieu.* And what was Harry's wife?"

"A tradesman's daughter." Alessa was enough her mother's daughter to feel shame at this revelation.

Sofia closed her eyes, then opened them suddenly and fixed her daughter with a piercing gaze. "Harry got her pregnant."

"Maman, please!"

"Quixotic fool. Didn't he know how such things should be handled?"

"Don't you dare blame Harry. He was honorable."

"He was an idiot. He's ruined your life. He's paupered your son. My grandson. Don't you know that, Alessa? Don't you care?"

"Of course I care." Tears stung Alessa's eyes, tears of anger and humiliation and a sense of outraged justice. "I care every time I hold my baby in my arms and know he will never be the Earl of Milverton. I care every time I look at Niki—and it's not his fault, I know it isn't—but I care every time I look at him and know that he's another woman's child. I care every time I remember that Harry didn't trust me enough to tell me of his first marriage. Oh, *Maman!*"

Alessa rose from her chair and flung herself on the floor in front of the settee, resting her head on her mother's lap. The tears came quickly now, unbidden, unremitting. She gave herself up to the luxury of weeping, feeling the comforting weight of her mother's hand on her hair, breathing in her mother's familiar scent.

Her tears slowed at last. "You have Michael, *Maman*. He loves you. Your children were conceived in love. But I—I gave my husband a son he doesn't need. I may never have another child of my own. I don't know what's to become of my marriage."

Sofia moved abruptly. "Get up, Alessa. I will not tolerate self-pity."

The words were cruel but effective. Alessa sat back in shock and dismay, then got quickly to her feet. "I'm sorry, *Maman*." She moved to a gilt-edged pier glass that hung above a small table of inlaid wood and studied the reflection of her ravaged face. Her eyes, enormous and dark, were not so very red, but her face was damp and streaked with the passage of tears. She wiped it carefully with a handkerchief, tidied her hair, and composed her features. Then, with head held high, she walked back to her chair and resumed her seat opposite her mother.

"That's better," Sofia said. "You have a right to be angry, Alessa, but you must use your head. Your husband has humiliated you and put you into an impossible posi-

197

tion, but there are always things that can be arranged."

"There is nothing to arrange, *Maman*." Her mother's brusqueness had had its usual tonic effect, and Alessa felt the full authority of her own twenty-three years. Then, remembering that other source of humiliation, she asked, "What do you know of the Countess Chernikova?"

Sofia went very still, and Alessa knew that her mother understood the full import of her question. "She is a friend of Harry's?"

"A very close friend."

"I see," Sofia said, watching her daughter for a moment. "She is said to be a virtuous woman. Or," she added wryly, "a very discreet one. Her husband was jealous of his honor."

"Her husband is dead."

"And you think that makes a difference? Alessa, Harry cannot have seen the woman for many years. She is in Russia, and he is not likely to see her again. You must not concern yourself with what he did in the past."

Alessa felt a flare of anger. "What he did in the past disinherited my son."

"Ah, there you are right," Sofia said, throwing open her hands in a gesture of acknowledgment. "It was a stupid comment. But you have nothing to fear from the Countess Chernikova."

Alessa was silent, feeling her heart resume its normal beat. She felt, absurdly, that she had got the upper hand. Her mother's fury at the start of their interview had aroused echoes of her own anger and despair and in an odd way had now freed her from them. The dreaded moment of revelation was over, and she could now pick up the pieces of her life and make of them what she could.

But if Alessa was ready to move on, Sofia was not. A moment later a knock on the door signaled the arrival of Harry, accompanied by Simon and by Sofia's husband, Michael Langley. "We thought you'd had long enough to sort it out between yourselves," Simon announced, "and it was time to have a family conference."

"Time indeed," Sofia said, ignoring her son's intrusion. "You have a lot to answer for, Harry Dudley."

Harry looked tired, but he walked toward Sofia and looked down at her with no trace of anger or remorse. "I see that Alessa has told you the whole. I am sorry, Princess. I was wrong not to tell her of my first marriage, but it was over long ago. It was a bit of youthful folly, and I had put it behind me. I knew nothing of the child, but improbably he exists."

Sofia's face had grown stormy, but before she could speak, Michael crossed to her side and took her hand. "Be patient, my love. It is not a cause for joy, but neither is it a cause for recrimination. Harry has done the honorable thing."

"Has he?" Sofia snatched her hand away, "He has humiliated my daughter before the world."

"I would not for anything have given my wife pain," Harry said, holding his temper in check with obvious effort. "I am sorry that I have done so. But Niki is my son. Would you have me deny him?"

"I would have you exert some reasonable caution." Sofia's voice was scathing. "You were told the child was dead and now this man Lychenko comes to you with a tissue-thin story that he is not dead after all, and you believed him at once. Have you asked yourself what Lychenko had to gain? Have you made any inquiries? How can you be certain that the boy is truly your son?"

It was the question Alessa had asked herself from the moment Harry told her about Niki. It was the question that had driven her to Elisabeth for help in investigating Lychenko, the question that still haunted her though she tried vainly to drive it away.

Harry, white-faced, was staring at her mother. Without thinking, Alessa rose and went to his side. "We're certain," she said. "Niki is Harry's son."

It was well past ten when Alessa escaped from the overheated drawing room and drew in a welcome breath of the chill air in the hall. She was being uncharitable, she knew that, but she could not bear another moment of Julia's preening and her air of self-congratulation. Alessa had tried hard to make a place for herself in Harry's family. She was fond of Georgiana and John, and she liked Harry's younger brother, Matt, though she had not seen him since their marriage, but Julia, who seemed to regard her sister-in-law with a mixture of envy, suspicion, and malice, had defeated all her overtures of friendship.

Alessa mounted the stairs slowly, her hand trailing on the cool wood of the banister, worn smooth by countless generations of Dudleys. The candle sconces on the wall made intermittent pools of light on the darkened treads. She wished Julia well, truly she did. She hoped she would be happy in her marriage. The look of joy and triumph on Edward's face boded well for her future. It was a love match, at least on his part. There was something to be said for love.

Alessa paused on the half-landing and looked down at the corridor below, listening for the faint sound of voices from the drawing room. The evening had not been as unpleasant as she had feared. After the scene in the blue saloon, she had gone to see her new baby sister, Michelle, and had envied her mother and Michael's happiness. Sofia had seemed somewhat mollified.

Dinner had been festive. Alessa had sat through endless toasts and smiled till her mouth ached and watched the happy couple with something approaching jealousy. Stupid, she would not be Julia for the world, and she hadn't the slightest wish to live in St. Petersburg.

No one had said a word about Niki or the disgrace Harry had brought upon the family. Alessa's mother, who knew her duty as a guest, had entertained the company with stories of life in the Russian court and had spoken to her daughter and son-in-law as though those charged scenes in the blue saloon had never taken place. Lady Milverton, looking like a well-groomed cat who has got at the cream, was more agreeable than usual and included even Alessa in her general benevolence.

Alessa was not deceived. Her mother had caught the look of surprise and gratitude on Harry's face when Alessa had come to his defense. She doesn't know, that was what her mother thought, she doesn't know for sure. And, more humiliating, she's loyal to her husband though she doubts his loyalty to her. Her mother saw entirely too much.

When the ladies retired to the drawing room after dinner, Sofia drew Lady Milverton aside. The two women had formed an uneasy truce on the occasion of their children's marriage, but tonight they seemed in complete accord. Alessa, responding to eager questions from Julia about Russian gowns and hats and hair styles, was in no doubt about the subject of their conversation.

A faint cry from above brought Alessa out of her preoccupation and sent her hurrying upstairs to the room adjoining her own. Alastair, bless his heart, had a splendid pair of lungs. Alessa forgot the two women plotting Niki's downfall in the drawing room below and entered the blissful state that nursing her son never failed to bring about. The curve of head and breast, the incredibly soft unblemished skin, the fine dark hair through which the skin shone faintly pink, the mewling sounds of contentment, the eyes that seemed to stare unblinking into her soul, all these created a world that shut out discord and pain. "I love you," Alessa whispered. "I love you more than I can bear."

Feeling as sated as her son, Alessa returned Alastair to Louise and entered her own room, where she made ready for bed and dropped off into an exhausted sleep.

She had no idea how long she had slept. She found herself sitting upright in bed, her heart pounding, listening to the sound of soft urgent blows on the door. Stumbling in the darkened room, she made her way to the door, guided by a strip of moonlight that poured across the floor through curtains carelessly drawn. She opened the door to see Galina, a ghostly figure in a white nightdress holding a flickering candle, her long blond braid falling over her shoulder.

"The children," Alessa whispered, her throat tight with distress.

"They had bad dreams, my lady," Galina said, an unaccustomed note of worry in her voice. "They are very frightened. I tried to calm them, but I think perhaps . . ."

"I'll come at once." Alessa silently cursed her mother. "Go back to them, Galina. I'll bring Lord Milverton."

It was instinctive, seeking Harry. Only when she stood before his door in her dressing gown and slippers, her hair falling in disorder about her face, did Alessa realize she had never gone to his room before. The shock on Harry's face when he at last answered her summons told her he was aware of that as well.

"What is it?" he asked, his eyes unfocused in the light of the corridor, his voice holding mingled surprise and concern.

"It's Niki and Zara," Alessa said quickly to cover her embarrassment. "They've had bad dreams and Galina cannot quiet them. Will you come?"

Without further speech, Harry took a candle from a nearby table, closed the door behind him, and stepped into the corridor. He was wearing a dark wool dressing gown, disarranged as if he had donned it hurriedly, and his face was drawn with fatigue. It had been a long day for both of them. Side by side, they mounted the stairs to the nursery floor, not touching, though Alessa was conscious that her billowing robe was brushing his legs.

"It's *Maman*," Alessa said, feeling as if the children's nightmares were somehow her fault. "Niki and Zara could tell she was upset when she saw them."

They were outside the door to the children's room. Harry stopped abruptly and turned to face her, the flame from his candle making a pool of light that insulated them from the surrounding dark. "It's my mother as well," he said. "And Julia, and all this . . ." He made a gesture to indicate the house and all the changes the children had had to undergo. "Let's go in."

202

The children were sitting bolt upright in Niki's bed, their faces turned toward the door as if in anticipation of the promised succor. Galina sat behind them, her arms embracing them both. On the table between the beds a candle burned, its flame wavering in the sudden draft from the open door, setting the spiky shadows on the sloping ceiling into trembling motion. The children were quiet but stiff and unyielding in Galina's embrace.

Alessa crossed the room quickly and drew Zara into her arms while Harry did the same to Niki. Zara clung tightly, tense with fear, her fingers digging into Alessa's skin. "Go to bed, Galina," Alessa said, rocking the little girl in a gentle rhythm, "we'll stay with them till they're asleep."

She felt the tension slowly leave Zara's body. The little girl whimpered, then buried her face against Alessa's breast. "It's all right, it's all right now," Alessa whispered, repeating the soothing formula over and over, conscious all the while of Harry on the other side of the bed, his arms folded about his son. She had never felt so close to her husband.

"Better?" Harry asked at last, putting Niki from him so he could look down into his face.

The boy nodded, but his voice trembled. "We don't want to go away."

Harry's jaw tightened. "Who told you you had to go away?"

Niki hung his head, his words so soft Alessa could scarcely hear them. "I don't know. We were on a boat, in the ocean. It was lost."

Harry forced the boy's head up. "Niki, listen to me. You're not going anywhere. This is your home. We're your parents now. No one can take you away from us."

Zara turned her head to look up at Harry. "The lady doesn't like us."

"The lady with the golden hair?" Alessa said in as light a voice as she could manage. Her mother had a lot to answer for. "You must pay no attention to her. She has nothing to

203

say about it. She's my mother, not yours. The thing is, she expected to see me with one child, not three. But I like having three children," Alessa added firmly, "and I won't give any of you up."

It was a greater commitment than she had ever made. The questions her mother had raised were a nagging pain, but she would not attend to them. Not with Zara in her arms and Niki close by looking at her so trustfully. It doesn't matter, she told herself. They're mine now, no matter whose children they are. They need me. It was wonderful to be needed by someone.

"As for *my* mother," Harry said, "you must pay her no heed either. She isn't used to my having any children at all, but this is my home and I will have as many children as I please."

Niki gave him a shy grin. Zara disentangled herself from Alessa's arms and bounced on the bed beside him. "Truly?"

"Truly," Harry said, giving her a hug.

The children were wide awake by now. Harry entertained them with stories of his boyhood, interspersing the Russian he spoke to them with the English words that were to be their new tongue. They followed him with avid interest, repeating the unfamiliar words and giggling over their strange sound till their eyes closed despite themselves and they were lifted, sleeping soundly, into their respective beds.

"Thank you," Harry said when he and Alessa were once more in the corridor.

"There's no need to thank me," Alessa said, annoyed that he saw her behavior as a favor to himself. "They're my children too."

"Still . . ." Harry smiled, a heartbreaking smile that left Alessa feeling totally undone. "I'm glad you're their mother." He lifted the candle to light their way and they turned toward the stairs.

It was cold in Moresby's endless corridors, but Harry's body gave off a heat that held the cold at bay. Her bedchamber would be cold too, its vast dark reaches stealing warmth and life from her. She did not want to be alone, not tonight, not now. The time with the children had brought her closer to Harry, and she was afraid to let him go.

Harry escorted her to her room and stood looking down at her, the light from the candle deepening the lines on his face. Alessa searched it for a sign, for help with the words she could not bring herself to say, but she saw nothing but fatigue and a kind benevolence. She did not want kindness, nor pity. Pity could not warm the chill that threatened her heart.

Alessa turned away and opened the door to her room. The candle she had left burning on the bedside table flickered in the draft. She could dimly see her bed, a large shapeless mass. There she would find warmth of a sort and oblivion. But not the oblivion she wanted.

She was about to close the door when Harry called her name. Surprised, she looked up and met his gaze. His eyes reflected the candle flame, and in their naked depths she saw a need as great as her own.

"Alessa," he said again. He set the candle down on a table that stood just inside the door and took a step toward her. Alessa held her breath, terrified at the sudden knowledge of how much he could hurt her.

If he saw her hesitation, he gave no sign. With a cry like a drowning man gasping for air, he drew her into his arms.

Chapter Thirteen

Desire shot through her body like lightning. She was sinking, drowning in a wave of heat. As velvet darkness enfolded her, some last vestiges of reason tried to struggle free of the force of her own longing. If she gave way now, her soul would be laid bare.

Harry's mouth moved against hers in demand and entreaty. Reason shattered like crystal. With a cry of surrender and need, Alessa parted her lips beneath his own.

The taste of his mouth, the roughness of his cheek, the scent of his skin were heartbreakingly familiar. But the hunger was new, the desperate hunger which seemed to rage through him, burning itself into her body and kindling an answering fire.

Harry tangled his hand in her hair, deepening the kiss and pulling her even closer until she thought she would be lost in the tide of his passion. Never, not even on the night Alastair had been conceived, had he kissed her like this. And never had she felt such a terrifying, violent need for him.

At last he raised his head and looked down at her, his eyes smoldering in the candlelight. Then, without speaking, he lifted her in his arms and carried her to the bed.

The feather bed was soft beneath her but his body felt hard and sure against her own. Fine wool brushed against her skin as his dressing gown fell open, and she felt the firm warmth of naked flesh. In the past Harry had always worn a nightshirt when he came to her. But he wore none tonight.

Perhaps he had donned it only in concern for her modesty.

There was a rustle of silk as he pushed her own dressing gown from her shoulders. The air felt cold against her muslin nightdress, but the urgent touch of his hands made her burn. When he fumbled with the buttons at the neck of her nightdress, her breasts went achingly taut. When his lips brushed the hollow at the base of her throat, she drew in her breath. And when his mouth closed over a nipple, she bit back a cry. Harry had told her once that it was all right to cry out, but she had never quite learned to believe him.

Liquid fire shot through her. Clutching his shoulders, she arched against him. Her leg brushed against the hardness of his arousal. Harry sucked in his breath. With quickened urgency, he pushed up the hem of her nightdress and slid his hand into the thatch of hair at the jointure of her thighs.

Alessa moaned, embarrassment lost in the deluge. Desire raced along her nerves. Her heart thudded against her rib cage and her breath came in quick, desperate gasps.

"Harry." His name was a sob on her lips as she twisted beneath him, trying to get closer.

Suddenly, Harry's hand stilled. With a shuddering breath, he pushed himself up on one elbow and looked down at her. His taut muscles told her how great was his effort at control, while his eyes showed how fragile that control was. "I don't think I can wait much longer, Alessa," he said, his voice rough. "But—the baby. Are you all right?"

Her throat too tight for speech, Alessa nodded. She was certain she would break in pieces if he did not take her now. Harry closed his eyes for a moment, as if he did not trust himself to move. Then he lifted her hips and drove into her.

As he began to move, he took her mouth in another deep, frenzied kiss. Alessa returned his kiss with an equal intensity, but she wished she could see into his eyes, wished she could tell if they held anything more than need, if he knew she had given him far more than her body.

But no matter how unequal the surrender, for the moment he was hers. Matching his urgent rhythm, Alessa was soon

207

conscious of nothing but the salty taste of his skin and th harsh sound of his breathing and the glorious feel of his bod filling her own.

Need blazed between them until she could not tell wher her own body ended and his began. For a moment she trem bled on a precipice of aching delight. Then the tension shat tered within her and she was blinded by glittering shards c light.

Harry's movements grew even more frantic. His face con torted with some emotion she did not understand and sh felt him shudder, spilling his seed into her. Overwhelmed b tenderness, Alessa wrapped her arms around him and hel him close.

Harry lay with his face buried in the crook of his wife' shoulder, shaken by far more than the spasm of physical re lease. Slowly his breathing returned to normal. He wa aware of the slow, soothing beat of Alessa's pulse and th clean, fragrant smell of her skin.

Pushing himself up on his elbows, Harry looked down a her. Her eyes were half-closed. With her lips red and swoller from his kisses and her dark hair tumbling in disarra against her pale skin and the paler linen of the bedclothes she looked at once very young and wholly seductive.

As he watched, she opened her eyes and smiled at him with a sweetness that drove the breath from his lungs. *I lov you.* The words came to him so naturally that he wondered he had denied them for so long. Yet he knew he could no speak them now. They would seem like one more demand when he had already taken so much from her.

Alessa looked up at him, her expression unexpectedly vul nerable. Harry's throat tightened as he recalled his lack o restraint. "I didn't hurt you?" he asked, scanning her fac with concern.

The wavering flame of the candle on the bedside table danced in Alessa's eyes. "Alastair is almost two months old Harry. Women recover from these things, you know."

"Yes, of course. That is, no, I don't know." Harry felt ab

surdly awkward. "I haven't much experience with—"

"Women just risen from childbed?" Alessa asked.

"Yes." Harry felt a quick, hard stab of guilt.

Alessa's eyes clouded, and Harry knew she, too, had remembered Nadia, who had borne his child and then died alone.

He withdrew from her carefully and rolled to his side, propping himself on one elbow. "My early experience wasn't nearly as extensive as some would have you believe," he said as lightly as he could manage. "I should have been gentler," he added in a more serious tone. "I'm sorry.

"I'm not a virgin anymore, Harry," Alessa said, turning her head on the pillow to look at him. "I wanted to, too, you know." Her gaze was steady, but her face was tinged with color.

Harry lifted his free hand and brushed his fingers against her cheek. "Nothing to be ashamed of in that."

"I'm not ashamed." Alessa's color deepened. "But . . ."

"But talking about it is always harder than doing it," Harry said, realizing they'd probably talked about it a good deal less than they should have.

Alessa smiled again. "Much."

Her smile made his heart turn over, a sensation he would have once sworn was anatomically impossible. Not trusting his own emotions, he leaned down and rested his face against her hair.

Alessa released her breath in a soft, contented sigh. For a long time, they both lay quietly. At length, the deep, regular sound of her breathing told him she was asleep.

Cautiously, Harry eased away from her and pushed himself up to a sitting position. Her arm still lay on the pillow near the imprint of his head, the frilled cuff of her nightdress falling over her hand. He had left her like this often enough in the past, yet what had once been commonplace now seemed an unspeakable wrench. His arms ached with a longing to gather her close and spend the night with his body molded to hers.

But having already invaded her body, to invade her bed seemed a fresh violation. Besides if he stayed, he knew he would take her again—already he could feel his own body stirring—and no matter what she had said, he was not sure he had the right to push her so far.

Harry eased his weight off the bed and pulled on his dressing gown. As he did so, his eye fell upon a dark mass in the shadows, the wrong shape to be a dressing table or chair. Alastair's cradle. Alessa moved it into her room at night. Harry felt a moment of embarrassment at the thought of having made such wanton love to his wife in his son's presence. Then he grinned at this puritanical attitude. Alastair seemed to be sound asleep and in any case he would probably see far worse sights in the course of his life.

Turning back to the bed, Harry felt the laughter die within him. The bedclothes were still disarranged. As he drew them up over her shoulders, Alessa stirred slightly but did not open her eyes. For a moment, Harry stood looking down at her, warring with his own demons. *Fool,* a voice said inside his head, *is it your wife you're trying to protect or yourself?*

Both of us. Acknowledging the answer, Harry leaned over to blow out the candle on the bedside table. Ever since Nadia he'd avoided actually spending the night with a woman. And instinct warned him to avoid such intimacy even—especially—with the woman he loved.

Alessa awoke to gray light spilling through the curtains and the sound of her son's cries. Moving automatically through a fog of sleep, she had stumbled to the cradle and lifted Alastair in her arms before the tenderness between her thighs reminded her of the events of the night before. Suddenly wide awake, Alessa sank into the armchair near the cradle and reached up from force of habit to undo the buttons on her nightdress.

It was already unfastened. Her body tingling with the memory of Harry's hands and mouth against her skin, Alessa settled Alastair at her breast. How odd that something as soothing as feeding a baby could be so like something as frenzied as lovemaking.

While Alastair swallowed his breakfast, his hands pushing softly against her breast, Alessa looked back at the bed. Harry had left long since, of course. He always did. It was foolish to think things had changed between them in such a fundamental way. "Your father is good man," she said, cradling Alastair's head in her hand. "He never promised me more."

In response, Alastair continued to nurse with undimmed enthusiasm. It was rather nice, Alessa thought, to have a confidant who didn't answer back. "Not sleepy?" she asked, holding him up when he had finished with both breasts. "For once I'm not either. At the moment I don't feel as if I'll ever be able to relax in that bed again." Alessa sighed. "I don't suppose I'll feel at all comfortable talking to you this way when you're old enough to understand. It's a pity."

"Ah-moo," Alastair said in reply, reaching for her cuff.

"A very sensible answer. Here, see if you can do this again." Alessa picked up a chased silver rattle, a parting gift from Elisabeth, and held it against the tips of his fingers.

Alastair grasped hold of the rattle, a new trick he had learned recently. "What a clever boy," Alessa exclaimed, marveling at the way he seemed to change with each passing day.

As she smiled down at him, an answering smile broke across Alastair's face. Not one of the simple curves of his mouth which Louise told her was only gas, but for the first time a real smile which lit his eyes and crinkled up his face.

Alessa let out a whoop of delight and hugged her son to her. Her first impulse was to tell Harry, but she had never barged into his chambers, and after last night she was even more hesitant to do so. Shutting from her mind the knowledge of the gulf that would probably always lie between her and her husband, Alessa devoted her attention to playing with Alastair until one of the maids arrived with the *café au lait* she drank in the morning in preference to tea or chocolate.

Recalling the events which had led to her night with Harry, Alessa made her way to the nursery wing as soon as she was dressed. She found Niki, Zara, and Galina breakfasting with Robby and his nurse. Alessa was relieved at the sight of her brother. At least *Maman* was not trying to keep him secluded from the other children.

"No more nightmares?" Alessa asked in Russian when she had joined them at the table.

Niki shook his head. His mouth was smeared with strawberry preserves and he seemed to have got some of it into his hair. Alessa took this as a sign of improvement. When he'd first come to them, he'd been much too neat. "Papa see us," he said in English.

"Papa came to see us," Alessa corrected, kissing him.

"Early." Zara looked up from her poached eggs on toast, clearly pleased at her mastery of the word.

Alessa kissed Zara as well, feeling a pleasant thrill of triumph. Apparently Harry had had as much trouble sleeping as she had.

"Harry told them a story," Robby explained, helping himself to another piece of toast. "I woke up and he said I could come in and hear it too. Harry tells good stories." Robby reached for the butter. "I'm your baby's uncle. Am I Niki and Zara's uncle too, 'Lessa?"

"I suppose you are. By marriage at least." Having decided Niki and Zara were her children, Alessa was determined to be consistent. "But it might be simpler if they just call you Robby."

Zara tugged at her sleeve. "Papa went on horse," she said in careful English.

"Yes, he likes to ride early," Alessa said, smiling down at the little girl, though she felt a pang at the realization that Harry had already left the house.

"Niki and Zara like horses," Robby told his sister. "Zara likes white ones best. Niki likes grays."

"They told you all that?" Alessa asked, surprised.

"Sort of." Robby took a swallow of milk. "I got out my

212

picture book and we pointed."

Alessa smiled, thinking how much more easily children solved these problems. She stayed in the nursery for another quarter-hour, then went downstairs to the breakfast parlor, a sunny room in the remodeled portion of the house, where she found her mother as well as Lady Milverton, Julia, Georgiana, and Miss Beaton.

"The men have all deserted us," Georgiana said. "John's working and Simon went out for a tramp with Mr. Langley. No one seems to know where Harry is."

"Riding," Alessa said, moving to the chair the footman was holding out for her. She saw a speculative look in her mother's eyes and realized they would think she knew Harry had gone riding because he had woken in her bed. Perhaps because the fact that he had not done so rankled so much, she was determined to set the record straight. "The children told me," she added. "I was just with them." She smiled at the footman as he poured her a cup of coffee, then turned to her mother. "Robby seems to be getting on famously with Niki and Zara."

Alessa meant the words to be a peace offering, but as frequently happened when she talked to her mother, there was more than a hint of challenge in her voice.

"Robby makes friends easily," Sofia said, her eyes showing that she understood the challenge very well. "He's like his father in that respect."

Michael Langley's sympathies were decidedly republican and he had acquaintances from a variety of walks of life, some of whom, Alessa knew, her mother did not think entirely suitable. Alessa set her cup down with care, though the tension in her fingers made it rattle against the saucer. "Niki and Zara had nightmares last night," she said, including Lady Milverton and Julia in her gaze. "Somehow they'd taken it into their heads that they might be sent away from here. Harry and I assured them that they wouldn't be and that no one at Moresby could wish to see them gone."

Lady Milverton continued to stir sugar into her morning

213

tea. "The children are your concern, Alessa. I see no reason to interest myself in the matter one way or another."

That was probably the best she could hope for from her mother-in-law. Alessa looked at her own mother, a question in her eyes.

"I'm sorry," Sofia said. "I didn't mean to upset them. They bear no fault for this business."

"Then at least we are agreed on something." Alessa, who still found the quantity of food served at an English breakfast rather sickening, helped herself to a piece of toast.

An uncomfortable silence was broken by Lady Milverton, who began to talk to Sofia about the neighboring families and the entertainments planned in the next few weeks.

Julia fidgeted with her napkin, a look of impatience on her face. "The country is horridly dull in October," she burst out when her mother paused.

"You're just upset because Edward has to go to London at the end of the week." Georgiana was at the sideboard, maneuvering a second helping of cold game pie onto her plate.

"Well of course I am," Julia said, and for once Alessa had to admit that her sister-in-law was not being unreasonable. "Besides, I need to begin ordering my trousseau, and there are all sorts of preparations to make for the wedding. You don't mean to stay immured here all autumn, do you, Alessa?"

"I haven't thought much about it," Alessa said truthfully. "I'm not sure what Harry's plans are, but I don't want to unsettle the children more than necessary."

Julia raised her brows. "I would never have thought you'd take motherhood so—"

"Seriously?" Alessa asked. "Wait till you have children of your own."

"I won't . . ." Julia broke off. "That is, it doesn't do to interfere in the nursery too much, you know."

"Very true," Alessa agreed. "I'm fortunate in my nurses. They don't interfere in the least."

Georgiana choked on her chocolate. Lady Milverton ignored the conversation, and Miss Beaton copied her example. Sofia pretended to do so as well, but Alessa sensed faint approval in her mother's gaze. Before Julia could reply, the door opened and Alessa's husband walked into the room.

Harry was in riding dress, his hair ruffled by the wind, a faint sheen of perspiration on his forehead. At the sight of him, Alessa's body tensed in disconcerting places. Their eyes met and Harry smiled, a faint smile but one meant only for her. Alessa smiled back and fervently hoped the warmth in her face didn't mean she was blushing.

"You must have gone out early," Georgiana said. "I went down to the stables at seven and you weren't there then. You didn't have nightmares too, did you?"

Alessa felt her face grow warmer under the pressure of Harry's gaze. "Something like that," he said, moving to the table. "Is it too much to hope that there's some fresh coffee?"

As Harry seated himself across from her, Alessa recalled the really important event of the morning. "Alastair smiled at me," she told her husband.

"A real smile?" Harry asked, and Alessa knew he'd been as anxious for one as she had.

"A real one," she assured him. "Wait till you see. It makes him look so handsome."

Harry met her gaze over the rim of his cup and in that moment it seemed to Alessa that there was an intimacy between them that went even deeper than what they had shared last night. Then her mother spoke and the moment was shattered.

"Now that I am becoming accustomed to the fact that my grandson is not Viscount Rutledge," Sofia said, spreading butter sparingly onto a piece of toast, "perhaps you will permit me to inquire what provision will be made for him." She set down her knife and regarded Harry with a look that had once made Alessa's stomach turn somersaults.

Alessa felt a renewed flash of anger, but Harry returned Sofia's regard with every appearance of good humor. "Certainly, Princess. As you know, the marriage settlement provides handsomely for any younger sons and daughters Alessa and I may have. In addition, I have a fair amount of property not covered in the entail or the settlement. I have a house at Croyden in Hertfordshire which I intend to be Alastair's."

Surprised, for Harry had not mentioned this before, Alessa sent her husband a look of gratitude. Sofia inclined her head as if to say that though she might not forgive Harry, at least she was pleased by his action in the matter.

Lady Milverton set down her cup with a quiet click that was somehow deafening. "Croyden has been in the family for generations."

"Alastair is my son," Harry said in the same pleasant tone he had used with Sofia. "It will still be in the family."

"You've never understood what it means to be entrusted with the Dudley heritage," Lady Milverton said.

"I understand the Dudley family has accumulated an unconscionable amount throughout the years." Harry poured himself some more coffee. "When Niki comes of age, I'm going to talk to him about modifying the entail."

Incredulity suffused Lady Milverton's face. "You wouldn't."

"On the contrary," Harry said, his voice almost gentle, "I've been thinking of it for some time. Acquiring three children simply made the matter more immediate."

Incredulity gave way to anger. For a moment Alessa actually thought Lady Milverton would hurl the Staffordshire breakfast dishes at her son's head, but all she said was, "You're a fool, Harry." The words carried the weight of countless past confrontations.

"Quite possibly," Harry agreed. "But it doesn't alter my decision."

Watching the look in her mother-in-law's eyes, Alessa felt a cold prickle down her spine. There was something even worse than anger in Lady Milverton's gaze. Revulsion.

"You were never an ideal heir to the earldom." Lady Milverton delivered this dispassionate assessment with the steely precision of a gunshot. She seemed to have forgot that there was anyone else in the room. "A pity, but it happens. You might have been molded into something. Instead, you made it a point to defy us at every turn. Your profligacy was bad enough. But now—God help him, if your father could see you, he'd say you were no son of his."

Harry heard his mother out in silence, then pushed his chair back with careful deliberation. "In that case, the least I can do is not inflict my presence on you further. Good morning, ladies."

As the door shut behind Harry, Alessa clasped her hands over her stomach, sickened and appalled. Lady Milverton sat in silence as her son left the room. Julia and Georgiana regarded her with stunned surprise. Miss Beaton stared at her plate. Sofia's face wore a look of faint distaste. For all her temper, she did not approve of scenes.

Her face once more its usual composed mask, Lady Milverton set down her napkin and got to her feet. "If you'll all excuse me, I have a number of things to attend to this morning."

Head held high, Lady Milverton walked to the door. The footman opened it for her, his face wooden.

"I say," Georgiana exclaimed when her mother had left the room, "I've never heard Mama sound so beastly. I mean, she and Harry never get on well but—"

"Georgiana," Miss Beaton said firmly.

Alessa pushed back her chair. Georgiana's words reminded her of something John had said three nights ago. *A set-to with his mother always affects him more than he'll let on . . . you're his wife. You'll know better than I.* Alessa still wasn't sure she did, but she knew she had to do something. Murmuring her excuses, she hurried from the room as well, relieved that there was no sign of Lady Milverton in the corridor.

There was also no sign of Harry. The footman on duty in the hall thought he had gone out. Alessa's impatience warred with the reality of an October morning. In the end, she went upstairs and snatched up a bonnet and shawl, then hesitated again, realizing she had no idea where Harry might have gone. Fumbling with the ribbons on her bonnet, she made her way to John's office.

"Where does Harry go when he's upset?" she asked while John was still murmuring a surprised greeting.

Comprehension showed in John's eyes. "There was another confrontation?"

"A battle royal," Alessa told him.

John grimaced. "When he disappeared as a boy, I always found him near the stream."

Not at all sure what she meant to say or even how welcome she would be, Alessa made her way along winding flagstone paths bordered by thick green grass and overhung by tangled oak until she reached the banks of the stream which meandered through the Moresby grounds. The sky was a heavy gray, but the air held the clean, cool scent of an English morning.

As John had predicted, she found Harry sitting on a low stone wall which ran along the path bordering the stream. He was leaning forward, hands linked around his knees. Something about the pose reminded her of Simon. He looked very young.

Alessa walked forward, very conscious of the sound of her footfalls on the flagstones, still damp from the morning mist. "Do you mind if I join you?"

Harry looked up and in that first unguarded moment she saw the wealth of pain in his eyes. Then he gave a strained smile. "I'm not the best of company just now."

"I know. That's why I came." Alessa perched on the wall, close but not touching him. That didn't seem right. Not yet. Last night she had taken his body inside her own, but this was a very different sort of situation. When it came to Harry's relationship with his family, she still felt she was in uncharted waters.

"I must confess I've never liked your mother much," Alessa said, her eyes on the red-brown leaves of the beech at the water's edge. "But I never actually hated her until this

218

morning."

To her relief, Harry laughed. "Poor Alessa. I should never have inflicted her on you." He hesitated a moment. "At the time, I didn't feel I could ask her to leave Moresby and Milverton House. I'm not sure I can make you understand . . ."

"I think I do," Alessa said. "Now. If you'd got on better with her, you might have asked her to go."

Harry looked at her, his eyes showing gratitude that she had understood. "I've always been a disappointment to her— that ought to be clear enough by now. I didn't feel I could add to it by tossing her out of her home. In any case, I thought I'd learned to be impervious. Christ." He brought his fist down on the rough gray stones of the wall with sudden violence. "What I hate more than anything," he said in a low, bitter voice, "is that their opinion still matters to me after all these years."

"Your mother and father?" Alessa asked. Harry rarely spoke of his father.

For a long moment Harry was silent, making Alessa acutely conscious of the rush of the stream and the scurrying of small animals in the grass along its banks.

"My earliest memory is of my father catching me climbing the hayrick and telling me future earls didn't make a spectacle of themselves," he said at last. "I think then and there I made up my mind that if that's what it took to be a proper earl I wasn't going to oblige him."

"And you spent the next twenty years proving it." Alessa felt as if, for the first time, she could begin to fit the fragments of Harry's life into a coherent pattern.

"With a vengeance. There seemed to be no escape from it, no chance to be anything but what they wanted me to be. My parents didn't visit the nursery often, but when they did, they didn't come to see me. They came to see the Viscount Rutledge."

Alessa thought of the burdens which had been placed on Simon almost from the day he was born. And then she thought of how insupportable those burdens would have been if not tempered by affection. "It's not an easy life to be born to," she said.

"Easier than most," Harry said with a wry grimace. "I used to tell Ned he was lucky to be a younger son. He'd tell me I was a fool." Harry stared down at his hands. "The devil of it was, I could never really believe it all."

"Believe what?" Alessa asked, watching him.

"That being born a Dudley automatically set me apart from others. That being my father's firstborn son gave me an inalienable right to all—all this." He made a vague gesture encompassing Moresby and all it represented.

Alessa was surprised. She had never questioned what it meant to be a Tassio, and though she knew Harry was reform-minded, she had never heard him speak in quite such terms before. "You sound like Guy Melchett," she said, thinking of Fiona's cousin, a playwright known for his radical views.

"My thoughts were hardly so coherent," Harry said. "I just couldn't take the whole thing quite seriously. It drove my father wild. He became even more determined to force me into his mold, and it became my primary goal in life to revolt whenever possible. I actually did organize a revolt at Eton, you know. Ten of us took one of the masters prisoner and wrote up a highly improbable list of demands. I'm sure I would have been sent down if I hadn't been a Dudley."

"Simon and Peter ran away from Eton," Alessa said. "It sounds an absolutely brutal place. Harry," she added, reminded of something which hadn't seemed particularly important until she'd had children of her own, "I don't want Niki and Alastair to go away to school."

"Nor do I. I see no reason we can't break another Dudley tradition while we're at it."

The humor in his voice was welcome, but Alessa did not want to stem this rare tide of confidences. "Was it the same at university?" she asked.

"More or less. I don't recall taking anyone prisoner and I

actually began to think a bit. All that reading does expose one to a remarkable number of ideas. When I had the chance a few years later, I got as far away as I could from Moresby and all it represented."

"Russia."

"Father didn't think his heir had any business joining the diplomatic corps, but considering the way I was behaving by that time, the senior generation of Dudleys agreed it might be best if I got out of England."

"Drinking, gaming, and wenching," Alessa said in a cheerful voice, though her chest tightened painfully at this last. "Typical behavior for any well-born young man, I would think."

Harry grinned. "It wasn't the behavior as much as the fact that I did it in low company. I was determined to enjoy my freedom while I could. At Oxford I began to understand that there might be more important things to do in life than battle with my father, but my main concern was avoiding the shackles of my position."

"What changed you?" Alessa asked.

"Nadia," Harry said, his eyes on the ground below.

Though she winced inwardly at the mention of Harry's first wife, Alessa subdued the impulse to draw in upon herself. Instead, she lifted her hand and placed it over Harry's. She felt a shock of surprise run through him. But when he disengaged his fingers from hers, it was only so he could put his arm around her and pull her to rest against him. Leaning into the warmth of his body, Alessa found she could hear him speak of Nadia without pain.

"My father had been lecturing me about the responsibilities of the earldom for years," Harry said, his breath stirring her hair, "but when Nadia came to me, I felt truly responsible for someone else for the first time in my life. I think it was then I decided to make something of being the Earl of Milverton, rather than rebelling against it."

Alessa thought with pride of the reforms Harry had instituted on his estates and the bills he had championed in Parliament. "You're a dangerous man, Harry Dudley."

Harry laughed, his arm tightening pleasantly around her. "My Uncle George said that to me once. I don't think it was meant as a compliment."

"You've done splendidly." Alessa let her head sink farther into his shoulder, determined to erase the sting of his mother's words.

"I don't think I've made a complete mull of it. And yet . . ."

"What?" The doubt in his voice made Alessa lift her head to look at him.

"It's just that in a perfect world there wouldn't be an Earl of Milverton."

Alessa was again brought up short. "The world isn't perfect," she pointed out. "And you are the Earl of Milverton. Besides, it seems to me that there are times when you like it."

"Like it? Oh, yes," Harry said with more than a trace of self-mockery. "It's just that I don't believe in it."

Alessa was not sure what answer to make. Before she could speak, Harry stood and swung her down to stand in front of him. "Enough self-pity for one morning, don't you think?" His face growing serious, he lifted his hand and laid it against her cheek. "Thank you, wife. Brooding alone is a thankless occupation."

It was the first time he had called her "wife." Feeling a welling of joy within her, Alessa covered his fingers with her own. They walked back along the path together, Harry's arm encircling her shoulders. By the time they reached the house, the feel of Harry's body beside her own had stirred some highly inappropriate thoughts about how they might spend the remainder of the morning. But Alessa was not yet so bold. Besides, she still wanted Harry to see Alastair smile.

"I'm going to take Alastair to the nursery to play with the children," she said as Harry held open a side door for her. "Could I persuade you to come with me?"

Harry grinned, the strain of a short time ago gone from his face. "I'll meet you up there. I want to look through the post first."

When they reached the end of the corridor, Harry drew her back out of view of the footman in the hall and kissed her. It was a light kiss, but his lips held the same desire which was wreaking havoc with her thoughts. Buoyant with unexpected happiness, Alessa went to her room and gathered up Alastair, then carried him to the nursery. If she could not have everything she would wish for from her marriage, it seemed she might have more than she had ever thought to have.

She was sitting on the nursery hearth rug, watching Robby, Niki, and Zara turn the pages of a picture book, when Harry came into the room. Alessa looked up, eager to have him beside her, and felt her happiness give way to a chill of apprehension. Harry's eyes told her that in their brief separation something had happened which threatened the new closeness between them.

Holding Alastair in her arms, Alessa got to her feet and went to her husband's side. "What is it?" she asked.

Harry smiled and Alessa felt the chill intensify. It was a smile of apology. Instinctively, she braced herself for painful news.

"This is a damnable time to tell you," Harry said, taking her hand, "but I've had a letter from Castlereagh. I'm afraid — it looks as if I'm going to have to go to Aix-la-Chapelle after all."

•

Chapter Fourteen

"I thought Harry wasn't going to Aix-la-Chapelle." Peter had ridden over from Sundon that morning and was walking with Simon along the stream that ran a quarter-mile north of the house. The stream boasted some fine fishing, but its attraction for the boys was its seclusion. Too far from the house to be considered part of the gardens, running between steep banks thickly planted with ash and willow and overgrown with gorse and blackthorn and bullace, its appeal was known only to the generations of Dudley children who had used it for exploration and mock battles and dreaming.

There was no sound save the trill of a thrush, the running water, and the crunch of their feet on the yellowed leaves. "He didn't want to go," Simon said, pushing aside the branches of a willow that overhung their path. "Then he got a letter from Lord Castlereagh urging him to come, if only for a few days." Simon looked back at Peter and grinned. "When the Foreign Secretary says you're indispensable, it's hard to say no."

They found a bare patch of ground just above the stream and stretched out, watching the play of quivering light on the water. The stream fell here, plashing over stones worn smooth by time, into a small pool. A dark shape darted in the depths and disappeared among the rocks. "Does your sister mind?" Peter asked.

"Alessa was furious. Harry had promised he wouldn't go

224

and then he broke his promise and left her to cope with *Maman* and Lady Milverton on her own. Then Michael had to go back to London, and that made *Maman* upset so she hasn't been in the best of tempers. And Edward had to go to London too, which made Julia go into a fit of the sulks. John's the only man about, but Lady Milverton makes sure he knows his place. I tell you, it's been devilishly fierce about here this past week."

"Women." Peter rolled onto his back and stared up into the trees. "Fiona's different. She's sensible. Radka's different too. She's not at all like Julia."

"She's not even like Alessa." Simon was very fond of his sister, but he spoke with the clarity of lifelong acquaintance.

"I like Alessa." There was a hint of reprimand in Peter's voice. "I feel sorry for her."

"Don't. She's stronger than you think. *Maman's* been determined to prove that Niki isn't Harry's son. She'd already written a letter to Cousin Sacha when Alessa put a stop to it."

"How?"

"By telling her she'd already enlisted Cousin Elisabeth's help. Not that anything came of that. And it made Harry furious. That's why they'd hardly speak to each other all the way back to England."

Peter sat up and wrapped his arms around his knees. "Marriage is so bloody awful. Most of the time. My father and Fiona are really happy. Maybe you have to try it twice to make sure it works."

"Maybe you shouldn't be in such a devilish hurry."

"It's different if you've found the right girl."

Simon stifled a clever retort. Peter's feelings ran dangerously close to the surface. Simon pulled the stalk of a weed and chewed it thoughtfully. "Yes, I suppose so."

Peter picked up a clump of the warm earth and let it trickle through his fingers. "Do you suppose we'll ever see her again?"

Simon hesitated, not wanting to raise false hopes. "It's not likely, is it?"

225

"It's so bloody unfair," Peter said, his voice throbbing with passion. "I can't bear to think of her married off to a lecherous old man. To think of his mouth—his hands—Oh, God Simon, why didn't we do something?"

Simon had asked himself the same question more than once. He had wanted to help Radka, but there hadn't seemed anything they could usefully do, and he felt his failure keenly. "We weren't very clever, were we?" Then he remembered what Fiona had told him when he was young. *If you haven't the power yourself, use the power of others.* "We'll talk to Harry when he gets back," he said with sudden decision. "Radka's uncle will be at the conference and Harry's bound to talk to him. He'll know how things stand. And then I'll ask *Maman* to write to Cousin Sacha."

Peter's face showed the dawning of hope. "Will she do it?"

"She will," Simon said with more certainty than he felt. "When she was Radka's age, she wanted to run off with Michael, but her parents made her marry my father instead. She'll remember how it feels. And if she won't remember . . ."

Peter grinned. "You can ask Michael to remind her."

Alessa put down her pencil and surveyed her drawing with a critical eye. The apple orchard at the end of the garden was well rendered, the gnarled trees that were old even by Moresby standards bowing their branches under the weight of autumnal fruit, but she was dissatisfied. Something was missing, perhaps the winy smell of the windfalls on the ground, perhaps the unexpected warmth of the sun on this mid-October day.

No, it wasn't the drawing. Lately nothing seemed right. It had been eleven, no, twelve days since Harry had left, and she missed him more than she cared to admit. She looked down at Alastair lying in a basket beside her, his mouth making contented sucking noises as he slept. Alastair should be enough. She had a beautiful son and two engaging older children besides, and a husband who was not totally indiffer-

226

ent. But Harry kept much of his life secret from her. He didn't need her, not in the way she feared she needed him.

Alessa looked toward the orchard where Niki, Zara, and Robby were chasing each other through the apple trees. On a nearby bench Galina sat bent over her embroidery, a cross-stich table runner heavy with red and black and gold thread, an echo of pieces Alessa had known from her childhood. Galina looked up from her work and gave her employer a searching look. "You are not feeling well?"

"I'm quite well," Alessa said, "only a little fatigued."

"Of course," Galina murmured, returning to her stitching. The shouts and laughter of the children echoed across the garden. "They are happy," Galina said, looking toward the orchard. "But I think you are not. Perhaps you miss your husband."

It was an unpardonable piece of impertinence, coming from a servant, but Alessa had long since ceased to regard Galina in that light. "I do miss him," she said, finding some relief in the admission. "The days are tedious."

A mischievous smile crossed Galina's face, "And the nights."

"Outrageous," Alessa said, not sure whether to laugh or cry. "Galina, you must not—"

"You're a merry pair." John came into the garden and regarded the two women. "What is it Galina must not do?"

"It's nothing," Alessa said quickly. "Only women's talk."

"Ah, then I should withdraw."

"Not at all. We were in want of company."

"As I was myself." John moved closer to the easel and studied the drawing in the open sketch book. "You have a gift, Alessa. Galina, what do you think?" They had been speaking in Russian, but he quickly repeated the question in English.

"I like picture," Galina said, the English words coming with difficulty to her lips.

"I like *the* picture."

"*The* picture," Galina repeated with an uncharacteristic blush. "I am trying hard to learn, Mr. Dudley."

"You're doing very well," John said, sitting down beside her. "She has a good ear," he told Alessa. "In six months she'll be chattering away just like every other English woman."

"You're making fun of me," Galina said, reverting to Russian.

"Never." John laid his hand over hers, then drew it away as he became conscious of Alessa's eyes on him. "You're my favorite pupil."

After the fair, John had taken it on himself to teach Galina English, and she was making remarkable progress. He was ostensibly tutoring the children as well, but Alessa had no doubt that Galina was the reason he so frequently neglected his desk. She prayed his gallantry was no more than that and that Galina, who was watching him with admiration in her wide blue eyes, would be sensible.

The children erupted from the apple trees laughing and screaming and threw themselves upon John, begging to be taken for a walk. John ruffled their hair and looked at Alessa in inquiry. "If your mother . . ."

He looked so wistful Alessa could not help but laugh. "Go John, go. I'm sure Harry would say the accounts can wait."

Galina had folded her embroidery with a haste that showed she intended to be one of the party. Alessa felt a surge of sympathy for the other woman. Playing child's nurse did not allow one much time for gaiety, and surely nothing untoward could happen when they were in the children's company.

Still their going left a void. Alessa picked up Alastair, who was beginning to stir, and carried him up to his room, where he claimed her attention for the better part of an hour. Then, leaving him in the company of Louise, she went downstairs, finding the house strangely empty. Simon had taken Georgiana to Sundon to visit the Carnes. Lady Milverton, Julia, and Sofia were paying a call on a neighboring family, but had failed to persuade Alessa to join them. Feeling an intense longing for her husband, Alessa paused on the half-landing, then ran quickly down the wide stairs to the ground

228

floor and made her way to his study.

She had not gone there often and then her attention had been on Harry. Now she saw the room for itself, stark and unadorned, its only decorative element a pair of watercolors of the stream where they had talked the day he told her he was going to Aix-la-Chapelle. The afternoon sun spilled through the casement windows, making bars of light on the worn Turkey carpet and the polished mahogany of the desk. The desk was bare save for a sheaf of writing paper and a silver inkstand.

Alessa moved behind the desk and pulled out the chair. Sitting there she could feel the ghost of her husband's presence. It was a comforting conceit, she thought, running her hand over the worn surface of the desk. There was little else in the room save a small table that stood against the wall near the door, two mismatched chairs for visitors, and a leather sofa in which her husband sometimes sprawled when fatigue or worry drove him away from his work.

Alessa smiled and pushed her chair away from the desk. It was then she noticed the central drawer was slightly ajar. In an impulse toward tidiness, she pushed it closed, only to find that the drawer would not move. Annoyed, she bent down and jiggled it, but to no effect. It's crooked, she thought, pulling the drawer out so she could straighten it. It resisted her pull, then all at once came free.

The drawer was filled with an assortment of papers, a few small, smooth-surfaced rocks that must have come from the streambed, a faded ribbon, and a bright blue feather from a jay. Harry's? Or his father's? Alessa gently pushed the drawer back, then stopped as she caught the signature on the letter that lay on top of the pile of papers. Castlereagh. It must be the letter that had changed Harry's mind and sent him off to Aix-la-Chapelle.

Curious, Alessa picked it up and read it through. It was, she conceded, a flattering plea. The Foreign Secretary thought much of Harry's experience and called his presence indispensable. For a few days only, Castlereagh said. In that

Harry had been truthful. He would not be kept away from England for long.

She was about to put the letter back when she caught sight of the one that had been lying beneath it. Her heart lurched and her throat went tight. It was a woman's writing, she would swear to it, and it was in French, dated only a few weeks before. Without thinking, Alessa laid down the Foreign Secretary's letter and picked up the other. *My dear Harry,* it read. *I have arranged it at last. I am going to Aix-la-Chapelle with my brother-in-law, Count Chernikov, who is accompanying the Emperor. I have your promise. Come, please come. I count on you not to fail me. With gratitude and affection . . .*

Alessa did not need to read the signature. She had noticed it at once. It was burned into her mind. Marina. He had gone to see Marina.

Something died within her. She felt shriveled and empty, like a husk of corn. The sun warmed her back but she was cold within. Once more Harry had lied. No, not lied, he had simply not told her the whole story. With Harry this seemed to pass for truth.

With great care Alessa returned the letters to their original position and closed the drawer. Then she rose, returned the chair to its exact position behind the desk, and left the room.

By the time she had walked down the hall to the great staircase, the chill had gone, to be replaced by a blaze of fury. Harry had betrayed her, was betraying her even now and the fact that she had given him this freedom when they made their marriage arrangements did not make it any easier to bear.

A thousand bird wings seemed to be beating in her breast. Alessa grasped the stair rail for support and slowly mounted the stairs. She was dimly conscious of voices from outside and the steps of a footman crossing the hall. As she reached the landing, she turned and looked down into the hall. Her mother had returned with Lady Milverton and Julia. Julia was talking in a high-pitched voice, but Alessa could not distinguish the words.

230

All at once her life at Moresby seemed insupportable. She would not spend another day enduring her mother's displeasure and Julia's whining and her mother-in-law's scorn. With a sense that she was at last taking control of her life, Alessa ran downstairs and confronted the three women. "Maman, I fear I must ask you to cut your visit short. I am returning to London."

In the event, it was the morning of the third day before Alessa was able to set off from Moresby. Julia insisted on accompanying her, and Lady Milverton, grumbling all the while about the unseemly haste of their departure, came along as a matter of course. Edward was in London, she said, and Alessa would be far too occupied with the children to serve as chaperone. Sofia, who had little choice in the matter, made no objection to leaving Moresby. She, too, chose London as her destination. Michael was there and she missed him. She did not say that she was also concerned about her daughter, but Alessa knew this was the case.

The prospect of the diversion of London lifted everyone's spirits, and the women of the house were far more in charity with each other than they had been since the departure of the men. John traveled with them, saying he had business to see to in London, though Alessa wondered if he would have been quite so eager if it were not for Galina. Only Simon had qualms about leaving the relative freedom of Moresby for the closer supervision he was bound to have in his mother's house, but on being informed that the Carnes would also shortly remove to London, he became reconciled to the event.

For a few days Alessa held her fears at bay. The problems of settling children, nurses, and Georgiana's governess and becoming reacquainted with the London staff took a great deal of her time. She began to make plans for Alastair's christening. There were bills to be paid, and squabbles among the servants, and some repairs to the house that should not be put off till Harry's return.

But the house and children soon ceased to occupy all of her attention, and she was faced with a return of her former agitation. In desperation she sought out Fiona, who had recently arrived in town, and poured out the story of Harry's betrayal. "I came to London in search of distraction," Alessa told her, "and I can't bear it any better here than I could at Moresby. We've had innumerable callers, and though the town is thin of company, there's no dearth of invitations. Lady Milverton and Julia are out almost every night and I use any excuse I can think of to avoid accompanying them. I loved parties, Fiona. You remember. And now I find them tedious beyond anything. I adored gossip and now it bores me. The truth is, I shall not be settled until Harry returns, and even then . . . Fiona, how am I to live with him knowing he went off to the Continent to meet another woman?"

Fiona gave her a look in which compassion was tempered with doubt. Without comment she refilled Alessa's teacup and pressed it into her hand. "Why are you so sure it's a tryst?"

"What other reason could there be?" The teacup rattled in its saucer and Alessa stilled it with her other hand. "Marina Chernikova is a beautiful woman and Harry admires her tremendously. If there were another reason for their meeting he would have had no need to keep it secret. I know she's older than he is, but that only seems to add to a woman's attraction. Adrian . . ."

She broke off, unwilling to pursue this line of thought. Adrian's mistress had been Gideon's first wife. Alessa swallowed a mouthful of tea, found it bitter, and set down the cup.

"I think," Fiona said thoughtfully, "that you must have this out with Harry."

Alessa clenched her hands. "And admit that I read his private papers? How could I?"

"You did nothing so very wrong. And if you did, it's noth

232

ing compared to this wound festering between you. You must ask him for the truth."

"I know the truth."

"Perhaps. Perhaps not. But you must hear it from his lips. And then you can decide how you want to get on with your life."

Alessa had hoped for more sympathy from her former governess, but like Sofia, Fiona was given to bracing reminders that the world must be taken as one found it. "I suppose you're right," Alessa admitted, thinking that she would rather die than confront Harry about his mistress. "I should do it. Yes, I must. I will." She rose abruptly and walked to the window which looked out on the garden in back of the house. The younger Carne children were playing hide and seek in the shrubbery. The sight brought painful reminders of how much more successful the Carne marriage was than her own.

She was still standing there when the door to Fiona's sitting room opened and a footman announced that Mr. Melchett had called and would like to see Lady Carne. "Which Mr. Melchett?" Fiona asked. She was half-sister to several Melchetts and she had Melchett cousins besides.

"Mr. Adrian, madam."

Alessa whirled round. Adrian? He was safely in India, where, she had prayed, he would spend the rest of his life. She had never thought to see him again. She had never wanted to see him again. And now, improbably, he was here, in the house he had once called his own.

Alessa looked at Fiona and read the shock in her eyes, no greater than the shock that must have been in her own. Fiona made an uncharacteristic gesture of helplessness. "I should see him," she murmured. "If you'd rather not . . ."

Of course Alessa would rather not. She could not bear to confront the first man she had loved, the man who had betrayed both her love and her trust, the man who had made it possible for her to enter into a marriage of convenience with Harry. She stared at Fiona, feeling the revulsion which

233

Adrian's name evoked, feeling too an unworthy curiosity to see him once again. Curiosity won out, aided by a desire to avoid any imputation of cowardice. If Adrian was in London, they were bound to meet sooner or later. Better here, in the safety of Fiona's sitting room, than in a public place where people who knew their history would be sure to gossip.

"No," Alessa said firmly, resuming her seat. "I will stay."

Fiona studied her a moment. Then, apparently satisfied by what she saw in Alessa's face, she turned to the footman. "Show him up."

The footman bowed and left the room. The women waited in silence. There was nothing they could say that would not be dangerous to speak, nothing that would fail to open old wounds. Alessa's heart beat faster, and she was grateful that she was seated with her back to the door. Holding herself very still, she listened for his entrance, wondering if he had changed, if he would seem as handsome as she remembered, if he would still have the power to hurt her.

The door opened, Adrian's name was announced, and Alessa heard his soft footfalls as he crossed the floor to the carpeted area where they sat. He made Fiona a graceful bow. "Thank you for receiving me."

His back was toward her and Alessa could not see his face, but the voice was the same and the erect carriage.

Fiona held out her hand to forestall a more intimate salute. Alessa envied her composure. "Why shouldn't I receive my brother?" Fiona said. "I'm very happy to see you."

"And I to see you again, though you may have reason to doubt me," Adrian said in a serious tone which surprised Alessa. He paused, then added, "I assure you, that's behind me now."

"Then we needn't speak of it." Fiona gestured toward Alessa. "You'll remember Alessandra di Tassio. She's Lady Milverton now."

Adrian spun round. There was shock in his blue eyes, but he recovered quickly and gave Alessa the smile that had once made her heart turn over with longing. His skin was a shade darker than it had been, the lines in his face a little deeper, but he was still slim, his fair hair set off by the yellow hangings in the room, his charm a palpable presence.

Alessa did not trust his charm. She gave him her hand to prove that she was now immune to his touch. "Hullo, Adrian."

He took her hand but held it only briefly. "Alessa." His voice was tinged with regret. "I must congratulate you."

"You must congratulate me twice," she said, holding his gaze. "I have a son."

"Then you are fortunate. You have my warmest wishes for your happiness."

It was a pretty speech. Despite her intentions not to trust him, Alessa could not but feel that it was genuine.

Adrian sat with them for the next half-hour, talking of his experiences in India. He had developed a taste for business, he said, and he had made a great deal of money. That put an end to Alessa's notion that he had come to Fiona because he was short of the ready. In the days when Alessa had known him, he had constantly overspent his lavish income. But now he had grown up. Or it seemed that he had.

By the time he rose to take his leave, Alessa was still not sure if she could believe his seeming transformation, but she felt more charitable toward him than she had on his arrival. And she could not but take pleasure in the obvious admiration in his eyes when he spoke to her.

"How are the children? Peter and Teddy and Beth," Adrian asked Fiona before he left.

"Very well," Fiona said, though it seemed to Alessa that she stiffened slightly. "Come, you can see them from the window."

He followed her across the room and watched the children silently. "The younger one is yours?"

"Yes, our daughter Fenella. She's three."

"She looks charming." He seemed about to say more, then thought better of it. Telling Fiona that he expected to remain in London and hoped to see more of her, he took his leave.

His departure left a feeling of emptiness in the room. Alessa saw Fiona's gaze upon her. "It's all right," she said. "It wasn't as bad as I feared."

"No," Fiona agreed. "Anticipation is always worse than the reality."

"India seems to have changed him."

Fiona looked thoughtful. "Perhaps."

She said no more, but Alessa was unwilling to let the matter rest. "How odd of him to ask after the children," she said after a moment. "He didn't know them well. Was he just being polite?"

A shadow of pain crossed Fiona's face. "I think not. I think he came to ask after the children. After Beth." Fiona clasped her hands in her lap. "Beth isn't Gideon's daughter, Alessa. She's Adrian's."

"Adrian's? I didn't know," Alessa whispered, a sudden pain constricting her heart. Aline had been dead before Alessa had known him, but she had discovered, almost too late, that he loved her still. Adrian and Aline. Harry and Marina. Her life seemed to have a way of repeating itself. Feeling doubly betrayed, Alessa took a hasty farewell of her friend and asked her coachman to drive her home.

When the coach pulled up in Portman Square, Alessa hurried into the house, eager to find a quiet refuge where she could think about Adrian and the storm of feelings his visit had unleashed. The footman informed her that the Dowager Lady Milverton and Lady Julia were out. Relieved, Alessa crossed to the hall table where the post was laid out and sorted rapidly through the letters, foolishly hoping there might be one from Harry. There was none. How stupid she was being. Harry had no way of knowing she was in London.

Telling the footman there was nothing she required and she did not want to be disturbed, she climbed the two flights of stairs to the suite of rooms that was her own. She closed the door of her boudoir behind her, tossed her letters on a table, stripped off her pelisse and bonnet, and threw herself on the chaise longue. At last she would have time to think. Or would if she were not a mother. Alastair's cry from the adjoining room claimed her attention for the better part of the next hour.

He was a healing force, Alessa decided when she at last returned to her boudoir. Her agitation had diminished and Adrian's return no longer seemed of such desperate consequence. She picked up the pile of letters and sorted through them once more. Feminine hands, all of them. They had to be cards of invitation. All save one, which was addressed in a bold but unfamiliar masculine scrawl. Curious, Alessa slit it open and unfolded the sheet of paper.

The language was French. Startled, Alessa glanced at the signature. *Captain Grigor Lychenko*. Lychenko, the man she had not trusted in Russia. Lychenko had no business thrusting himself into their lives in England.

A tremor of alarm went through her and she crushed the letter in her hand. Forcing herself to stay calm, she sat down on the chaise longue, smoothed the paper carefully, and read what he had to say.

My dear Lady Milverton, he began. *I find myself unexpectedly in London. A misunderstanding with a fellow officer made me judge it wise to leave Russia for a time. But I am happy to be in England, for I think perhaps I can be of service to you. I have information which you will find curious and of undoubted value. If you are interested in your son's future, please meet me at my lodgings tomorrow afternoon between three and five o'clock. I will not call upon you, for I do not care to meet your husband.* Then he didn't know that Harry was on the Continent. *The information is for you alone. I am at the Golden Cross in Charing Cross Road. Tomorrow, without fail. I remain your obedient servant . . .*

Alessa read the letter twice, then laid it aside. Grigor Lychenko could have only one reason for seeing her and not Harry. Niki was not Harry's son, as she had suspected from

237

the beginning. Alastair was his heir. Alessa felt a surge of happiness, tempered by guilt at the thought of the little boy of whom she had grown so fond. Lady Milverton and her own mother would be beside themselves with joy. But she would not abandon Niki, not for the world. He was their son and they would raise him as their own.

But what would Harry say? There would have to be proof, irrefutable proof, before he would believe Niki was not his son. Even then he would be devastated. She had seen his eyes glow with the pride of fatherhood when he looked at Niki. Perhaps he would blame her for what Lychenko had to say.

Alessa clenched her hands, recalling their quarrel in Russia when Harry had learned of her inquiries about Lychenko. But for Alastair's sake, she had to keep this appointment. Her farce of a marriage could be no worse for whatever she might learn.

When Lady Milverton and Julia returned, Alessa pleaded a blinding headache. She would not join them for dinner, nor would she accompany them to the Warwicks' rout, but she trusted they would have an enjoyable evening. This done, she escaped to her room, where she had her dinner on a tray and enjoyed a few precious hours of solitude.

Alessa could not sleep. It was past eleven when she made her way to the library, thinking to distract herself with the latest novel by Philippa, the clever sister of her friends, the Davenports. She had just started down the stairs to the ground floor when she heard a commotion in the hall and then the unexpected sound of her husband's voice. She stopped, her heart beating wildly in her chest. Harry. He had come home. Uncertain how she was to face him, she hesitated. So much had happened that drove a wedge between them—Marina's letter, Lychenko's, even Adrian's return.

But her need was too great. She ran down the stairs and

238

stopped once more, her legs trembling with shock. Harry was there, but he was not alone. A woman was beside him, a slender woman in a fur-lined cloak, its hood framing and concealing her face. The woman was turned toward Harry and her gloved hand rested on his arm in an intimate gesture. Alessa had seen that gesture before, in the ballroom at Tsarkoe Selo. It wasn't possible. He would not dare.

But he had. The woman moved away from Harry and turned her head. It was Marina Chernikova, and behind her stood her daughter, Radka.

Chapter Fifteen

"I didn't expect you," Alessa said, walking carefully down the last two steps and across the wide expanse of hall toward her husband. By a miracle her voice was calm, as though it were an everyday matter for her to receive his mistress under her roof. By another miracle her hands did not tremble, though she feared her body would tear asunder from rage and chagrin. "Welcome home, Harry." She inclined her head slightly. "Countess. Radka."

For an instant Harry's face showed a look of blank surprise. Then he smiled, a smile as false as hell. "Alessa. I didn't expect you."

"No, I don't suppose you did. We've been in London over a week. Your mother and Julia are out tonight. I'm afraid John has gone to bed. Are you staying with us, Countess?"

The question was pointed and unnecessary. Not all of the luggage littering the hall was Harry's. A look of dismay passed across Marina's face. She turned to Harry, a question in her eyes, but before she could speak he intervened. "The countess and her daughter will be our guests, Alessa. Until things are settled."

Settled? What was to be settled? "Then in that case I must see that your rooms are made ready. Harry, take our guests to the drawing room. Would you like some refreshments, Countess? You've had a long journey. Some wine? Tea?" Alessa turned to Radka, toward whom she felt more charita-

240

ble. The girl seemed to be wilting, no doubt from fatigue, though her eyes were frightened. Alessa's voice grew warmer. "Are you hungry? I can arrange a light supper."

Marina put an arm around her daughter. "Please do not trouble yourself, Lady Milverton. We've upset the household enough as it is. One room will be enough for tonight. Radka will sleep with me."

The statement was meant to reassure. Alessa would have her husband to herself for this night at least. Or perhaps it was meant to give Harry time to tell his wife that he intended to install his mistress in London. Or that he was through with playing at marriage.

Alessa glanced at Harry, who was giving some instructions to one of the footmen. "Then if you'll excuse me," she said in a carefully modulated voice, "I'll just speak to the housekeeper."

She rejoined them in the drawing room some twenty minutes later. She had debated giving Marina a room as far away from Harry's as possible, then giving her one near her own suite so that she might know when the countess was receiving visitors. In the end she was sensible and told the housekeeper to prepare the yellow bedchamber, a small but sunny corner room, the best of the guest rooms the house had to offer. If Harry wanted to visit Marina, he would find a way to do so, no matter where she placed her.

The drawing room was quiet when she entered. Radka was sitting erect on a small bentwood chair, but she seemed in imminent danger of falling asleep. Harry was sprawled on a sofa which had ample room for another person, but Marina had chosen a chair near her daughter. So, they were going to observe the proprieties, at least in public. It was something to be grateful for.

"Your room should be ready in a few minutes," Alessa said with a sympathetic glance at Radka. "I've had your luggage sent up. There's a room adjoining which will be made up tomorrow for Radka. Is there anything I can get you?"

241

Marina rose. "Thank you, no. You've been more than kind."

"Not at all," Alessa said, cutting short any talk in this vein. She had not been kind at all, and Marina, who seemed a perceptive woman, was sure to be aware of it. "If you'll come with me, I'll show you the way."

Marina picked up her cloak and prepared to follow Alessa. "Radka."

The girl had risen too, a pale wraith in a white dress who looked insubstantial next to her vibrant mother. Alessa, who had never had any doubt about her own attractions, felt she could forgive Marina everything but her beauty.

"Good night, Harry," Marina said with quite unnecessary warmth. "Thank you. Thank you for everything." Then she followed her daughter and Alessa out of the room.

"I am so happy to be in England," Radka said with some return of animation. "Is your brother here, Lady Milverton?"

"He's in London," Alessa said, disliking the ties that bound the Chernikovs to her own family, "but he lives with our mother."

"I would so like to see him again. And his friend Peter."

Alessa had noted Peter's infatuation with the young girl but did not know if Radka harbored any tender feelings for either Simon or Peter. Radka's artless comments did not make her preference clear. Please God, let it not be Simon. It would be too much to have both her husband and her brother bewitched by the Chernikov women.

"They're both in London," Alessa told Radka with some reluctance. Then, because she was not without sympathy for the girl, she added, "I'm sure they'll want to call upon you."

Alessa escaped at last to her own room, having said a formal good night to Marina and forestalled any further expressions of gratitude. Her head ached and her throat was tight with unshed tears. She was too restless to sleep and too agitated to sit still, so she paced the room, which seemed to be closing in upon her like a cage. Lost in thoughts that repeated themselves over and over in her brain, she was not at first aware that the noise she heard was someone rapping at the door. She stopped suddenly, listening, then walked quickly to the door and pulled it open. It was Harry.

He came in without asking leave, forcing her to retreat before him. His face showed uncertainty and concern and determination. He knew she was angry and her anger fed his own. But he knew also that he owed her an apology and he quickly made it.

"I'm sorry," he said, "I did not mean to overset you. Even had I known you were in London, there was no time to warn you of our coming." Harry hesitated, then made a gesture as though he would put his arms around her. Alessa retreated another step. It was like a slap. Harry saw it and his tone grew more formal. "I'm sorry if you've been inconvenienced."

"Inconvenienced? Is that what you call it?" The agony she had suffered in the last hour erupted in a blaze of passion. "Harry, how could you? How could you bring that woman here, to our house? Why are you trying to humiliate me in this way? I hadn't expected much from our marriage, but I thought I could expect discretion on your part."

"Discretion?" Harry stared at her as though she had gone suddenly mad. "Good God, what is it you accuse me of?"

"Search your heart, Harry. What do you think?"

The blood rose in his face. "I thought I knew you. I thought we—"

"I thought I knew you too. It seems I did not." Alessa drew her shawl more closely around her shoulders. "I don't want to talk about it, Harry. Tell me what you want of me and I'll try to be a dutiful wife. But don't expect me to connive in this farce you seem bent on playing."

In two strides Harry was before her, his hands clutching her arms in a painful grip. "You're a fool. But by God, you'll put this poison from your mind and hear me out."

Confused, Alessa turned her head away. "No."

Harry pushed her into a chair, none too gently, and stood before her so she could not escape. "You will listen to me, Alessa. I have a story to tell you."

She looked up and met his gaze. He was as angry as she had ever seen him, but the anger was tempered by sorrow and fatigue. Her own anger had abated. Feeling bewildered and lost, she made a gesture of acquiescence.

Harry stepped back. "Very well." He drew a breath. "This isn't about Marina. It's about Radka."

"Radka?" Alessa's voice was hoarse with spent passion.

"Radka. Her guardian is her uncle, her father's brother, Count Chernikov. He controls her fortune and her person. He's an ambitious man and intends to use Radka to further his ambitions. He's already arranged her marriage. The man is nearly three times her age."

Alessa was appalled. "Radka is only fifteen."

"That doesn't matter to Chernikov. She comes from a good family and her dowry is substantial. Radka is terrified at the prospect. Marina fears for her daughter's happiness, but she has no say in her future. She thought to take Radka out of Russia but knew Chernikov would not allow it."

"She went to Aix-la-Chapelle."

"How did you know?"

Alessa could not bring herself to confess that she had read Marina's letter. "That's where you went. You did, didn't you?"

"Yes, there was the conference, and I had a request from Castlereagh I couldn't ignore. But I went too because of Marina. Chernikov was attending on the Emperor, and Marina begged him to take her and Radka with him. Radka had never traveled out of Russia, she said, and if she was to marry, she should have some experience of other countries. Marina was making herself agreeable and Chernikov consented."

Alessa thought of the visits Harry had made to Marina's dacha. "You planned it when you were in St. Petersburg."

"Yes, but we didn't know then that it would succeed. Marina's letter arrived the same day as Castlereagh's. If I hadn't gone on his request, I would have gone on hers. I'd given her my pledge."

As he'd given his pledge of fidelity on his wedding day. Not that Alessa had intended to hold him to it, but there had been things between them since that had led her to expect him to take his vows seriously. If Radka had to be brought to England to escape an unwelcome and too-early marriage, the fact remained that Marina was in England as well.

"How did you arrange it?" Alessa said, feeling some curiosity on this score.

Harry smiled. "It was simple enough. Marina and Radka left one morning on an excursion to Cologne. Chernikov did not expect them back until that evening. I met them in Cologne and drove them to the coast. We embarked straightway for Dover and have been traveling ever since."

Alessa found herself caught up in the story. "With Chernikov at your heels. Harry, he'll follow you. How can you keep Radka from him?"

"I don't know," Harry admitted, his brows drawing together. "But I'll manage somehow."

Alessa was silent, unsure how to broach the question Harry had not answered. He had given her a reason for bringing Marina and Radka to London. But had he given her the whole? She looked up into his face. He was standing near the grate where a small fire burned fitfully against the chill of the October night. The shadows cast by the fire and the flickering candle on the table near her chair showed his features in harsh relief. His expression was somber. "And now, wife," he said, "we will talk about this matter of discretion."

Alessa stiffened, remembering when he had last called her 'wife,' remembering the pleasure she had taken in the name and their moments of intimacy by the stream.

Harry came forward and looked down at her, his eyes

darkened with anger. "You believe I am Marina's lover? You believe I brought her to London for my own pleasure? Is that the reason for this tantrum?"

Alessa was out of her chair, trembling with indignation. "Tantrum? No. Honest outrage. What am I to believe, Harry, after your behavior in St. Petersburg? I've seen the looks that pass between you. I've seen the intimacies. If you are not bedding her now, then you will. But not in my house, not in my sight."

Harry took her by the shoulders, hard, as though he would shake her. "Do you take me for a fool?" His fingers dug into her flesh, the pain sharpening her rage and her fear. Then his hands dropped, leaving her feeling curiously bereft. Their anger at least had been a bond between them.

He stepped back, putting space between them. He seemed to have retreated a vast distance. When he spoke, his voice was as cold as his eyes. "If I ever choose to ignore my marriage vows, madam, be assured that you will see and hear nothing of it. Nor will I ever bring my mistress into your presence."

Alessa stared at her husband, knowing she had made a terrible mistake. "Harry," she said. She could not form the words of apology.

"Marina Chernikova is my friend. I had hoped she would be your friend, too, but I do not require friendship on your part, only courtesy and common humanity. She has been terrified for her daughter. She has risked everything to protect her—property, possessions, Radka's dowry. I have done what I can to help her. I will not abandon her now."

Alessa kept her eyes on her husband's face, wondering which was worse, the betrayal of the body or of the mind. Marina was his friend. She would almost rather have had her his mistress. She forced herself to speak. "I would not expect it of you."

"Then for once you are wise." Harry hesitated. His expression seemed a shade less grim, though it might have been a trick of the flickering candlelight. "There is something else you should know. I did not wish to speak of it because it is a private matter, one which you should hear from Marina. She is to be married. That's why she chose England as her refuge."

Alessa's voice was barely a whisper. "Who?"

"Jeremy Barrows. You know him?"

Alessa nodded. A quiet man of independent fortune with a collector's passion for painting. A young man. "But he's—"

"Scarcely older than I am myself. Believe me, it doesn't matter."

No, it would not. Aline had been years older than Adrian when he became her lover. Alessa pushed the thought aside, trying to remember what else she knew of Barrows. "He went to Russia."

"Two years ago. That's when they met. He was devoted to Marina, but her husband was alive and nothing could come of it."

"She was widowed. Why didn't he return to Russia then?"

"She forbade it. She feared Radka would be taken from her if she married a foreigner. But now that she's in England . . ."

"Can he protect the child?"

The lines in Harry's face deepened. "I hope to God he can."

He looked so weary and so beset that Alessa longed to comfort him, as she had when he had told her about his father. But the time for comfort was long past. Alessa had said words that could not be recalled, words that Harry would never forgive. He had gone too far away, far beyond her reach. "Harry," she said, wondering if her voice could bridge the chasm between them.

He stiffened, and when he spoke, his voice was devoid of emotion. "I trust matters are now clear between us. If you'll excuse me, I'll retire. It's been a long day."

"Harry," Alessa said again to the empty room. Then again, her voice breaking with despair, "Harry."

Between remorse and Alastair's demands, Alessa slept badly that night. The next morning she rose early, took a long look in her mirror, and made her toilette with more than usual care. She took care too in her choice of dress, choosing at last a blush-colored Parisian silk whose warm hue lent some color to her pale face. Then, knowing she must take responsibility for the shambles she had made of her life, she descended the stairs to the breakfast room, where she found her husband making a solitary meal of toast and coffee.

It was a sign that Harry was no more rested than she, an observation that was underscored by the dark smudges beneath his eyes. Alessa dismissed the footman and walked forward. "Harry, I'm so sorry," she said, abandoning her well-rehearsed speeches. "I was fearfully jealous, and I was wrong." She sat down abruptly and leaned toward her husband, her arm extended on the table in a conciliatory gesture.

A faint smile crossed Harry's face. "It's over. Let's say no more about it."

Alessa could not let it go. "I know I jumped to conclusions," she said, "but Edward had too."

Harry raised his brows. "Ned? No, he knew there was nothing between Marina and me. I told him so myself."

"But he told me that there was," Alessa insisted. "Not in so many words, but there was no mistaking his meaning. He'd have no reason to do that unless he believed it were true. Unless . . ." Alessa broke off, recalling the conversation she had had with Edward. She looked at Harry, challenge in her eyes. "Unless he was deliberately trying to make trouble between us."

"Good God." Harry threw down his napkin and rose from

the table. "Ned's my friend. You misunderstood him, Alessa. You heard what you wanted to hear."

Baffled, Alessa stared at her husband. She knew what she had heard. "Perhaps," she said, taking a cup and pouring herself some coffee. There was no point in making an issue of it now. Harry would not believe her. His friends came before his wife, and the knowledge stung her.

"I have to go out," Harry said. He was still angry but she knew he wanted her help. "I'll be back in midafternoon. Would you tell my mother . . ."

"About our guests? Of course. I'll see that the countess and Radka are not neglected. In fact, I think I'll send a note to Simon. He and Radka became quite friendly and she'll be lonely."

There was a slight softening in Harry's expression. "Thank you," he said, then turned and left the room.

Alessa almost went after him. She had meant to tell him about Grigor Lychenko's letter, but he had not believed her about Edward and in his uncertain mood he might dismiss it as a fabrication or an attempt to extort money. No, it would be better to see Lychenko alone, pay him if she must, and learn what he had to say. Time enough then to judge whether or not she should speak to Harry.

There was a great deal to do before her appointment with Lychenko, and Alessa did not linger at the table. She left instructions to be called as soon as the countess and her daughter were up, then paid a brief visit to Niki and Zara and a somewhat longer one to Alastair, whose demands for food seemed to increase daily. When he was settled once more, she went to her sitting room and penned a note to Simon and another to her mother, asking them both to call that afternoon.

She had no sooner given the notes to a footman for immediate delivery when Georgiana found her and demanded to be told something about the new guests. Word had spread among the servants, but Georgiana, who spent as much time below stairs as above, always knew what was going on.

"They're friends from St. Petersburg," Alessa said, careful not to designate them as Harry's guests, "and they came unexpectedly. They'll be with us for a while."

"A countess, they said."

"The Countess Chernikova and her daughter, Radka." Alessa hesitated. Georgiana was sure to ferret the story out sooner or later, and it might be best to tell her now, before the gossip had time to grow and be distorted. "Radka's uncle wanted to marry her to a much older man, and her mother brought her to England to keep her from him."

"I heard she was very young," Georgiana said, plainly intrigued by the story.

"She's fifteen."

Georgiana looked at her in astonishment. "I'm thirteen." Eighteen, when one could properly be considered marriageable, must seem a vast distance away, but fifteen was nearly the same as her own age. It was clear that Georgiana was not yet ready to leave childhood. "Will her uncle come after her?"

"He might." It was what Alessa feared, which was why she hoped to enlist her mother's help. "Georgiana, you must not talk of this. It may make things more difficult."

"I won't tell Mama," Georgiana assured her. "She's likely to spread the story all over town. But I think we should tell the servants. If Radka's uncle tries to get in the house, they'll know to keep him out."

"I don't think . . ." But Georgiana was right. The servants might be their best defense. "Very well. I'll tell them that if Count Chernikov calls, they're to deny all knowledge of the countess and her daughter. I'm afraid I'll have to tell your mother, too. I'm sure she'll understand."

"Oh, Mama knows how to keep a secret if she likes," Georgiana said. "There are lots of things she won't tell me."

Georgiana was an unlikely ally, but Alessa felt she could trust her. How quickly they had become caught up in a conspiracy. They would have to tell Julia and John as well. Marina's stay in their house must be kept quiet, at least till they knew whether or not Chernikov intended to act.

Georgiana, who was lonely for company of her own age, was delighted with Radka, who seemed to her both delicate and exotic. Radka knew little English, but Georgiana's French was fluent though ungrammatical, and the language did not seem to be a barrier. Alessa told Miss Beaton that her charge was to be free of the schoolroom that day so she could companion their young guest.

Lady Milverton and Julia were taken aback by the abrupt arrival of Marina and her daughter, but they seemed to blame Alessa rather than the countess for failing to warn them of the unorthodox visit. A countess, a Russian countess, could not but be a welcome guest, and Marina knew how to flatter. She assured Julia that members of the diplomatic community were very welcome at court, that the social life was lively and unremitting, and that the weather was no worse than one could expect in England. Well, perhaps the north of England. All the nobility spoke French and it was not absolutely necessary that she try to learn the Russian tongue.

By the time their morning visit was over, Lady Milverton was more than reconciled to the unexpected visitors. She was only sorry that Marina did not care to go into company, for there were many people of rank she would like her to meet. Marina told her frankly of the reason for her desire to be secluded. "Barbarous," Lady Milverton murmured when informed of Count Chernikov's plans for Radka, and she very willingly agreed to keep the countess's presence a secret.

Lady Milverton and Julia were engaged for the afternoon, which left Alessa free to make her peace with Marina Chernikova. It was not a task she relished, but she owed it to Harry. More important, she owed it to herself. *Maman* rarely admitted error, but Fiona had taught Alessa that confessing one's misdeeds lightened the soul. Hers could stand some

251

lightening. She felt bowed down by the weight of her stupid jealousy.

"I must apologize for my behavior last night," she told Marina when they were alone. They were strolling in the garden, an activity that allowed one to carry on a conversation without having to look the other person in the face. "I'm afraid your reception was not very cordial."

Marina stopped to admire a late-blooming rose. "Nonsense. It was late and you'd had no word of our arrival. I don't wonder that you were overset." She bent her head toward the rose, then moved on. "Harry should have told you what he intended."

"Harry knew better," Alessa said, determined to make her faults clear. "I would have made a scene."

"Ah, I see. May we speak frankly, Lady Milverton?"

"That's what I am trying to do. I'm making rather a mull of it.

"Not at all. Let me try. You misinterpreted the friendship between Harry and myself."

Alessa looked up and saw Marina regarding her with sympathetic eyes. "To tell you the truth, I was fearfully jealous."

Marina laughed, but there was neither malice nor condescension in the sound. "And no wonder. You had made a difficult journey and given birth to a son, only to find that the heir you presented to your husband so proudly was not the Milverton heir at all." She sighed. "Harry is a dear man, but he is inclined to be pigheaded. He had no business keeping you in ignorance of his first marriage. He should certainly have told you there was a child, even if he believed the child dead. You must have been furious."

"I was. I love Niki, but even now, when I look at Alastair, sometimes . . ."

"You wish Niki at the very devil. Of course, you wouldn't be human if you did not. It does not alter your love for Niki by one jot. Come, sit by me." Marina pulled Alessa to a nearby bench.

Alessa scuffed the gravel with the toe of her slipper. "Harry never told me much about his life. He had so many secrets. And when I saw him with you at Tsarkoe Selo, I thought you were another. Even worse, he wanted me to welcome you."

"No wonder you looked as though you wished me at the furthest reaches of hell. Believe me, if I had been Harry's mistress, I would never have allowed the introduction."

Alessa glanced at the other woman. "Was it so obvious?"

"Not to everyone. But I know the signs. My husband was often indiscreet and in the early years of our marriage, before I learned not to care, I suffered endless humiliations. When I met Harry, I was grateful for his friendship."

"I'm not much used to friendship between men and women."

"Believe me, it can occur." Marina was silent for a moment. "It can even exist between husband and wife."

Alessa twisted the wedding band on her finger. "I suppose so," she said without conviction, thinking of the moments when she had thought such a thing was possible between Harry and herself. She turned to Marina. "At least I won't be jealous any longer, not of you."

"Harry told you, didn't he? That I am going to marry Jeremy Barrows. I'm very much in love with Jeremy."

"I have to confess it makes it easier," Alessa admitted. "Understanding your friendship with Harry. I envy you that, your talent for friendship. And for love."

A look of distress and concern appeared on Marina's face. "Oh, my dear child, you have that talent in abundance. Be patient. I'm sure things will come right."

Alessa forced herself to smile. At the moment she was not sure they ever would.

"I don't see why you wanted me to come," Georgiana complained as Simon shepherded her through the hall and up the stairs. "I've seen babies. I don't need to see him again."

"They want to be alone, bratchet. At least Peter does. He likes Radka."

Georgiana stopped and gave him a shocked look. "You can't mean — But you do, don't you. Don't you know Radka's too young for that sort of thing?" She turned and continued up the stairs. "So is Peter, even though he thinks he's nearly a man. And so are you," she added in an accusing voice.

Simon grinned. "There I agree with you. I'm not going to get entangled with women for a bit yet. Not even with girls. Not even with you."

Georgiana sniffed. "I should hope not."

They walked down the corridor to Alessa's rooms. Alessa was closeted with her mother and the countess in the small drawing room. Peter and Radka were walking in the garden. Simon, out of sympathy for his friend and what was clearly Radka's preference, had dragged Georgiana away on the pretext of visiting his nephew.

They entered Alessa's boudoir and Simon walked at once to the door of Alastair's room and scratched softly on the panel. When Louise bade him come in, he slipped inside, dimly aware that Georgiana had remained behind. He spent a pleasant few minutes holding his nephew, who was awake and in a contented mood, then handed him back to the nurse and returned to the sitting room.

He stopped abruptly on the threshold. "I don't think you should be reading my sister's letters," he said, controlling his outrage.

Georgiana quickly dropped the letter she had been reading. She showed not one sign of guilt. "If I didn't read other people's letters and listen to other people's conversations, I wouldn't know what's going on in this house."

"You could ask."

"No one ever tells me anything."

Simon felt a moment of pity for the girl. "Even so, it's wrong."

Georgiana gave him a shrewd look. "If I hadn't listened at the door, I wouldn't have been able to write Alessa and tell her Harry was going to Russia."

Simon knew when he had met his match. "Come along," he said, taking her arm. "We'll go see Niki and Zara."

Simon was bothered by the incident, but an hour later he was forced to admit that Georgiana's penchant for prying into other people's affairs could be useful. They had collected Galina and the children and joined Peter and Radka in the garden where they were discovered by Harry on his return home. Radka's face was radiant. "It has been a lovely day," she told Harry. "I am so happy in England."

Harry's face relaxed into a smile. "Where is your mother?"

"I believe she is still with the Princess Sofia."

Harry turned to Simon. "The footman told me Alessa went out," he said in a low voice. "Do you know where?"

"I do," Georgiana said triumphantly. She drew Harry aside and Simon followed, ready to protect his sister's interests. "She went to someplace called the Golden Cross," Georgiana continued when they were out of earshot of the others. "She went to meet a man called Grigor Lych—"

"Lychenko?" Harry's voice was sharp.

"That's it. He had something to tell her about Alastair. Or maybe it was about Niki. Anyway, it had to do with Alastair's future."

"God in heaven," Harry breathed. He looked at Simon. "I'm going after her."

"Shall I come?" Simon asked.

"No. No, stay here. We shan't be long."

Simon watched Harry stride across the garden and disappear into the house. His disappointment was reflected in Georgiana's face. "What's happened?" she demanded.

"I don't know." Simon could guess, and he was troubled. He looked at Georgiana and summoned a smile. "Don't worry," he said, "when I find out I promise I'll tell you."

255

Alessa's hands gripped the edge of the carriage seat. The streets were crowded, the drive was interminable, and her anxiety was rapidly mounting. Whatever Lychenko had to say, it was bound to disturb the precarious balance of her life. What it would do to her and Harry she dared not contemplate.

The carriage pulled up at last. The footman helped her down the steps and escorted her to the inn. He would have followed her inside, but she dismissed him at the front door, telling him to have the carriage wait. The servants would gossip enough as it was, and she did not want Captain Lychenko's name bandied about belowstairs.

The Golden Cross was a large coaching establishment, a five-story brick building on a narrow cobbled street off Charing Cross Road. Alessa stood in the entrance hall a moment, buffeted by the crowd inside, attracting no little attention from the men who were entering and leaving the inn. But she was not her mother's daughter for nothing. Pushing her way through the throng, she stopped a harried waiter with a gesture and asked for the innkeeper. The waiter, taking in the quality of her attire, promised to fetch him immediately.

A few minutes later the innkeeper was leading her up the stairs. "The last door on the left," he told her as they reached the third floor. "Shall I inquire . . ."

"It won't be necessary," Alessa said, dismissing him with a smile. "I am expected."

The innkeeper gave her a long look, then disappeared down the stairs. Alessa proceeded down the corridor, wondering what damage the visit was doing to her reputation. Not that she cared. The only one concerned was Harry, and he would know the truth soon enough.

She knocked firmly on the last door and waited. She knocked again, and then, annoyed because Lychenko had been clear about the time, she knocked once more. There was no answer and no sound from within, though the noise of raised voices from the hall below came clearly up the stairs. Alessa tried the knob of the door and found it turned readily in her hand. She pushed the door open and called, "Captain Lychenko."

It was a dark, depressing room, furnished with bed, dresser, table, and chairs, but it appeared to be empty. A coat was thrown across the bed and there was a smell of spirits in the air. Had the man drunk himself into a stupor? Angry and alarmed, Alessa moved into the room and stared down at the figure sprawled on the floor near the table. Devil take him, he was drunk.

Furious, she dropped to the floor at his side and put out her hand to rouse him. Then she stifled a gasp and withdrew her hand. Lychenko's waistcoat was drenched with blood and his blue eyes stared unseeing at the ceiling. The man was not drunk. He was dead.

Chapter Sixteen

Harry made his way down the inn corridor toward the room to which the maidservant had directed him. The door was ajar, though to Harry's surprise no voices came from inside. Not feeling any need to stand on ceremony, Harry pushed the door open and saw his wife kneeling on the floor beside Grigor's recumbent form.

Alessa looked up in alarm, then released her breath. "Harry." There was no surprise in her voice, only relief. "I think he's dead."

Holding his shock at bay, Harry knelt on the carpet by his wife. The sickly stench of dried blood washed over him. He felt for a pulse, but the body had already stiffened. "He is. For some hours it appears."

Harry looked up and took Alessa by the shoulders. Her face had gone as white as the lace on her gown. "Let's go downstairs," he said, pulling her to her feet. "You can wait in a private parlor. Then I'll—"

"No." Despite her pallor, Alessa's voice was steady. "I'm not going to collapse, Harry. It's just that I've never seen anyone dead before. Except my father and he was laid out in his bed." She drew another breath, as if trying to order her thoughts. "Who could have done this?"

"I don't know." Harry released Alessa and knelt beside Grigor again. The cause of death was plain enough. There was a bullet hole in Grigor's chest, singed around the edges, as if the shot had come at close range. Grigor's face wore a look of surprise, suggesting he had been taken unawares. His blue eyes had grown cloudy. Harry closed them gently. It was impossible to hate Grigor now that he was dead. Harry felt only a vague contempt tinged with pity. No man should meet his death this way.

"Harry," Alessa said, her voice taut with her effort to maintain control, "I think you should see this."

Getting to his feet, Harry saw that she was pointing toward the fireplace. The light coming in through the window glinted off something metal. Something which looked very like the barrel of a pistol.

"Someone was careless," Harry said. He walked to the fireplace and looked down at the small pistol which lay half concealed by the fender. The carving on the handle stirred a chord of memory. "It's Grigor's," he said.

"How do you know?" Alessa asked.

"Because he threatened me with it five years ago when he found out about Nadia."

"Then"—there was a tremor in Alessa's voice—"who fired it?"

Harry glanced about the room. An overturned glass on a nearby table and a patch of damp on the carpet below accounted for the reek of spirits in the room. There were marks in the carpet, as if the table had been shoved back suddenly.

"I'd hazard a guess Grigor got into a fight with someone and drew the pistol himself," Harry said, recalling the unleashed violence Grigor had shown at their last meeting. "There seems to have been some sort of struggle. The pistol may have gone off accidentally. Since the weapon was Grigor's, there was no need to hide it. Grigor's visitor simply threw it away and ran."

Alessa rubbed her arms, as if to ward off the cold horror of Grigor's death. "Who?" she asked again.

"God knows. Grigor was capable of fighting with just about anyone. A chance-met acquaintance he invited up for

259

a game of cards. A woman he brought up for other reasons. Or—"

"Someone who knew him better," Alessa said in a flat voice.

"Possibly, yes." Crossing back to her side, Harry put his arm around her and urged her toward the door. "There's nothing more we can do here."

This time Alessa made no protest at being led from the room. By the time they reached the corridor, she had begun to tremble. Shutting the door on the ugliness within, Harry drew his wife into his arms. "It's a foul act and a foul sight," he said, his voice muffled by the plumes on her bonnet. "Enough to overset anyone."

Now that the immediate situation had been dealt with, a wave of nausea rose up in Harry's throat. This was the first time he had confronted violent death. He felt an intense gratitude that his efforts at rebellion had not led him into the army.

Alessa clung tightly to him, her fingers clenching on the fabric of his coat, but at length her trembling eased and he felt her heartbeat return to its normal pace. "I'm all right, Harry," she said, drawing back to look up at him. "But—"

"I know." Harry touched her face. "God knows I wasn't fond of Grigor, but I wouldn't wish such a fate on anyone."

Alessa shivered. Then her brows drew together. "How did you know I was here?"

"Georgiana told me," Harry said, remembering that he and Alessa had a number of things to discuss which had nothing to do with Grigor's death. "She saw Grigor's letter to you."

"She . . ." Indignation flared in Alessa's eyes, then faded. "In the circumstances, I suppose I should be grateful to her. Harry . . ."

"No." Harry laid a finger over her lips. "Not now. There's too much to be done."

He drew her toward the stairs, keeping his arm close around her. In the face of death, life seemed all the more precious. "I have to speak to the innkeeper," he said when they reached the ground floor. "Do you want to—"

"I'll come with you," Alessa said in a firm voice. "I'm the one who found him."

The innkeeper, who looked harried and distracted, was shocked at the news. It was the first time, he said, that anything of that sort had happened at the Golden Cross. He immediately dispatched one of the waiters to the nearest Public Office, then took Harry and Alessa to a private room and served them his best claret with his own hands.

"A horrible business," he repeated, his hand shaking slightly as he set down the bottle. "You say the man was a relative of yours, Lord Milverton?"

"My first wife's cousin." Harry sipped the wine, wondering how much of the story would have to become public. "Neither Lady Milverton nor I had seen him since his arrival in England."

Harry glanced at Alessa in concern and was relieved to see that some of her color had returned. When the police officer arrived, she told him calmly that she had come to the Golden Cross in response to a note from Captain Lychenko. She said nothing about the reason for their appointment. Officer Howell, a round-faced young man who appeared as shocked by the business as the innkeeper, did not press her.

"I should go up and look at the, ah, the body," Howell said, closing his notebook. "Lady Milverton . . ."

"You want me to come with you and tell you what I found." Alessa got to her feet, holding herself with the same composure Harry had seen her adopt in confrontations with her mother. "Of course."

The innkeeper led them up a back staircase to Grigor's room where, with the same composure, Alessa described how she had entered the room—the door had been unlocked—and knelt beside the body. Harry added an account of his own arrival, showed Officer Howell the gun, and explained his theory about a struggle. Howell seemed inclined to agree. Leaving the body to be examined by the doctor he

261

had summoned, Howell suggested they return downstairs.

"Must have been a terrible shock for you, my lady," he said to Alessa when they were out of the room. "No doubt you are eager to get home."

Alessa started to protest, but then admitted that she should get back to her baby.

"I'll stay and see if they're able to learn anything more," Harry promised when he had escorted her to her carriage. "I'll see you at home this evening."

He hesitated, leaning against the open door of the carriage. There were unmistakable shadows of strain on Alessa's face. In addition to everything else, Harry realized, she had got little sleep the night before. There was much to be said between them, but this was no time for it. Instead, he lifted her hand and pressed it briefly to his lips, then went back into the inn.

An hour later an exhaustive questioning of the inn staff had yielded only the information that the Golden Cross was a very busy establishment and that while no one had seen Captain Lychenko receive any visitors last night — when, in the opinion of the doctor, death had occurred — no one could swear that he had not. Apart from Harry and Alessa, no one seemed to have asked for directions to Grigor's room, but Grigor could have taken a visitor up himself or received someone who already knew the location of his room. No one had heard the gunshot, but this did not seem improbable as the room next to Grigor's was empty, there had been a great deal of noise downstairs, and the shot had been fired at close range.

By the time the questions came to an end, one of the maids had succumbed to hysterics, two patrons had left the Golden Cross in evident agitation, and a knot of curiosity seekers had gathered outside. There would be an inquest, Officer Howell told Harry, a note of apology in his voice, and most likely both Lord and Lady Milverton would be required to testify. He would keep Lord Milverton apprised of any developments.

Despite his youth and the fact that he had never handled such an investigation before, Howell seemed to know what he was about. Harry left at last, satisfied that he had done all he could. There was a throbbing pain in his temples. The cold shock of horror warred with a numbing sense of disbelief. It seemed impossible that someone had taken Grigor's life, yet the sight of his body had been all too real. Harry could still see the surprised grimace on Grigor's face and feel the clammy cold of his skin.

By the time Harry returned to Portman Square, it was past six. The footman informed him that Lady Milverton was in her rooms. Not bothering to inquire the whereabouts of the rest of the family, Harry made for the stairs. He found Alessa sitting on a small rose-colored settee in her boudoir with Alastair at her breast. After the horrors of the day, the simple warmth of the sight washed over him with physical force. He closed the door, drinking in the familiar fragrance of rose potpourri which always filled his wife's chambers.

"Did you learn anything?" Alessa asked, her eyes dark with concern.

"Not a great deal." Wanting nothing more than to gather Alessa and Alastair to him and forget the whole afternoon, Harry dropped down on a giltwood chair and told her what Howell had learned from the inn staff.

By the time he had finished, Alastair had done so as well. Alessa carried the baby to Louise in the adjoining room, then returned to the settee. "Does Officer Howell think the murderer was someone Captain Lychenko knew well?"

"It was certainly someone Grigor let into the room. Beyond that, I think Howell is as much in the dark as we are. He asked me whom Grigor knew in London. Howell was very polite, but I suppose I could be considered a suspect myself. I certainly would be if Howell knew the full story."

Alessa clasped her hands. "How much of the story does he have to know?"

"As little as possible, I hope. As neither of us killed Grigor,

I think it unlikely that his death has anything to with the children."

"Yes." Alessa adjusted one of the embroidered cushions beside her on the settee.

Harry settled back in his chair and folded his arms. He was curiously reluctant to speak, yet he feared that if he did not do so now, he never would. "Why didn't you tell me you were going to see Grigor?" he asked.

Alessa's chin shot up, the way it always did when she was challenged. "I wanted to find out what Captain Lychenko had to say first. Besides . . ." She looked away.

"What?" Harry asked.

"You didn't tell me why you were going to Aix-la-Chapelle," Alessa said, meeting his gaze.

Harry was not sure whether to laugh or to curse. "Is that it?" he asked. "An eye for an eye? I thought we were beyond that, Alessa."

"You didn't feel able to take me into your confidence," Alessa said, her warm brown eyes turning cold.

"Oh, Christ." Harry ran a hand through his hair. "You know that isn't how it was."

"You didn't tell me about your letter from the countess until she reached London. I was no more secretive about Captain Lychenko's letter to me." Alessa folded her hands in her lap, concealing the gold of her wedding band. "I might ask why you followed me."

"Because I wouldn't trust Grigor with anyone, let alone my wife," Harry said at once. "And because anything he had to say about Niki concerns me as much as you."

Her eyes told him that this last statement had cut home. For all her pride, Alessa did not flinch from the truth. "I may have been wrong. But last night I wasn't thinking too clearly."

"Nor was I." With a stab of guilt, Harry recalled his own loss of temper the previous evening. "It's been a bloody awful twenty-four hours, hasn't it?" he said.

Alessa's mouth curved in a ghost of a smile. "I've known better," she admitted.

It was a truce of sorts. Harry hesitated, afraid to push their fragile accord. The soft chimes of the porcelain clock on the mantel reminded him that it was nearing the dinner hour. "I must go and tell the rest of the family about Grigor," he said, getting to his feet. "Howell promised to keep the investigation quiet, but there'll be an inquest and it's sure to get into the papers."

"We'll have to tell the children as well," Alessa said. "They're bound to hear about it from someone."

"I know. First thing tomorrow. At least we know neither of them was overly fond of Grigor."

"No." Alessa smoothed her skirt carefully, not meeting his eyes. The subject they had both carefully avoided hung heavily between them. Grigor's letter had raised new questions about Niki's parentage. Grigor's death had robbed them of the answers.

Alessa looked up, her eyes filled with anguished uncertainty. Though his impulse was to take her in his arms, Harry knew that would do nothing to destroy this new barrier between them. Just as he knew it was very likely they would never know the truth.

"I'll see you at dinner," he said and left the room.

Alessa smoothed the embroidered Brussels lace at the neck of Alastair's christening gown. "What a good little boy," she murmured, walking carefully down the stairs. "I know you're ready for a nap but this is your party, and everyone wants to see you."

As soon as they had returned from the church, Alessa had taken Alastair up to feed him. By now, most of the guests had gathered in the drawing room. Alessa paused at the base of the stairs and drew a breath. This day, which should have been one of the happiest of her life, had been fraught with tension from the first. The story of Grigor Lychenko's murder had caused both her mother and Lady Milverton to renew their questions about Niki's parentage. And then there

265

were Alessa's own doubts, which she kept bottled up tight inside. As she had stood at the christening font, it had been impossible not to wonder if the Honorable Alastair Dudley should really be Viscount Rutledge.

Still, this was Alastair's day. Determined to present a happy appearance, Alessa crossed the first-floor hall to the drawing room.

A discreet murmur of conversation punctuated by children's laughter greeted her when she entered the room. Cheerful light and a crackling fire brightened the long room with its high-coffered ceiling and classical friezes.

A small hand caught hold of Alessa's pearl-embroidered skirt. "Mama," Niki said. "Is 'Stair better?"

"Much better," Alessa assured him. Niki had been alarmed when Alastair had started crying as they left the church. "He just wanted some food," she said, bending down so Niki could see his little brother.

"Don't be afraid," Niki said, gently smoothing Alastair's hair. "Everyone likes you." He looked up at Alessa. "He doesn't know what's happening, does he?"

Alessa swallowed, her mouth dry. "No."

"There's my godson," Fiona said, coming forward with a smile Alessa found very heartening. "Are you looking after him, Niki?"

"He cried," Niki said in English, looking up at Fiona. "He's all better now. Mama made him better."

"Mothers are good at that," Fiona said.

Alessa straightened up with one child in her arms and another clinging to her skirts, her chest constricting with the sickening pull of divided loyalties. Her attention on the children, she did not see her husband approach.

"I'm glad Alastair isn't going to miss his own party," Harry said with an easy smile which Alessa envied. His gaze met her own and she had the sense that he read more than she wished in her face. "Come on, Niki," Harry said, taking his son's hand. "Let's find Zara and the other children."

Niki made no objection. Before he led his elder son off

Harry looked down at the younger. "Bear up, old chap. You'll have to meet the family sooner or later." He brushed his fingers against Alastair's cheek, then laid his hand briefly on Alessa's arm, sending an unexpected shiver along her nerves.

"Alastair seems to be bearing up remarkably well," Fiona said, her gaze tactfully on the baby.

"Training for public ceremonies. It starts early," Alessa said, and then bit her lip, for public ceremonies would have been more important in Alastair's life if he had been the eldest son. She glanced at the corner of the room where Harry had taken Niki to join the other children. Gideon was there as well, with Fenella on his lap and his arm around Beth. Watching them, Alessa recalled Fiona's revelations about Beth's true parentage. Gideon knew the truth, yet he was devoted to the girl. But then, Beth was not his heir.

If Fiona noticed Alessa's discomfort, she gave no sign of it. "So much nicer to have a small gathering," she said, glancing about the room. "It's never made sense to me to turn a party for a child into something overpowering."

"With a younger son, less formality is required." Lady Milverton joined them, her tone courteous, but her eyes holding the expression of disapproval she had worn ever since Alessa and Harry's return from Russia.

The ever-present pain again stabbed through Alessa's chest. "How very true," she said, forcing a smile to her lips. "In that sense, my son is fortunate not to share the burdens of his elder brother."

"Of course," Lady Milverton murmured, her tone implying that she knew perfectly well that Alessa was trying to put the best face on the situation.

Between the news of Grigor Lychenko's murder and Alessa's decision to keep the christening party informal and include children among the guests, she and Lady Milverton had got on worse than usual in the past week. Alessa, who did not feel equal to coping with her mother-in-law at present, was relieved when various friends and relatives crowded round to get a glimpse of the baby, preventing further conversation with Lady Milverton. Not much above thirty people had been invited, but many of them hadn't seen Alastair save at the church earlier in the day. Alessa was grateful that John's parents were in Northumberland, visiting their daughter, who had recently had a baby herself.

By the time Alessa escaped to one of the matched green velvet sofas which were grouped about the room, Lady Milverton's attention had been claimed elsewhere. "I said Alastair was holding up remarkably well," Fiona said, sitting beside Alessa. "It might be more to the point to ask if his mother is."

"Fair to middling." Alessa settled the delicate folds of Alastair's christening gown. "The inquest about Captain Lychenko was yesterday."

"Yes, I saw the report in the paper. Was it very bad?"

Alastair stirred in Alessa's arms and made a whimpering sound. "I daresay it could have been a great deal worse," Alessa said, giving him her finger to suck. "It was held in the common room at the Golden Cross—I've never actually sat in a common room before—and Harry and I were treated with the greatest deference. If you saw the report in the paper, you must know the verdict was murder by person or persons unknown. Which it had to be."

Fiona touched Alessa's hand. "I'm sorry."

"It seems rather a shame to make such a fuss over him when he's too young to remember it," Georgiana said, appearing beside the sofa. "Wouldn't it be more sensible to postpone christenings till we're four or five at least? Verity agrees with me," she added, turning to the girl who was standing beside her.

"The idea does have its merits." Alessa smiled at the girls both wearing white dresses, both thirteen, poised between childhood and maturity. Both Alastair's aunts. For Verity Drake was Alessa and Simon's half-sister, the result of an affair between their father and an Englishwoman. Though the relationship was not generally known, Alessa and Simon had

268

seen a good deal of Verity since they had come to England. Alessa invited Verity and her foster parents, Lord and Lady Windham, to the christening as a matter of course.

Verity was looking at Alastair with curiosity. Like Georgiana, she seemed intrigued with the idea of being an aunt. "Would you like to hold him?" Alessa asked.

"He won't mind?"

"No, he's a very agreeable baby. Here, sit beside me."

Verity's smile as Alessa placed the baby in her arms told Alessa she had made the right suggestion. Verity, who had a young foster sister and brother, handled the baby with easy competence. "I think he looks a bit like you," she said, coaxing Alastair to grasp hold of her finger.

"He has his father's chin," Alessa said, but she was looking not at Alastair but at Verity. Despite her pointed features and light brown hair, there was something about her mouth and eyes which had a distinct stamp of the Tassios.

Alessa glanced across the room where her mother sat conversing with one of the Dudley cousins. *Maman* had always been very matter-of-fact about Verity's existence, but surely it had been painful to learn *Papa* had been unfaithful.

Unless she had already been well aware of his infidelity. Nails digging into the palms of her hands, Alessa looked from her mother to Harry, who was standing beside a white marble pillar, talking to Marina and Jermy Barrows. Harry had not been Marina's lover, but that did not mean he had been faithful. The idea of him with another woman was more than Alessa could bear.

"It's awfully nice to have a party you're allowed to stay up for if you're under eighteen," Georgiana said, perching on the elaborately carved and gilded arm of the sofa. "This week is splendid—first the christening, then the wedding."

"Wedding?" Verity asked.

"The Countess Chernikova's. Radka's mother. She's going to marry Jeremy Barrows, that handsome dark-haired man," Georgiana said, gesturing toward the countess and Jeremy. "They've been madly in love for two years, but they couldn't marry because the countess was already married and then because her wicked brother-in-law was keeping them apart. They're going to be married the day after tomorrow, and we're going to protect Radka from her uncle while they go on their wedding journey."

Verity nodded, as if this disjointed account made perfect sense. Alessa met Fiona's questioning gaze with what she hoped was determined confidence. Privately, Alessa was still not sure what they would do if Count Chernikov arrived at Milverton House demanding that they return his ward.

"I say," said Georgiana, who was too excited to focus long on any one thing, "what do you suppose Mama and Lord Sutton have been talking about for so long?"

Relieved at the distraction, Alessa followed the direction of Georgiana's gaze and saw Lady Milverton sitting beside Edward's father, Lord Sutton, a tall, lean man in his midfifties with dark, silver-streaked hair.

"Isn't he an old friend of your family's?" Verity asked.

"An old friend of my father's," Georgiana said. "I never thought Mama liked him very well. She always seems uncomfortable when he's about."

Alessa considered this, then dismissed it. Lady Milverton had always appeared to her to be on good terms with Sutton. Georgiana had a vivid imagination. But the reference to Sutton reminded Alessa that she had unfinished business with his son. In the past week she had had far more important things to worry about than Edward's misleading remarks about Harry and Marina, but now she saw a chance to clear up the misunderstanding.

However, it was not until later in the day that she had her chance. When Alastair had been taken up to the nursery and the christening breakfast had been consumed and the immediate family and close friends had gathered back in the drawing room, Alessa found herself standing in the bow window alcove overlooking the back garden with Edward beside her and no one else nearby.

"I'm sorry Will and his family couldn't be here," Edward told her.

"So am I," Alessa replied automatically. Edward's elder brother spent most of his time on his father's estate in Buckinghamshire.

"This is a happy day," Edward went on. "You deserve one after all that's happened."

"Yes, there's been a lot of trouble. And misunderstanding." Alessa looked up at her husband's friend, fumbling for the right words. Finally she decided a direct attack would be best. "Edward, why did you make me believe Harry had been the Countess Chernikova's lover?"

Edward's blue eyes widened in astonishment. "Why did I do what?"

"You must remember our conversation at the reception at Tsarkoe Selo. You told me that whatever was between Harry and the countess it ended a long time ago. Yet if Harry is to be believed, you should have been able to assure me that there had never been anything between them.

"My dear Alessa . . ." Edward stretched out a hand, then let it fall to his side in a perfect display of awkward confusion. "You've gone through so much these last months," he said, his voice gentle. "I don't wonder that it's difficult for you to remember all that's happened."

Alessa was not fond of being told she was wrong. "I remember the conversation perfectly," she said. "It's not the sort of thing a wife easily forgets."

"No, of course not." This time Edward reached for her hands, but Alessa drew back. Edward smiled as if to say he understood her discomfort. "There has been so much discord between you and Harry," he said softly "Naturally, you would be willing to assume the worst."

"Perhaps," Alessa acknowledged. "But that doesn't change what you said. Why Edward?"

"Alessa . . ." Edward gave a helpless shrug. "Please believe me when I tell you that I said no such thing."

Looking into Edward's frank, open face, it took Alessa a

moment to realize he had just told her a bold-faced lie. The look of sincere concern on his face almost made her doub her own memory. Then she recalled again the pain of tha night at Tsarkoe Selo and knew she was not mistaken. Fo reasons she could not understand, Edward had lied to he then and he was lying to her now. It was as if someone sh trusted had unexpectedly doused her with cold water.

Confused, hurt, and more than a little angry, Alessa sup pressed her desire to shake the truth out of Harry's friend. "I seems we can't reach an agreement," she said, with a coo smile. "A pity, but fortunately there's no harm done. I know the truth now."

Before Edward could respond, Alessa moved out of the al cove. Harry was sitting in front of the fireplace with Nik and Zara on his lap and the other children gathered around He seemed to be telling them a story. Alessa longed to go t him, yet Harry had already made it clear that he would tak Edward's word over her own.

This knowledge stung even more than Edward's lies Needing a few moments to compose herself, Alessa made fo the door and slipped out into the hall. Why, she wondered raising a hand to her burning cheek. Why would Harry' friend have sought to make mischief between Harry and hi wife? Had his words at Tsarkoe Selo been an honest misun derstanding? Was he now lying to hide his embarrassment But if he had known the truth about Harry and Marina a along, why hadn't he simply told her? Unless, of course, i was Harry who had lied about not being Marina's lover.

No, Alessa told herself firmly, even as fear lanced throug her. For despite all the times Harry had not taken her int his confidence, he had never lied to her.

Perhaps if she could sit down for a few minutes, she coul order her thoughts. Alessa crossed the hall and opened th door of a small antechamber. On the threshold she froze i astonishment. John and Galina stood in a patch of bright clear sunlight, locked in a passionate embrace.

John's fingers were tangled in Galina's loosened hair. Ga

lina's arms were wrapped close around him. They seemed oblivious to the opening of the door. Alessa hesitated, uncertain whether to retreat or to demand an explanation.

Before she could decide, she heard footsteps behind her and the matter was ripped from her hands. "What in the name of heaven is going on here?" Lady Milverton demanded.

Chapter Seventeen

John and Galina broke apart at once.

"I can explain," John said, raising a hand to adjust his crumpled cravat. His face was flushed but his voice was steady.

"That will hardly be necessary. The situation speaks for itself." Lady Milverton closed the door behind her with firm finality. "I'm surprised at you, John. I would have thought you knew enough to keep these affairs belowstairs."

John's face went from red to a cold, angry white. He stepped forward and put himself in front of Galina. "If you imagine—"

"This is not the sort of thing to be discussed in front of the servants," Lady Milverton said, not even deigning to look at Galina. "The girl had best—"

"You'd best go back to the children, Galina," Alessa intervened. "We can sort all this out after the guests have left."

"Of course, Lady Milverton," Galina said in careful English.

As she stepped forward, John caught her by the wrist. Galina laid her hand over his and shook her head. John glanced at Lady Milverton and Alessa, then looked back at Galina. "Very well," he said. "Perhaps it's best. This isn't the time." Drawing Galina's arm through his own, he turned to Alessa. "I'm sorry if we've made a scene. Believe me, that wasn't our intention. If you'll excuse me, I'll escort Miss Yuskaya back to the drawing room."

"Thank you, John," Alessa said, even as Lady Milverton drew in her breath to protest.

Seeing the determination on John's face as he held the door open for Galina, Alessa was forcibly reminded that he was Harry's cousin. Galina carried herself with quiet composure, neither defiant nor embarrassed. Alessa smiled at her as she moved past, but she sensed that Galina was not in need of comfort.

Lady Milverton stood in silence until the door had closed. "I know that this is now your house, Alessa," she said, her eyes showing her disgust for the scene they had just witnessed, "but it is plain that that girl isn't fit to have the charge of children. I insist that you dismiss her."

"Do you?" Alessa found she almost relished the open confrontation with her mother-in-law. A polite facade had hidden their skirmishes for too long. "I thought you took no interest in Niki and Zara."

"I take an interest in having a well-run household." Lady Milverton adjusted a porcelain figurine on a nearby table, as though to establish her position as mistress of Milverton House for thirty years. "I knew no good would come of bringing foreigners into the house."

"I see," Alessa said, raising her brows as she had often seen her mother do when confronted by those of whom she disapproved. "Are you referring to Galina or to me?"

Lady Milverton had the grace to flush. "Don't be ridiculous, Alessa. You know I didn't mean anything of the kind. I take it you will dismiss the girl?"

"I will do no such thing. And you might remember that your nephew is at least as much at fault in the matter as Galina."

"That," said Lady Milverton, "is a remark of sheer impertinence. I'm sure you know better than to put their behavior on the same level. But I will certainly speak to Harry about John's conduct."

"No," Alessa said, filled with a liberating sense of power, "I will. Please don't concern yourself with this any further,

275

Lady Milverton. As you so rightly pointed out, I am mistress of Milverton House."

Harry groaned. "I was afraid of this. I've never seen John so taken with a girl. But I'd hoped he'd have the sense . . . I should have remembered it's damnably hard to be sensible at that age."

Alessa was aware of a strong wish that Harry would be less sensible where she was concerned. She firmly pushed this thought aside. For once she and Harry were not dealing with their own concerns.

"I've sent Georgiana to sit with the children and asked Galina to join me here in a quarter-hour," Alessa said, settling back on the settee in her boudoir. "I suppose I must find out how far things have progressed between them. But I will not dismiss Galina, whatever she tells me."

"Of course not." Harry, who had been frowning at his hands, looked up with quick assent. "I'll speak to John," he added with a grimace.

"It's rather horrid to have to interfere in these things, isn't it?" Alessa said. "It makes me feel like my mother."

"Yes, I have the lowering sense that if I'm not careful, I'm going to start sounding pompous." Harry gave one of the smiles which always warmed her.

Alessa smiled back, realizing that in the last few minutes, with their attention diverted from their own problems, they had been more comfortable with each other than they'd been all week. "There's one other thing," she said. "I'm afraid I had something of a confrontation with your mother."

"Did you?" Harry asked, an appreciative look in his eyes. "What did you say?"

"I told her that this is my house now. Our house," Alessa added.

"Which it is." For a moment Alessa thought Harry's eyes held the same yearning she felt for Milverton House and Moresby to become real homes. Then he stood abruptly.

"Galina will be here soon. I should go find John. We can talk when we know more."

Harry walked to the door, but stopped, gripping the handle, and looked back at her. "I know today wasn't easy for you," he said quietly. "For what it's worth, you have my thanks."

Alessa swallowed over the constriction in her throat. "We would have had to deal with Galina and John sooner or later," she said.

"I wasn't talking about Galina and John," Harry said, and left the room before she could respond.

Alessa raised her hand to her face, feeling her eyes smart. Harry's understanding was almost enough to undo her. She forced herself instead to think about the scene with Galina, recalling how, under different circumstances, *Maman* had lost her temper and dismissed Fiona without a reference. It was one of the most infuriating things *Maman* had ever done. Alessa was pleased to have the chance to prove she was different.

Galina arrived a few minutes later, at precisely the specified time, appearing as self-possessed as she had in the antechamber.

"Please sit down," Alessa said, gesturing to a nearby chair and wondering where to begin. She had never had any trouble speaking to servants in the past, but she had never spoken to a servant about such an intimate matter. And she had never had a servant who was as close to being a friend as Galina was.

"I'm sorry, Lady Milverton," Galina said, seating herself. "John and I were indiscreet, and we have put you in an embarrassing position."

"No," Alessa said. "That is, that isn't the problem." She clasped her hands in her lap, feeling like a schoolgirl again. Save that as a schoolgirl she'd been a good deal more confident. "Galina . . ."

"You wish to know if I am John's mistress." Galina's gaze was open and steady. "At present I am not."

277

"I see," Alessa said, disconcerted by Galina's use of "at present." She looked at Galina, neat as usual in her dark print dress, her best in honor of the christening. Her blond hair was once again twisted into a smooth knot. Her blue eyes held a quiet maturity which Alessa envied. Yet Galina was little more than twenty and in a foreign country. "Lord Milverton and I feel responsible for you," Alessa said. "After all, we took you from your home . . ."

"My home was scarcely sheltered," Galina pointed out.

"No, but . . ." Alessa leaned forward and spoke as she might to Verity or Georgiana. "We don't want to see you hurt."

Galina smiled. "I have little experience in the matter, but I fear people in love are frequently hurt."

Alessa drew in her breath, surprised by this last as much as anything. It had not occurred to her to put Galina and John's relationship in those terms. "Are you in love with John?" she asked.

For the first time Galina colored. "Yes," she said simply. "Very much." She hesitated, looking down at her hands. "My parents died when I was young. With John, for the first time I feel as if I have someone of my own."

The eloquence of those words turned the awkward scene into something far more poignant. Alessa found herself wishing she could express her feelings for Harry so directly. All her assumptions about the need to separate John and Galina were shaken, yet what was she to do? Give tacit consent to an illicit love affair?

"The world isn't very fair to women," Alessa said, repeating something her mother had once said to her. "Our indiscretions are viewed differently."

"I'm not a child, Lady Milverton." Galina looked up and met Alessa's gaze. "I saw what happened to the girls at the inn who formed liaisons with officers. I know the risks. I know I cannot marry John. But I learned long ago that life is not perfect. I have always tried to make the best of what is offered to me."

She sounded in command of herself. Yet by her own admission, Galina was a woman in love and Alessa knew all too well how love could play havoc with one's judgment. She thought of Fiona, forced to fend for herself in London with scant money and no references to enable her to find other work. "I know how it must seem now," Alessa said, "but a woman in your position must remember—"

"You think I am so very different?" Galina sprang to her feet, her sharp clear voice filling the small room and taking them both by surprise.

"Forgive me, Lady Milverton," Galina said, the quick rise and fall of her chest betraying her emotions. "But do you think because my father was a peasant I do not have the—the same feelings as you? The same needs? The same passions?"

Alessa gripped her hands together, thinking of Harry's lips against her skin and Harry's body filling her own. If anyone tried to make her give Harry up . . . Not that it was the same, of course. For all the anguish she felt over Alastair and Niki, at least she knew both of them had a name. "It isn't only a question of your own future," Alessa said. "There might be consequences."

"A baby." Unexpectedly, a smile crossed Galina's face. "Fond as I am of Niki and Zara, I would like to have a baby of my own. I would like to have John's baby. Whatever happens, I do not think he would let either of us starve."

"No," Alessa agreed, quick to defend Harry's cousin. "Of course not. But—"

Galina laid a hand on the back of her chair as though to steady herself. "It is no use, Lady Milverton. If John wants me, it would take more than convention or morality to stand in my way."

Alessa was at a loss for an answer. She should urge Galina to caution, yet she could not help thinking that if John cared for Galina as much as Galina did for him, their liaison might be far more honest and genuine than the contract she had entered into with Harry.

The silence was broken by a rap at the door. Relieved at the interruption, Alessa crossed the room and opened the door to find her husband and John standing in the corridor outside.

"I'm sorry to intrude," Harry said, "but John has something important to say to Galina. I think we should leave them alone together."

Alessa looked at her husband in bewilderment. He appeared a trifle bemused but much more cheerful than he had half an hour ago. Behind him, John looked at once determined and surprisingly exhilarated.

"Trust me," Harry said, taking Alessa's arm and drawing her out into the corridor.

"Thank you, Harry," John murmured, his eyes on the room beyond. "I won't forget this." Nodding briefly to Alessa, he strode through the door and pulled it shut behind him.

"Harry?" Alessa said. "Are you going to tell me what all this is about?"

Improbably, Harry collapsed against the corridor wall and let out a whoop of delighted laughter.

"Harry," Alessa persisted, wondering if he had drunk more at the christening breakfast than she had realized, "what does John have to say to Galina?"

Harry grinned. "He's going to ask her to marry him."

Alessa stared at her husband in disbelief, which gave way to annoyance. "Don't joke about this, Harry. Galina deserves better."

"She most certainly does," Harry agreed. "And I'm perfectly serious. So is John."

"But . . ." Alessa bit back the words as she saw the laughter die in Harry's eyes. "Harry," she protested, "you must see . . ."

"What?" Harry folded his arms and regarded her, as if daring her to voice objections.

Alessa turned away with a burst of impatience. Surely even Harry understood how unsuitable the match was. Galina wasn't Fiona, who even before her legitimacy was proved had been unquestionably a gentleman's daughter, raised and educated in a gentleman's house. Galina's parents had been peasants. And John was first cousin to the Earl of Milverton. The idea of marriage between them was utterly mad.

Even madder than Harry's insistence on marrying a shop-keeper's daughter. The situations were very like, Alessa realized, staring at a porcelain bowl which stood on a marquetry side table beside her door. An honorable, well-born young man insisting on standing by a woman of lower station. Save that Galina was not pregnant.

"But John hasn't even touched her yet," Alessa said, turning back to Harry. "Not in that way. There's no need for marriage."

"If that's all marriage means, perhaps there isn't," Harry said in a cold, flat voice. "John feels differently." He pushed himself away from the wall. "If you'll excuse me, I promised John I'd break the news to my mother."

Watching Harry stride toward the stairs, Alessa felt as she had as a girl when she had failed to meet Fiona's expectations. "Harry," she cried, running down the carpeted corridor after him with no very clear notion of what she meant to do or say.

"Yes?" Harry stopped and looked down at her, his expression not softening.

Alessa sought for some words or action which might bridge this new gulf between them. "May I come with you?" she asked.

Lady Milverton made a sound halfway between contempt and incredulity. "I never thought that madness ran in the Dudley family. It seems I was mistaken. I trust you disabused John of this foolery."

Feeling a faint weariness at the prospect of the coming confrontation, Harry rested his arms along the back of a wing chair in his mother's sitting room. Ever since the scene in the breakfast parlor at Moresby, battles with his mother had lost their edge. Nothing else she said to him could be quite that painful. "I didn't presume to try," he told her. "Madness aside, we Dudleys can be quite damnably stubborn, you know."

"Don't be impertinent, Harry," Lady Milverton said. "Even you will hardly consent to a match such as this."

Harry looked at his mother, seated across from him on a carved mahogany settee. One did not think of one's mother in such terms, but he supposed most would account her beautiful. Dark hair, fine bones, aristocratic carriage. Like Alessa, Harry realized, comparing them consciously for the first time. His gaze went to his wife, sitting quietly a little to one side. She was still dressed in the gown she had worn to the christening, as was Lady Milverton. Alessa wore white lace embroidered with pearls, his mother lavender silk, but the overall impression of well-groomed elegance was the same.

As was their reaction to John and Galina's betrothal, save that his mother had voiced what Alessa had not dared put into words. Harry looked away from Alessa, unwilling to acknowledge how much he wanted her to understand.

"Harry." Lady Milverton's voice was tinged with the faintest anxiety. "You will forbid the marriage."

"I'm hardly in a position to do so," Harry pointed out. "I am not John's guardian, and in any case he is of age."

"You are the head of the Dudley family," Lady Milverton said firmly.

"Indisputable, but I don't think that would stop John. Assuming, of course, that I wanted to."

Alarm flickered across his mother's face. "Next you will tell me you favor the match," she said with an exclamation of disbelief.

"As a matter of fact I do," Harry said truthfully. "Galina is a fine, intelligent young woman who's survived things most of us haven't even dreamed of. Any young man would be lucky to have her."

Lady Milverton rose in one swift, economical movement. "The girl is a peasant."

"So were our ancestors, if you go back far enough."

Their eyes met. They were standing so close that Harry could smell his mother's scent, an elusive fragrance which had stirred conflicting emotions from nursery days.

Lady Milverton drew in her breath, then released it very slowly. "I don't know why I expected any differently," she said in the even voice with which she always made her most painful attacks. "It's little different from your own sordid affair. It seems John has aped more than your subversive ideas."

Harry's fingers dug into the upholstery of the chair back. "On the contrary, John is a far better man than I am. I married Nadia because I felt responsible for her. John is marrying Galina because he loves her."

"This is no time for vulgar sentiment, Harry. I take it the girl is pregnant. That's the only possible explanation for such lunacy."

"No." Alessa got to her feet, her voice sharp. "You wrong them both. John has not taken Galina to his bed."

"How do you know?" Lady Milverton asked.

"Galina told me."

"And you believed her?" Lady Milverton's brows rose. "These creatures will say anything, my dear. I don't doubt the girl is a clever liar."

Alessa stood very still, but the pearls on her gown shimmered in the late afternoon sunlight, betraying her trembling. "Galina would not lie to me," Alessa said. "She has too much pride."

"You're being soft-hearted, Alessa," Lady Milverton told her in a tone of mild reproof. "Don't make the mistake of thinking that persons of that sort feel as we do. The girl would hardly allow pride to interfere with her self-interest. Fortunately," she added, turning back to Harry, "the matter does not lie in your hands. If John persists in such a disastrous course, his father will cut him off without a shilling."

"He may," Harry agreed. "But I think I can compensate for any difficulties John may encounter by increasing his salary."

His eyes on his mother's outraged face, Harry heard the soft rustling of Alessa's dress as she came to stand beside him. "We hope John and Galina will make their home with us after they are married," Alessa said, giving Lady Milverton a smile of supreme confidence. "We would be sorry to lose either of them."

Lady Milverton stared at her daughter-in-law as if she had never seen her before. "I would not have expected you to take such a position, Alessa," she said at last. "It seems marriage to Harry has changed you."

Alessa linked her arm through Harry's and looked up at him with a smile which warmed his heart. "Yes," she said. "It has."

"I've never seen such a kick-up." Georgiana sprawled on the leather-covered library sofa and licked the jam from her fingers. "It's almost a pity Uncle George is in Northumberland. There really would have been fireworks if he'd been here."

"Nicer this way for John and Galina, I would think," Peter said, thinking of the obvious happiness on the young couple's faces. He glanced at Radka, who was sitting beside him. He hadn't seen her since her mother's wedding two days ago and each separation from her became more difficult than the last. Today Simon had taken pity on him and suggested they invite the girls for a drive, but by the time they reached Milverton House it had begun to rain, so they had taken refuge in the library with a plate of scones and a pot of chocolate. They were conversing quite comfortably in French, the only language in which they all were fluent.

"The betrothal is very romantic, is it not?" Radka said. "In Russia such a thing would not happen."

"In England it doesn't happen very often," Simon told her.

Georgiana helped herself to another scone. "Harry and Alessa were wonderful. I don't think Mama will ever forgive them."

Simon grinned. "I'd have expected it of Harry, but Alessa surprised me. Harry must be having a good influence on her."

"That's just the sort of horrid thing brothers always say," Georgiana said, pretending to throw her napkin at him. "But I do think she and Harry have been getting on better since all the fuss about John and Galina's betrothal. Do you know," Georgiana exclaimed, leaning forward and gesturing with the scone, "they seem to get on better whenever they quarrel with Mama. Do you suppose we should—"

"No," Peter and Simon said almost in unison.

"Oh very well." Georgiana subsided and took another bite of the scone. "But if things take a turn for the worse . . ."

"No," Simon said firmly.

"Well, perhaps it won't be necessary," Georgiana conceded. "Do you think now they might finally admit they love each other?"

Simon looked down into his cup and Peter knew his friend was still worried about his sister. "I doubt they'd do anything so easily," Simon said.

"But why not?" Georgiana demanded. "It's so obvious to us, and it would be so simple."

"But it is not simple at all, Georgiana," Radka said, leaning toward the younger girl. "When a marriage is arranged, how is one ever to believe the other person would have married one for oneself? It was an arranged marriage, was it not?" she asked, looking back at Peter.

Peter swallowed. He'd been hopelessly distracted by the way Radka's gown pulled across her breasts when she leaned forward. Now that she had turned to him, he found her violet scent equally distracting. "Yes," he managed to say. "That doesn't mean they don't love each other now."

"Sometimes arranged marriages work out like that," Simon said. "But don't ever let anyone tell you it works all the time."

285

"No," Radka agreed in a quiet voice. "I know it does not. I saw my parents."

Peter laid his hand over hers in a gesture of comfort. His skin burned when he touched her own and then the warmth went deeper within when she gave him a smile of thanks.

"They still don't know who killed that Russian captain." Georgiana, who never let a lull in the conversation last too long, drew her feet up onto the sofa. "Harry's been to talk to the police officer and the magistrates but they don't seem to have learned anything. You don't suppose he was killed by anyone we know, do you?" she asked, sounding both intrigued and appalled.

"I doubt it," Simon said calmly. "If he had proof Niki wasn't Harry's son, no one would have had reason to get rid of him. Quite the reverse in fact."

Georgiana's face grew serious. "Do you think Niki is really Harry's son?"

"I think," Simon said in a quiet voice with an undercurrent of determination, "that we had all better make up our minds to it that he is."

"Do you think Alessa can do that?" Georgiana asked.

"I don't know."

Radka looked with sympathy at Georgiana's troubled face, then turned to Peter. "Georgiana and I are so looking forward to the party at your house." Fiona was giving a party the next day to introduce Niki and Zara to other families with young children. "Are we not, Georgy?" Radka said to Georgiana.

"Of course we are. Except that Julia's decided to go. I can't think why, for it's not at all her sort of thing. I suppose it's because she likes the idea of going to that beautiful, enormous house. I'm glad Edward's coming along to keep her occupied." Georgiana leaned forward to pour herself some more chocolate. "You don't think if we got Harry and Alessa alone at the party . . ."

Simon laid a hand on her wrist. "Sometimes," he said, "people have to solve things for themselves."

286

Georgiana opened her mouth to protest, but before she could speak, the library doors opened with an exuberant crack that did not sound like any of the footmen.

Peter looked round to see a tall, carelessly dressed young man with red-tinged hair stride over the threshold. The man looked familiar, but it was not until Georgiana flung herself forward with a cry of "Matt!" that Peter realized the new arrival was Matthew Dudley, Harry's younger brother, who spent most of his time looking for antiquities in Egypt.

"What are you doing here?" Georgiana demanded, hugging her brother. "Why didn't you tell us you were coming? How was Egypt?"

"Hot and dusty," Matt told her. "I'm here because the last time I checked it was where my family lived and I have a certain passing fondness for them, and I didn't tell you I was coming because I wasn't sure when the ship would dock and I hate to write letters." He held her at arms' length and surveyed her. "I swear, you never seem to stop growing, brat."

"You always say that," Georgiana objected, dragging him forward. "You remember Simon and Peter, don't you? Radka, this is my brother Matt who's just come back from Egypt. Countess Radka Chernikova, Matt. She's staying with us because her mother's on her wedding journey, and she has a wicked uncle who wants to marry her to someone horrid."

"Delighted to meet you." Matt sketched a bow in Radka's direction and smiled at her with rather too much charm for Peter's peace of mind. "If it's any consolation," Matt said to Radka, "when it comes to keeping wicked uncles at bay, I doubt you could find a better man for the job than my brother."

Radka, who was beginning to learn English, nodded as if she had followed this speech. "Thank you, Mr. Dudley."

"Her uncle, Count Chernikov, is supposed to be on the Continent," Georgiana told Matt. "But we're afraid he may come looking for Radka. If he does, you're to deny all knowledge of her."

Matt laid his hand over his heart. "You have my solemn promise." He grinned at his sister. "Been having rather a busy time of it, haven't you?"

"Oh, that's nothing," Georgiana said. "Julia's finally going to marry Edward, and John's going to marry a Russian peasant girl, and Harry and Alessa have a baby, and they have two more children as well because it turns out Harry was married before and his wife had a baby that didn't die like Harry thought it did, and the baby has a cousin and . . ." She broke off and looked at her brother with smug satisfaction.

"Well," Matt said, "it sounds as if things have been less dull at home than usual. Perhaps I'd better have a drink before you tell me the details."

Alessa leaned back in her chair, basking in the warmth of the fire and the sound of children's voices and the comfort of being surrounded by people who were interested in Alastair and Niki because they were children, not contenders for the earldom. Everyone Fiona had invited to the party was connected in one way or another to her own family or Alessa's, and all of them seemed to prefer talking about their children to relating the latest gossip. At one time, Alessa would have found such a party dreadfully flat. Now she could not imagine anything more pleasant.

It was difficult to believe this was the same room she had entered five years ago as Adrian's prospective bride. The dark wainscotting was the same, and the gilt-framed pictures and rose velvet upholstery, but the atmosphere could not be more different.

"The children have done wonders for this house," Alessa said to Fiona. They were gathered near the fire with some of the other women.

"Children do wonders for anything," said Nicola Windham, Verity's foster mother, one eye on her small son, who was crawling across the carpet with gleeful determination. "I

288

just had a letter from my friend Francesca Scott. She used to send me accounts of Parisian fashions, but now all she writes about is rattles and colic. And to think Francesca used to tease *me* that I'd gone soft over Verity. Charles," Nicola added in sudden warning as her son crawled dangerously close to a brass-inlaid table leg.

Charles Windham bent down and scooped up his son just in time to avoid a collision.

"Is Charles happy to have a son?" Alessa asked, envying Nicola for having been able to give her husband an heir.

Nicola looked thoughtful. "He insisted it didn't matter," she said, "though I suppose most men like the idea of having someone to follow them. After all, I'd like it if one of the children took to music as I did."

"Magnus tried to pretend it didn't matter, but I knew he wanted a son desperately," said Margaret Melchett, glancing affectionately at her husband, who had joined Charles and Fiona's brother Robin.

Alessa looked at the quiet dark-haired young woman who held the title that might have been her own. It was Margaret's husband who had become Marquis of Parminter when Adrian was proved illegitimate. It had always bothered Alessa that Harry had never seemed as concerned as most men with the importance of an heir. For the first time she realized that he had lifted an enormous burden from her shoulders.

"There's something to be said for marrying a man who already has two sons." Fiona leaned forward to pass round a plate of cakes. "What about you, Rachel?" she asked the fifth woman present, Magnus's sister Rachel.

Rachel Melchett, an attractive auburn-haired woman who managed her own theater company and was as enviably self-assured and competent as Fiona, gave a wry smile. "I expect Guy would like one of the children to follow in his footsteps and be a playwright, but I'm sure he'd maintain that girls can write plays just as well as boys."

Rachel's husband, Guy, was known for his radical views.

He and Harry had become great friends, but though Alessa liked him too, she was never quite sure what to make of Guy's cheerful and often quite outrageous attacks on the world as she knew it. Lately, however, her world had been so turned upside down that she found she would rather welcome his perspective.

Sometime later in the afternoon, Guy came over to offer his congratulations to John and Galina while Alessa was talking to them. There was no surprise in Guy's voice as he spoke to the couple, merely sincere wishes for their future and genuine delight at their happiness. He even said a few words to Galina in Russian.

"I didn't know you knew Russian," Alessa said to him when John and Galina had moved off, though it was difficult to be surprised by anything Guy Melchett did.

"The merest smattering," Guy said with one of the engaging grins which made his blunt-featured face seem devastatingly attractive. "There was a Russian actor at the theater in Paris where I worked for a time."

Alessa adjusted her embroidered silk scarf. "You're happy about John and Galina's betrothal, aren't you?" she said, her eyes on the scarf's lace edging.

"Love's a dangerous state, but I'm always happy to see two people willing to risk it. John's a good fellow," Guy added in a more serious tone, "and Galina seems charming."

"I was shocked when I first learned of the betrothal," Alessa confessed, twisting the end of the scarf around her finger. "I didn't think such a marriage was possible. I suppose you think that's horrid," she added, looking up at Guy.

"No," said Guy, his gray-green eyes honest, "but I'm impressed that you changed your mind. It's difficult to go against the training of a lifetime."

"Harry does," Alessa said. "Constantly. I think I saw that the day he asked me to marry him, though I didn't understand it until later. Perhaps that's what . . ."

"What drew you to him?" Guy asked.

"Yes," Alessa said, grateful to him for putting it so tact-

290

fully. "Do you quite despise people like us?" she asked abruptly, voicing the question that had troubled her for years.

"Despise you?" Guy asked in surprise. "No, of course not. I'd look impossibly arrogant if I did, wouldn't I? How could I despise the work Harry and Gideon and Windham have done in Parliament? Or the school Fiona started? I'm even more than passingly fond of my cousin Magnus, though I disagree with him about a number of things. We're all trapped to some degree by the circumstances of our birth."

Alessa reached up and touched the cameo brooch at her throat. "When I was eighteen, I thought I knew precisely what was important and how the world should be ordered. Now I feel as if I'm standing on shifting sands."

Guy laughed. "When I was eighteen, I thought I knew everything. With each passing year, I feel I know less."

"But the sort of life you wanted hasn't changed so very much, has it?" Alessa said.

"On the contrary. It took me years to realize how much I wanted Rachel," Guy said with a warmth in his eyes which Alessa longed to see on her own husband's face. "People do change," Guy continued in a more thoughtful voice. "When Rachel's sister was eighteen, she thought she wanted a title. Later she had a chance to be a duchess, but instead she married a merchant's son with a crippled leg and persuaded him to stand for Parliament."

"Because she fell in love?" Alessa asked.

"Do you know," said Guy, an odd note in his voice, "I rather think she did. But I also think she decided she wanted power more than a title. She's been the making of her husband."

"I'm not sure what it is I want," Alessa said. "Everything seems hopelessly confusing."

"Good," Guy told her, "I'm all for confusion. There's nothing like complacency to foil change."

He smiled, but his eyes were genuine and Alessa knew he

291

was not mocking her. She returned the smile, feeling in some obscure way more comfortable with herself.

They were interrupted by laughter as Beth Carne hurried by, accompanied by Rachel's daughter, Jessica. Jessica stopped and looked up at Guy. "You haven't forgot you promised us a story later, have you, Daddy?"

"Have you ever known me tô go back on my word?" Guy said, ruffling his stepdaughter's hair before she ran off with Beth.

"You think of Jessica and Alec as your own children, don't you?" Alessa asked him.

"Yes," said Guy without hesitation. "More to the point, they seem to think of me as their father, though it took some time."

"It doesn't matter to you that their name isn't Melchett?"

Guy grinned. "I must confess I've never had a proper appreciation for the Melchett name."

Across the room, Alessa saw Magnus Melchett lift his young son up onto his lap. "If you and Rachel have a son, will you view him differently than Alec?" she asked, recalling her talk with the other women.

"I hope not," Guy said. "I don't view our daughter differently than Jessica. But then I don't have an inheritance to worry about. That has a way of complicating things."

Alessa felt a leaden weight settle about her shoulders. "It certainly does."

Guy touched her arm lightly. "Let's join the children. They have a way of putting things in perspective."

Alessa smiled gratefully at him. They found the younger children sitting on the carpet near the fireplace under Peter and Radka's supervision.

"I remember when I found out I was going to have a baby brother," announced Susanna Windham, a four-year-old with her mother's red-gold hair. "I wasn't even three."

"It's a game," Peter whispered to Alessa. "Who can remember back the farthest. It keeps them occupied for hours."

Robby looked up at Alessa. "I remember your wedding."

"Are you sure?" Alessa asked, looking at her brother doubtfully.

"I do. You had a dress with lots of lace and there were flowers and *Maman* kept telling me not to squirm. I was only two."

"You were almost three," Alessa told him. "It seems you and Susanna are tied."

"I remember when Juliet's balcony fell down. How old was Daddy?" Corisande Melchett asked, tugging at Guy's trouser leg.

"Just past two if memory serves," Guy said, dropping down on the floor and pulling her onto his lap.

"I remember something," Zara said in Russian. Radka went over to translate, but Alessa hurried forward, brushing past the settee where Edward and Julia were sitting together far more closely than Lady Milverton would allow.

"What is it you remember, darling?" Alessa asked in Russian.

"My mama in Russia took me in a barge on the river."

"Do you know how old you were?" Alessa asked.

Zara shook her head. "It was when my other papa was still alive."

"Then you can't have been more than two," Alessa said. "It seems you're tied with Corisande."

The game continued and Alessa gave herself up to the enjoyment of the children. Guy was right. They helped put things in perspective. She was feeling happier than she had in days when a footman slipped into the room and stopped to speak with Fiona, who had joined the group around the children. "Excuse me, my lady," he murmured, "but Mr. Adrian Melchett has called again."

Fiona glanced quickly at Alessa, then nodded to the footman. "You'd best show him up, Thomas. It is a family party, after all."

Chapter Eighteen

Harry's hands clenched into fists as Adrian Melchett was shown into the room. This was the man to whom Alessa had given her heart, the man she had almost married, the man who had betrayed her trust. Thanks to Adrian's lies, Harry feared Alessa would never believe him if he told her he loved her.

Though they had met years before, Harry had not remembered how strikingly handsome the other man was. He had his sister Fiona's golden hair and finely drawn features, and if he did not have her understanding, he appeared to possess abundant charm. It was no wonder Alessa had been infatuated with him.

It would be no wonder if she still was. Harry cast a quick glance at his wife. She was sitting very still, her face pale, her eyes dark and expressionless, her arms clasped around Zara who was on her lap. Whatever else Alessa felt, she was clearly not unaffected by Adrian's arrival.

Nor, Harry realized, was she surprised to see him. Alessa must have known Adrian was in London. Perhaps she had already seen him. And she had said nothing of it to her husband.

"You must forgive me," Adrian said as Fiona came forward to greet him. "I did not realize you were entertaining." His manner was engagingly boyish though Harry knew Adrian was three years his senior.

"It's just family," Fiona said, with a smile which was friendly if a trifle fixed. "I think you know everyone."

"Hullo, Adrian." Gideon moved forward, his hand extended. He, too, was smiling, but Harry thought there was something protective in the way he positioned himself beside his wife. "It seems India agreed with you."

"I haven't done badly for myself." Adrian clasped Gideon's hand, and for a moment Harry could have sworn he saw the echo of some long-ago conflict between the two men. "I brought some presents for the children," Adrian continued, "but I thought it best to leave them with one of the footmen."

As Fiona drew Adrian toward the rest of the company, Harry glanced again at Alessa. He was desperate for some clue to her feelings, but she seemed determined not to betray them. He could have sworn there was no anger in her eyes. Had Adrian's charm made her forget his betrayal?

Adrian nodded to his brother Robin, then walked over to Magnus and shook his hand. "I understand you've built a Parminter House of your own," Adrian said, "and that you're planning a country house that will rival Sundon."

"One must needs have the trappings to play the part." Oddly enough, Magnus, who had taken Adrian's title, seemed more comfortable with him than Gideon had been. "I don't believe you know my wife," Magnus added, putting his arm around Margaret.

"No, but I'm delighted to meet the new Lady Parminter." Adrian bowed to Margaret with the smile which must once have won Alessa's heart.

"Our son is over there," Magnus said with obvious pride, indicating the area near the fireplace where the children were still gathered, watching the scene with curiosity.

"The next Marquis of Parminter. I'm sure my grandmother is pleased." There was a trace of amusement in Adrian's eyes but no resentment. Harry found himself wishing the man would behave with less grace. There was something dangerously attractive about a reformed prodigal.

Adrian remained for most of the afternoon, speaking quietly with various of the guests, not making himself conspicuous or disrupting the party. He even spent a good half-hour talking about India to an interested group of the older children. There was nothing to take exception to in his manner, and that, Harry thought with savage frustration, made it all the worse.

Only pride kept Harry from staying close to Alessa's side while her former betrothed was in the room. Pride told him he could not follow his wife with his eyes for the entire afternoon. Pride was shattered when, in the midst of a conversation with Rachel Melchett, he looked up and had a clear view of Adrian carrying Alessa's hand to his lips.

Alessa was looking down, so that their heads were only inches apart, her dark curls almost brushing the burnished gold of his hair. When Adrian straightened up, she smiled at him with a confident assurance which made Harry's blood run hot with anger, then ice cold with dread.

"May I say something wholly impertinent?" Rachel asked quietly.

Harry forced a smile to his lips. "I can't imagine you being impertinent, Rachel."

"My husband always has a quote for every occasion," Rachel said, her voice light but her eyes serious. "In this case I rather think he'd say something about the green-eyed monster." She laid a hand on Harry's arm. "Jealousy is a terrifyingly destructive emotion. Believe me, I know from experience."

Rachel's gaze spoke volumes. "Thank you," Harry said, touching her hand. She was right, he knew. But that did not make the thought of Alessa and Adrian any easier to bear.

Drawing on all the skills he had acquired in his years of diplomacy, Harry carefully schooled his feelings until most of the guests had departed. The Milverton party lingered so that Alessa could go upstairs to feed Alastair. Fiona and the younger children went with her, and the others took them-

ves off for a game of billiards, leaving Harry alone in the
drawing room with his brother and Gideon.

Harry leaned back in his chair and massaged his temples,
feeling the strain of the past two hours settle like a dull ache
behind his eyes.

"A nice party," Matt said, stretching his legs out in front of
him. "Perhaps there is something to be said for the delights
of domesticity."

"It helps to find the right woman," Gideon told him.

"Yes, I would think so. Though Harry managed to do it
without even trying, damn his eyes."

Harry dropped his hands. He was very fond of Matt, but
he did not care to have his younger brother know the state of
his marriage. "In your case the choice is somewhat limited,"
he told Matt. "I wonder how many women there are who
would put up with a husband who has an insatiable interest
in people who've been dead for thousands of years."

"Can't be any worse than putting up with politics and the
London Season and running a mausoleum of a house," Matt
said cheerfully.

Harry regarded his brother with affection, thinking that
Matt's form of rebellion against being a Dudley was far less
destructive than his own. Instead of lashing out, Matt had
simply developed his own interests. Interests which took him
well away from England and the family. Being a younger
son, Matt had been able to stay away.

Matt pushed himself to his feet. "I suppose I ought to go
find the others," he said. "I promised Simon a game of billiards. Do I need a map to find my way to the billiard room,
Harne?"

"Depends on how good you are at geography," Gideon said
with a grin.

While Gideon saw Matt to the door and directed him to
the billiard room, Harry contemplated the wavering flames
of the fire and brooded over the image of Adrian Melchett
pressing Alessa's hand to his lips.

297

"You can stop torturing yourself," Gideon said in a qui voice. "Adrian didn't come here to see Alessa."

Harry looked up and met his friend's gaze. "That obviou was it?" he asked, torn between amusement and despair. appreciate the effort, but if you're going to try to tell me h just came here to deliver presents to the children . . ."

"Hardly," Gideon said, moving toward a chair. He seeme to be limping more than usual, and his face was shadowe with weariness. "Adrian came to see his daughter."

Harry sat up in surprise. "His daughter?"

"Adrian was my first wife's lover," Gideon said, easin himself into an armchair. "I thought you knew. Everyone i London seemed to at the time. Haven't you ever wondere why Beth looks so like Fiona?"

Harry had an image of Beth Carne with her long pale gol hair and dark gray eyes. Used to thinking of Fiona as th young Carnes' mother, Harry had never given the matte much thought, but Beth did look far more like Fiona tha Gideon. And Adrian Melchett looked like Fiona as well.

Though Gideon rarely spoke of his first wife, Harry kne the marriage had not been a happy one. He now understoo that moment of challenge when Gideon and Adrian ha shaken hands. "And here I was resenting his attentions t Alessa," Harry said. "It's a wonder you even receive th man."

Gideon gave a dry smile. "My first marriage was damage beyond repair while Adrian was still a young whelp at Cam bridge." Gideon leaned forward. "To his credit, Adrian genu inely loved Aline. Nearly a year after her death, I heard hir break down and admit no other woman could ever mean a much to him. Alessa was there as well. That's why she brok the engagement."

My fiancé pretended to be in love with me and I was silly enough believe him. It was an embarrassing experience. I trust you woul never make the same mistake. "Bastard," Harry said, recallin Alessa's words the day he had asked her to marry him.

"As a matter of fact, he is," Gideon agreed. "But it's hardly fair to blame Adrian because his mother committed bigamy."

"I suppose I must acquit him of complicity in that event," Harry admitted with a reluctant smile. "It's a pity. I spent the afternoon longing for an excuse to plant him a facer. The fellow is too damn, well behaved."

"His years in India seem to have had a good effect on him." Gideon stretched his legs out in front of him and stared at the toes of his boots. "I forgave Adrian for Aline a long time ago. But I couldn't stomach the idea of his laying claim to Beth."

"Did he?" Harry asked.

"No." Gideon's dark eyes were thoughtful. "Before he left, he took me aside and said he was grateful for the chance to see her, but he wouldn't interfere. I felt almost charitable toward him."

They were silent for a few moments until the crackling of the fire broke the stillness. "You haven't learned anything more about Lychenko?" Gideon asked, shifting his position in the chair.

Harry shook his head, relieved to be talking of something else. "I've made some inquiries myself in the vicinity of the inn, but it seems not a soul paid attention to Grigor's doings the night of his death. Even if we learn who killed him, I doubt we'll ever know what Grigor wanted to tell Alessa." Harry hesitated, staring down at the rich, glowing colors of the carpet which echoed the intricate pattern of the painted ceiling overhead. "I love Niki. Nothing could change that. But every time I look at him . . ."

"There's nothing more damnable than uncertainty," Gideon said.

"I'd have thought so," Harry agreed. "But after what you told me about Beth . . . Perhaps knowing another man fathered the child you thought was your own is even worse."

"No," Gideon said with sudden force. "It isn't. Believe me."

Harry looked up at his friend, suddenly aware of the cool

shadows of early evening spilling into the room. "You mean not being certain about Beth was worse than knowing the truth?"

"No," Gideon said again. "I knew from the first that Beth wasn't mine." He leaned over and picked up a carved wooden horse which one of the children had left on the floor. "Ever since I learned about Niki, I've wondered if I should tell you," he said, turning the horse over in his hands. "It's not a story I'd share with many, but it seems we share a common predicament."

"It's all right," Harry said, feeling awkward. "There's no need—"

"On the contrary," Gideon said, meeting his gaze squarely. "Judging by what I've seen of you in the past weeks, I'd say there's every need." He ran a finger over the worn wood of the horse, scarred from many nursery battles. "This was Peter's originally. I gave it to him when he was little older than Fenella. God, but I was proud of him. I'd always had my doubts about Teddy's parentage, but Peter, I thought, was the one unsullied thing to come out of my marriage. Then one night Aline decided to disabuse me of the notion."

Though he had seen the revelation coming, Harry drew in his breath. "It wasn't . . ."

"No," Gideon said, "not Adrian. He wasn't that precocious. The man's name doesn't matter," he continued in a quick, even voice. "Suffice it to say, Aline had a lover before we were married. In her anger, she tried to convince me the lover was Peter's father. But the truth is, none of us could ever know for certain who had fathered him."

A host of images sprang to Harry's mind: Gideon and Peter walking together across the grounds at Moresby, their stride strikingly similar. Peter, his face intent, trying to best his father at chess. Gideon looking on with pride as Peter delivered a particularly clever piece of reasoning. How many times Harry had envied the easy camaraderie between Gideon and Peter, something he had never known with his own father. He could not think of two other men who seemed so unquestionably father and son. "In God's name how did you learn to accept it?" he asked.

Gideon gave a brief, self-derisive laugh. "At the time I didn't. I committed one blunder after another. Finally I went off to the Peninsula and turned my back on everything, including my children, which of all the mistakes I have made in my life is probably the most criminally stupid. I don't think," he added, his voice low and bitter, "that I will ever forgive myself."

"But you came back," Harry said.

"Yes, I came back. Out of duty at first. Aline was dead by then and I was all the children had. I soon realized that they were mine, whoever's bed they'd been conceived in."

"Do you think Peter suspects?" Harry asked, remembering Niki's nightmare and wondering how much his own son was aware of.

A spasm of anger crossed Gideon's face. "Peter knows. When he was twelve he overheard a conversation that should never have taken place. I thought then that I might have lost him for good. I was bloody terrified."

Harry thought of the bond he had felt the moment he saw Niki. And then he remembered the look on Alessa's face at the christening party when she had held Alastair while Niki clung to her skirts. "Does it ever bother you that if Fiona gives you a son he won't become Lord Carne? That your heir isn't really your son?"

Gideon smiled, all traces of anger and self-mockery gone from his face. "That's just it," he said very gently. "Peter *is* my son."

Edward set Julia down in Portman Square, declined an invitation to come in, pleading unspecified business, and drove off, his heart beating fast with panic. Who would have thought a child could have such a clear memory of some-

301

thing that had happened when she was barely two? Yet if Zara remembered the barge ride, it was all too likely that she remembered other events on that day. Or that, if she did not remember them now, she would in the future. She might even realize she had seen Edward before.

Harry was no fool. If Zara remembered anything at all, Harry might begin to unravel the whole story. Edward's palms grew sweaty as he again saw Grigor sprawled on the floor at the Golden Cross, so suddenly robbed of life. There could be no turning back now. What had started as revenge had become a matter of self-preservation.

Zara would have to be got rid of. Edward didn't want to hurt the girl, but she must be permanently removed from Harry and Alessa's household. Her disappearance would raise new questions, but there was no reason anyone should suspect that Edward, who would be as distraught as the rest of the family, had had anything to do with it.

Losing Zara would be hard on Niki, but the boy would recover. In time, the fuss would die down. Niki would remain Harry's firstborn son and heir, but Harry would always wonder about the boy's true parentage. And that, after all, was exactly what Edward wanted.

Feeling better, Edward forced his hands to ease on the reins and began to plan Zara's disappearance.

Alessa climbed the staircase slowly, aware of the echo of Harry's footsteps on the marble stairs behind her. The rest of the family had already gone up. For the first time since they had returned from the Carnes', she and Harry were alone together. But even now he kept his distance from her, though the staircase was certainly broad enough for them to walk abreast.

When she reached the landing, Alessa hesitated, one hand on the cool, polished mahogany of the stair rail. Though she and Harry had been easier in each other's company since John and Galina's betrothal, Harry had not visited her bed

Alessa sensed that he was waiting for her to give some sign that she would welcome him there, and she did not know how to do it. Especially not when he was acting as aloof as he was tonight. Yet the urges of her body grew harder to deny with each night that passed.

Harry stopped on the last step but one. As their eyes met, Alessa shivered and knew it was not because of the night air or the thin silk of her gown.

Harry drew in his breath, as if making a decision. "Alessa . . ."

"Yes?" she said, praying he would initiate what she was not brave enough to ask for herself.

"You've seen Adrian Melchett before today, haven't you? Since he's been back in England."

Disappointment washed over her. "Yes," she said, rubbing her arms to ease the chill of loneliness, "he called on Fiona while I was visiting her."

"You said nothing about it."

"It was while you were on the Continent. By the time you came back, there were so many more important things to think about."

"More important than seeing the man you first loved?"

Alessa stared at her husband in surprise. His eyes were dark and unreadable in the shadows, but she could not have mistaken his words or the edge to his voice as he spoke them. "You're jealous," she said, laughter welling up inside her.

"Is that so surprising?" Harry demanded. "I didn't much care for the way Melchett kissed your hand."

"You've seen dozens of men kiss my hand," Alessa retorted, relishing the knowledge that she could stir such feelings in him.

"Not men to whom you've been betrothed. Not men you smiled at in just that way. I know jealousy isn't the most ennobling emotion," Harry added as her laughter bubbled up again, "but I wouldn't call it funny."

"Oh, Harry." Alessa walked forward, her hands extended.

"I'm not laughing at you. Do you really think I'd have been able to smile at Adrian like that if I'd still been the least bit in love with him? Even seeing him that first time wasn't as bad as I expected. And today, when he kissed my hand, I didn't feel *anything*. That's why I smiled. It was as though I'd been liberated. Adrian can't hurt me anymore."

"Adrian had damned well better not try," Harry said, gripping her hands tightly. His face lightened. "Do you think me an utter fool?"

"No, though it is a relief to know you can be just as idiotic as I was about Marina. Harry . . ." Alessa looked up into his eyes, searching for the right words.

Harry smiled but said nothing. It was still up to her to make the first move. She could not bear it if he left her now. "Harry," Alessa said again, staring fixedly at his cravat, "will you come to my room?"

Harry released his breath as if he had been holding it. "I was beginning to think you'd never ask," he said, his voice not quite steady.

The distance from the stairhead to her bedchamber had never seemed longer. Thank God she had fed Alastair less than two hours ago. He should sleep for at least two more. It was only when she opened the door of her room that Alessa remembered that her maid was waiting to help her undress. "It's all right, Phillips," Alessa said, aware of Harry standing behind her, "I won't be needing you this evening."

"Very well, my lady." A brief smile flickered across Phillips's composed face, not the sly smile of a maid snickering at her mistress but the friendly smile of one woman to another. Since Alastair's birth, Phillips had unbent remarkably. Or perhaps, Alessa thought, she herself was the one who had changed.

As the door shut behind Phillips, Alessa turned to Harry, feeling as if she had run a long distance very quickly. It had been one thing to ask him to come to her room on the shadowy landing. It was another to face him in the bright lamp light of her bedchamber. Save for that last time, when passion had overwhelmed constraint, Harry had always come to her when she was already in bed, with a single candle burning discreetly on the bedside table. Now they were standing several feet apart, both fully clothed, and Alessa was not at all sure what she was supposed to do next.

"Not having doubts, are you?" Harry asked, stepping toward her.

"No," Alessa said, feeling even worse. If she were behaving correctly, he wouldn't want to leave her. She thought of Marina Chernikova, who had not been Harry's mistress but could have been. Marina would know what to do in such a situation. "I'm sorry," Alessa blurted out. "I know I'm not very good at this."

Harry stared at her as if she had lost her wits.

"There's no sense in pretending," Alessa said, folding her arms protectively. "I know men prefer women who are more experienced, and—"

"Who the devil told you that?" Harry demanded.

"Well, it's pretty obvious Adrian preferred experienced women, isn't it?" Alessa said, feeling defensive.

Harry drew in his breath sharply. "Adrian . . ." He bit back whatever opinion he had been about to deliver of Adrian Melchett. "If I understand correctly, Adrian was in love with someone else," Harry said, placing his hands on her shoulders. "Not that it excuses what he did to you."

"He was still in love with Aline Carne," Alessa said, distracted by the pressure of Harry's hands. "But after she died he took another married woman as his mistress, even though he was courting me at the time."

Harry's eyes darkened with anger and then with something else that made her pulse race. "Enough of Adrian." He lowered his head and kissed the tip of her nose and the hollow of her jaw and the corner of her mouth. "Don't you know you drive me mad, wife?" he murmured, his breath warm against her skin.

This was what she had wanted him to do all along, yet just when she could finally lose herself in his arms, Alessa sensed that their conversation was not finished. "I know you want me," she said, drawing back. "But perhaps that's just because when you come to me you've been without a woman for a long time."

She could see she had taken him by surprise, but he did not immediately brush aside her words, as she had half hoped he would. "Tell me," he said in a mild voice, "do you have a such a low opinion of men in general or merely of me?"

"I never asked you to be faithful to me," Alessa said, watching him carefully.

"No," Harry agreed. "You more or less told me you expected me not to be, as I recall."

Alessa's heart lurched. She feared she might be in for more honesty than she wanted.

Harry lifted his hand and traced his finger over her lips. "Don't be a fool, Alessa," he said very gently. "I haven't taken another woman to my bed since I asked you to be my wife."

For a moment, Alessa's happiness was so great that she could not speak. Then, just as Harry reached for her, she was assailed by doubt. "That doesn't mean you've taken one somewhere else, does it?" she asked, putting out a hand to forestall him.

To her relief, Harry gave a shout of laughter. "No," he assured her. "Not on the drawing room carpet, or in a hayloft, or beneath the stars, or . . . my imagination fails me." He drew her to him, and this time Alessa willingly allowed herself to melt into his arms. But instead of kissing her, he began to undo the fastenings on the back of her gown.

"What are you doing?" Alessa demanded.

"Undressing you," Harry said, his voice muffled by her hair. "It seems a sensible prelude to whatever we're going to do next."

"But we're in the middle of the floor," Alessa pointed out.

"Mmm," Harry agreed, slipping his hand beneath her chemise and trailing his fingers along her bare skin. "You aren't by any chance still shy after two years of marriage, are you?"

"No," Alessa said, drawing in her breath as he touched the sensitive flesh at the nape of her neck. "But we've never—"

"There's a great deal we've never done," Harry said, raising his head and looking down at her. "My mistake, I think. Do you want me to turn the lamps down?"

"No," Alessa decided, aware of more than a little curiosity. After all, she'd never got a proper look at Harry without his clothes on. "But if you're going to strip me naked, you might at least take your coat off."

"Gladly." Harry shrugged off his coat and tossed it over a nearby chair. "But," he added, returning his attention to her gown with a skill which made Alessa remember that, however faithful he'd been since their marriage, he'd had considerable experience before, "I've no objection to your helping."

Startled and a little hesitant, Alessa raised her hands and tried to undo the folds of his cravat. Her fingers were trembling and the fine linen seemed treacherously smooth, but she felt an intoxicating sense of power when the cravat was finally untied. Made bold, she pressed her lips against the pulse at the base of his throat and felt his heartbeat quicken in response.

The heavily embroidered bodice of her gown slipped down over her arms, and she realized Harry had unfastened the dress completely. His hands brushed her shoulders in an aching caress as he eased the soft silk folds to the floor.

Freed of the gown, Alessa felt her shyness return. She wore only a thin chemise beneath, and Harry had never seen her in so scant a garment. The air felt cool against her bare skin, and when she looked down, she saw her darkened nipples pressing against the linen fabric.

Harry's gaze skimmed over her with a hunger which made her skin feel tight and painfully sensitive. Then, as if to show he would surrender as much as she, he proceeded to strip off his waistcoat and shirt.

The lamplight played over his skin, accentuating lines of bone and muscle, picking out unexpected strands of gold in the hair on his chest. Alessa's gaze dropped lower to where tawny flesh met the biscuit-colored kerseymere of his breeches. There was no doubt that he was aroused.

Feeling her face grow warm with color and her body grow warm for other reasons, Alessa met Harry's gaze. Harry grinned at her with an ease which made her own embarrassment seem foolish. Then he took her hand and drew her to the bed.

Sitting on the edge of the damask coverlet, untying the ribbons on her slippers and unrolling her silk stockings, it was impossible to be shy. But then she looked up and saw Harry standing in front of her, completely and magnificently naked. Alessa let one of her slippers thud to the floor. Classical statues could not possibly compare with a living, breathing man. Not with Harry anyway.

Harry gently touched the muslin frill at the neck of her chemise and slid his hand lower to cup her breast, a question in his eyes. Wanting him to see her as she had seen him, Alessa lifted her arms so he could pull the chemise over her head. But as he grasped hold of the fabric, she put out her hand to stop him.

"What is it?" Harry asked.

"I've had a baby," Alessa said. "I don't look . . . I've got marks and my stomach isn't flat and . . . Oh, I wish you could have seen me before."

"I wish you could have seen me when I spent my days playing cricket, not sitting behind a desk," Harry said, and without further ado pulled the chemise over her head.

She was naked, absolutely stark naked, and it was glorious. She knew that as soon as she saw the warmth in Harry's eyes. With a cry of delight, Alessa flung her arms around Harry and drew his lips down to her own.

The taste of his mouth flooded her body and sent delicious heat coursing through her. Harry pushed aside the bedclothes and fell back on the smooth linen sheet, cradling her on top of him, which was even better. Then, taking her face between his hands, he pulled the pins from her hair so that it fell like a curtain over both of them.

"Not feeling shy now, are you?" he asked, the teasing note in his voice belied by the need in his eyes.

In answer, Alessa ran her fingers over his skin, finding the nipples hidden in the mat of hair on his chest. She might not be experienced, but she had learned something in two years of marriage.

Harry drew a sharp breath. He gripped her shoulders, then eased to a touch that was feather light. His hands drifted down over the swell of her breasts and the curve of her waist, so slowly that she was moved to protest. She wriggled on top of him, determined to wreak equal havoc on his senses.

With a more compelling touch, Harry caressed her between her thighs. But then, instead of rolling her onto her back as she'd expected, he grasped her hips and lifted her above him.

"Harry?" Alessa said uncertainly.

Harry grinned up at her, his face framed by the fall of her hair. "There's more than one way to do this, you know," he said, carefully easing her onto him. "Even in a bed."

As his flesh filled her own, Alessa shuddered with relief and longing. Some things were the same whatever position they took. But it seemed very odd . . . She moved experimentally and felt the response that ran through him.

"Christ." Harry's voice was hoarse. "Don't stop, Alessa. And don't say anything more about not being good at this."

At once frightened and intoxicated by the power she had discovered, Alessa let her instincts take over. Groaning, Harry pulled her tight against his warm, sweat-drenched skin. He kissed her or she kissed him, it scarcely mattered anymore. Her body seemed to be moving of its own volition. She felt wanton and utterly shameless.

And she liked it. Just as she admitted this to herself, the first tremor of release coursed through her, sharp and dazzlingly sweet.

The breath torn from her lungs, she clung to Harry, aware of him still moving inside her. Then his hands clenched and his body convulsed and at last they both lay still, her hair spilling over his chest, his arms wrapped close around her.

The air was heavy with the scent of their lovemaking. Harry's chest heaved beneath her and her own breathing was harsh and erratic. Cool air washed over her, but she didn't want to move. Finally, her lips against his skin, she said, "Harry?"

"Hmm?" Harry asked, trailing his fingers through her hair.

Alessa lifted her head. "I think I like it that way."

"That was fairly obvious," Harry said, his mouth curving in a smile.

It was amazing how easy it was to talk to him all of a sudden. Even so, Alessa hesitated before asking her next question. "But if you—if you wanted me and there wasn't anyone else," she said, tracing the whorls of hair on his chest, "why didn't you come to me more often?"

Harry hesitated, his face growing serious. "Because the terms of our marriage weren't conducive to intimacy. And perhaps because . . ."

"Because of what?" Alessa persisted.

"Perhaps because I was afraid to grow so close to you." Very gently, Harry disengaged his body from her own and rolled to one side.

The loss of intimacy unnerved her. Alessa looked into his eyes and knew he was going to leave. If not at this moment, then as soon as she fell asleep, as he always did. She put her hand on his arm. "Stay with me tonight, Harry. Please."

His eyes showed surprise and something else she could not

quite fathom. For a moment they were both very still. Alessa knew that, for all they had shared, if he left now, their marriage would remain incomplete.

Harry lifted his hand and brushed the hair back from her shoulder. Then, without speaking, he drew the covers up over both of them. "You may regret this," he warned, pulling her against him. "I'm a restless sleeper."

"I don't mind," Alessa said, warmed by blankets and happiness. "Besides," she added, snuggling back against the curve of his body, "perhaps there are some more things you can show me before morning."

Alessa rearranged the sketches spread out on the writing table in her first-floor sitting room and tried to school her thoughts. She was supposed to be selecting pictures which might do for the Russian history book she and Fiona were planning, but memories of the night before kept intruding. Even now, at the sedate hour of half past two, she could still feel the imprint of Harry's body on her skin.

She had woken in his arms this morning, and if she had woken not to his caresses but to Alastair's demands, when she returned to bed she had learned that making love in daylight could be every bit as enjoyable as making love at night.

Reminding herself of the task at hand, Alessa picked up one of her better sketches, a rendering of the Palladian bridge at Tsarkoe Selo. The memory of the quarrel she and Harry had had on the bridge came sharp to mind. For a moment, the unanswered questions about Niki intruded on her happiness, but she pushed them aside. Life might not be perfect—for all they had shared last night, Harry had not said he loved her—but she was not going to spoil her hard-won happiness.

Alessa set the sketch to one side with the others she planned to use. She ought to be making better use of her few hours of free time. Alastair was asleep, Niki and Zara were

311

napping as well, Radka and Georgiana had gone to the park with Peter and Simon, and Harry was meeting at Brooks's with Gideon and some other colleagues. She turned her attention to a sketch which showed a longer view of the lake and the palace grounds. Something about the perspective bothered her.

She was still puzzling over it a few moments later when there was a knock on the door. Alessa's pulse quickened with the hope that Harry had returned early, but it was one of the footmen.

The look on his face brought Alessa to her feet. "What is it?" she asked. "The children—"

"No, my lady," the footman said quickly. "It's a visitor. He says his name is Count Chernikov."

Chapter Nineteen

Chernikov. Alessa had almost forgot the danger of the count's appearance. She looked at the footman, a strapping young man quite capable of showing any number of Chernikovs the door. "Did he ask for the countess?"

The footman grinned. "What countess, my lady?"

Cheeky young fellow. Lady Milverton had complained of him on more than one occasion, but Alessa found his presence reassuring. She suppressed a smile. "Did he?"

"No, ma'am. He asked for Lord Milverton. When I told him his lordship was not at home, he asked for his lordship's wife. Is your ladyship at home?"

Alessa frowned. It would do no good to deny Chernikov. They would have to confront him sooner or later, and perhaps better she than Harry. "Show him up. And Charles, when you have done so, do you think you could intercept my brother before he returns. He's taken Countess Radka and Lady Georgiana driving in the park. He'll be coming back by Portman Street. Tell him the count is in London. He'll know what to do."

When the footman had left, Alessa rose, walked to the mirror that hung between the windows at the far end of the room, and studied her reflection. Her hair was immaculate, her gown flattering. She practiced a stern expression, then thought she might have more success if she were cordial. Leaving the mirror, she settled herself on the green satin sofa that was the dominant piece of furniture in the room. It was a trick she had learned from her mother. She would not receive her visitor at a disadvantage.

"Count Chernikov," Alessa said with every appearance of delight when he was shown into the room. "What a pleasant surprise. I did not expect to see you in England."

"I did not expect to come," Chernikov said as he bowed over her extended hand. He was a well-groomed man in his middle forties whom some might have accounted handsome. Alessa did not. He had a well-trimmed dark beard framing a thin-lipped mouth that seldom smiled and his deepset eyes were cold. He was said to be enormously ambitious. She suspected he was vain as well.

"Please," she said, indicating a chair she knew was not particularly comfortable.

"Thank you." Chernikov sat down, then carefully adjusted his position in the chair. "I trust you are well, madam. And your little son."

"He is thriving," Alessa said truthfully. "I am sorry my husband is not at home. You were at the conference? Perhaps you saw him there."

"I did." Chernikov laid his hands on the arms of the chair. "Madam, I must be blunt. Your husband left Aix-la-Chapelle most abruptly."

"I would not say so. It was never expected that he would stay long. He went only to consult with Lord Castlereagh."

The count fixed her with a stern gaze and continued as though she had not spoken. "As did my sister-in-law, the Countess Chernikova, and her daughter."

Alessa decided it was time to play the outraged wife. "Sir, are you suggesting there is some connection between the two events?"

Chernikov threw up his hands. "I suggest nothing, madam. The countess and her daughter accompanied me to Aix-la-Chapelle. I had every reason to think they would return with me to St. Petersburg. I fear they have run away, and I am deeply concerned. I am guardian to Radka and responsible for her future."

"I am Lord Milverton's wife and I am responsible for his good name."

Count Chernikov concealed his anger with obvious difficulty. "I am not impugning your husband's name, Lady Milverton. Only his good sense. He was well acquainted with Marina Chernikova when he was stationed in St. Petersburg. He called upon her more than once on his recent visit. The countess and her daughter embarked upon a ship bound for England. Yes, madam, I have traced them thus far. I strongly suspect that Lord Milverton aided their escape. Make no mistake about it, an escape it was."

Alessa's outrage was genuine. "The countess is assuredly her own woman."

The count rose abruptly. "Her daughter is not, and her daughter I intend to recover. I have arranged her betrothal. She must return to St. Petersburg. If you will not tell me her mother's whereabouts, Lady Milverton, I must return and put the question to your husband."

Alessa left the sofa and took a few steps toward the count. "My husband knows nothing."

Chernikov regarded her with something bordering on contempt. "Your loyalty does you credit, madam, but you are a foolish woman if you refuse to see what is before your nose."

"There is nothing to see." Alessa lifted her chin and looked the count full in the face. "I do not know the whereabouts of the Countess Chernikova and neither does my husband. We have heard she is in England, but I doubt that you will find her in London. I believe she is on her wedding journey."

The count blenched. Alessa felt a small surge of triumph. At last she had succeeded in piercing that self-satisfied armor. She stepped around him, walked to the bellpull, and gave it a firm tug. Chernikov's voice followed her. "The girl. Surely she would not take the girl with her."

Alessa turned round and studied the shaken figure standing across the room. "I have no idea what arrangements the countess may have made for her daughter."

315

Chernikov strode toward her. "How long? How long will she be gone?"

"I don't know," Alessa said, dismissing the matter with a shrug. "These things commonly take four or five months."

"Months?" Chernikov's face darkened with fury. "I cannot wait months."

"That is hardly my problem. Count Chernikov, I have told you all that I can. The countess has clearly not run away from you but towards another man. You came here to accuse my husband of running off with her. You have insulted him, and you have insulted me. You will not be received in this house again."

The count looked as if he had been struck, which was the effect Alessa had intended. "Charles," she said as the door opened and the footman appeared, "show Count Chernikov out."

Chernikov retrieved his hat, made her an abrupt bow, and walked toward the door. Before he reached it, he turned to her once more, his face contorted with anger and the need to beg for favors. "For the love of God, tell me his name."

"The countess's husband?" Alessa decided she could afford to be generous. Chernikov could learn it soon enough. "Jeremy Barrows. He may have rooms in London, but I have no idea where. He resides mostly in the country. Good day, Count."

He gave her a thunderous look and followed the footman out the door.

After her visitor had left, Alessa paced the room, her heart pounding. It was part elation at having routed the count, perhaps for good, part fear that despite her efforts he would succeed in finding Radka and forcing her back to Russia. Radka would not be safe till he had left England, and even then Alessa feared his power. Chernikov had right on his side. He would likely go to the Emperor, the Emperor would complain to Count Lieven, his London ambassador, Count Lieven would go to the Regent, and the Regent, not wanting to offend an ally, would go to the Foreign Secretary, who would decree that England had no hold on Radka.

But no, Cousin Sacha would surely listen to *Maman*. She must write to him at once. The price of Radka's safety might be her dowry, but that would be a small price to pay. Alessa had great faith in Sofia's ability to order events as she pleased.

Her heart had ceased its pounding. Alessa put her hand on her breast but could feel nothing but the rise and fall of her breath. She thought of every exchange in her interview with Chernikov. How easy it was to lie. And how satisfying when done in a worthy cause.

Peter strolled with Radka along one of the quieter reaches of the Serpentine, far from the cries of children and nurse-maids and the laughter of young men who found a walk along the river an occasion for hilarity. Simon, with admirable tact, had set them down a quarter-hour before. He had promised Georgy to let her handle the ribbons, and he did not think Peter and Radka would want to continue in the carriage.

It was a pleasant day, not too cool for comfort, but with the hint of autumn in the air. There was little to be heard save the lapping of water and the occasional bark of a dog in the distance. Peter was very conscious of the girl at his side. She was quieter than usual but did not seem unhappy with his company.

"A penny for your thoughts," he said.

Radka looked up, her face bewildered.

"I beg pardon?"

"Just a saying we have," Peter said, reverting to the French in which they usually conversed. "It means, oh, you seem thoughtful. Preoccupied. Are you worried?"

"Worried?" She laughed and his heart turned over. "Oh, no," she went on, "I was just thinking about my mother."

Peter thought he understood. "It will be different now, won't it?"

Radka gave him a grateful smile. "Dear Peter, you do understand. I am not sorry that she has married again. I am very happy for her, because she is so happy. And Mr. Barrows seems like a good and kind man. It's only . . ." She turned to the bank and stood looking out over the water.

"It's only that there were just the two of you for so long, and now there are three."

Radka sat down, her feet curled under her, and pulled idly at the grass. "Yes, that is it exactly. My mother now has a life apart from me. It seems strange. We were always so close."

They were quiet for a while. "Families change," Peter said. "Sometimes it's for the better."

Radka turned her head and studied him. "You are fond of your stepmother."

Peter nodded. "I like Fiona. But it was different for me. My mother died, but my father was off at war and there was only me. And the younger ones, of course. It was like I became a father instead of a son."

"But then your father came back."

"Yes, that was strange. I hardly knew him, and I was angry most of the time. But then Fiona came too and we were a family again. I never had my father to myself, not like you and the countess."

"Poor Peter. You have had a hard life."

The sympathy in her eyes washed over him like a warm caress. "So have you."

"Well then, we have had hard lives together."

If only they could. Peter felt such a welling of desire and longing that he could hardly breathe. "I'd give my life to protect you."

Radka gave a shaky laugh. "Yes, I think you would."

They leaned toward each other, not quite touching. Peter was intensely aware of the softness of her skin, the clean smell of her long hair, the curve of her brows, and the shadow cast by her lashes. She had a small mole just below her ear, a small marring of perfection which only intensified her beauty. He leaned closer and felt the warmth of her breath. Scarce daring to move, he bent his head and pressed his lips to hers.

They parted beneath his own, soft and warm and yielding. Peter closed his eyes, drowning in sensation. For a moment the world disappeared. Then, sensing a slight withdrawal on Radka's part, he moved away, terrified that he had gone too far.

Her eyes were veiled, as though she, too, had been lost in a dream. Her mouth, still parted, curved in the faintest semblance of a smile. Peter held his breath, not daring to speak. Words would destroy what was between them. It was too new, too fragile. He had taken a liberty he dared not take again, but something had passed between them, a promise, a pledge. He would redeem it one day, not now, it was too soon, but in the future.

They sat without speaking, side by side, gazing out over the water. Peter was filled with unspeakable joy. Surely the air was sweeter, the light more golden. Anything and everything was possible. He was changed forever.

Georgiana's shout recalled him to the world he had left behind. Harry's sister was running toward them across the grass. "Peter, I did it! I drove them! They didn't even try to run away."

Full of her newfound mastery, Georgiana gave no sign of noticing that Peter had changed. Nor Radka. Peter rose and gave Radka his hand. She smiled at him, but it was no different from the smile she had given him when he helped her into the carriage. Disappointed, he realized that perhaps it didn't show. On reflection, he was glad that it did not. He could not share with anyone what had happened by the river. Not even Simon.

Georgiana's high spirits infected them all, and they were very merry during the drive home. As they entered Portman Street, Simon slowed the horses, preparing for the turn that would lead them to the mews behind Milverton House. A burly young man in shirtsleeves hurled himself at the carriage, waving his arms and shouting at them to stop. Fearing some harm to the girls, Peter urged Simon to drive on. Instead, Simon reined in the horses, and Peter then recognized the man as one of the Milverton footmen. He looked different out of livery, but there was no mistaking the urgency of his voice.

"Lady Milverton sent me," he panted, out of breath from running. "I've been waiting an hour or more. You mustn't go to Milverton House. Count Chernikov called this afternoon. Lady Milverton said you would know what to do."

Radka made a small sound of dismay. She might not have understood all of the footman's words, but she had heard Chernikov's name clearly enough.

Peter took her hand. "It will be all right," he said, though he felt far from certain this was the case. Surely there was someone he could slay to protect her.

"I understand. Thank you, Charles." Simon pressed some coins into the footman's hand, then turned the horses and drove back the way they had come.

"Where are we going?" Radka asked.

Simon looked back at her and smiled. "Where Alessa and I agreed we would go if this happened. To my mother's."

Alessa stared at her mother in disbelief. "You asked Count Chernikov to call *here*?" It was the third day after Radka's removal to the Langley house in Bolton Street. Alessa had called to visit with the girl and was now closeted with her mother in a sitting room done up in the princess's favorite shades of blue.

"It would have looked odd to meet him anywhere else," Sofia said calmly. "And you needn't worry about Radka. She's in the nursery with Robby, and she has strict orders to stay there until the count's visit is over."

"But why see him at all?" Alessa had convinced herself that it was only necessary to wait until the count had tired of his search and gone home.

"Because he is a tenacious man of no imagination who alvays expects to get his own way. I've met him before, Alessa. He'll not leave England, and he can cause endless trouble. Radka can't spend her life fearing to show her face out of doors. I thought it time to put an end to it." Sofia looked in the teapot, decided it had brewed properly, then poured a cup, which she handed to her daughter. "You needn't stay if you don't want to."

"*Maman*, I'm not afraid of the man." Alessa set down her cup, added a half-teaspoon of sugar, and stirred it with more vigor than was necessary. "I haven't the slightest intention of leaving."

Sofia smiled. "I thought not. You got him addled, you know. He's not thinking properly. He's been to Somerset House to check that the marriage actually took place, he's gone to Sussex to learn where Jeremy Barrows took his bride and learned nothing for his pains, and he's been twice at the embassy. Both times he came away with the most thunderous expression. Don't look surprised, Alessa. I've had him followed."

Alessa laughed and set down her cup. "I'm not surprised. I'm impressed with your enterprise."

"It's nothing. I know a number of people, including most of the embassy staff. Fortunately, Count Lieven is at the conference. When he returns, he'll be forced to act unless we can persuade Chernikov to leave."

Sofia took another swallow of tea and set her cup aside. "But enough of this odious man." She regarded Alessa with appraising eyes. "You and Harry have come to an accommodation, haven't you?"

Alessa felt her face grow warm. Accommodation seemed a very paltry word to describe what had passed between her and Harry in the last few days. And nights. Alessa reached up and touched the knot of satin ribbon pinned to her dress, Harry's gift to her at the Moresby fair. Then she picked up her cup, wondering how much her mother could read in her face.

"I'm glad," Sofia went on. "However badly Harry has be-

321

haved—though I must admit he has conducted himself we
where Radka is concerned—I do not like to see you unhapp
or lonely."

Alessa looked up quickly, realizing the word "lonely" wa
meant to encompass a number of activities.

Sofia settled back on the sofa. "Don't look so surprised
Alessa; mothers notice these things. Now, tell me about m
grandson."

Talk of babies occupied the next quarter-hour, and by th
time Chernikov was announced, Alessa was relaxed an
quite prepared to meet him. The same could not be said c
the count. He started visibly when he was aware that she wa
in the room. Then his face assumed a mask of cordiality an
he advanced into the room and made Sofia a low bow. "Prir
cess, how delightful to see you after so many years. We hav
missed you at court."

"How kind of you to say so. You know my daughter, Lad
Milverton?"

Chernikov executed another perfect bow, his face impas
sive.

"Please sit down, Count. I've rung for fresh tea. I long t
hear the news from court."

Alessa could not have admired her mother more. For th
next half-hour Sofia plied the count with tea and with ques
tions about her friends in St. Petersburg, scarcely allowin
him time to answer and foiling all attempts to raise question
of his own. Chernikov grew more and more agitated. Bead
of sweat appeared in a faint line above his collar. Finally, h
could stand it no more. "Princess, I must talk to you abou
my late brother's wife, the Countess Chernikova."

"Ah, Marina," Sofia said with evident delight and em
barked on another lengthy reminiscence.

"She is gone," Chernikov said, his eyes desperate.

"I understand she has married an Englishman," Sofia sai
calmly. "As I have myself."

Chernikov withdrew a pristine handkerchief and moppe
his forehead. "I beg your pardon, Princess. I meant no disre

322

pect. But she has taken her daughter with her, or hidden her way." He glanced at Alessa. "Lady Milverton has been unable to tell me where she may be found. Madam, can you help me? I am her guardian, and she must return with me to Russia."

Sofia made a grimace of distaste. "Surely you would not be so cruel. I'm sure the child is much attached to her mother."

Chernikov assumed a sterner posture, as though he had found more certain ground on which to stand. "She is no longer a child, madam."

"Fourteen, is she not?"

"Fifteen, and soon to be a young woman. She is to be betrothed. I have arranged a brilliant marriage for her, a marriage of which any girl would be proud. It will take place next year."

Sofia gave a heartfelt sigh. "So soon. So young."

Chernikov's mouth tightened. "Quite old enough for what is required."

"I cannot agree with you, Count Chernikov. I was eighteen when I was married to the Prince di Tassio. He gave me two beautiful children, but the marriage was not a happy one."

"With all respect, madam, marriage is not intended to make one happy. And again, with all respect, Radka's future is my own affair, not yours."

Sofia sat forward. "I am afraid, Count that I have made it my affair." Though her expression remained pleasant, her voice had acquired a hint of steel. Chernikov showed signs of erupting from his chair, and she held up a hand to warn him off. "I think you should hear me out, for like it or not, I am now concerned in the matter."

She rose and walked to a small writing desk that stood near the window. Taking a large sheet of heavy paper from a drawer, she returned to the sofa, indicating to Chernikov that he should resume his seat. "Before her marriage, I had a long conversation with Marina Chernikova. I do not know

323

where she is at present, nor do I know what arrangement she intended to make for her daughter. What I do know is that she is unalterably opposed to having Radka forced into marriage with a man nearly three times her age. The idea fills her with revulsion, as it does me."

Sofia glanced down at the folded paper in her hand, then raised her eyes to meet the count's hard gaze. "I was moved to write to my cousin, the Emperor Alexander, on her behalf. He remembers my distress on the occasion of my first marriage, and I knew he would be sympathetic to my plea."

Chernikov made a strangled noise. His gaze went to the paper on Sofia's lap.

"Yes, Count, this is his reply. You will recognize his hand." She opened the paper and held it up for Chernikov to see. Alessa, who was seated an equal distance away, could not make out the words, but Alexander's signature stood out in bold relief.

Sofia turned the paper and perused it quickly, as though to make sure of its contents. Then she raised her eyes to Chernikov. "This is what my cousin Sacha proposes. First the betrothal will not take place. No promise has been made save your own, and you will explain the matter to her intended husband."

Chernikov half rose from his chair, his eyes wild. "No."

"Sit down, Count, I have not yet finished. Second, the monies set aside for Radka's dowry are to be transferred to an English bank. The property that would have come to her may remain in your possession. Neither Marina nor her daughter intend to return to their homeland."

"But the money, I cannot raise it."

"No? Then you must sell some of the property. Finally, Radka's guardianship is to be transferred to her mother."

Chernikov's face was ashen, his eyes dead. "I do not believe it. It is a trap."

Sofia folded the paper and tucked it behind a cushion. "Do not be distressed, Count," she said, her voice now cajoling. "The Emperor will be most grateful for your acquiescence in his affair. Those were his last words. He has always valued your loyalty and your service. I know the Emperor. You will not lose by agreeing to these terms."

A host of warring emotions passed across Chernikov's face. They gave way to a gleam of calculation. Chernikov stared at Sofia as if weighing her credibility. Sofia bore his scrutiny with every appearance of calm. Alessa watched them both, afraid to breathe.

After a long moment Chernikov stood up. "You have won, madam. I must bow to the Emperor's persuasion." He made her a curt bow and took his leave.

After the count's departure, Sofia remained sitting on the sofa, her eyes focused on nothing in particular, a bemused expression on her face. A dreadful thought crossed Alessa's mind. There had scarcely been time for Cousin Sacha's reply to reach London. *"Maman,"* she said, "let me see that letter."

Sofia gave Alessa a sharp look, then retrieved the letter from behind the cushion and held it out to her daughter. Alessa looked at the seal. It was the Emperor's. She opened the sheet and studied the signature again. There was no doubt it was from Alexander, and it was written from Aix-la-Chapelle. But the substance of the letter had nothing to do with Radka Chernikova.

"Maman, how did you dare? Suppose Chernikov had asked to read it?"

Sofia reached for the letter and carried it back to her writing desk. "I would have refused, of course. There were personal matters in it I had no wish to share with Count Chernikov."

"You are incorrigible."

Sofia returned to the sofa. "I had hoped I was clever."

"That too. Cousin Sacha has not yet written, is that right?"

"There's scarcely been time."

"But when he does . . . suppose he does not agree to what you have proposed?"

A faint look of doubt appeared on Sofia's face. "Oh, he

will. And if he does not, I must write to him again and te
him that he already has. In fact, I must do so in any case
lest Chernikov returns to Aix-la-Chapelle and demands a
audience. Alessa, you must leave. The letter must be sent to
day. You may tell Radka that she is safe and that she ma
return to Milverton House."

Alessa spent half an hour with Radka, who was overjoyed
then arranged for her to remove to Milverton House the nex
day. When Alessa at last left Bolton Street, her feelings wer
in some confusion. Her mother was arrogant, she was high
handed, she demanded her own way in everything. And ye
she could be kind, and clever, and caring. She had taken i
Radka, a child she scarcely knew, and lied and cheated t
protect her. On balance, Alessa admired her mother. An
wonder of wonders, for once she did not feel diminished b
the admission.

Harry pulled up his curricle at the Golden Cross, left hi
horses in the care of one of the stableboys, and entered th
inn to look for Officer Howell. Howell had sent him a not
that morning indicating that they might, at last, have infor
mation about the death of Captain Lychenko. Harry praye
it was so. The police investigation, to say nothing of his own
had turned up no information at all, at least none that wa
useful. In the three days he had been at the Golden Cross
Lychenko had proved to be a friendly man with a fondnes
for brandy, but he had spoken only a few words of Englisl
and no one had had what might be called a conversatio
with him.

Howell was seated in a far corner of the coffee room, bu
he was not alone. He rose at Harry's entrance and his com
panion did as well. As he approached their table, Harry too
in the features of the other man. He was tall and somewha
stooped, with a narrow face and scant dull brown hair. Hi
eyes, Harry saw when he drew closer, were blue, but of sucl
a pale color they seemed to be without expression. Not

326

emorable face or figure, save for his height, yet Harry had
e impression of watchfulness and a keen understanding.

"Lord Milverton." Howell had the relieved air of someone
ho is finally able to relinquish responsibility. "May I
esent John Burley of the Bow Street Office."

Harry held out his hand. Burley's eyes showed a flicker of
rprise, then he extended his own. His handclasp was sur-
isingly firm.

"I didn't expect Bow Street," Harry said, motioning the
o men to be seated.

"The Home Office called us in," Burley said. "Lychenko
as an officer. They want some answers before Count
even returns from the Continent and raises inconvenient
estions."

"Will you take something to drink, my lord?" Howell
ked.

The two men were drinking coffee. Harry shook his head.
want to know what you've learned."

"Someone asked for Lychenko the night he was killed,"
owell said. "Burley turned him up. It wasn't our doing."

It was a handsome admission. Burley shrugged. "Our in-
rmant is rather shy of the police. We know him, you see.
e isn't employed here regularly, but his sister works in the
tchen and they took him on that night as they were short of
lp."

Harry leaned forward. "Go on."

Burley swallowed some coffee and pushed his cup aside.
e was passing through the entrance hall when a man
ked him for Captain Lychenko. The name caught his at-
ntion. It was odd, not being English, and our informant
ades in oddities. So he noticed the man who was asking for
e captain."

Burley seemed to have all the time in the world, and
arry cursed his slowness.

"Tell me, Lord Milverton," Burley went on, his voice quiet
ut his fingers beating a soft tattoo on the table top, "do you
now a man of somewhat more than middle height, thick

dark blond hair, carefully dressed, eyes of a medium blue, a open face, pleasing features. A gentleman, you understand Not arrogant, but used to being served."

Ned. The image of his friend came to Harry's mind, un welcome and unbidden. "The description could apply to an number of people," Harry said cautiously.

"I understand," Burley said. He leaned back and sprea his long fingers on the table. "But we are not interested i any number of people, Lord Milverton. Only those peopl you may know. I daresay, people you may know well. Yo are our only link, you see, you and Lady Milverton. W have no reason to believe Captain Lychenko had other busi ness in England."

Harry refused to accept Burley's conclusion. Lychenk could well have had other fish to fry. To gain time, he asked "Is your informant to be trusted?"

There was a slight movement in the corner of Burley' mouth. "Not in the least. But he's an observant lad."

"I see. Then there's no more to be said." Harry got to hi feet.

Burley's eyes were fixed on Harry's face. "Do you kno him, Lord Milverton?"

"I might," Harry admitted, feeling like a traitor. "I ca swear to nothing. You will have to give me more time."

Burley nodded. "I understand." He stood up slowly an came around the table to stand close to Harry. "But a wor of advice, my lord. Be careful. A man has been killed."

Chapter Twenty

Harry returned to Portman Square in an unsettled frame
of mind. Burley had upset him. The description of Grigor's
visitor matched Edward, but Edward would have had no reason to seek the other man out. Or if he had, it might have
had nothing to do with Grigor's letter to Alessa and Grigor's
subsequent death.

It couldn't have been Ned. He had known him all his life.
They had played together as boys, they had gone to school
together, they had shared rooms in St. Petersburg. Of all
Harry's friends, only Edward had known about Nadia.
Edward had been present at their wedding, had kissed the
bride and danced with Nadia's sister, Irina. In fact, the four
of them had been on several outings together in the days
after Harry had promised to make Nadia his wife. Edward
had met Grigor at the wedding and Grigor had gone to
Edward about Niki, but Edward would have no cause to seek
Grigor's company now.

There must be a simple explanation. He would have to see
Edward at once, but first he had to speak to Alessa. He had
promised to tell her the results of his meeting with Howell.

Charles opened the door for him, took his hat, and informed him that Lady Milverton was waiting for him in the
small sitting room. Dreading what he must tell her, wondering if he would in fact mention Edward's name at all, Harry
hurried up the stairs to see his wife.

Alessa was not alone. Galina got up hurriedly at his entrance. "Don't go," Alessa said as the girl showed signs of leaving the room. "Galina has something to tell you," she said to Harry. "But first tell us what happened. What did Howell say?"

"He's called in Bow Street. Or the Home Office have. They're afraid Count Lieven will make some complaint about Lychenko's treatment on English shores."

The women sat down and Harry threw himself into a chair. Galina was having difficulty following the conversation and Harry switched to Russian. "Lychenko had a visitor on the day he was killed. The Bow Street man, Burley, turned up someone who had seen him."

Alessa leaned forward, her lips parted. Harry had an incongruous desire to kiss her. Her words drove the thought from his mind. "Who was he, Harry? What did he look like?"

The words had been etched in his mind with acid. Harry knew he could not lie. "More than middle height," he said slowly. "Thick dark blond hair, carefully dressed. Blue eyes. Pleasing features and an open face. A gentleman, not arrogant, but used to being served."

Galina turned startled eyes to her mistress. "It sounds like—"

"Edward," Alessa finished, "Harry, it was Edward."

"It could have been anyone," Harry pleaded. "It could have been a friend of the man whose wife Lychenko had debauched. It could have had nothing to do with Lychenko's letter to you, nothing to do with Niki."

Alessa would not let him off so easily. "Or it could," she said with calm certainty. "Galina, tell Lord Milverton what you told me."

Galina folded her hands in her lap and sat up very straight. "It is not much, my lord. John and I were talking about Captain Lychenko when we went driving this afternoon. I was trying to remember everything I know. Captain Lychenko came often to Krasnoe Selo, mostly with the other

330

officers. But one day he had a visitor and they met in a private room. I did not see him, but the boy who waited on them came racing down to the kitchen with a scared face. He had taken them vodka, which was Captain Lychenko's drink, but the visitor wouldn't touch it. Lychenko was very angry because it was not the first time the visitor had come and the boy should have known he always took brandy." Galina pressed her hands together, the only sign of her disquiet. "In my experience, all Russians drink vodka, though I learned later this is not always true. At the time, I thought Lychenko's visitor was a foreigner."

"Edward detests vodka," Alessa said quietly. There was no hint of triumph in her voice.

"It's not proof," Harry insisted. Grigor had called on Edward in St. Petersburg to ask him how to get in touch with Niki's father. Edward had said it was the only time he had seen Grigor since the wedding. Harry gnawed at his knuckle, remembering Alessa's conviction that Edward had lied to her about the relationship between Marina and himself. He hadn't believed her, but he no longer knew what to believe.

Harry stood up and looked down at his wife. "It's not proof," he said again, "but I'm going to talk to Ned. It's time to put an end to this speculation."

"Harry, let me go with you." Alessa was standing before him, her eyes asking for his trust. "I know you're friends, I know it would be easier for you to see him alone, but this concerns us both."

Harry hesitated, but he could not deny her. "Very well. Ten minutes then, in the hall. I'll order the carriage." He turned and strode toward the door, but before he left the room, he looked back at John's betrothed. "Thank you, Galina. You've been very helpful."

Edward was not at home. The footman who answered the

door at Lord Sutton's house did not know where he had gone or when he could be expected to return. Frustrated, for he could now not wait to have matters out with Edward, Harry asked for Lord Sutton. The footman hesitated and looked confused. "I am not sure," he said. "Lord Sutton has a visitor. If you will wait a moment . . ."

The footman moved down the hall. "Tell him it's urgent," Harry called after him.

"What do you think Edward's father can tell you?" Alessa asked.

Harry ran a hand through his hair. "I don't know," he said. "Something. Anything. Maybe nothing at all."

They stood in silence till the footman returned and told them Lord Sutton would see them in the library. "Lord Milverton, Lady Milverton," he announced, then closed the library door behind them.

It was a familiar room. Harry knew the Sutton house nearly as well as his own, and he had always felt the library to be a comforting place. Well-cared-for books, a shabby rug, deep leather chairs with book-strewn tables placed conveniently nearby. Lord Sutton was seated near the windows. He rose at their entrance and waited for them to come forward.

His visitor, who proved to be a woman, turned round and regarded them with disapproving eyes. "You look dreadful, Harry," said Lady Milverton. "Whatever is the matter?"

Harry started, then mumbled an apology for their precipitate entrance. "Not at all," Lord Sutton said, waving them to a nearby sofa. "We've been discussing Edward and Julia's wedding. But we're about through. What can I do for you, Harry?"

Harry leaned forward, hands clasped between his knees, and stared at the floor, wondering how to begin. Then he looked up and met Lord Sutton's gaze. A kindly man, if a somewhat remote one. He might be puzzled, but he would not be angry at what Harry had to say.

"I've known Ned all my life," Harry said. "Tell me, sir, what reason would he have to hate me?"

Harry heard his mother gasp. Lord Sutton continued to regard him with grave eyes. "I take it you have some cause to ask this extraordinary question."

"Cause, yes, but certainty, no," Harry said. "I don't know that Ned is implicated in these events. But if he is, it can only be from a wish to do me some injury."

"Harry, you're being outrageous. Edward is about to become your brother-in-law." Lady Milverton glanced at Alessa, then looked back at her son. "Who's been filling your head with poisonous lies?"

Harry put his hand over Alessa's, but she withdrew it and clasped her hands in her lap. "I suppose I have," she said calmly. "When I was in St. Petersburg, Edward was at some pains to tell me there was an adulterous relationship between Harry and the Countess Chernikova. I believed him and only recently learned that the accusation was false. You'll be happy to know that Harry did not believe me when I told him. He thought I had misunderstood."

"And because of this taradiddle, you've come here to—"

"Not at all." Harry interrupted what promised to be one of his mother's tirades. "Hear me out, ma'am. And you, sir, if you'd be so kind. There's a matter of a death involved."

Lady Milverton turned pale. "You mean that Russian, that—what is his name?"

"Lychenko." Harry turned to Lord Sutton. "I'd best tell you the story, sir. I don't know that you've heard it. Captain Lychenko was a cousin of my wife. My first wife. Earlier this year he came to Ned to tell him that my son, the child whom I thought had died at birth, was in fact alive. Lychenko wanted to know how to get in touch with me."

"And my son wrote to you. That seems reasonable." Lord Sutton was growing impatient.

"I went to St. Petersburg and had several meetings with Lychenko," Harry continued. "I confess that some money

333

was involved in the transaction. He was not a man to let an opportunity slip by."

"Fool," Harry's mother said under her breath.

Harry ignored her and went on with his story. "But in the end Lychenko put Niki in my care. My son, you saw him at the christening. I brought him back to England. I brought his cousin Zara as well."

Alessa stirred by Harry's side. "I think I should tell you, Lord Sutton, that I was suspicious of Captain Lychenko from the beginning. I had just given birth to my own son, you understand, and I did not like to see him displaced by another child. I had Lychenko investigated, but found nothing save that he gambled and drank and was fond of women." Alessa faltered. Harry knew how much these admissions were costing her. She went on in a firmer voice. "Harry would have nothing to do with my suspicions. He has never doubted that Niki was his son. And I have learned to believe as he does."

Harry gave her a grateful look, then turned to Lord Sutton, who was moving uneasily in his chair. "I do not see what this has to do with Edward," Sutton said.

"Nothing beyond the fact that Edward was an intermediary between Lychenko and myself. Bear with me, sir, I am coming to the matter. Lychenko came to England and sent a letter to my wife. He begged her to call on him. He had information for her, he said, information that had a bearing on her son's future."

Lady Milverton half rose from her chair. "I knew it. I knew that little upstart could not be your son. He was going to admit it, wasn't he? Why wasn't I told what was in this letter?"

Harry felt the blood rush to his face. Alessa put a restraining hand on his arm. "We don't know what Lychenko had to say," Harry continued. "Alessa kept the appointment and found him dead. He was shot in the chest. I came a short time later and found her bending over the body. He had been dead several hours."

334

"Remorse?" Lord Sutton suggested. "He took his own life?"

"No. There had been a struggle in the room. The pistol that killed him was found several feet from where he lay."

Harry's mother had subsided in her chair. "So we'll never know."

"No, I fear we will not. And I fear that may be the reason for his death, to keep us from knowing."

"Edward." Lord Sutton's voice was taut with impatience.

Harry clasped his hands, as though that could stop the pain. "Lychenko had a visitor the night he was killed. The visitor was seen, and his description matches Edward's."

"No." Lady Milverton's voice was sharp. "It couldn't have been Edward. A man like Lychenko was bound to have enemies. It could have been anyone."

"That's what I thought. That's what I kept telling myself. But as far as I know, Lychenko knew no one in London save Alessa, Ned, and myself. He spoke little English. He had but the one visitor in the three days he spent in London." Harry turned to Lord Sutton. "If it was Ned who called on him, there's bound to be an explanation. I came here to see him, but he's out and no one knows when he'll return. I'll ask him directly, and if he tells me he had nothing to do with Lychenko, I'll believe him. But for the love of God, sir, tell me first, does Edward have any reason to wish me harm?"

An extraordinary look of pain appeared on Lord Sutton's face. He leaned back in his chair and closed his eyes for a moment, as though wrestling with some inner temptation. Then he turned and spoke, not to Harry, but to Harry's mother. "I'll have to tell him."

Lady Milverton shook her head, a look of great distress upon her face.

"He has a right to know," Lord Sutton said quietly.

Startled and bewildered, Harry watched this byplay between the two older people. He felt Alessa stiffen beside him.

"I have my own story to tell," Lord Sutton said to Harry.

"It's not a pretty story, and I'm afraid it reflects badly on you father."

Lady Milverton made a sound somewhere between laugh and an exclamation of contempt. "Harry is no strange to his father's faults."

Harry, remembering the passionate battles between hi parents when he was young, was not surprised by her out burst. "Go on, sir," he said. "I'm prepared to hear anythin you have to say."

"Hmm, yes," Lord Sutton continued in a mild voice "Henry Dudley had a temper, you were aware of that, but i most things he was an abstemious man. Except wher women were concerned."

"Harry understands," his mother said. "It's a common fail ing. Though his father had none of Harry's romantic natur and certainly none of his attacks of conscience." She was talk ing about Nadia, of course, but Harry scarcely felt the stin in her words.

"He was a handsome devil, I'll give him that," Lord Sutto went on. "My poor Lucilla easily fell prey to his charms." A flush of color appeared on Lord Sutton's normally pale face It was as close as he ever allowed himself to come to an ex pression of anger. "I didn't know, of course. I didn't know until she lay dying and confessed it to me on her death bed She told me then of the affair and its consequences. Will i Henry Dudley's child."

"My God," Harry breathed. "Your heir." Harry was more shocked by the revelation than he could admit. How could his father have done it. Lord Sutton had been his closes friend. And why Lucilla Clifford, who had been a timid woman with only a pallid prettiness to recommend her, no at all his father's type.

Lord Sutton's mouth twisted in a painful grimace. "Wha could I do? Will had already come into his majority. thought of him as my son. How could I deny him? Hov could I besmirch Lucilla's name?"

336

Harry's fingers beat rapidly on the arm of the sofa. He remembered Burley's mannerism and forced himself to be quiet. "Edward knew?"

"In time. One night I drank too much and told him the story. He was very bitter. He'd always envied you, I think, being the firstborn son. But then to find he'd been cheated out of the same place, and all because of your father's damnable lechery." Lord Sutton drew a handkerchief from his pocket and wiped his face. "Forgive me," he said. "I cannot think of it with equanimity."

"Don't torment yourself," Harry said quickly, feeling sympathy for the other man's pain. "It was not an easy story to tell." Would it be enough, he wondered, to explain Ned's behavior. From nursery days, Ned had teased Harry about being an elder son, and for all their friendship the teasing had had an edge to it. Could Ned and Grigor have concocted a scheme to present an imposter as Harry's son? It would be revenge of a kind on Ned's part. An unknown child, perhaps a bastard, as the Dudley heir to pay for the bastard Will Clifford who would one day be Viscount Sutton, the bastard who had cheated Ned of his rightful title. Harry looked at the others. They were all thinking it, he was sure, but none of them was willing to speak.

It was Lord Sutton who at last put it into words. "You may not call it just, but there may have been times when Edward hated you."

"We must be fair," Harry insisted. "We can't condemn Edward out of hand. I won't believe he had anything to do with Lychenko till I hear it from his own mouth. And even then—"

"You're a good man, Harry," Lord Sutton said. "Do you want to wait here till Edward's return?"

"If I may."

Lady Milverton rose and gathered her reticule and shawl. "I must go," she said. "I am much distressed."

Lord Sutton got up and took her hand. "But it was not so

337

very bad, was it? It's best to have these things in the open. And Harry knows how to hold his tongue."

He walked with her to the door, but before they reached it, the footman appeared once more. "Forgive me, my lord," he said. "There are several young people in the hall. The Prince di Tassio and Lady Georgiana and two others whose names I didn't learn. They want to see Lord Milverton. They say it's most urgent."

Lady Milverton did not give Lord Sutton time to answer. "Georgiana, here? Send them in at once."

Georgiana burst into the room ahead of the others and stopped abruptly at the sight of her mother. "Mama, what are you doing here? Oh, Harry, I'm so glad we've found you. It's so dreadful. We didn't know what to do."

By this time Simon, too, was in the room, followed closely by Peter and Radka. "It's Zara, Harry," Simon said. "She's gone."

Harry was on his feet in an instant. "What do you mean? Where?"

Even as he spoke, Alessa hurried forward, her eyes wide with shock. "What happened?"

Simon took her hands and squeezed them hard. "The children were out with one of the maids. Maggie, is that her name?"

"Yes, she helps in the nursery. Galina went driving with John this afternoon."

"Maggie was near hysterical, but I think I followed her story. They were coming home from their walk when a carriage pulled up alongside. The coachman jumped down, picked up Zara, and flung her into the carriage, then drove off like all the fiends in hell were after him. Maggie was helpless with shock, but Niki ran after the carriage till it was out of sight. Maggie took him home." Simon paused. "I'm afraid Niki's gone mute again. Galina's with him now."

Alessa turned to Harry, her face drained of color. "Edward?"

"God help us," Harry said. "I'm afraid so."

"But why Zara?" Alessa's voice shook with passion. "Why not Niki?"

Harry shook his head. He had no answers, only question piled upon question. At the thought that Ned had taken Zara, Harry's bewilderment over his friend's actions gave way to cold anger.

"What's Ned got to do with this?" Peter asked.

"I don't know," Harry said. "But I've got to find him." He turned to Lord Sutton. "Where would he go, sir? Where would he take her?"

"I don't know—" Sutton began.

"Oh, I know where Edward is," Georgiana said. "Or where he said he was going. Julia told me," she added in response to a disapproving look on her mother's face. "She was in the most dreadful temper. Edward sent her a note to say he couldn't take her to Lady Swinnerton's rout tonight."

"Georgiana." Harry was trying hard to curb his impatience.

"Hertfordshire. He had business in Hertfordshire, and he was spending the night."

"He's gone to Wyncross then," Lord Sutton said, naming one of the smaller of his properties.

"I'm going after him," Harry said. "We're going after him," he added when Alessa clutched his arm.

"Shall I come?" Simon asked.

"No, take the others home. Spend some time with Niki. He needs comfort. Tell him we're doing our best to get Zara back."

"What about me?" Georgiana asked. "I was the one who told you where to go."

Harry ruffled her hair. "You're going home, too, brat. You've been a big help."

Georgiana scowled. "But I'm in the way. I know." She stood on tiptoe and pecked Harry on the cheek. "I'll do my best with Niki."

When the young people had left, Harry turned to Lord Sutton. "I'm sorry, sir. It may not be Ned, but I have to go."

Lord Sutton seemed to have gained some firmness of purpose. "I'm going to Wyncross too. He's my son."

"I'll go with you," Lady Milverton said.

Lord Sutton looked at her in surprise, but she bore his scrutiny without flinching. "Very well," he said. "I'll order the carriage. Harry, we'll meet at Wyncross."

Chapter Twenty-one

Wyncross was a small manor house of no particular distinction with several tenant farms attached. It was one of Lord Sutton's several properties—he had land in both England and Ireland—but it was not entailed and had been made over to Edward on his majority. This much Alessa had been able to learn from Harry in the course of their journey north from London. They had been on the road nearly three hours and for most of that time Harry had been silent, wrapped in his private misery. Unfair, Alessa thought, but she dared not comfort him or seek comfort of her own. Harry blamed himself for Zara's abduction, and he had condemned Edward for it. It had to be Edward. Alessa could not bring herself to think of an unknown enemy, nor, she guessed, could Harry. But Edward, his friend, Julia's soon-to-be husband . . .

The coachman turned the barouche into a gateway flanked by stone pillars. It was late afternoon and the autumn sun cast long shadows on the tree-lined path. "We're here," Harry said unnecessarily. He sat forward on the seat as though he would leap out before the carriage had come to a halt.

They pulled up before a small house of weathered brick smothered in ivy. White pilasters framed a narrow door surmounted by a fanlight. The windows, symmetrically placed, reflected the dying sun. As Harry helped her down from the carriage, Alessa put up her hand to shield her eyes from the glare. The drapes had been drawn inside, giving the house an uninhabited look.

Without ceremony, Harry pushed open the front door. Alessa was conscious of a flurry of activity, as though the house had just been brought to life. A maidservant disappeared behind the green baize door at the end of the hall, another could be seen on the stairs, and a footman in his shirtsleeves was passing through the hall. Startled, he stopped at the sight of the visitors. "My lord," he said in some confusion, dropping a cloth he was carrying, then bending to pick it up. "You weren't expected."

Alessa realized that Harry was known as well here as he was in Lord Sutton's house. "Is Clifford here?" Harry asked, checking his headlong stride.

"In the study, my lord. Shall I—"

But Harry was already before him. He moved quickly across the hall to a door at the rear of the house and flung it open. Before she could follow, Alessa heard his voice. "What have you done with her? Where is she?"

Alessa reached the study and saw Edward standing behind his desk, his face contorted with bewilderment and shock. "What the devil are you talking about?"

For an instant Alessa believed in his innocence. But Harry did not. Or else he scarcely heard Edward's denial. "Zara," he said, his voice near choking on the name. "Zara's been abducted."

"Good God." Edward sat down abruptly. "Who would want to do such a thing?"

Alessa had a sudden image of the maidservant she had seen on the stairs when she entered the house. The maid had been carrying a tray, and on the tray there had been a glass of milk. Without waiting to hear more, Alessa fled the room and ran toward the staircase. The men were too engrossed in their game of accusation and denial to notice her absence. She doubted that Edward was even aware that she was in the house.

There was no one in the hall. Alessa ran up the stairs to

the first floor and began opening doors. There were only half a dozen rooms and she quickly found that they were all empty. She opened the door to the back stairs leading down to the ground floor, but she saw no sign of a stairway leading up.

Balked, Alessa stopped and drew upon her first image of the house. She was sure there had been another floor, at least over the central portion of the house. She remembered the three squat windows under the roof, nearly hidden by ivy. There must be some way up.

It took only a few minutes to find it, a door tucked away just beyond the linen cupboard. Alessa opened it and saw a flight of narrow steps rising before her. "Here now, miss, you can't go up here." The maidservant she had seen earlier blocked her way.

Alessa drew herself up and fixed the woman with a piercing gaze, rendered less effective because she was standing a good two feet below her. Alessa moved up one step. "I am Lady Milverton and I will go where I please."

The maid gasped. "It's as much as my position is worth if I let you into our rooms."

"It's as much as your life is worth if you do not." And with a fierce disdain that did credit to her mother's upbringing, Alessa pushed past the maid, forcing her against the wall, and continued up the stairs.

She found a single low-ceilinged room, sparsely furnished with two dressers and four narrow white-covered beds. The tray with the milk stood untouched on one of the dressers. The room seemed to be empty. "Zara," Alessa called softly.

There was no reply. "Zara," she called again, then held her breath, thinking she heard the sound of movement from a dark corner beside one of the beds. She went toward it and saw a small huddled figure on the floor. "Zara," Alessa cried.

The child lifted her head, revealing a face that shone white in the gloom. "Mama?"

In an instant Alessa was on her knees, and in the next Zara's thin arms were wrapped tight around her neck and

Zara's soft hair brushed her face.

"Ma'am?" The maidservant stood just above them. "Ma'am, there must be some mistake. It's the little girl that's going to Ireland."

"Ireland?" Alessa was appalled. She twisted her head free of Zara's grip and looked up. "There's no mistake," she said fiercely. "This is my daughter and I'm taking her home to London." She stood up, holding the child tight in her arms. The maid was frightened and was not to blame. "Get below," Alessa said in a gentler voice. "Get below and stay there. You haven't seen me. You know nothing of this."

Murmuring softly that all would be well now, Alessa carried Zara down the narrow stairs to the first floor, down the main staircase to the hall, and into Edward's study. The room was crowded, for Lord Sutton and Lady Milverton had arrived, and everyone seemed to be talking at once. "Harry," Alessa said in a low voice which brought him round instantly.

"Thank God," Harry breathed, his hand cupping Zara's hair. She turned her head and smiled, then buried her head once more in Alessa's shoulder.

Harry cut off Edward's protests. "It's no use, Ned. We've found her."

Lord Sutton stepped aside, his face working with suppressed emotion, leaving Alessa with a clear view of Edward. He was pale and wide-eyed with shock. Lady Milverton, who had believed none of their story, was in little better condition.

"I'm going to take Zara to the kitchen and get her something to eat," Alessa announced. "Edward, I expect to hear an explanation when I return."

She went back to the hall and made her way through the green baize door and down the stairs to the working part of the house. It was fully as crowded as the study. The cook, a pleasant-faced woman of middle years, was stirring something in a large pot on the stove. A kitchenmaid was chopping potatoes and listening to the story told by the maid

344

Alessa had met in the attic. A second maid was there as well, along with the footman, a bootboy, and Cowper, the coachman who had driven the Milverton barouche to Wyncross.

They fell silent at Alessa's entrance. "There's been a dreadful mistake," she said to them, "but it's being put right. The child's name is Zara and she's daughter to Lord Milverton and myself. No one is sending her to Ireland. She will go home with us to London after we have talked with Mr. Clifford." As she spoke, Alessa repeated each sentence in Russian so that Zara would know exactly what was being said.

"Zara has been very frightened, but she won't be frightened now," Alessa said into the silence which greeted her words. "She knows you all wish her well." Alessa seated herself on a bench beside Cowper and placed the child between them. "I'm sure she's hungry and tired and would like something to eat."

The words brought a flurry of activity and expressions of concern. Zara was soon provided with bread and soup, which she ate eagerly, talking all the while with Cowper, who was a great favorite with her because he sometimes let her sit astride the horses. Alessa meanwhile suggested that tea be provided upstairs, as the Dowager Lady Milverton had had a long journey, and then suggested that some whisky would also not go amiss.

Alessa left the kitchen a quarter-hour later. Zara seemed much recovered from her ordeal, and though she was reluctant to see Alessa go, she was willing to accept Cowper as a substitute. Alessa left him with strict instructions not to let the child out of his sight. But indeed there seemed no further danger. The servants understood that the little girl was a Dudley, and Edward would not dare make off with her now.

Ireland indeed. Alessa shuddered as she made her way up the service stairs to the hall. The servants had told her Zara was to be sent to the Cliffords' Irish estate the next day with the daughter of one of the tenant farmers, who was returning to Ireland to be wed. "One of Mr. Clifford's by-blows, that's what we thought," the cook had told her. "He said as how her mother was dead, and he wanted to see the lass provided for. He always seemed a kind gentleman."

"It was a mistake," Alessa had said, repeating the fiction she had invented earlier, but she knew none of the servants truly believed it. No matter. Edward would be exposed, and he could never harm them again.

When she reached the hall, the footman told her she would find Mr. Clifford and the others in the parlor. It was a comfortable room facing the front drive, made incongruously cozy by the presence of a tea tray and another tray with decanters and glasses. No one was talking. Edward stood looking out the window, a large glass of whisky clutched in his hand. His father held another. Lady Milverton, the only one seated, was sipping tea as though the hot beverage could warm the chill in her body. Harry drank nothing at all.

They had been waiting for her, Alessa realized, the time since she had left them filled with the ritual of refreshments and settling into the larger room.

Harry looked up as she entered. "Zara? She's all right?"

Alessa allowed herself a small smile. "She's being cosseted by the servants and looked after by Cowper, who will not leave her side." Her smile vanished. "Harry, he was going to send her to Ireland."

Lord Sutton's mild temper deserted him. "Good God, sir," he demanded of his son, "what did you think you were about?"

Edward turned round, his face haggard with the strain of the past half-hour. He grimaced. "I don't suppose I can say it was a mistake."

"Edward." Lord Sutton's voice held a warning.

"No, I suppose not." Edward took a healthy swallow of whisky, refilled his glass, and threw himself into a large upholstered armchair. "I'm not sure where to start."

Harry took a chair nearby and leaned forward, hands on his knees, forcing his friend to meet his gaze. "Why Zara, Ned? Why not Niki?"

"Because it was Zara who . . . You remember the Carnes'

346

party, the children were playing a game, seeing who could remember the furthest back."

Alessa tried to recall what it was that Zara had said. "She was with her mother, wasn't that it? They were going someplace, yes, they were on a barge. Why was that important, Edward? Were you there?"

Edward twirled the glass back and forth between his hands, watching the swirl of amber liquid. "Not on the barge, but I saw them that same day. I thought the child might remember."

"You're evading me." Harry shook his head in frustration. "What did it matter if you'd met Irina? Because you told me you hadn't seen her since before Nadia died, is that it? Because I might catch you in a lie? It's been all lies, hasn't it? Lies from the beginning. Tell me, Edward, is Niki my son?"

Alessa drew a sharp breath, her body going tense.

Edward raised his eyes, now cold and hard. "It hurts, doesn't it? I wanted to hurt you, Harry Dudley."

"Be damned to you, Edward Clifford. Answer me. Did my son die in childbirth? Or is Niki my son?"

"The child didn't die." Edward took a long swallow of whisky. "Nadia had a daughter. Zara. Irina didn't want you to know. She wanted the girl for herself."

Harry stared at him, his face white with shock. "And Niki?"

"Irina's son."

There was a long exhalation of sound from Lady Milverton, a sigh of relief, perhaps, or a murmur of vindication. Alessa felt a great upwelling of joy. Alastair, her beloved Alastair, was Harry's heir, the next Earl of Milverton. She felt a small pang for Niki, who by Edward's few words had been displaced, but comforted herself with the reflection that Niki knew nothing of earls or properties and he would still be their son, as Zara had been their daughter. She glanced at Harry. He was deathly quiet. He wasn't thinking of Alastair; he was thinking of Niki.

An ormolu clock ticked quietly on a table by the window,

its sound preternaturally loud in the silence of the room. "Was it your idea or Grigor's?" Harry asked at last.

"Grigor." Edward spat the name. "Grigor was a fool. He had no imagination."

"He came to you because Irina died, is that it? He wanted to know if I might be induced to take on responsibility for my daughter."

"And he thought you might be willing to pay for the knowledge. Grigor always had an eye on the main chance."

Harry eyed his friend coldly. "But you had a better idea, didn't you? If Harry Dudley could be induced to acknowledge a daughter he didn't know he had, why not do the same with a son. A son, an heir, no, not a bastard heir, you couldn't manage that, but a false heir. What a great joke on Harry Dudley."

Edward began to laugh, a low rumbling sound that erupted into bubbles of laughter spilling from his mouth. He wiped his hand across his face, swallowed the last of his whisky, and stood up to refill his glass. His legs were not quite steady, but his hand did not falter as he poured.

"Did it make up for Will?"

Edward spun round, looking down at Harry with shocked eyes.

"I told him," Lord Sutton said. "This afternoon. What a paltry revenge, Edward. What an abysmally stupid, childish thing to do."

"Stupid?" Edward turned on his father. "Stupid Edward, is that it? Too stupid to know his own rights. You cheated me, Will cheated me, my foolish sainted mother cheated me, and so did that bloody whoremonger Henry Dudley."

"Edward!" Lady Milverton was outraged.

"No, I've been cleverer than you. Than all of you. Do you hear me? Clever Edward who devised the perfect revenge. Symmetry, an eye for an eye, a tooth for a tooth . . ."

"A bastard for a bastard," Harry finished. "Oh, my God. Niki wasn't Varsenin's child. He was yours."

Edward gave a whoop of laughter. He jumped onto the

sofa and perched on its back. "You see it, don't you, Harry. You appreciate the beauty of it. A Dudley bastard inherits the Sutton title and estates. A Clifford bastard becomes the Earl of Milverton. It was perfect, wasn't it? I would have told you eventually, but by then it would have been too late."

Lady Milverton gave a small cry, but she waved off Alessa's attempts to come to her aid. Alessa could not but admire her. A lesser woman would have called for hartshorn.

Harry's hands were clasped between his knees. He shook his head, seeming bewildered less by Edward's revelations than by the venom in his voice. "You and Irina. God help me, I was blind."

"Blind, yes." Edward's voice was gleeful. "Blind, stupid Harry. Didn't you know the little bitch was jealous because her sister had snagged an English gentleman? She was all over me. I crooked a finger and she fell. Well, why not?" he added defensively. "She was a sweet little bit, not all weepy like your Nadia."

"You got her pregnant."

Edward swallowed the last of his whisky and hurled the glass into the unlit fireplace. Lord Sutton made a move of protest, but Harry waved him off, as though to say he did not want to stem the tide of Edward's confession.

"Takes two for that," Edward said. "Or so I've heard. But I wasn't about to get caught." He turned to Lady Milverton. "Not like our noble Harry. Marry Varsenin, I told Irina, and she did, and I daresay was as happy as most women of her kind. Varsenin thought the boy was his."

"Edward," Lady Milverton said in a broken voice. "Julia . . ."

The mention of Julia made Edward flinch, but his mocking expression soon returned. "Sweet Julia. Nothing like melding the two families, is there? Our elders and betters did it, so why shouldn't we? Dudleys and Cliffords. Cliffords and Dudleys. All one happy family."

Edward bounded off the sofa and stood before Lady Milverton. "Does this mean the marriage is off, mother soon-to-be-mine? No need, you know. My quarrel is with Harry, not Julia. Stupid Harry who didn't want to be an earl, witless Harry who didn't appreciate his good fortune. I would have liked to be an earl. By rights I should be a viscount and Julia my viscountess. But no matter. Clifford's revenge has fallen on a child's recollection. It's forgot. It need never have been. None of us here will care to speak of it."

"By God." Harry was on his feet, his fists clenched. "If you dare approach Julia again . . ."

Edward clutched his chest in mock dismay. "What? You'll withdraw your consent? Too late, old cock, the papers have been drawn up and the terms agreed to. You'll not go back on your word. Julia must have her dowry. I insist on the dowry."

Lady Milverton was chewing her knuckle, a sign of discomposure Alessa had never seen. "Edward, stop."

"Stop, mother dear? I've just begun. I liked you once, Harry Dudley. God help me, I did. I don't like what you've become. Julia doesn't much like you either, but I doubt you care for that. We'll be off to St. Petersburg in a month and you need never see us again. But you'll know I'm part of your family, Harry, won't you? You'll never be rid of me."

Harry cried out, an inarticulate sound of rage, and hurled himself on Edward, pushing him back across the table where the decanters stood. Taken by surprise, Edward fought back, his hands around Harry's throat. The decanter overturned and the sharp fumes of whisky filled the air. Lord Sutton tried vainly to drive a wedge into the jumble of bodies and arms and legs.

Lady Milverton was on her feet. "Stop it, stop it at once!"

It must have been the voice of their childhood, for she succeeded where Lord Sutton had not. The men slackened their grip and lay panting across the table, one atop the other. Then Harry pushed himself away and Edward staggered to his feet.

"You used to do that when you were children." Lady Milverton's voice was sharp with disapproval. "You're chil-

350

dren no longer." She righted the decanter and looked at Edward, her breast rising and falling rapidly. Alessa had never seen her so agitated. "You think you're clever? You with your petty nursery envy. You're your father's son, that should be enough for you. Don't you know that revenge has a price? When I think of what I've had to live with, when I think of what I've done . . ."

She broke off, breathing rapidly. Alessa had a glimpse of the passionate young woman Lady Milverton must have been in her youth. The others saw it too. Lord Sutton was staring at her in dismay. Edward had lost his fire.

"Yes, Mother," Harry said into the ensuing silence, "what is it you have done?"

Lady Milverton's voice shook with passion. "Nothing. Everything. My God, if you knew . . ." She sat down abruptly and clenched her hands to still their trembling.

Harry's face was without expression, and when he spoke, his voice was dangerously quiet. "Madam, you owe us an explanation."

Lady Milverton looked up at her son with something that might have been pity, but her ravaged face did not soften. "I owe you nothing."

The sting of her words was like a slap. "I didn't ask to be born."

"No, you did not." Lady Milverton spoke quietly, her passion spent. There was a look of intense pain on her face. "I've been unfair to you." She turned to Lord Sutton. "And to you, William."

"Barbara, in God's name . . ." Lord Sutton's distress was palpable.

"No," Lady Milverton said, her voice firm with decision. "Harry has a right to know. As do you."

Lord Sutton retreated to his chair, clasping its arms as if for support. Harry and Edward, no longer driven apart by Edward's hatred, sat on the sofa.

"You all know the story of Will's parentage," Lady Milverton began. "I don't need to repeat it. Needless to say, it was not the first time my husband had broken his marriage vows. I would have minded less if he'd contented himself with dancers and milliners, like other men of his station, but he was a man filled with conceit and oblivious to danger. He took delight in despoiling my friends. He humiliated me beyond belief."

Alessa glanced at Harry. It must pain him to hear his father spoken of so, but beyond a faint tightening of his mouth, he showed no reaction at all.

"We were at a houseparty one winter," Lady Milverton went on. "Henry left my bed to go to the room of my closest friend. I didn't have to follow him. He told me, you see. He boasted of it." Lady Milverton spread her fingers across her lap to ease their tension. A faint smile appeared on her face. "In those days I had a temper. If he would serve me thus . . . the following night I proceeded to seduce his best friend."

It took Alessa a moment to realize that Lady Milverton was speaking of Lord Sutton. That mild, inoffensive man seemed an unlikely target for a passionate liaison, but the flush that rose in his face left no doubt that he was the man she meant. Alessa looked again at Harry and realized he was not surprised. The cool, controlled woman that she knew was not the mother of his youth.

"Lord Sutton was not unwilling, but I absolve him of all blame. The fault was mine." Lady Milverton clasped her hands again. "As I say, I had a temper. Henry and I had dreadful fights. During one of them I told him what I had done." She laughed, but the sound was without mirth. "He was furious, as I had intended he should be. I didn't know then how far his fury would take him. Shortly after that, he seduced Lord Sutton's wife, Lucilla."

"And my brother, Will, was born," Edward said in a now quiet voice.

"Will was born," Lady Milverton repeated. "Henry told me the boy was his. I was furious, and I begged Lord Sutton to meet me secretly. I was going to tell him the truth." She glanced at Edward. "I wish now that I had."

352

Edward drew a long breath. "Yes? What then?"

"Your father misunderstood my intentions. And when I realized what he had in mind, I conceived of a greater revenge. I had told my husband I was pregnant, and at the time I had thought I was. Then I had some bleeding and assumed I had made a mistake. I saw no reason I could not get pregnant again and present my husband with the heir he longed for. I said nothing of Will to Lord Sutton, and in time Harry was born. It was only eight months later, but he was a small baby."

Harry stared at his mother with a stunned expression. Then he turned and looked at Lord Sutton, the man she had just claimed as his father. Sutton shook his head in denial and bewilderment.

Edward was laughing softly. "So Harry is a bastard. My brother Will, the future Viscount Sutton, is a bastard, and so is the Earl of Milverton. My God, it's rich."

"It's not a matter for levity." Lady Milverton was once more her disapproving self.

"But don't you see—Harry, *you* of all people must appreciate the irony—Lady Milverton, it's the perfect revenge, better than anything I could have devised."

"I did not devise it, Edward. It happened. And it was certainly not intended for your amusement."

But she had devised it, of course; it was exactly what she had intended. Alessa looked at her mother-in-law with wonder. What a passionate woman she must have been. What had happened to all that passion? Or had the fruits of that passion shocked her into some semblance of remorse?

"You told me you were already with child." Lord Sutton's voice broke. "All those years . . ."

"I'm sorry, William," Lady Milverton said with more genuine feeling than she had shown in the entire recital. "I used you, just as Henry used Lucilla. We've both been paid back for our folly."

Harry had been silent throughout all of Lady Milverton's tale, his face an expressionless mask. "I always suspected you didn't really like me," he said. A look of intense pain suffuse his countenance and Alessa's heart broke for him.

"I feared you would be like Henry," Lady Milverton said "and that I couldn't bear. Then later I feared that you woul not. Henry understood what was owing to his position though he could not understand what was owing to his wife She closed her eyes, looking unutterably weary. "Mistakes so many mistakes, so much useless passion," she murmured A moment later she opened her eyes and looked at her son "I paid for it, you know. And I took care that my next chil dren were Henry's." She turned to Edward. "You shoul have been my son. We are alike, you and I, and we will bot live to regret it."

"I never meant to hurt the little girl." Edward seemed so bered by Lady Milverton's declaration. "She would hav been well cared for."

"You have a black soul, Edward." Harry's tone was bitter Edward smiled. "Not black. Unredeemed. Julia—"

"There's no question of Julia," Harry said sharply.

"But nothing happened." Edward's tone was that of a smal boy caught in some mischief. "It's over. Things are as the were."

Harry stared at him, his eyes disbelieving. "You're mad Grigor's dead."

"Oh, no." Edward abandoned the sofa and put some dis tance between himself and Harry. "You'll not blame me fo that."

Harry strode toward his onetime friend and gripped him by the shoulders. "Edward, you were seen."

For a second Edward's composure deserted him. Then h pulled away, in command of himself once more. "I don't hav to answer to you, Harry Dudley."

"You'll have to answer to Bow Street."

Lord Sutton stepped between the two men. "Don't be an egregious fool," he said to his son. "For the sake of whateve duty you owe me, tell me the truth. Tell me now. Tell me al of it. I won't abandon you."

Edward went very still. Alessa saw calculation in his eyes, then uncertainty, then something that might have been fear. "It was an accident," he said, his voice so low they strained to hear it. "An accident," he repeated in a hoarse voice, moving to the sofa once more.

"Was it the Russian?" Lord Sutton asked, trying to get his bearings.

"Yes, Captain Lychenko," Harry said quietly.

"Grigor sent me a note," Edward went on. "He was in trouble. He wanted money. He said he'd written to Alessa and was going to tell her everything if she'd pay him enough. But since we were friends—friends, hah!—he'd be quiet if I would take care of him." He looked up. "Is there any whisky left?"

Harry poured out what was left in the decanter and handed it to Edward.

"That's better." Edward cupped the glass, inhaling its fumes. Then he took a healthy swallow and continued. "I went to see him, but I was damned if I'd pay him another farthing. I told him so. I threatened him with the police. Then the fool came at me with his pistol." Edward looked at his father as though seeking absolution. "What was I to do? Let myself be shot? We struggled, the gun went off, Grigor was dead. Stone dead. Irremediably dead. Bloody fool. I left him there. Afraid if I was found, it would give the game away."

"An accident," Lord Sutton said. He seemed to be speaking to himself. "Yes, an accident. Edward," he went on hurriedly, "you'll have to go to the police. I'll go with you. There'll be no problem. I'm not without influence."

Lord Sutton put an awkward hand on his son's shoulder. Then he looked back. "Harry?"

Harry's face lost some of its tightness. "It's all right. We have Zara back. That's all that's important."

It was nearly ten when the barouche pulled up in Portman

355

Square. They had not dined. No one had the stomach fo food. Zara fell asleep in Alessa's arms as soon as the carriag pulled out of the Wyncross gate. Lady Milverton, who a companied them, sat beside Alessa, silent but outwardl composed.

Harry, seated opposite the two women, tried to reconcil the shifting images of his mother, her fierce temper, her o casional bursts of tender feeling, the constraint under whic she now lived. He could not but admire her self-contro Considering what she had revealed that evening, she ha cause for anger, for regret, for shame, but she showed non of these emotions. He could not tell what she was thinking of the past or of the present, of Henry Dudley and Willia Clifford, who had been friends in their youth and had bot betrayed that friendship, or of Julia and Alastair and Nik whose lives would be altered by Edward's perfidy and he own confession.

Alastair. Harry had felt a stab of pain when he learne Niki was not his son. But he still had a son, and for Alastair sake—and for Alessa's—he was glad. Alastair would be hi heir, as Alessa had fully expected at his birth. Harry ha cheated his wife, and now he could make it right.

Save that he was no longer the Earl of Milverton. For th first time, Harry realized the full implications of his mother story. The title belonged to Matt, who was the legitimate so of the man Harry had thought to be his father. While Harr Dudley, who should properly bear the name of Harry Clif ford, was not legitimate at all. What a sorry mess he ha made of Alessa's life. She had married a wealthy earl and wa now shackled to a bastard son with little to call his own sav his brother's charity.

Harry looked across the carriage at his wife. She met hi gaze and smiled. Surely she must realize what had happene in the sitting room at Wyncross, but perhaps she had not ye taken it in. She had Zara back, and for the moment that wa enough. Harry suppressed a groan. He would have to talk t her tonight, and tomorrow he would talk to Matt.

When they entered the house, Georgiana and Radka raced out of the library door. "You found her," Radka said, breathless from her run down the hall. "Is she all right?"

"She's all right, but she's tired." Alessa brushed her hand against the fair hair of the child who was now resting in Harry's arms. "We're going to put her to bed," she added, forestalling Georgiana's questions. "Then we'll come down and tell you all about it."

Harry shifted the child's weight and followed Alessa up the stairs, dimly aware that Matt and Simon and Peter were also in the hall. He heard his mother's voice asking after Julia.

At the sight of Zara, Galina crossed herself and mouthed a silent prayer. John, who had been waiting with her, gave Harry a heartfelt grin. They were all quiet, lest they wake Niki, but the stir of movement as they undressed his cousin roused him. "Zara?" he asked, sitting up abruptly in his bed.

"She's here. We brought her back." Alessa smoothed his mousled hair. "It's all right, Niki. It's not going to happen again."

Niki turned and reached out his hand, as though to assure himself that Zara was in fact really in the room. Then, exhausted by the events of the day, he fell asleep.

"Explanations downstairs," Harry said as they left the nursery.

John gave him a searching look. "You needn't if you don't want to."

Harry grimaced. "I must. There'll be talk all over the house, and I have to find some way to curb Georgy's tongue."

They had nearly reached the first-floor landing when they heard a piercing shriek followed by the slamming of a door. A moment later Julia pushed by them, her tearstained face distorted with anger and dismay. "That's part of it," Harry said, feeling keenly his sister's distress. Perhaps he should not have forbade the marriage. But then, he realized belatedly, he now had no right to forbid anything at all.

Lady Milverton emerged from the small drawing room and started slightly at the sight of the four adults on the landing. "I'm tired," she said to no one in particular. "I'm going to bed." Without another word she, too, passed up the stairs.

The next half-hour was a painful one. His mother's story of course could not be repeated, but Harry gave the group in the library a full account of what had happened in Russia and, more recently, in London. His first marriage, the birth of his daughter, the intelligence that the child had died, Edward's scheme and Grigor's involvement, Grigor's accidental death. He omitted only Edward's seduction of Irina and Niki's parentage. As far as anyone knew, Niki was a Varsenin.

When Harry had done, John drew a deep breath. "So you have a daughter and not a son."

Harry smiled. "And a nephew rather than a niece."

"It doesn't matter," Alessa said fiercely. "They're both our children."

Harry gave her a grateful look. He could not have asked for a more loyal wife. And yet he would soon have to test that loyalty. She did not know that he planned to unfold the full story to Matt.

No one spoke much after Harry was finished. Even Georgiana was quiet. Peter and Simon took their leave, and Harry suggested the others must be tired after their long vigil. Matt picked up a book and tactfully shepherded the two girls to the door. "What about you?" Alessa asked Harry. "Aren't you tired, too?"

Harry looked into his wife's beloved face. Her hair had come loose from its pins, there were dark smudges under her eyes, and there was a greasy stain on her collar where Zara's hand had clutched her. She had never looked more beautiful. "I am," Harry said, longing to hold her in his arms. "But we have to talk."

Chapter Twenty-two

The firelight cast warm, flickering shadows over Alessa's face as she looked up at him in inquiry. Harry hesitated, carefully committing the picture to memory—the angle of her head, the curve of the dark hair swept back from her face, the soft amber folds of her dress. Whatever passed between them in the next few moments, he would at least have this to remember.

"Harry . . ." Alessa held out her hand to him. "I'm so sorry. I wish there was something more I could say."

Her voice was warm with sympathy, but Harry wondered if she had realized the full extent of the upheaval caused by the day's revelations. Subduing the impulse to seize her hand and pull her into his arms, he moved to a chair several feet away. He needed distance for what he was going to say, and she deserved distance in which to hear it.

Alessa watched him, waiting for him to speak. Her eyes reflected the firelight. Harry forced himself to look into their depths. "I've done you a great wrong, Alessa."

"Harry, no."

There was a note of shocked surprise in her voice. She didn't understand then. Yet. That was going to make this even more difficult.

"But I have," Harry insisted, keeping his voice level. "The conditions of our marriage were very clear. You would be my countess, and our son would be my heir. I violated those conditions when I forced Niki on you. "Now it seems Alastair is my firstborn son after all. But I have no right to call myself Earl of Milverton."

Alessa's eyes widened. "I hadn't thought . . ." she said softly. "You must think me very stupid. You're going to tell Matt?"

"I have to." The words came out with more force than Harry intended. "There've been too many lies in this family," he said, moderating his breathing. "I can't live with more."

Alessa gave a strained smile. "You're an honorable man, Harry."

Guilt closed painfully around his chest. "I'll be sure the children are provided for," he told her. "That is . . ." Harry ran a hand through his hair, realizing he had not considered the process of turning the title over to his brother. "I suppose I haven't a penny to my name, but I'm sure Matt will make some sort of settlement. We won't starve."

"Of course not," Alessa said. "In any case, we'll still have my money."

Her voice was composed, her feelings carefully concealed. The air felt heavy with restrained emotion. Harry found himself wishing Alessa had gone into one of her rages. Then at least he could confront the pain she must be feeling. The pain he had caused her.

"If there were any way to let you out of this, I would," he said, desperate for honesty. "You must believe that."

"Let me out of it?" There was a tense note in Alessa's voice that had not been there before.

"I've failed my side of our bargain," Harry said, looking steadily at her. "By rights you should be released from yours. But there's no precedent for ending a marriage on such grounds."

For a moment Alessa stared at him in silence. Her eyes darkened, not with anger, he could have sworn, but with pain. Before he could speak, she pushed herself to her feet in a single swift motion. "Is that what you want, Harry? Are you regretting your lost freedom?"

"Don't be ridiculous," Harry said, springing to his feet as well.

"Is it so ridiculous?" Alessa's voice trembled. "You're free of the burdens of the earldom for the first time in your life. Do you wish you were free of your wife and children as well?"

"*No.*" Without knowing he had moved, Harry seized her by the shoulders. "God in heaven, Alessa," he said, looking down at the face he could trace from memory, "do you know me so little?"

Alessa's breathing had quickened, but her eyes were uncompromising. "*You* thought I'd want to be free of you."

"That's different."

"Is it?"

"Of course." Harry forced himself to ease his hold on her. "Can you honestly say you'd have listened to my proposal if I'd been plain Harry Dudley? Or Harry Clifford? Not merely untitled, but a bastard to boot."

"I . . ." Alessa broke off, but her stricken look was answer enough.

"No one could possibly blame you," Harry said, releasing her and stepping back.

"Harry—"

"It's all right." Harry turned away, fearing his face would betray him. He could not bear to be an object of pity. "I understand."

"No. No, you don't understand at all." Alessa's voice was sharp with urgency. "Harry, please, you have to listen to me."

Her hand closed on his arm, sending a shock of longing through him. Steeling himself to hold all feeling at bay, Harry turned and met her pleading gaze.

"You're right," Alessa said. "I used to think birth and fortune mattered. When I was young, it never occurred to me to think otherwise. I thought I was in love with Adrian, but I probably wouldn't have considered him as a husband if he hadn't come from an old family and had a splendid title. When it turned out Adrian didn't love me at all, I decided

361

my heart wasn't to be trusted. Perhaps birth and fortune were the only guides to a suitable marriage. But that was before . . ."

"Before what?" Harry asked, the breath tight in his throat.

"Oh, a hundred things. Before I realized I could love Niki and Zara no matter who had borne them. Before I realized how wrong it was to try to keep John and Galina apart. Before . . ." She swallowed and he felt a tremor run through her. "Before I knew I loved you."

A coal fell against the fender. A gust of acrid smoke filled the room. Alessa's hand was firm and solid on his arm, yet her words seemed a fragile illusion which would shatter if he moved or spoke. Willing the moment to last, Harry lifted his hand and gently traced the line of her jaw. Then, unable to contain himself any longer, he crushed her to him and covered her lips with his own.

Her mouth was warm and her fingers tangled in his hair and he knew it was not an illusion.

"We have each other and the children," Alessa said at last, tilting her head back and smiling at him. "The rest doesn't matter."

Harry took her face between his hands, recalling her joyful expression when she had learned Alastair was his heir. "Alastair will never be an earl," he reminded her.

"I know." There was a flicker of sadness in Alessa's eyes, quickly gone. "But he'll be your son and mine. That ought to be enough of a heritage for any child." Alessa gave an unexpected smile.

"What is it?" Harry asked.

"Has it occurred to you," Alessa said, her eyes bright with laughter, "that I almost married Adrian and it turned out he wasn't really the Marquis of Parminter. Then I married you and it turns out you aren't the Earl of Milverton. I must be positively dangerous."

That she could laugh about it was more than he had dared hope for. Light-headed with relief, Harry pulled her close, breathing in the smell of jasmine and tuberose and that indefinable scent that was Alessa herself.

Several moments later, her head resting on his shoulder, Alessa said, "You'll be sorry to give it up."

"You wouldn't think so, would you?" Harry said, smoothing her hair. "I've spent most of my life rebelling against the earldom."

Alessa drew back and touched his face. "That was before you made it your own."

Harry thought briefly of visiting his tenants, planning improvements on the estate, making his first speech in the Lords. The sense of loss was sharper than he would have believed possible. "It never was my own," he said.

Alessa shook her head. "It was. And it had nothing to do with your birth."

"Coming from a Tassio, that's a remarkable statement," Harry told her. "Don't distress yourself, my darling. I can always try to get myself elected to the Commons. That way I can spend my days debating Uncle George."

Alessa smiled. "The prospect almost makes the whole thing worthwhile. Harry," she added, wrapping her arms around his neck, "are you going to tell Matt tonight?"

Harry had been planning to, but one look at Alessa's parted lips and delicately flushed skin was enough to change his mind. "Matt's waited twenty-five years to be Earl of Milverton," he said, sinking his fingers into her hair. "It won't hurt him to wait till morning."

Harry disengaged himself from his sleeping wife and slipped out from beneath the covers into the chill morning air. He did not want to wake Alessa, who had been up early with Alastair. Besides, he would as soon she was sleeping peacefully while he had his interview with Matt.

Alessa was lying on her side, her mouth curved in a smile. Smiling himself at his memories of the night before, Harry dropped a light kiss on her hair and subdued the urge to linger. Matt usually rode early in the morning. Harry wanted to speak to him before the rest of the family were stirring.

Pushing his tangled hair from his eyes, Harry fished his breeches and shirt from the trail of clothes on the floor and shrugged them on for warmth. When he had straightened Alessa's clothes as best he could and bundled the rest of his own clothes up in his arms, he walked over to the cradle and looked down at his sleeping son. Like his mother, Alastair looked peaceful and contented. Harry watched his son's even breathing. As he grew older, Alastair would know that Harry had given up the Milverton title. Harry wondered if his son would understand. And then he wondered how he would ever face Alastair or Niki or Zara if he did not tell Matt the truth.

Harry made his way quickly to his own room and rang for Lytton, who was becoming used to seeing his master's bed unslept in. A quarter-hour later, shaved and dressed in fresh clothes, Harry walked downstairs. As he had hoped, he found Matt sprawled on the library sofa, still in his riding clothes, a cup of coffee beside him and the *Morning Chronicle* in his hands. It occurred to Harry that Matt was going to be as unconventional an Earl of Milverton as he had been himself. He found the thought comforting.

"Hullo, you're up early," Matt said by way of greeting. "Come to fight me for the paper?"

"No, just to talk," Harry said, closing the door behind him.

Matt let the paper fall abruptly. "I'm a blundering idiot. You must be feeling pretty miserable after yesterday. I don't suppose it would help if I said I never liked Ned Clifford much. He was always too damned good-natured."

"If nothing else, he was a superlative actor." Though he still found it difficult to think of Edward, Harry smiled, grateful that at least he and Matt were free of the jealousy which so often plagued brothers. Of course, Edward was his brother too.

"By the way," Matt said, tossing the paper on the table beside the sofa, "it's fairly obvious that there's more to what

Ned did than you let on. But I don't suppose you have any intention of telling me, so I won't ask questions."

"On the contrary," Harry said, moving to a chair. "I came here to tell you the rest of the story."

Matt pushed himself up on the sofa. "I won't pretend I'm not curious."

Harry considered a number of prefaces to the story, but abandoned them as inadequate. With as much accuracy and as little emotion as possible, he recounted what he had learned from Sutton and his mother on the previous day.

Matt listened in silence, first intrigued, then startled, then plainly shocked. "Good God," he exclaimed when Harry had finished. "It makes that racy French book with all the letters look positively tame, doesn't it? Who would have dreamed Mother was so passionate. In every sense of the word."

"I think it was pride as much as passion," Harry said, leaning back in his chair. "She couldn't bear the fact that Father had humiliated her."

"And to think of Father and Sutton acting as though they were the best of friends all these years . . ." Matt shook his head, trying to sort out the story. Then he looked at Harry. "I'm glad you told me."

"I could hardly have done otherwise," Harry said. "You have the right to know."

"What stuff our parents were really made of? By that token you ought to tell the girls as well."

Matt still didn't understand. But perhaps it was no wonder. The shock of the story could well obscure its implications.

"Think," Harry said, leaning forward. "Mother made it quite clear that you at least are legitimate. You're Father's firstborn son, Matt. His firstborn legitimate son."

It was a moment before Matt understood. Then he sat bolt upright, a look of stupefaction on his face. "Bloody hell, you can't be serious."

"I'm utterly serious," Harry assured him. "I've no intention of keeping the earldom under false pretenses."

"Why not?" Matt demanded. "It's done in the best of families. Look at William Lamb. He's an honorable man but you don't see him offering to step aside and let Frederick or George be the next Lord Melbourne."

"That's different. No one believes Frederick and George are Lord Melbourne's sons any more than William is. Besides, Lord Melbourne acknowledged William."

"Our father acknowledged you."

"But he didn't know the truth," Harry said, thinking that this was one final way he had disappointed the man he had called father.

"Is that why you're doing all this?" Matt said in a tone of disbelief. "For Father's sake? You never used to think he deserved such consideration. And that was before we knew he cuckolded his best friend's wife."

Harry laid his hands firmly on the arms of his chair. "I'm doing this so our family won't be as divided as the Cliffords are."

"Well that's a nice compliment, I must say," Matt exclaimed in an aggrieved tone. "Just because Edward Clifford didn't have enough imagination to see there are better things in life than a viscountcy, you expect me to go plotting behind your back."

"Don't be an idiot, Matt," Harry said, feeling a wave of affection for his brother. "You might go to great lengths for a pottery bowl. You wouldn't take such risks for anything as paltry as an earldom. But your children might feel you had deprived them. Not to mention your wife."

"You may be sure that any woman I marry will have more important things to think about. So will our children." Matt looked sharply at Harry. "Speaking of wives, have you told Alessa about this?"

"I have. She agrees with me."

"Does she?" Matt grinned. "Marrying her is one of the more sensible things you've ever done, Harry."

"The most sensible," Harry said, feeling an answering smile break across his face.

"Though as I recall," Matt added, "at your wedding you adn't quite realized how lucky you were."

"Don't taunt me with my mistakes. You're still my youn-er brother, even if you are going to have the title."

"But I'm not." Matt pushed himself to his feet. "This is nadness, Harry," he said, taking an impatient turn about the oom. "How do you propose to go about it? Bring the matter efore the Lords and drag Mother's name through the mud? may not be the most devoted son, but that's not a prospect I elish."

Harry was brought up short for the first time in the inter-iew. Between the shock of his mother's revelations, the joy f Alessa's avowal of love, and the knowledge that he would ose the heritage he had come to value, he had not consid-red anything beyond his talk with Matt.

"Even if you could find some way to do the thing quietly," Matt continued, "I'll fight you to the end. Don't think I'll tand by quietly and let you ruin my life."

"Ruin your life?" Harry repeated.

"You don't think I *want* to be the Earl of Milverton, do ou?" Matt said in an incredulous tone. "I'll admit I enjoy he odd visit home now and again, but living here all the ime? Tramping about the estate and sitting in Parliament nd entertaining the tenants at Christmas? Either I'd stay ome and be miserable or I'd spend my time abroad and ave everyone saying I neglected my duties. I'm not cut out or it like you are, Harry."

"Cut out for it?" Harry gave a shout of laughter. "Good God, Matt, haven't you been listening to what everyone's aid about me practically from the cradle?"

"Who?" Matt demanded. "Mother? Father? Uncle George? When have I ever listened to them?"

"In a way they may have been right," Harry said, getting o his feet and facing his brother. "I hated the idea of being Lord Milverton for years. I learned to make the best of it."

"You hated the idea of being what Father wanted you to e." Matt's eyes were serious and he suddenly looked far

older than Harry was accustomed to think him. "I'
watched you, Harry. I may not pay a lot of attention to th
family, but I've seen you these past years. You *like* talkin
about land improvements and crop yields. You ma
speeches that energize people instead of putting them
sleep. You could find your way around any of your estat
blindfolded."

Harry swallowed, aware of a disconcerting ache in h
chest. "That doesn't change the facts," he said.

"Oh? And what are they?" Matt asked, striding forwar
"Mother thought she was carrying father's baby. Her cours
started. She lay with Sutton. You were born eight montl
later."

"A small baby," Harry reminded him.

"Which doesn't mean you were premature. Hell, Harr
you're supposed to know more about these things than I d
Women can bleed even though they've conceived, you kno
The truth is, even Mother can't be sure whose child you are

Harry thought of Gideon's words about Peter's parentag
But Peter was Gideon's son because Gideon loved hin
Harry could not say the same of his own father. "We'll nev
know," he said, "but we'll always wonder."

"Then as the eldest, I insist that you assume the burden
doubt," Matt said. "Personally, I have better things to worr
about than whose beds our parents were sharing thirty yea
ago."

"You're twenty-five, Matt," Harry said, looking at h
brother. "You may regret this."

"I doubt that," Matt said, his gaze steady. "But I know tha
if you proceed with this madness, we'll both regret it for th
rest of our lives."

Time seemed to have become unbearably slow. Afraid t
admit how much he wanted what Matt was offering hin
Harry breathed in the musty air of the library and looked a
the ranks of books collected by generations of Dudleys wh
might or might not be his ancestors.

"You're not being very consistent," Matt told him. "You'v

always claimed you didn't believe in inherited privilege."

"And that makes it all right for me to hang on to privilege I didn't inherit?" Harry asked dryly.

"Someone has to." Matt stepped forward and laid his hands on his brother's shoulders. "You're the rightful Earl of Milverton, Harry. Not because of who your father is. Because you've earned it."

Zara carefully conveyed a spoonful of porridge to her lips. "Cowper said I could sit on the horses today," she said, reverting to the Russian in which she was still most comfortable.

"I'll come with you," Niki said, setting down his cup of milk.

"I'm sure Cowper will let you ride the horses too," Alessa told him.

"It's not the horses," Niki said, with a determination which reminded Alessa of Harry. "I don't want anyone to take Zara again."

Alessa looked at the two children sitting at the nursery table and felt a wave of protectiveness. The day after Zara's disappearance, Niki seemed more disturbed by the event than Zara herself. "No one's going to take either of you anywhere," Alessa promised.

"Mr. Clifford isn't going to come here anymore, is he?" Zara asked.

"No," Alessa said, her throat tightening. "He won't come anywhere near you."

Zara seemed to accept this without question. It was wonderful, the trust children placed in you. Wonderful and rather frightening.

Alessa clenched her fingers together beneath the table. The thought of Edward reminded her of the talk Harry must now be having with Matt. She could not say that she would not miss being Countess of Milverton and mistress of Moresby and Milverton House. Yet if it had not been for yesterday's revelations, she might never have found the courage to tell Harry she loved him. Alessa swallowed, feeling a pang which had nothing to do with the loss of the earldom. Harry had still not said *he* loved *her*. Not that she would have wanted him simply to echo her own admission. But she longed more than anything for the words of love she had once warned her husband never to speak to her.

Determined to turn her thoughts in a more constructive direction, Alessa talked to the children and Galina about their plans for the day until she heard the nursery door open. Before she had a chance to turn round, a smile broke across Zara's face and Niki exclaimed, "Papa."

Alessa met Harry's gaze. He looked far happier than she would have expected. Perhaps it was merely the relief of having told Matt. He smiled at her, a private sort of smile which made her breathing quicken, but it was impossible in front of the children to ask him what Matt had said.

When they finally left the nursery, Alessa looked at Harry in inquiry, but he merely laid a finger over his lips, took her by the arm, and steered her down the corridor to her own apartments.

Shutting the door of her boudoir firmly behind them, Harry turned to her and lifted her hand to his lips. "It seems," he said, "that you are still a countess, though perhaps a bogus one."

Alessa stared at him. "You told Matt?"

"Oh, I told him. Matt threatened to fight me tooth and nail if I tried to palm the burden of the earldom off on him."

"He doesn't want the title?" Alessa asked. Somehow such a thing had not occurred to her.

"He was horrified at the prospect. He also pointed out that I could hardly pass the title on to him without plunging the family into scandal. And," Harry added, his mouth twisting with self-mockery, "that the reproductive system is not infallible and we'll never know for certain who my father is."

"That's true, you know," Alessa said, looking at him in concern.

"Yes, I suppose it is. It won't stop me from wondering. But for better or worse, it seems the earldom is ours. I won't pretend I'm sorry."

"You deserve it," Alessa said, laying her hand against his cheek.

Harry gave a wry smile. "Matt said something of the sort. You must both be sickening with something."

"No," Alessa said. "We're just perceptive." She smoothed the hair back from his face. "I'm proud of you, Harry."

Harry caught her hand and pressed it to his lips again, this time with greater intensity. "If I'd known what I was getting the day I proposed to you, I'd have been too bloody terrified to ask you to marry me."

Alessa laughed, the relief of the moment washing over her. "If I'd known how different you were from the safe husband I thought I wanted . . ."

"Perhaps there's something to be said for getting to know each other after the wedding." Harry looked down at her, the mockery in his eyes replaced by a look of tenderness that did uncomfortable things to her breathing. "Speaking of which . . ."

"Yes?" Alessa said, a little too quickly.

Harry took both her hands in his and gathered her to him with a leisurely care that made her shiver. "When we became betrothed, you forbade me to speak of love. Are you determined to hold me to that promise?"

Happiness welled up in her throat. Alessa stood frozen, not daring to breathe, not daring to believe he had actually said it. Then she looked into his eyes, so warm, so filled with naked emotion, and wondered that she could have ever doubted his feelings for her.

Laughter spilling from her lips, Alessa wrapped her arms around her husband and pulled him close. "I think," she said, reaching up to plant a kiss beneath his jaw, "that I might be persuaded to change my mind."

Epilogue

Moresby
December 1818

"I was beginning to think they'd never come round." Georgiana ducked beneath a leafless branch still laden with the morning's rain. "It seemed to take Zara going missing to make them finally come to their senses."

"Children can do that," Peter said, thinking of his father and Fiona, though his eyes were on Radka, who was walking beside him, her cheeks flushed in the cold air, her fair hair curling against the white wool of her cloak.

"I don't quite see how, but at least it seems to be working. They haven't quarreled in nearly two months. Of course with Harry and Alessa you never know." Georgiana looked anxiously at Simon. "Do you think they'll start acting foolish again?"

"No," Simon told her, "not this time. Or if they do, it won't be like before. Things have changed between them."

"Thank goodness," Georgiana said, stepping around a puddle of rainwater on the flagstone path. "Though I'm still not sure I understand it all."

Radka smiled. "Nor do I," she said in careful English. But," she continued, with a smile which made the breath catch in Peter's throat, "I hope one day I am happy as they are."

373

"You will be," Peter promised, catching hold of her hand.

Radka glanced up at him with one of the private looks they exchanged more and more frequently. Wishing he could kiss her, Peter breathed in the damp, chill air and savored a moment of almost perfect happiness. Radka's mother and stepfather were spending the holidays at Moresby, close enough to Sundon that he could see her practically every day.

"Moresby's a different house these days," Georgiana said after a tactful interval had elapsed. "Though I expect that's partly because Mama's gone."

"You don't miss her?" Radka asked. Peter knew she had been very glad to have her own mother returned home.

"Not really. Not at all actually." Georgiana turned and looked back at Radka. "Do you think that's horrid?"

Radka's eyes glinted with humor. "No. I know your mother."

Georgiana grinned as though relieved. "I never saw all that much of her actually, and when I did she mostly looked disapproving. Besides, she'll only be at the Dower House, though I expect she and Julia will go visiting a lot. They're going to spend Christmas in Surrey with Cecilia."

Peter exchanged glances with Simon. The events which had brought Harry and Alessa together had if anything widened the rift between Harry and his mother.

"It's probably easier that way," Simon said gently, his eyes on Georgiana. "For everyone."

"Oh, much," Georgiana agreed in a remarkably cheerful voice. "Especially for Alessa. She and Mama never could agree about who was supposed to run the house. And I don't suppose Julia wants to be anywhere near anything that reminds her of Edward."

"It must be very hard for her," Radka said, her fingers tightening around Peter's hand.

"Yes, for the first time I actually feel sorry for her." Georgiana rubbed her arms. "It makes me a bit sick, thinking about how Edward lied to all of us."

Simon's brows drew together in a quick frown. "I still think we should have seen through him."

"Seen through *what?*" Georgiana demanded, stopping in the middle of the path. "We still don't know exactly what it is he did. Or why. Except that obviously he was jealous of Harry." A look of pain crossed her face as she said this last, reminding Peter that Edward had been like a brother to the Dudleys.

Simon touched her arm. "We'll probably never know the whole story. Not," he added with a smile, "that I don't admit to an insatiable curiosity."

Georgiana didn't return the smile. "Do you think Edward had anything to do with Captain Lychenko's death?" she asked.

It was the question none of them had quite dared put into words in the past two months. The air seemed colder than before, and the rush of the stream and the stirring of the wind in the branches suddenly sounded deafening. Peter drew Radka closer to him.

"Well?" Georgiana persisted. "Captain Lychenko must have had something to do with switching Niki and Zara. And the inquiries into his death seemed to stop right about the time we learned the truth about Edward."

"Mr. Clifford has gone back to the embassy in St. Petersburg," Radka said. "If the police suspect—"

"The police were convinced Lychenko's death was an accident, whoever killed him," Simon pointed out. "If Edward's father used his influence to hush matters up, they might have been persuaded to let the matter drop."

Georgiana nodded slowly, as if acknowledging that she would have to be content with this, but Radka watched the younger girl with concern. "Your mother went to John and Galina's wedding," Radka ventured as they neared the banks of the stream.

"She decided it would cause more talk if she stayed away," Georgiana explained. "We Dudleys believe in family solidarity. At least on the outside."

"More to the point, John's father didn't disown him," Peter said, recalling the conflicting emotions on George Dudley's face at the wedding.

"That," said Simon, "is because Alessa got *Maman* to make a point of fussing over Galina. I think she had John's parents half convinced that Galina was secretly connected to the Russian nobility. Imperial connections do have their uses."

Peter grinned at his friend. "Careful, your excellency, we lowly commoners might decide to throw you in the stream."

Simon adopted his most princely expression. "You lowly commoners might *try*."

"Imperial connections were a help with my uncle," Radka said, looking up at Peter. "I still cannot believe Princess Sofia persuaded him to transfer my dowry to England."

"It's amazing what you can accomplish if you invoke the name of an emperor," Simon said.

Radka colored. "I am sorry your mother had to take such a risk on my account."

"Oh, I didn't mean it that way," Simon assured her. "*Maman* knows what she's about. Cousin Sacha would have backed up her story in any case. And as it happens, when he finally answered her letter, he more or less said what she'd already told Count Chernikov. I'll say this for my mother, she's good at getting things done."

"Like Alessa," Georgiana said.

"No," Simon said, a slow smile crossing his face, "Alessa's not really like *Maman* at all. Not anymore."

"So you see, it looks as if Alastair will be the Earl of Milverton after all, but he may have absolutely no right to the title." Alessa carefully returned her teacup to its saucer and looked up at Fiona, scarcely able to believe she had finally brought herself to tell her friend the story.

"Judging by what you've told me," Fiona, said, "he has as clear a right as anyone."

"Which is to say not clear at all." Alessa gripped her hands

376

together. "The whole thing's a fearful muddle. I own I was terribly relieved when Matt told Harry he didn't want the title. I could have been happy with Harry no matter what, but I quite like being Countess of Milverton. Yet there are times when I feel the most awful fraud."

"And that bothers you?" Fiona asked.

Alessa was taken aback by the question. "Well, of course it does. If Harry is another man's son, then he hasn't any right to be Earl of Milverton, and I haven't any right to be countess."

"That depends on what you call right," Fiona said. "It all comes down to a question of an accident of birth."

Alessa bit back the obvious retort, recalling moments in the schoolroom when Fiona had said things equally disconcerting. "I was brought up to believe that birth mattered above all," Alessa said. "Simon and I were always Tassios before we were anything else."

"In that respect I think I've been luckier than you." Fiona paused, a thoughtful look on her face. "Didn't you once tell me the Emperor Alexander's father was commonly thought to be illegitimate?"

"Yes," Alessa said, though it had not occurred to her to equate events which had taken place before she was born with her present situation. "But no one denied he was the Empress Catherine's son."

"And yet the Empress didn't rule by right of birth," Fiona pointed out.

"That's true. Of course, you could hardly call the imperial succession an ideal model," Alessa said, thinking of the bloody history of her mother's family.

Fiona looked down at her hands and lightly touched the gold of her wedding band. Then she sat back in her chair and regarded Alessa for a moment. "On that night at Sundon five years ago, you heard some unpleasant things about Gideon's first wife. You must know there's some question about Peter's parentage."

Alessa drew in her breath. She did remember, though on

the night in question she had been too shattered by her disillusionment with Adrian to pay attention to much else. "I never knew if it was true," she said. "Gideon and Peter have always seemed so close . . ."

"They are." Fiona smiled. "Peter is very like Gideon. But as to who actually fathered Peter—we'll never know. Gideon learned to accept that. So did Peter. But it wasn't easy for either of them."

Fiona spoke quietly, but there was a note in her voice which reminded Alessa that other people had suffered pain that was perhaps far stronger than her own. "But if you and Gideon have a son," she said, "won't it bother you that Peter will inherit?"

"No," Fiona said, taking a sip of tea. "But then I long ago stopped believing birth mattered above all else."

"I'm not sure I do either anymore," Alessa said. The admission, which would have shocked her a few months ago, came easily to her lips. "I really do think of Niki and Zara as my children. I've stopped seeing Galina as a servant. But . . ."

"The earldom is different?" Fiona asked.

"Harry should be the Earl of Milverton. He's filled the role admirably since he came into the title. It's just that . . ." Feeling the need to occupy her hands, Alessa picked up her plate from the table between them. "It all seemed so straightforward when I married Harry," she said, crumbling the remains of a biscuit between her fingers. "He was the Earl of Milverton and therefore a suitable husband for a Tassio. I never questioned the fact that either of us had an unshakable right to the life we were born to. I never questioned that our children would have that right as well. But if birth doesn't matter . . . well, our whole way of life rather becomes a house of cards, doesn't it?"

"Then perhaps," Fiona said, leaning forward to add some more milk to her tea, "that's what makes you feel like a fraud, not the question of Harry's birth."

Alessa met her friend's gaze, realizing there might be

more than a grain of truth to what Fiona said. "Guy Melchett would be proud of me," Alessa said, with a laugh that was part relieved, part despairing. "He told me he was all for confusion and I'm certainly confused. I thought far more clearly in the schoolroom, didn't I?"

"On the contrary," Fiona said. "You were distressingly inclined to be literal-minded. I flatter myself that some of my efforts paid off. You're not at all the girl you were at thirteen, Alessa. You're not even the woman you were a year ago."

The note of pride in her former governess's voice cheered Alessa more than anything. "Niki and Zara may have the best attitude toward all of this," she said. "Harry and I were terribly worried about telling them it's really Zara who is Harry's daughter, yet it scarcely seemed to make any difference to them. They've always thought of each other as brother and sister, and they both still think of us as their parents."

"Perhaps you should take note of their example," Fiona suggested.

Alessa smiled. "Perhaps I should."

Nothing had really changed, but Alessa felt as though her talk with Fiona had lifted a great burden from her shoulders. She busied herself refilling the teacups. In the past few minutes Moresby had somehow become more her own. Thank goodness her mother was talking with Marina, giving Alessa and Fiona a chance for this tête-à-tête.

"*Maman* and I don't seem to be clashing as much lately," Alessa told Fiona. "It's partly that Alastair is Harry's heir after all. But it's also that I've realized I'm different from her. That makes her much easier to put up with."

"I'm eternally grateful to her for what she did for Radka," Fiona said, as Alessa handed her back her cup. "I've grown very fond of the girl."

Alessa smiled. "That's fortunate considering the way she and Peter look at each other." She took a sip of the fresh tea. "It's nice to see young people in love."

"It's very heartening," Fiona agreed. She paused and her

379

face grew serious. "Have you had any more news about Julia?"

"In her last letter Lady Milverton said Julia seemed in better spirits," Alessa said. "And Harry's sister Cecilia sent along a note saying Julia is receiving a good deal of attention from two of the young men in the vicinity and doesn't seem wholly impervious to it."

"Admiration can be an excellent cure for a broken heart." Fiona adjusted her cashmere shawl. "Should I take it as a favorable sign that Lady Milverton writes to you?"

"Oh, she's very good at observing the forms," Alessa said, her voice sharpened by the bitterness she always felt when speaking of her mother-in-law.

"So is my grandmother," Fiona said in a thoughtful voice. "It's kept our relationship smooth on the surface, but it hasn't done much else for it."

"It's one thing to forgive Lady Milverton for an indiscretion thirty years ago," Alessa said, her fingers clenching on the delicate porcelain cup. "It's another to forgive her for how she's treated Harry all these years. I don't think she could forgive herself for giving her husband a bastard heir, you see. And she took it out on Harry."

"Can Harry forgive her?" Fiona asked.

"More than I can, I think," Alessa said, taking a sip of the soothing tea. "At least he says he understands her. But I don't know if matters will ever be mended between them. Still, it's easier now that everything is out in the open. And," Alessa added with a pang of mingled guilt and relief, "now that she's decided to have her own household."

"Does Georgiana mind her mother being gone?"

"I don't think so. She practically begged Harry and me to let her stay with us."

Fiona smiled. "It sounds as if she's longing for the chance to be part of a family."

Alessa nodded, determined that Georgiana's childhood would not be as troubled as Harry's had been. Then she remembered that she had some really important news to share

380

with Fiona. "Alastair can push himself up on his arms now," she said. "Oh, and I wanted to ask you, when did Fenella start eating solid food?"

Talk about the children changed to talk about the book of stories from Russian history which they planned to finish early in the new year. They had moved to a table against the window and were pouring over Alessa's sketches when the door opened on a medley of youthful voices. Alessa turned to see her husband standing in the doorway with Alastair in his arms and Niki, Zara, and Fenella clustered around him.

" 'Stair woke up," Niki said in English.

"But he doesn't need to be changed," Zara said, speaking in English as well. "We checked."

Harry smiled at Alessa. "I think he's hungry, though he quieted down when I picked him up."

Alessa walked toward her husband and children. Whatever doubts she had experienced in the past weeks, Harry had only to smile for them to be replaced by simple, sustaining joy.

Zara ran forward and flung her arms around Alessa's legs. Alessa bent to hug the little girl, then tousled Niki's hair before she went to look at Alastair. He was lying contentedly in his father's arms, his gaze fixed on the shiny buttons on Harry's waistcoat.

"It looks as if he just wants to be cuddled," Alessa said.

"Of course. I should have realized even babies need that." Harry looked searchingly at her. He knew she had been going to tell Fiona the story today. "All right?" he asked softly.

Alessa glanced at Fiona, who was bending over her own daughter, then looked back at Harry and smiled. "More than all right," she said, meaning every word of it. Alessandra di Tassio had grown up at last.

Historical Note

Alessa, Simon, and their mother, though related to the imperial family in this book, are entirely fictional.

Accounts of Russian court and diplomatic life are based on the correspondence of Lord Granville Leveson Gower (London: John Murray, 1916), who was the English ambassador to Russia in 1804-6 and in 1807; on the letters of Sarah, Lady Lyttelton (London: John Murray, 1912), who visited St. Petersburg in 1813-14; and on information found in *The Congress Dances* by Susan Mary Alsop (New York: Washington Square Press, 1985).

Information on the conference at Aix-la-Chapelle comes from the issues of the *Morning Chronicle* published in 1818.

THE ROMANCES OF LORDS AND LADIES
IN JANIS LADEN'S REGENCIES

BEWITCHING MINX   (2532, $3.95)

From her first encounter with the Marquis of Pender-leigh when he had mistaken her for a common trollop, Penelope had been incensed with the darkly handsome lord. Miss Penelope Larchmont was undoubtedly the most outspoken young lady Penderleigh had ever known, and the most tempting.

A NOBLE MISTRESS   (2169, $3.95)

Moriah Landon had always been a singularly practical young lady. So when her father lost the family estate over a game of picquet, she paid the winner, the notorious Vis-count Roane, a visit. And when he suggested the means of payment—that she become Roane's mistress—she agreed without a blink of her eyes.

SAPPHIRE TEMPTATION   (3054, $3.95)

Lady Serena was commonly held to be an unusual young girl—outspoken when she should have been reticent, lively when she should have been demure. But there was one tra-dition she had not been allowed to break: a Wexley must marry a Gower. Richard Gower intended to teach his wife her duties—in every way.

SCOTTISH ROSE   (2750, $3.95)

The Duke of Milburne returned to Milburne Hall trust-ing that the new governess, Miss Rose Beacham, had in-stilled the fear of God into his harum-scarum brood of siblings. But she romped with the children, refused to be cowed by his stern admonitions, and was so pretty that he had the devil of a time keeping his hands off her.